I.R.I.S.

By

MATTHEW NEWELL

Copyright © Matthew Newell 2020
This book is sold subject to the condition that it shall not, by way of trade or otherwise, be lent, resold, hired out, or otherwise circulated without the publisher's prior consent in any form of binding or cover other than that in which it is published and without a similar condition including this condition being imposed on the subsequent publisher.
The moral right of Matthew Newell has been asserted.
www.matthewnewell.co.uk
ISBN: 9798670529037

This is a work of fiction. Names, characters, businesses, organizations, places, events and incidents either are the product of the author's imagination or are used fictitiously. Any resemblance to actual persons, living or dead, events, or locales is entirely coincidental.

CONTENTS

I	1
II	11
III	22
IV	32
V	40
VI	47
VII	59
VIII	69
IX	81
X	95
XI	106
XII	116
XIII	126
XIV	139
XV	150
XVI	160
XVII	174
XVIII	192
XIX	203
XX	216
XXI	229
XXII	252
XXIII	270
XXIV	283
XXV	294
XXVI	306
XXVII	315
XXVIII	324
XXIX	337
XXX	350
ABOUT THE AUTHOR	362

I

'I don't worship gods and I certainly don't follow leaders, hell, I have trouble trying to embrace new technology, let alone working with the current advancements.'

'Why?'

'Because I believe that the more we sync with our digital revolutions, the more we become primitive and lazy, allowing ourselves to be dictated to by those that are slowly enslaving us from behind our screens, using the very tech we idly use, without question.'

'You mean, our leaders?'

'Our so-called chosen deities, you mean. We are so easily manipulated through advertising and propaganda from our churches and our governments that we forget just what it is to be human and to think for ourselves.'

'But that is the way of the world now, you either adapt and change, or you get left behind.'

'Fuck that! It's better to learn from our ancestors than from officials in power that wish to govern us, pushing us further into declension.'

'But why don't you believe in a god?'

'Because a god would not let its chosen disciples be ruled over by greed.'

A heated conversation is taking place on the 12th floor of the I.R.I.S. HQ in Canary Wharf, London. A city where the only buildings to exist now are those that serve businesses. Residential dwellings across the whole of the former United Kingdom are all now mobile homes that are constantly on the go, allowing for more green open spaces. The narrow green belt from a long time past, which circled London, has now spread to the city and has made it a flourishing metropolis where nature has taken hold once more.

The near future

'Stephanie Coulson, this job requires that you understand the core concept behind our future plans.'

'This is not what I signed up for five years ago, Dom.'

'If you can't agree to the new terms of your contract, then you can't hope to efficiently do your job to the best of your abilities further down the line. You either sign the contract or you walk out of the door. The choice is yours, Steph, this contract is now protocol.'

'Fuck your protocols and your mandates, Director Dominique.'

'I'll ignore that, Agent. Look, the public will have access to this new concept very soon, depending on how this trial goes, obviously. But we cannot sit back and let our competitors beat us across the finish line by getting their patent in before us.'

'I have been more than efficient in my job role up until now, why can't you just tell me what I need to know? Why do I have to be your case study?'

'Because this is ground breaking, it will change the face of our business and the world in which we inhabit for the better.'

'But it's intrusive and I don't want to wear it. In truth, I can't see the public getting behind the idea either.'

Stephanie Coulson is gesturing to you, hiding behind a contact lens embedded with a gold ring floating in sterilisation fluid, your window, currently into her world.

'If it's the procedure that is bothering you, let me assure you that—'

'It's not the operation, Dom. I get how it works, you put me under on some operating table and slice away my natural lens lining and then graft the new smart contact lens into place, using lasers and God knows what other kind of tools to permanently change my perspective of the world through enhanced vision, am I right?'

'Well yes, a simple and safe procedure. I fail to see the problem.'

'Didn't you just hear me? It's immoral and a step too far, surely you and they must see this?'

Your view of the Director and Agent Stephanie Coulson is clouded by the substance that swirls around your vision.

'I don't care what they believe, this is the right direction for you to better deal with any future assignments. Trust me when I say you will see things clearer, literally! It will improve your already impeccable skill set.'

'It will make me a slave to the system and that goes against all I stand for.'

'You're already a slave to the system, Steph, you work for chits and pay taxes, you've already been sold!'

'When I left university five years ago, I believed when I landed this job that I could make a real difference to the welfare of others and for a while I did, but this, this is not within my comfort zone, Dom.'

'You're thinking negatively, Steph. This programme will enhance you in ways that you cannot fathom, I promise.'

'Fuck, Dom. Why me? Why do I have to trial it?'

'Because you are our finest agent and we can capitalise on that and make you our most prized asset, the poster child for I.R.I.S.'

'You can be a charming bastard when you want to be, you know that?'

'I try.'

'Okay, fine. Fuck it. Don't make me regret this decision, Dom. If this turns into a clusterfuck then I'm going to bail from this programme, do you understand me?'

'Some people would kill for this opportunity, Steph.'

'Then they are delusional, primitive apes.'

'Embrace the light and step out from the dark ages, Miss Coulson.'

'You are such a prick sometimes.'

'Can't argue with you on that one, now come, shall we take you next door and get the doctors to prep you for the op?'

'Fine.'

'You know, I can't wait for our Watchers to get started, so they can run their analysis and observations. I look forward to their assessments.'

Director Dominique flashes a grin in your direction but all you can make out is a distorted shadow.

'Who are the Watchers exactly, Dom?'

'Those that are out there watching and listening to us right now from behind the lens floating currently in that sterilisation fluid in that pot beside you.'

Stephanie looks rigid as she looks wearily at you encased in the contact lens of tomorrow, which you are growing accustomed to.

'You mean they have heard everything we have discussed?'

'Yes. But I wouldn't let that bother you. They will be permanently attached to your retina very soon.'

'You still haven't told me who the fuck they are. Don't hold out on me, you owe me that much.'

'That's confidential information, Stephanie, not even I have access to that. They could be from any walk of life for all I know. Black, white, straight, gay, female, male, non-gender. What does it matter? They are here to observe you and when they're done I'm pretty sure they will have a better understanding of the future potential of our product.'

'Military?'

'Again that is above my pay grade, but yes, I am sure that some of our investors are indeed military. They have invested quite heavily into our programme already to date.'

'No surprise there then, huh? But what if I need to pee or have some personal time with my partner, you know, stuff I don't want to share with the world or with them?'

Stephanie turns away from you as the fluid starts to clear, slowly allowing your picture of her to come into focus, showing you her slender young frame with her brunette, long flowing hair, trailing down her back and over her navy suit jacket that is fastened up tight around her waist.

'Ha, trust you. Look, all you do is send a voice command to power down the contact lens or shut your eyelid to block out what you see through your chosen eye. They cannot witness anything that you don't want to divulge. You have chosen a preferred eye, I presume?'

'Shit, does it really matter? My right eye, Dom, okay? But if I forget they're there, do I risk a voyeuristic, shady collective of so-called officials masturbating over my sex life?'

'There is an override that monitors you closely. The moment it senses any kind of sexual behaviour it will suspend data collection, unless of course you choose otherwise.'

'So wait. Not that I would, but, what if I wanted to record and replay my past antics?'

'Then you can do so. All you need to do is freeze the Watchers out and then save the recording into a locked file within the lens data storage. It's all quite simple really. I have an encrypted E-manual for you to digest when the operation is over that explains all the functionalities of the device.'

'Okay, I trust you, Dom. At least they won't be able to read my thoughts.'

'But they can read your actions, so just remember that.'

'Oh I certainly will, I'll act like some bacteria under a fucking microscope! I do have one last question.'

'Hmm, which is?'

'Can they gain full access of my life if I die in service?'

'If you're dead then what does it matter?'

'There may be some sick fucks out there who might get off on watching my death unfold over and over on playback.'

'Do you forget where we work, Steph?'

'No, Director, I do not. We are I.R.I.S. Information Retrieval Investigation Service. The cutting-edge technology of the future and investigators of our own product's misuse for illegal criminal reasons. Innovators of the safety and personal welfare of all denizens that wear our brands and assistants to the ease of living with tomorrow's technology today, and our slogan is "We have our sights on your vision for the future."'

'Slightly condescending, but straight out of the graduate's training manual. I'm impressed, in short that means we uphold the values and privacy of anyone that wears our product... including you.'

'You really are a self-righteous prick, you know that?'

'That's why I earn the big chits.'

'Okay, enough of this bullshit, where do I sign?'

'Take this stylus and sign the pad here.'

'Yup, done. Now let's get on with the show, shall we?'

'After you, Steph. I won't be far behind.'

You see Stephanie Coulson exit through an electric sliding door from an obscure angle to your right.

'Okay. To you, the Watchers out there, I will rejoin you shortly once we have Miss Coulson settled and then I will address you all directly before we integrate you into her left eye, or was it the right? I can't seem to remember, anyway, thank you for your patience.'

Director Dominique exits through the threshold and twenty minutes wane before the Director enters once more.

'Sorry to keep you all waiting for an explanation and I apologise for Miss Coulson's outburst earlier. Let me reassure you that she is one hundred percent committed to our cause, it is just pre-op jitters.'

Director Dominique towers above you at over six feet tall, wearing a red chequered suit with a white shirt beneath, and sporting a plain gold-coloured tie. His features are sharp and his eyes are sunken. You watch as he pulls on a pair of rubber gloves from a box just outside your peripheral vision.

'Now then, let me just scoop you onto my finger and bring you up to my face so you can better get acquainted with me. It still fascinates me that no matter which way up the lens is, you, the Watchers, can still see out the right way.'

The overhead strip lighting is bouncing off the Director's thinning head of hair and obscures your perception of the world you see.

'So, for those of you wondering what we actually do here and for those of you curious whether to make another, or new investment by the time the trial expires, let me explain our core values.'

Dominique approaches a large black padded armchair located in the corner of the room and sits himself down. The glare from the light shifts, returning an ambient light to proceedings once more, allowing you to see him clearer.

'Here at I.R.I.S, we pride ourselves on delivering breakthrough technology, cooked up from our talented team in our Research and Development department. What you are looking through is our most advanced, electronic smart contact lens to date using microchips and nanotechnology combined, to deliver our prototype lens that will change the world and your perspective of it. You will witness first-hand what I believe is a launch that can redefine your lives.'

The Director lifts you up and takes you to a row of overlarge windows, that look out from the high rise across New Canary Wharf where less buildings now remain and more wooded areas have flourished. The sun is beginning to set on the horizon.

'The first contact lens we created revolutionised the way people perceived the world. No more glasses to be worn or contact lenses that had to be taken out daily, they quickly became a thing of the past, a relic to how we once lived.

'Now they are only found in antique shops from yesteryear and a bygone age. Our first lens had 2020 vision that also allowed the user to zoom in to great distances that were otherwise out of reach with the eyewear of yesterday. Then came our second phase with crisper clarity and the added bonus of a built-in health A.I. that only the wearer could see or hear and interact with in ways that were mindblowing at the time.'

Returning to his seat with you still perched upon his index finger, Dominique spins you around, making you dizzy.

'The A.I. was fantastic. You gave her or him a name depending on your gender preference and the A.I. would respond to your questions of the state of your body, from your blood sugar levels to your heart rate and the sensing of danger or emotions of people around you. It could even repair your tissue, commanding the nanos within you to give you a chance of more life by preventing heart attacks and the like, thus cutting down on visits to the medical centre and not having you drain the resources of the NHS. A win-win situation all round.

'Sigh, that was a real boost for us, until our competitors from abroad tried to out-think us and create better technology using other methods...

'...But still we keep pushing the envelope and today I would like to share with you phase three of our plan, one that will blow all other companies out of the water and I hope will have you invested in our vision for a brighter future.

'Like before, you will still get the aftercare package where we employ people like Stephanie to assist and investigate any misuse or issues that you have, in turn cutting down on the dwindling resources of our deteriorating police force, always being able to get to the scene first with the already built-in tracking GPS and transmitter embedded into the device.'

Dominique pauses for a long moment.

'Now we have record and replay function for phase three. That's right, a function that constantly records your every move and action. But don't be put off by that insignificant revelation, as to accompany this new trait we also have the ability to let you share the data of your still, captured images or recordings direct to like-minded users via transfer between the same style lens. Also, as well as all the above, you get fully integrated augmented reality. Let that sink in a moment...'

Dominique closes his eyes and breathes in and out gently before addressing you once more.

'Imagine if you will that there are fond memories you once had that have faded over time that you could only replay in your mind using photos or recordings on an old television that we once had, to jog your memory. Now imagine that you can replay those memories in your mind's eye like you were actually there again using the lens. There is no comparison, is there? This lens is truly unique but that's not all, for you can share that memory to your partner for instance, who can see through your eyes and gleam a different perspective than what they had. How great is that? Now picture that you are afraid of flying or you are housebound. Imagine that you can access your colleague or partner's lens and relive their holiday by having them share with you their adventure, with their consent of course. Or better yet being able to pay for someone to holiday for you and let you look through their eyes and have them partake in whatever you want to experience all from the comfort of your own home.'

Holding you above his head, Dominique smiles at you.

'Sounds too good, you say. What about Stephanie's view on the legalities? Well we have fail-safes in place, we wouldn't roll out our programme if we didn't. Look, we have the Power Down function to override so what could possibly go wrong?'

A squat, cheery nurse enters the room; her cheeks are flushed and she has perspiration across her forehead, looking like she has hurried from afar to get here.

'Director, I am to inform you that we are now ready for the integration, sir.'

'Thank you, Bonnie, I will be right along.'

Bonnie smiles at you and then hurries off back through the door with her chest heaving rapidly.

'Lastly, before we part ways let me give you one more example. Imagine your employee is having trouble with the job he or she is undertaking and seeking your assistance. Now you can look through their eyes and assess or assist them whilst you are sunning it up on the other side of the world. So I don't need to express anymore how exciting the possibilities are, for I'm sure you are already thinking about it now. But for this trial I must ask that you keep it all secret and please don't share your findings as we can't have an outside agency stealing our ideas, can we?'

Dominique carries you on his finger and takes you through the sliding door where you end up in a long white corridor with large windows to your right looking out across the city. To your left are glossy white sterile walls bathed in the rays of the dying sun shining in from outside and throwing silhouettes across their smooth surface from passing, rolling clouds.

'There is one more addition I would like to share with you all. That is, this smart lens also has some other cool features that I cannot disclose to you just yet, as I want you to experience them first-hand when Stephanie takes you out into the field. But believe me when I say that you will all have the experience of your lives and that's a promise. The next time we meet will be through Stephanie and not me direct, so I will end this conversation on wishing us all a very successful trial.

'Once Miss Coulson has healed in around three days or so, then we will see you on the other side, Watchers. So for now, Power Down.'

The contact lens fades out of focus and plunges you into darkness.

II

'Power On!'

Stephanie Coulson is reclining on a swivel tub chair, with her bare feet up on a black smoked glass table in front of her. She is riding in her driverless and fairly spacious, fully electric, class A mobile home that is travelling at great speed across the M25.

'Hi everyone and welcome to my home. Sure, it's probably not that great compared to other affordable six-wheel mobile homes on the market, but it suits me just fine. Maybe one day I could afford a class S Toterhome, eight-wheel behemoth like Director Dominique's, but anyway here we are. So this is my living room that leads away to my compact kitchen, interconnecting with my restroom to the left and to the right my bathroom and utility room. Beyond those rooms lies my main lobby with exit to the outside world.'

Stephanie looks up and you see the vehicle's glass roof surround, with rain splashing across its surface from outside on a dark and dreary, usual overcast day.

'As you can probably gather the operation was a success and now we are fully unified, so I guess this trial is now well and truly live.'

You hear sarcasm laced with regret in her tone.

'Sorry if you were expecting me to power up sooner but I had to get my head around this strange set-up first and to acquaint myself with the E-manual. Having gotten used to some of the features first-hand, I am now confident that I can literally take you out on the road with me to our first assignment.'

Stephanie sits forward and brings her feet in beneath her before swiping a finger across the black smoked glass table that pulls up an electronic qwerty keyboard across its surface. She types a message: *Voice Command and Full Three Degree View on*, before hitting enter and leaning back. Sensors in each corner of the room switch on and emit a soft hue of blue radiating light.

'Access email sent today from Director Dominique and play attached file. Watchers, I have already heard this but I will replay it for your benefit.'

Each sensor's light beams an arc into the centre of the room that quickly take on the shape of Director Dominique's head and shoulders as they fuse a colourful three-degree image together.

'Hello Watchers, sorry I can't attend proceedings today but by the time you get this recording I will be crossing the checkpoint at the border to my birthplace of Scotland. I have recently acquired a plot of land that looks out across Loch Lomond, a beautiful and breathtaking vista that is very sought after.

A 360-degree panoramic view of the Loch appears as Dominique's image fades away.

'I was lucky enough to outbid some very wealthy people to secure the spot. It will be a wonderful place to unwind at the end of each day from the hustle and bustle of work in London. I certainly don't miss the static mortar and brick houses of an overcrowding time long ago. That's the great thing about our mobile society now, we can travel wherever we like, when we like. By the time I've changed into my casual clothes and sunk a few alcohol beverages whilst watching the streaming shows from the comfort of my sofa and then showered and got ready for bed, my driverless home has driven me six hours to my tranquil destination just in time for me to open the door and soak up the dying rays of sunset over the Loch whilst I have a final nightcap. I may even have time to get in some fishing.'

Stephanie rolls her eyes and for a second you see the inside of her eyelid.

'Then when I awake in the morning my home has already driven me five hours back during the night. When my alarm goes off I am only an hour away from Canary Wharf, to give me enough time to dress and have breakfast before I start another gruelling day at the office. The best thing of course is that I don't get hampered by border control, seeing as how I am a Diplomat.'

Stephanie rubs away at the lens causing your imaging to pixelate before returning to normal.

'Anyway, I digress, you all already know this, sorry everyone, back to business. So early this morning we took a live message from a Gloria Day, yes, that is her real name, who had reported some alarming news about her father, Sebastian. It seems that he has been unseen for a little over three weeks now. The reason that she had not reported him missing sooner was because he had just got divorced from Gloria's mother, Christine, and he had decided on a whim to take off in a rental mobile to clear his head.'

'Pause.'

The image of Loch Lomond vanishes and Director Dominique's face is scrambled midway in returning to full 3D. Water begins to cascade down across your vision.

'Apologies, Watchers, but my eye is weeping, let me just dry it here, it has to be the healing process that has caused this.'

A crinkled ball of tissue is thrust into your vision as the traces of saltwater tears are soaked up.

'Sorry. Continue playback.'

Dominique's animated face takes shape and begins to speak again as the tissue is removed and discarded to a nearby bin.

'Apparently Gloria left him many concerned messages but received none in return, until this morning that is, when a prerecorded message from him found its way to her, dated two days after he had left in the rental. Now here's the real mystery, it would seem that he is a black market seller of our phase two smart contact lenses, one of which he was wearing himself that he might have got modded, but that information we need to investigate. Anyway, he was in the process of outsourcing our lenses to one of our unknown competitors, possibly to raise some quick chits to settle his quite substantial divorce settlement that was looming. How do we know this? Well, we have his last message to his daughter to play for you, see attachment.'

Dominique's image minimises and a tired look from a bearded man with a bloodshot eye fills the void as he comes into focus wearing a grave look upon his face.

'Gloria, my precious daughter. I am so sorry that I have not contacted you sooner but what happened to your mother and I really hit me hard. I know that you will never forgive me for what I did to your mum but I swear to you that I was not myself. I believe now that the A.I. in this infernal contact lens was what had put the thoughts into my head and made me react the way I did. I never meant to beat on her, you must believe me. The A.I. made me suspicious and paranoid about the close relationship with her boss at work. It sounds incredulous, I know, but I'm sure it drove a wedge between us, so that's why I accepted the online divorce and took off. I am a danger to be around right now and time is short.'

The message pauses and Director Dominique's image enlarges until it matches side-on to the face of Sebastian's. Dominique looks to the paused face of the troubled father and then looks directly at you.

'Absolute nonsense, I assure you. There is no way that our A.I. would become self-aware. Now this can only lead to one assumption: A, he was not meant to wear our lens because our psych evaluation team would have deemed him unstable to wear it to begin with, so he must have acquired it on the black market, or B, it has been modded by an outside source, which would explain that the A.I. has been tampered with and made therefore dangerous. This would in fact invalidate the warranty if it were bought legitimately. But as he was not on any of our programmes, I can only assume that he has purchased the lens from the black market which is worrying, for that would mean that our tech is being stolen and could be sold on to our competitors, who might take the phase two lens and find out how to improve on our design, in turn beating us to phase three.'

'Pause.'

Stephanie stands up and you find her transporting you to a coffee machine. She sighs and pours herself a mug before returning to her tub chair and placing the hot mug on a glass cabinet to her side. She pulls a bottle of eye solution from her pocket and squeezes three drops across your field of view.

'Sorry to pause but I have an itchy eye, I'm still getting used to the graft, I think.'

Stephanie rubs a finger across the underneath of her eye with the lens in.

'Well I don't know about you but I can see why that would be a real concern for us. You would be surprised how many times that I come across wearers of our brands that have had them illegally modded whilst in their eye, sometimes with very messy results. This, however, is new to me. I've not come across anyone that has had a backstreet op to implant a lens that could only have been stolen, how dangerous is that? I will need to visit our Manufacturing Lab for answers. They have records of all lenses created with their unique IDs. Anyway, resume playback.'

'So this is why we are making this case our first assignment for Miss Coulson to undertake. We need to find Sebastian and investigate him further, but I fear we may be too late. The last part of his message that I am about to play is very worrying indeed and if I'm right, then the consequences to the threat delivered will mean that Miss Coulson may have to extract his eye and bring it back to the lab for testing. Anyway, you decide. Stephanie, report to me your findings when you have enough evidence. Dominique out.'

The digital image of the Director fades away and the message from Sebastian plays once more.

'I'm sorry I cannot be there for you, my precious daughter, in your time of need, but I hope this message finds you and gives you some small comfort. I have enough to get by so don't worry about me, I have sold a case of contact lenses to someone very important and I am just awaiting payment. The only trouble is I think someone is out to get me by using my personal A.I. against me, I just hope that I'm not being set up by the seller, there seemed something off with him, he...'

You notice that he looks spooked and a little paranoid, that he may have said too much.

'I really do love your mother and I deeply regret what I have done to you both.'

Sebastian's face changes and his eyes squint. It looks as though he is experiencing a sharp migraine.

'Stop! No, shut up. I won't let you do that to me. My life is not yours for the taking. Enough is enough, your silence will be my retribution.'

He reaches out to grab something off-camera.

'Nooooo!'

The message is sounding distressing as Sebastian shakily brings a gun up to his head; he is restraining against the gun being brought up to his temple and tears are rolling down his cheek.

Blood is oozing from his eye where the contact lens is embedded.

A loud bang rings out and brain matter splatters across the recording of where Sebastian's face once was. Then the message abruptly ends.

Stephanie turns away and you realise she is deeply troubled.

'It's worse the second time around that I watch it! Do you think that this is a tad concerning? I know I do. Well that's why I have decided if I didn't already have my reservations about this fucking contact lens before, then I do now. There is no way on earth that I'm taking my A.I. off standby, like ever. It's a shame because I named her Sybil, after a woman in ancient times that uttered the prophecies of God. I thought that was quite amusing at the time but now I know that we will not be activating that part of the programme, so I apologise, Watchers, but I hope you understand why.'

An automated female voice sounds from a built-in speaker behind you. 'Fifteen minutes to destination.' Stephanie checks her watch.

'Good, we will shortly be arriving spot on time then. I took the liberty before bringing you online, Watchers, to track down Sebastian Day's vehicle and instruct the law enforcement to close a section of the highway off to bring his mobile home to a stop. I believe there will be two police drones on the scene now awaiting our arrival as per usual.'

Stephanie picks up her mug of coffee and drinks from it, causing condensation to cloud your vision. She returns the mug to the table and reaches out to type once more on the keyboard that spells out a command: *Access outside sensors and beam in nearby, mobile fast food restaurants*. The condensation quickly evaporates.

The built-in speaker resonates the voice once more. 'Two mobile fast food chains nearby, first is Italian and the second is Indian. What will you require, Stephanie?'

'Since I've been feeling queasy most mornings, I seem to always hunger for an Indian at this time of the day, but I think I quite fancy an Italian for a change. Alexa, access reviews for the Italian and bring up the menu please?'

'Would you like to play their advert?'

'No, the menu and reviews will do, thank you.'

The sensors in the four corners of the room beam in a two-dimensional view of the Italian's menu accompanied by various reviews for the restaurant left on Trip Advisor. Stephanie quickly makes her selection and the holographic screen closes.

'Order placed. Time to arrival of meal ten minutes, time to destination ten minutes.'

Getting up, Stephanie walks over to a handle protruding from the exterior wall of her mobile home, set in a square frame. She gives it a twist and pulls it down, letting the rush of the outside world whistle through the now open hatch. She then turns away and grabs a large holdall from a nearby desk.

'Right, let me just unzip my bag and make sure I have the eye extractor within here.'

You see that the cotton holdall is compartmentalised inside with each section housing gadgets and tools of many different shapes and sizes.

'Okay, this looks like the baby, it's a little outdated and primitive compared to today's standards, but it works well and suits my tastes just fine. If we have to remove his eye, depending on if he is dead of course, then this beauty will do a fantastic job.'

Stephanie turns it over in her hand and you notice that it resembles a hand gun with a curved grip. It is comprised of stainless steel and has a trigger attached beneath a razor-sharp scoop at the barrel end. Stephanie gives the trigger a squeeze and the scoop retracts back in on itself, sliding into the barrel. She stows it into the belt around her trousers and pulls her blouse down to conceal it.

A clunk followed by a thud is heard as the voice from the speaker crackles into life once again. 'Takeaway delivered, depositing funds from account.'

Retrieving the carton from the hatch and shutting it back up, silencing the wind rushing in from outside, Stephanie picks the fork away from the packaging and removes the lid, listening as the delivery vehicle pulls away.

'Hope you don't mind and I'm sorry if I eat this in front of you, but I'm starving.'

'Warning, warning. Dog loose on road one mile ahead, safeguarding in process, braking, braking, stopped.'

The vehicle gently comes to rest.

'For fuck's sake, what now? That's all we need. I do love the advanced warning and safety methods employed on our pressure-sensitive smart roads, but I wish it didn't happen today of all fucking days. Okay, fine, we walk from here. Sorry Watchers but you will realise I don't have much patience when I'm on a case.'

Abandoning her takeaway to the side, Stephanie bends down and pulls her shoes out from underneath the black smoked table where she then pulls them over her feet. She then takes you through the interconnecting rooms and into the lobby at the front of her mobile home.

'Open door.'

The steel door opens outwards and glides down gracefully, creating a ramp that Stephanie steps out onto. The rain is falling hard and she swipes a purple rain mac from beside the threshold that she throws on. A dog is barking in the distance.

'What do you reckon? Shall we try out the zoom function now? What was it again, blink once for photo and twice to auto zoom, was it? Sybil, activate voice commands from standby!'

Instantaneously the zoom function takes effect and magnifies to a scene in the distance of two flying police drones, three feet in length and covered in the metropolitan police markings, with blue flashing LED lights circling around their white-painted, hardened steel bodies. Behind them is a six-wheeled vehicular mobile home similar to Stephanie's, standing static in a part of the motorway's lane that has now been powered down. To the right is a high grass embankment with rows and rows of small headstones peppered along the vast expanse of the M25's outer rim.

Stephanie closes the eye that conceals you and cloaks you in darkness for a brief spell. When she opens her eye again, your view has returned to normal.

'Whoa! That is way too trippy for me. I thought I was having an out-of-body experience for a second there. One second, if you will.'

You follow Steph as she falls to her knees and watch as she projectile vomits onto one of the concrete lanes that houses a continuous strip of solar running through its centre and snakes off in both directions into the distance, following the contours of each lane of the motorway.

'Sorry about that. Just give me a moment to adjust, I guess it will take me a while to get used to this. I don't suppose it helps that I'm nauseous most mornings.'

Standing up, you see Stephanie wipe away the bile from the corner of her mouth.

'Okay, let's get off the road, shall we, as I'm just as guilty now of holding up the traffic as much as that dog is, wherever it is. I see it's only the fourth, fast lane that has the stoppage. Lane one for recharging is fine and I see lanes two and three for leisure and business are still flowing freely.'

You look up across the embankment and follow her gaze as she climbs up and onto the top of the sodden wet grassy verge, narrowly avoiding the row upon row of small headstones that litter her path.

'Wow. I've never stood here before. Look at all these plots containing cremated remains. I mean I knew that cemeteries and crematoriums ceased to allow interring and burials long ago through lack of space and that new methods were employed now that we have far greener lands. But I never knew this was the alternate method. There are so many flowers laid here, it's almost beautiful. Look at this marker.'

It reads: *Here lies Nathan and Sally Palmer, brother and sister reunited in death as they were in life. Rest in peace.* A tear is forming in the corner of Steph's eye.

'How sweet is that? Anyway, we've lost too much time already, so let's get to Sebastian's mobile home, shall we?'

She wipes the tear away.

The bark from the dog rises in intensity as Stephanie nears closer to the vehicle. The enforcement drones scan Stephanie on arrival and seeming satisfied, they retreat to the distance with their blades humming menacingly as they slink away into the deluge of rain.

'Sybil, activate Thermal Imaging. I wish to scan this six-wheeler before I break and enter.'

'You wish me to activate?'

'No, I wish you to stay in standby and I want you to activate Thermal Vision please?'

'Thermal activated.'

Your vision changes the spectrum of colours that you see, swapping out the natural dark grey daylight for deep blue and yellow and green saturated palettes, infused with dark orange and reds.

'Damn, I can't see any heat signature from within the mobile. I reckon that we will have to expect the worst, I'm afraid. Okay Sybil, back out to Normal Vision.'

'Blackout confirmed.'

'No, wait, what's happening? I said back out. Is it me or is the air getting thinner?'

Darkness begins to take hold as Steph starts to gasp for air, bringing her hands up to her collar to loosen it and sinking to her knees.

'Bloody voice recognition, that's the trouble with not bringing my A.I. fully online. Arghh!'

Steph's brain shuts down through lack of oxygen and casts you into darkness, like a power cut shutting down a moving image on an old television set.

III

The first thing you see when Stephanie regains consciousness is a giant Alsatian dog's tongue licking its way around her face and across the surface of your window.

'Eww! Get the fuck off me, you slobbering mutt.'

You see Steph getting to her feet and pushing the dog away.

'What the fuck was that? What just happened here? Do you have any idea, Watchers? Because I'm coming up short on them right now. This could not have been a coincidence.'

The sodden wet Alsatian dog looks directly at you as it tucks its tail between its legs, before whimpering and scampering away, wearing a neglected demeanour. Steph starts rubbing her temples.

'You know what boils my piss? When the goddamn police are never around when you're in need of them. Where the bloody hell have those drones gone?'

Looking around you see the traffic is speeding past in the three lanes to the left of Sebastian's home and those that were held up by the road closure are now being automatically switched to the free lanes, by unseen data transfer between the smart road and vehicles that are fast approaching, making a seamless transition. Stephanie uses the Zoom Function and spots the police drones a mile down the road directing the traffic away from the scene.

'Cool, I'm getting used to this function. Ah, they're a long way off now, oh well, fuck it, it's too late now anyway. So this day keeps on getting better, Watchers. Let's hope that's the worst of it, hey? Think

I might need to have myself checked out when we get back. Come on, let's get back at it, shall we? I really need to look inside Sebastian's motorhome. I have a strong feeling that we may be on to something big here.'

The section of road that Sebastian's class B rental motorhome is parked on is semi-bathed in darkness, the only light that spills across the mobile exterior is emitted from passing vehicles zipping along the neon green, red and blue strip lighting from the solar strips of each lane that run adjacent to the powered-down section, flickering as each vehicle drives across them.

'I almost bought one of these models. It's slightly more rounded than mine and it has a complete section of smoked glass roof that runs the entire length of the home. But I think the whole cigar shape put me off, you know? Glad I upgraded to something better. The mortgage is fucking steep though.'

Approaching the front door of the mobile home, you see Stephanie pull away her rain mac and reach into her jacket pocket to remove a small, black digital fob that she pushes up against the lock on the front of the hatch door to Sebastian's home. A red LED light turns green and the mechanism within clunks. Slowly the hatch gently opens to double up as a ramp leading up to the confines of the home as it hits the road.

'My job does have some benefits I guess... Oh my god, the smell, it's fucking awful! Well if the stench is anything to go by then I can safely presume that Sebastian is truly dead and that the recording of him we played was definitely not doctored in any way. It pays to check the details, you know.'

Stephanie uses her rain mac to mask the smell from her nostrils as she tentatively makes her way up the ramp. Flies buzz around you as they swarm past and out into the rain-soaked sky. You continue inside to the darkness of the tomb as Stephanie fumbles around in the cold, dark interior.

'Well Watchers, is this your lucky fucking day or what? Guess we will have to shed light on proceedings then because it will be way more fun than flicking on the light switch. Sybil, turn Night Vision on, please.'

'Night Vision activated, Stephanie.'

Pushing through the threshold of the lobby and further into the confines of the mobile home, you notice that each room Stephanie looks into is well maintained and spotlessly clean, like a showroom that has not been lived in yet. A kaleidoscope of various green colours from the Night Vision show up the appliances and cupboards in the kitchen area that Stephanie looks into first, bathing them in an eerie wash of a green glare.

'All clear in here. Let's check the bedroom next, shall we?'

The bedroom yields nothing further, so Stephanie looks into the washroom followed by the utility room, until finally you end up in the living quarters at the rear of the vehicle having not seen anything suspicious. Sure enough, laying on his side, keeled over onto the sofa with a gun in his twisted hand, lies the maggot-ridden body of Sebastian Day. The maggots are wriggling and writhing in both of his eye sockets, bathed in bright green light from the lens. You realise what Stephanie must do.

Dark green blood spatter covers the room and streaks across the glass ceiling to the drips stained dry down the four walls. The neon rain is battering the roof and flies are choking the air creating a luminescent illusion.

'Bollocks, I have to remove the maggots first before I can extract the eye. Kind of glad I'm not viewing this in natural light.'

Stephanie goes to pull out the eye extractor from her belt when she suddenly thinks better of it.

'Wait, what's this here then?'

A message is displayed flashing on the table with a constant bleeping. 'Play me.' Stephanie reaches out and taps enter on the black smoked keyboard in the centre of the room which comes as standard in these styles of motorhomes. The backup generator kicks in and activates the sensors in the corners of the room, bathing the dark room in a soft gentle blue light, causing Steph to squint.

'Sybil, back out of Night Vision please?'

'Night Vision disabled, Stephanie.'

'That's better.'

A black silhouette of a figure materialises from a recording stored in the hard drive. The voice is masked to protect the identity of the speaker.

'Welcome, Stephanie, and may I extend my warmest of welcomes to you too, Watchers.'

'The fuck?'

'Like you, there are those of us that have observed from afar the advancements that these so-called smart lenses bring with every incarnation. But some of us believe that with every new upgrade comes a new found risk to humankind. Some of which we know that Stephanie agrees with.'

'You what? How the fuck do they know this?'

'Sebastian here has flaunted the law and the advancements by his own admission of greed. He was sold a batch of your so-called phase two lenses but they were modded with recording technology from your trial phase three. I guess someone wanted to release the trial early. I would look close to home, Stephanie, if I were you to unravel who the seller is, for we don't have this information.'

'You've got to be shitting me.'

'Now what I can do is to share with you what we do know. Sebastian Day was the middle man in the transaction, he has sold the lenses on to one Olivia Redfield. So yes, Stephanie, before you ask the question to your Watcher friends, we are already investigating her. All you need to worry about is who the seller is. As for our part in all of this, well I'm afraid I cannot reveal that to you yet, so we have taken precautions... begin timer.'

'Begin what now?'

'May we have the pleasure to see you soon, Stephanie. Oh, and one last thing, we cannot afford you the privilege of tracing the data on Sebastian's lens back to us. If you try to remove the lens, it will send a signal to a bomb located beneath your feet in the water storage tank.'

You can tell that Stephanie is agitated as she begins to race around the room, upturning the furniture and trying to locate the tank. A faint bleeping has started.

'I suggest you exit now, Stephanie. You have just ten seconds.'

'Fuck!'

In a blind panic and forgetting to turn on the Night Vision again, Stephanie stumbles back toward the exit of the vehicle, banging and crashing into the doors and walls. She just makes it out and heads for the high grass verge, when an explosion from behind erupts and sends you flying through the air and crashing down upon a row of hard concrete tombstones. You hear Stephanie wincing in pain and then watch through her as she pulls herself along the ground and her eyes begin to shut. You hear a voice just before she blacks out.

'Trauma detected. Override initiated. Sybil fully functioning and online.'

Moments later, Stephanie's eyes snap open accompanied by a long groan. You see that an image of a female digital avatar has appeared in the corner of your peripheral vision, sporting a white coat. She has a slender, gentle face with her hair up in pigtails, with no trace of make up on and she is wearing a cheerful look. You watch as Stephanie pulls herself up and staggers back through the torrential rain and back to her mobile. You wonder if she can see what you can.

Groaning and in pain, Steph goes to enter her mobile but then casts a look back to the twisted scrap of metal and searing inferno that engulfs the now destroyed home of Sebastian Day. Two police drones hone in and start scanning the wreckage for survivors, causing the flames to fan as they dart backwards and forwards overhead. Stephanie turns away and enters her home.

'Now they show. Typical. Wait a minute, who the hell brought you online! Sybil, I didn't activate you. I order you to Deactivate.'

You realise she can now see the medical A.I.

'Trauma detected. Request denied.'

Stephanie grabs her side in pain and makes for her living room.

'Well then patch me the fuck up and then Deactivate.'

'Scanning bone, muscle and tissue, one moment please.'

'Didn't you just hear me? I said—'

'Vitals stable.'

'Bollocks to it, well at least I won't need to explain what happened, seeing as how I've got recordings and playback functions as well as witnesses, hey? Sybil, just send the last half hour of recorded footage back to I.R.I.S. and Scotland Yard when you have finished your assessment.'

'Scanning complete, priority health assessment done. Now creating folders and compiling footage for secondary objective. Data transferred and files complete. Sending files as requested, Stephanie Coulson.'

'Thank you, Sybil, I guess.'

'Trauma detects one broken rib, minor cuts and bruises and light concussion. Nanobots commanded to repair damage. Please rest whilst self-healing takes place.'

'Sure, just hold on a second. Let me just get this and go lie down on my sofa.'

Stephanie retrieves her cold veggie Italian dish in its container and makes for the sofa, where she then falls back into it with her meal held tight into her lap.

'Further assessment detects child in womb. Baby shows no trauma. All functions are normal.'

Stephanie having barely rested, suddenly sits upright in shock and spills her takeaway to the floor.

'What the fuck did you just say, Sybil?'

'Child in womb shows no trauma, all vitals are normal.'

'What child? What the hell are you talking about?'

'You are with child, Stephanie Coulson. My calculations put it to being around five weeks old. Would you like me to assess its gender for you?'

'No, I do not want you to tell me shit. Wait, hold on just one fucking minute, I can't be pregnant because you can't tell a baby's sex until around twenty weeks with an ultrasound, so nice one, I didn't realise you could express humour, Sybil.'

'Nanobots can probe and assess the foetus from early on so you can find out much easier now.'

'Enough, I want you to Deactivate right fucking now, do you understand me?'

'Negative. New life indicates around-the-clock monitoring. Would you like to hear the baby's heartbeat?'

'Hell no! I don't want to hear the heartbeat. I want you to Deactivate right fucking now.'

'Denied. Child's welfare takes precedent over that of the mother's life.'

'I think I'm going to be sick.'

'Would you like me to counteract your sickness?'

'Shut up! Just shut the fuck up already.'

Gently caressing her stomach and seemingly lost deep in thought, Stephanie looks around the room and you see her reach for a bottle of pink gin, nestled between the cushions on the sofa. She unscrews the lid and takes a deep swig of the alcohol.

'Two units exceeded. Counteracting.'

'You what?'

Rolling from the sofa with her knees landing in her cold meal, Stephanie clutches her stomach and doubles up on all fours as she starts to convulse and vomit onto her royal blue carpet.

'No more than two units can be consumed per week whilst a mother is expecting. You have exceeded the limit. Your body is being flushed of toxins.'

'You've got to be kidding me.'

Stephanie throws up again before groggily pulling herself back onto the couch and burying her head in her hand. You can just about see between her fingers to the clear bile on the floor.

'Alexa, call Jack Mintlyn.'

'Calling Jack Mintlyn.'

After a short delay the dialling tone echoes around the room and the sensors in the four corners come alive once more to beam a 3D image into the centre of the room, showing a young man in his mid-twenties with a head of blond curly hair and chiselled looks.

'Shit, Steph, you look terrible.'

'Yeah, thanks, I gather that.'

'What do you want?'

'We need to talk?'

'Well, can you make this quick as I'm a little busy right now.'

'No, I can't make this fucking quick, Jack. There's, there's something I need to tell you.'

'Goddamn it, Steph. Why can't you ever be reasonable?'

'Jack, just shut up and listen, okay?'

'You see what I mean? I can never get a word in, can I? I bet it's about the bloody operation again. I told you where I stand. I swear if you've gone ahead and done it then you and I are finished. It's over, or did I not make myself clear the first time?'

'You selfish bastard!'

'Whatever, I told you I don't want my life scrutinised by whoever is pulling your strings from behind the scenes.'

'I did have the operation but that's not it, look, this is important.'

'Wow, after all we discussed you went ahead anyway, are you off your head? Don't you realise what you have signed up for? Did we not watch the same news coverage of the marches taking place from the protesters, against the dangers of the revolution that you are wrapped up in?'

'Yes I did, and yes we did, but that's not what I—'

'Wait, does that mean that I'm being observed right now?'

'Well yes, but I can—'

'I can't believe you chose your work over us.'

'Jack, please.'

'No, I've heard enough. See you around, Steph.'

'Wait... I'm pregnant.'

'Seriously? I never took you for cheap tricks like that! '

'It's true, my A.I. Sybil, told me.'

'Your who? You know what? I don't care. Fuck you, Steph.'

'But—'

'Goodbye.'

The image of Jack fades and the blue beams of light dim from the sensors, returning them once more to standby.

'Motherfucker! Alexa, run trace on Olivia Redfield, let me know when you find her.'

'Of course Stephanie, I will alert you when I have found her.'

'Also set me a reminder to call Dom six hours from now.'

'Reminder set.'

Stephanie stands up and makes her way to her restroom where she proceeds to stare into a digital mirror on the wall.

'I'm sorry about that, Watchers. I can't believe that I'm pregnant, I can't be, I was careful, I don't... Anyway, you know what really pisses me off? I'll tell you, it's this whole situation with the creepy voice from the recording in Sebastian's motorhome. Who the fuck was that? And why is he or she helping my case? I can't have a devil on my back when I'm trying to dance, do you know what I mean?'

Stephanie is absentmindedly pushing you around her eye and for a moment from the reflection in the mirror, it is like you are staring into her very soul.

'I think I need a hot shower then get myself off to bed for a while. I need private time now, Watchers.'

'Agreed, you must rest now, going into rest mode.'

'Piss off, Sybil. Later, Watchers. Power off!'

[override] 'Power on.'

Stephanie is standing naked in the shower with a jet of hot water spraying across her ample frame as she is lathering herself up. Steam is clouding your vision as she washes herself down with a sponge, caressing her breasts and wiping the suds away from her stomach and the dark bruising on her ribcage.

You notice that she has a small tattoo of the Union Jack flag tattered and in flames with a large O at its centre with a large A through the middle of it, inked between her breasts. You recognise that it is the symbol of Anarchy.

Stephanie has no idea that you are watching her as you observe her dry off then drag herself off to bed where she is quick in closing her eyes. It is only then that you experience darkness once again.

IV

An alarm clock sounds through the darkness and your vision slowly returns as Stephanie opens her eyes. She gradually pulls herself up in the bed and brings a pillow up behind her to rest on.

'Alexa, stop alarm.'

Stephanie yawns and stretches.

'Well fuck me, Steph, it looks like you might have really needed that sleep, you're feeling quite refreshed, girl.'

'That is because you are fully recharged and the nanobots have healed you, Stephanie Coulson.'

'For fuck's sake, I forgot all about you, Sybil. Look, from now on you only speak when I fucking ask you something, do you understand?'

'Do you require me to run background monitoring?'

'If it will shut you up then yes.'

Stephanie pulls herself out of bed and checks her side; the bruising has gone and the cuts have scabbed over. She rifles through her wardrobe and puts on her bra and knickers before rolling on deodorant and getting out a crisp white shirt and grey suit.

'Alexa, how far have we got on tracking down Olivia Redfield's automobile?'

'We are currently cruising at matching speed behind the registered vehicle to Olivia Redfield, at a safe two hundred yards behind.'

'Thank you, Alexa. It's nice to know that one computer is doing as I ask.'

'Would you like me to intercept?'

'No thank you, continue as you are.'

'Request granted.'

'Where are we currently, Alexa?'

'At present we are on the M4 coming up on Bristol.'

'Thank you.'

Going into the rest room and now fully clothed, Steph washes her face and then brushes her teeth, before padding her face dry with a towel. She then proceeds to apply her makeup in the digital mirror using an overlay of different makeup applications that are being presented to her on screen. Stephanie settles on an overlay of subtle skin tones and applies her foundation and lipstick to copy the image.

'Sybil, do you have access to power up my lens?'

'Negative, that function is restricted to you alone.'

'Okay, that's fine. It's just I have a strange feeling that I am being watched, without my permission.'

'Would you like me to set up a time stamp when power mode is toggled?'

'What, you can do that?'

'It is in the E-manual, Stephanie Coulson.'

'Don't fucking condescend to me, Sybil. Okay, look, never mind. Yes please, I would like you to set up a time stamp.'

'Time stamp activated.'

Pulling her long auburn hair up into a bun and pushing through bobby pins to keep it in place, Stephanie then smiles into the mirror at her freckled complexion before turning and walking back into the living room, she then looks up through the glass ceiling and realises that it is now night time and the sky has cleared.

'Alexa, what time is it?'

'21.43, Stephanie.'

'Thank you. Alexa, please call Dom.'

'Calling Dominique Hastings.'

As the dial tone echoes around the room, Steph picks up the bottle of eye drops from the side and puts three drops in, blurring your vision. The rinse starts to wash away and your sight slowly returns.

'Power On.'

'Good evening, Watchers. I'm guessing some of you are back or will be very shortly so I'll be frank, I read in the E-manual that once I power on, a notification signals to you to say that I am back online. So, here we are again. Developments that I should make you aware of are that we have intercepted Olivia Redfield and are now tailing her. I wanted you online before we engage, so we can get to the bottom of this mystery and get some questions answered.'

The dialling tone cuts into a prerecorded image of Dominique accompanied with a message from the Director, beamed in from the four sensors located in the corners of the wall.

'I'm sorry, I cannot answer your call right now, but if you would like to leave a message stating your business, then I will get back to you soon.'

'Alexa, hang up.'

'Hanging up.'

Dominique's image fades and the blue shafts of light die as the sensor's projectors go back into Standby Mode.

Stephanie approaches her black smoked glass table and pushes a button at the side of the console that tilts the table at a 45-degree angle. She types the command: *Access front facing exterior cameras.* A live feed displays on the table of Olivia Redfield's Toterhome driving along the road in front of you.

'Shit! I'm actually quite worried about Dom with all that's happening right now. Anyway, fuck it, I'll try again later.'

Steph begins to bite her nails to the quick.

'You know, the more I think about it, the more I realise how dependent I am on this bullshit technology that is supposed to make our lives easier. The truth is though, I believe that it just complicates matters really, don't you agree? When I'm done with this cock-sucking trial, I swear I'm going to go off-grid and live off what the land provides.'

An almighty crash and screeching of grinding metal on metal comes from out of nowhere and rocks Steph's motorhome, sending her flying across the living room and into a glass drinks cabinet at the side of her sofa. She ends up sprawled across the floor. You notice that her eye is millimetres away from the sharp corner of the glass surround edge.

'Bugger me, what the fuck was that?'

Pulling herself up and scrambling across the sofa to access the console of the table, Steph types another command: *Access all exterior cameras*. Instantaneously, three new images show up on the table's OLED display, in turn minimising the front camera which is tracking Olivia Redfield to the top left window. The right side camera just shows an empty lane and the rear camera shows traffic way off in the distance. But the left camera is now damaged.

'I can't...'

A black mobile home appears on the front camera in the left lane accompanied by another that passes the right camera in the right-hand lane as they catch up to Olivia Redfield's Toterhome and hem her in on either side, sandwiching closer and closer.

'...This isn't good.'

You watch on as the event plays out.

Sparks begin to fly as the black mobile vehicles rub up against Olivia Redfield's home on opposing sides, slowly twisting and contorting strips of panelling that begin to peel back like a knife through butter. The vehicles persist until at last they bring her home to an abrupt standstill and force Steph's home to take an emergency procedure.

'Evasive measures, braking, braking, stopped.'

Then without warning, the two unmarked black vehicles with their tinted-out windows and angular shapes, open their spacious boots at their rear in unison, releasing four heavily weaponised black sleek drones to the skies each, before taking off at great speed and disappearing into the distance.

'Who the fuck are they? Military perhaps, I didn't catch any markings.'

Stephanie is gripping the console with dear life, as you and her watch helplessly on.

'No, no, no! I'm being fucked over here.'

You can sense the impending doom mounting as the drones hover above and all around Olivia Redfield's home. Suddenly they open fire and begin to rain down traces of speeding bullets into the Toterhome, ripping it apart with every bullet that tears through its hull, peppering it with holes.

'You fucking tin can wankers.'

Tears are welling up in Steph's vision as she shakily types another command into the console: *Zoom in camera one, track movement.*

You watch and notice just as Steph does that there is movement from below Olivia's Toterhome. A large hatch has opened under the belly bringing down a lift with a small bright red car resting on it with a female passenger at the wheel; you gather it must be Olivia.

Now having been safely deposited to the road, lights appear on the vehicle, signalling that it has been started.

'Yes, come on Olivia, get the fuck out of there.'

The noise from the car's engine alerts the drones overhead and they quickly swing round and drop down low where they begin to sweep around looking for a clean shot as the hatch retracts.

Stephanie runs for the door and makes her way through her adjacent rooms to the lobby. She commands the door to open, releasing the hatch to the outside, where she then runs flat out down the ramp waving her hands in the air.

'Okay Watchers, this is going to seem suicidal but she needs a distraction. Over here, you fucking morons.'

It looks as though the drones are about to turn on Steph when all of a sudden they swing their turrets round and let loose hot lead into Olivia Redfield's Toterhome's wheels and axles. The projectiles tear through the rubber and metal drive shaft, sheering them to bits across all eight wheels.

Then with a large groan the crippled Toterhome buckles under its own weight and crashes down upon the car with Olivia having just exited it and about to run for cover.

The look of horror is imprinted into Olivia's eyes as her Toterhome comes crashing down upon her, ending her life. All that remains visible is her head with a face frozen with fear and an outstretched arm in a death pose of someone reaching out for help.

'You motherfuckers!'

Screaming and cursing, Steph falls to her knees and looks defiantly to the drones as they form a V flock formation above. They are not paying her any attention as they turn to the approaching police drones and the sirens wailing in the distance, sounding from the advancing law enforcement.

Steph crawls over to the deceased Olivia and begins to cry; your vision becomes blurred again.

'Why? Why the fuck have they done this?'

Stephanie looks away from the drones in disgust and back to Olivia's lifeless body. It is then she notices that one of Olivia's bulging eyes is harbouring a lens exactly like hers. It is without question a phase three lens, notable by the golden ring around the iris that denotes the technology built within it.

You see Steph slide out the eye extractor from her belt and force the scoop into Olivia's eye socket where she then pulls the trigger with a sickening squelch. She pulls out a zip bag from her pocket and releases the trigger, sliding the bloody eye into the bag which she then zips up before sliding it back into her pocket and the bloody extractor back to her belt.

'We've got to get the fuck out of Dodge right now, Watchers.'

Stephanie stands up and faces the approaching police drones as the black drones fall down to her side with their weapons trained on the enforcement drones before them.

Steph looks bewildered to the four sleek black drones on either side of her and she starts to tremble.

A cold and hollow message sounds from one of the two police drones that hovers in to view.

'Stand down your drones, Miss Stephanie Coulson, so we can resolve this peacefully, or an arrest warrant will be granted for your capture.'

'Are you fucking shitting me? These drones aren't mine, look I...'

But her words trail off as the black drones open fire once more and obliterate the police drone in front you, showering Stephanie in hot metal shards as she ducks in fright. The second police drone that was further back suddenly turns and flees the scene.

'Fuck, fuckity, fuck, fuck.'

The black drones then rise into the sky and emit one collective solitary message in a digital voice as they swirl into a funnel like formation.

'We warned you, Miss Coulson, but you would not listen. Find the seller, find the answers.'

You can tell that Steph wants to speak but the drones then explode all around you, forcing Steph to run for the sanctum of her home as the debris rains down.

'Now I'm in deep fucking shit. Sybil, send an encrypted message to Dillon back at the lab in I.R.I.S. HQ. Tell him I'm sending him a package, tell him I'm in trouble and will explain later but more importantly, tell him that he must investigate the package. He will know what to do, do you understand?'

'Yes Stephanie, message has been sent.'

'Good.'

'I see your blood pressure is high, would you like me to bring it down for you?'

'Are you bloody serious? Did you not see what just happened? No, I'm perfectly fucking fine. There's only one person that can help with my boiling blood, Sybil, and he isn't answering his goddamn calls right now, shit!'

Entering her mobile home, Steph gives the command to close the door which brings the hatch up and then she makes for the living room without stopping.

'Alexa, set course for Loch Lomond, and get me there as quick as possible, I have a bad feeling about Dom.'

'Granted. Would you like me to track his whereabouts?'

'No, I know where he will be. I'll give you the coordinates for his home shortly.'

[Override] 'Power Off.'

V

'Power On.'

'You know, I just don't get it, why would my lens shut down on its own?'

'I do not have sufficient data to answer that, Stephanie, time stamp just confirms power off.'

'Yes, thank you Sybil, we ascertained that. Thing is, all I can gather is it's hacked in a similar way to what happened to Sebastian Day. But why? It must be something to do with the assisted suicide of Sebastian and the assassination of Olivia. I really need to see Dom.'

'You must restrain caution, Stephanie. Someone knows that you are now time stamping and they have gone offline before they are uncovered.'

'Yes, someone knows that we were on to them, so you could be right, but my lens is legit. It's not some black market hack. I'm missing something.'

Stephanie returns to her sofa and presses a finger down on a file on the screen that is named E-manual.

'Maybe I'll find the answers here. If I really am pregnant then I can't afford to be quite so reckless now can I?'

'No Stephanie, you cannot. There are two lives to look after now.'

'Thanks for reminding me, okay, silent now please.'

'Hello again, Watchers. Sorry but this is a serious start to our conversation, I'm afraid. You see, there is a point I really need to hammer home to you, so I hope that none of you have infiltrated my lens as that is a serious offence.

'That kind of bat shit is up there with rape. I swear to God if I find out it's happening to me and I'm compromised and one of you are involved, then I will track you and I will fucking, fuck you up, I swear. Anyway, now that is out of the way I can resume business.'

A female voice comes over the airwaves from the hidden speakers built into Steph's motorhome walls. 'Next passenger please.'

Steph's class B motorhome is currently stopped at the border to Scotland where occupants' passports are checked and the row of motorhomes are being queued for inspection. An open expanse of motorway has widened into eight lanes to quicken the amount of time it takes to process traffic across the border. Accompanying large electronic booths surrounded by solar panels and totally automated are scanning each vehicle as they pass through.

Abandoning her work station for now, Steph approaches her tilted console and waits as a ghost image of a passport appears on screen. You see Steph turn her passport over and push it up against the screen.

Moments later a sound pings indicating a successful scan along with a green tick to be quickly replaced by an outline of a face denoting where to line your eyes up. A retinal scan then gets under way as you are met with an infrared shaft of light that bathes you in a crimson glow as it reads Steph's eye to make sure it marries up to the records on a biometrics file from the automated machine's database.

'Welcome to Scotland, Stephanie Coulson, is your stay business or pleasure?'

'Business.'

'How long will you stay?'

'Umm! One day at most.'

'Please state your business.'

'I.R.I.S. business, confidential.'

'You are free to pass. Enjoy your stay.'

'Thank you.'

Steph waits for the screen to go back to black with the built-in digital console appearing once more.

'Fuck me, that was nerve racking. I guess that my warrant hasn't been issued yet then, Watchers, if it had then we would have been boarded for sure. Well I guess that buys us some time for now, so where were we? Oh yes, the dreaded manual. Alexa, proceed to coordinates please.'

'Coordinates locked. Solway Firth to Loch Lomond time and distance are one hour, twenty-five minutes for one hundred and one miles.'

'Okay, Alexa, what's the time now?'

'3.45 a.m.'

'Good, so we should be there around sun-up.'

'Estimated time on arrival will be 5.10 a.m.'

'Thank you, Alexa. What time did you send the package?'

'I sent the drone with the package at 22.45 p.m. You have one drone left in the storage hold.'

'Good, that means I can spend some time going back over this hefty manual then.'

You see the text currently displayed on the screen in front of you outlining the procedure for the lens graft that is discussed in great detail. It outlines the method for cutting away the natural lens with fluid then being injected into the eye that fuses with the artificial lens capsule as it solidifies on insertion.

The smart lens then takes over the job of focusing light on the retina and it is also laced with tiny nanobots that disperse into the blood stream and travel around the arteries of the body at the point of entry, where they then start communicating with the lens's built-in transmitter to the A.I., like drone bees working for their queen bee in the hive.

'I'm sure I read somewhere in here about a firewall and malware programme that prevents any unauthorised access controlling the lens through the built-in transmitter, but I can't seem to find it.'

Flicking her finger across the screen, digital text on pages begins to turn over as Steph skims through the manual's pages.

A melody rings out from the speakers and alerts Steph to sit bolt upright, suspending her reading.

'Incoming call from Dillon Fletcher.'

'Alexa, enable Hologram Video Chat and connect.'

The sensors whir back into life and beam in a 3D rendered live feed of Dillon Fletcher above the console in the centre of the room.

He is wearing a flat cap that hides his eyes but you can just about make out the outline of his round face with a goatee beard.

'Do you realise how much trouble you're in, Steph?' His voice is hushed but bitter.

'Hello to you too, my favourite geek.'

'This isn't time for pleasantries, do you know what kind of trouble you've got me involved in?'

'I know it looks bad, but this is important, did you get my package?'

'You need to go into I.R.I.S. HQ and sort this mess out, Steph.'

'Can't, I'm too wrapped up in this case right now, so did you get it or not?'

'Of course I received it, that wasn't at all subtle was it? Sending one of your drones right up to my front door.'

'And?'

'And nothing, Steph, this is way above my pay grade.'

'Oh come on, Dilly, I know you wouldn't be able to resist checking it out.'

'I may have done, but look, I'm not comfortable with this.'

'I'll throw in a hand job if you share with me what you know.'

'This isn't funny, Steph.'

'Come on, I'm just fucking with you, lighten up and tell me what you found?'

'You don't get it, this is some dark shit. I would really like to outlive those that I've wronged, Steph, so they can't speak ill of me at my funeral in front of my loved ones, and right now you're putting me in the firing line.'

'Ooh! I'm intrigued now. So much so that my panties are really wet with anticipation.'

'Back off, Steph, I mean it. I'm not prepared to hold this conversation with you over the airwaves but I will say this. The eye you sent me, oh, and by the way, thank you for that gruesome surprise, the one belonging to Olivia Redfield who is now dead by the way, murdered by your hands nonetheless, has grafted into her eye a lens that is not one of ours.'

'Fuck off! I could have sworn it was the same as the one I'm wearing. If not ours, then whose?'

'That's not my job to find out, that is solely your responsibility. But Steph, this lens is as advanced as our phase three is.'

'Fuck me, is it? Hmm.'

'Lucky for you I can send a copy of the recorded events dating back three weeks ago of her meeting with Sebastian Day and send the data directly over to your lens. I warn you though that you won't like what you find, in fact it made me sick to my stomach. I have a family, Steph, and I have to say I'm feeling pretty traumatised after what I have witnessed.'

'It can't be that bad, can it?'

'It's worse! You're lucky I'm off tomorrow. Anyway, I've zipped the folder and it's now being sent to you.'

'File received, Stephanie. Would you like me to open and sync?'

'Not right now, Sybil. I'll access it later.'

'Who are you talking to, Steph?'

'Sorry Dilly, my A.I. just informed me that she has received the folder.'

'Well make sure you have a stiff drink handy for when you've finished viewing the footage and I would suggest that your A.I. filters out the chaff and just plays what's important.'

'How did you get through it all so quickly anyway?'

'What can I say? I'm a workaholic. Seriously though, I skipped through a lot of unpleasant stuff and I suggest you do the same.'

'Okay, well I guess you came through for me, so thank you.'

'I hope you find what it is that solves your case, and I wish you all the best in clearing your name, Steph.'

'Clearing my name?'

'Have you not seen the news? You're a wanted fugitive now, breaking news and riveting stuff! I suggest you tune in, it makes for excellent viewing. Especially the way you controlled those drones to shoot down that police interceptor.'

'You what?'

'I never took you for the studious type, Steph, but I'm obviously wrong. The way you paired your A.I. with those drones to control them is world class.'

'What? You mean you can actually do that?'

'Don't play coy with me, Steph, it's in the manual. I'm glad you executed that monster even if you didn't realise what she was. But the police drone was a step too far in my opinion. Now you have the whole of Scotland Yard on your heels. That's going to complicate things for you.'

'But how come I got through the border without being flagged?'

'Red tape I presume, Steph. Be careful and hopefully I will see you when you have cracked this case. I need to go now as I think I can hear my boy stirring in his bedroom and I don't want to wake the wife.'

'One last thing though, what have you done with Olivia's eye and lens?'

'Oh, I have sent that back on ice with your drone, I don't want anything of that monster's. You can call it your insurance.'

'Okay, Dilly. Thanks again.'

'One last thing, Steph. I've also sent your drone on its merry way with a parting gift for you, I thought it might come in handy later. I have activated the drone's homing beacon, so if you can transmit your receiving signal then it will find its way back to you through your lens's GPS tracker.'

'Yup, I know how to do that, thankfully, so what is it you're sending me?'

'It's... Sorry Steph, the boy's crying. I have to go, take care and good luck.'

The image of Dillon fades to black and the sensors dim once more leaving the only light in the room shining from the glass table's heads-up display. Steph types in a command: *Play news bulletin.* The footage begins to stream and you see the previous events that Stephanie has partaken in beam her antics around the country.

'So they're saying I'm a goddamn terrorist, are they? That I'm wanted in connection with Olivia Redfield's murder, to use extreme caution if anyone comes into contact with me. Bastards! That's fake news right there, Steph, from the very people that govern you and spread lies through their media. Poetry in fucking motion and you're right at the heart of the action.'

VI

Time passes as the highlands roll by and small farming towns off-grid fade to the distance. Steph has her head down reading the E-manual on a section concerning the nanobots that are swarming within her veins.

'It says here that these nanobots are 0.1 micrometre in size each and that they are constructed of molecular components. Thousands of them would have been injected into my bloodstream where they then spread out around the inside of my body to monitor and seek out any detection of threats against my life. If they do find anything, then they communicate with one another to regroup and begin to repair any damage on the advice from Sybil as to the state of my condition and what internal operations to carry out. Fascinating stuff.'

'We are coming up on the position of Dominique Hastings, I am not permitted to park in a space next to his position.'

'Umm, you won't, Alexa, we haven't paid for that luxury. Locate visitors' car park and find a space there.'

'That requires that we leave the circuit. There is possible chance of battery depletion within twelve hours' time.'

'That's fine. I have no intention of staying that long, just do it.'

'Granted.'

Closing the console before you, Steph then gets up and stretches, before looking around the room. Eventually she walks over to her kitbag, snatches it up and slings it over her shoulder.

'Okay Watchers, now we go to work again.'

Steph exits her home and strides across the car park surfaced with loose chippings. The small pebbles crunch underfoot as she makes her way over to the large solar grid car park in the distance, separated by a painted red boundary marker. Dom's Toterhome is tucked in between a row of similar homes overlooking the loch, fanning around a sweeping expanse of water. His private registration reads: D0MH45T.

'I know it's the weekend but I really hope he is at home.'

Ringing a doorbell with a camera above it, you sense Steph becoming agitated as the melody sounds inside.

'Come on, Dom, for fuck's sake, I really need your help right now.'

Silence. Steph starts pounding on the large steel hatch.

'Answer, Dom! I'm really fucking worried here.'

'Hello there, can I help you?'

Spinning around in fright, Steph is taken aback by the sight of a dark-haired, middle-aged woman wearing a straw hat, sitting in a deck chair on an exposed area of her Toterhome that has split its front end into three segments to create an open-top room, right next door.

'Sorry. Yes. My name is Stephanie Coulson. I work for I.R.I.S.'

You see Steph pull her I.D. card out from her inside pocket and flash it at the lady, before slipping it away again. The woman gives her a curt nod.

'I am here on official business looking for my boss. His name is Dominique Hastings and this is his Toterhome, but it doesn't look like he's in. I don't suppose you know him, do you? Or have at least seen him around here, he is—'

'Well of course I know him. He is my husband after all.'

The woman laughs and takes a sip from an iced drink in a tall frosted glass.

'Oh, fuck me. Sorry. I, I have heard so much about you but we have never met. I thought that you worked overseas.'

'Well yes I do, but I am on vacation at this present time. That is why Dom leased this spot, so we can meet here when we can. It was

I.R.I.S.

the very spot that he proposed to me.'

'Okay that's erm, well, that's lovely. I'm sorry but I really must see him as it's very important. I wouldn't come all this way if it wasn't urgent.'

'I'm sure you have your reasons, Miss Coulson.'

'If I could just see him then I can get away to leave you in peace. I'm sorry if I've disturbed your time alone.'

'Not at all. I have heard all about you, Miss Coulson. Dom tells me that you are his finest agent, won't you join me?'

'Stephanie, I sense that you are experiencing what is referred to as a hot flush, may I recommend that you drink a cold beverage to bring your temperature down?'

'Piss off, Sybil.'

'I'm sorry, what did you say, Miss Coulson?'

'Ahem, nothing. Sure, of course I will join you. Thank you.'

Mrs Hastings reaches for a remote control and jabs a button which activates the front side hatch to extend down to ground level, creating a ramp. Steph catches sight of it and makes her way up to join her as an amber glow from the sun is rising from behind the hill tops.

'Please won't you join me, would you like a glass of margarita?'

'Yes, thank you. Isn't it a little early in the morning for alcohol though?'

'I'm on vacation, so time means very little to me. Besides, what better way than to see the sunrise with a cold margarita in hand?'

'I suppose.'

Taking a sip, Steph sits beside Mrs Hastings on a matching chair and rubs a finger around the rim of the glass.

'Sorry but where did you say Dom is?'

'I didn't. But I can tell you as it's no secret. He is out somewhere on the loch fishing. He has purchased a little rowing boat that he was very keen to sail out on. He asked me if I would join him but I didn't want to get in the way of him and his new toy.'

'I see.'

'Indeed. Now tell me, Miss Coulson. How come you have two different coloured eyes? One is blue and the other has a golden tinge to it I see, how is that even possible?'

'Oh right, of course, that's nothing. You see my left natural eye colouring is blue and my right eye is a smart contact lens, the golden colour you see is the receptor ring that is built into it.'

'Is it the new phase three lens by any chance? How exciting.'

'Yes it is. I'm sorry but how do you know about phase three? I thought it was confidential.'

'Well of course it is. Dom was never one for keeping a secret from me though, would you mind if I have a closer look?'

'Yeah, that's fine I guess.'

Mrs Hastings leaves her chair and squats down in front of you; her white summer dress is clinging to her well-toned body. She takes Steph's face in her hand and gets right up close and personal to look deep into the lens that you are looking out from. You notice that Mrs Hastings has goosebumps across her arms caused from the cool wind spilling across the loch.

'Ego sum vita in manibus.'

'Sorry, what now?'

'It means you have your whole life ahead of you.'

'Oh I see.'

'Codice primi ante christum 00.1.'

'I'm sorry but you what?'

'You must be overjoyed to have such a gift of enhanced sight.'

Steph wriggles away and goes to stand up, feeling really uncomfortable.

'Excuse me, but I really have to go, Mrs Hastings, thank you for your time.'

'But we haven't got to know one another yet.'

'I know but I really must find Dom, I will come back and see you when I have my situation sorted.'

'Stephanie, before you go.'

'Yes?'

'Invadere uterum.'

A strange feeling of dread creeps up on Steph and a dull ache shoots through her stomach making her double over in pain. You look at Mrs Hastings and Steph blinks hard.

[Photo taken]

'I really must go. Mrs Hastings, thank you once again. See you soon, I promise.'

You can tell that Steph is in a lot of pain as she is clasping her stomach.

'Operatio tuam.'

The dull ache begins to subside as Mrs Hastings starts to laugh. 'Goodbye, Miss Coulson.'

Steph retreats to the beach and begins to hurry along the coastline looking out to the loch half cloaked in the shadow from the hill tops, as they reflect across its still surface. The sun is slowly rising up and glinting off the loch further downstream.

'Well this day just got fucking strange, Watchers. Who the hell drinks at this time of the morning let alone talks in some fancy language?'

'Sybil, you have access to Alexa, right?'

'Yes Stephanie, I do.'

'Then can you please send her the photo I took of Mrs Hastings and ask her to bring up her details please? Also ask her what language that was and to translate what she said to me.'

'Relaying information, Stephanie.'

'In the meantime, can you show me my heads-up display please?'

'Displaying HUD.'

'Thank you.'

An overlay of information is displayed in your field of view in digital text. In the top left of the window is displayed the time 6.30 a.m. and in the right is the image of Sybil. Across the bottom is a row of six dots with numbers affixed to them, one through to six. In the bottom right is an image of a folder.

'Information received from Alexa, Stephanie.'

'Okay, play back message.'

'The language that you requested is Latin. Translated, the segments read in order of dialogue first to last. The first reads: I have your life in my hands. The second reads: Activate code 00.1. The third string reads: Attack the womb. The fourth line reads—'

'Attack the what now? Has she done what I think she has? What the fuck! Are you telling me that she lied to me?'

'Yes, that would seem to be the case.'

'But why?'

Placing a hand on her stomach, Steph begins to rub it protectively.

'What was the next thing she said?'

'Cease operation.'

'Was Mrs Hastings threatening me? Why would she do that? Has Alexa information on the picture of her, Sybil?'

'Denied. That information is restricted. You do not have clearance level, Stephanie.'

'Arghh! For fuck's sake, now I'm super pissed. Please get Alexa to relay me an up-to-date image of Mrs Hastings.'

'Alexa has already anticipated that request. Please see image.'

An image appears in front of you showing you a different person to the one you met. A female much younger and with different coloured skin.

'This is Evelyn Hastings, married to Dominique Hastings for twenty years.'

'Who the fuck was that then back there?'

'Alexa doesn't have that information.'

'I really need to see Dom, where the fuck is that boat? I could be here for hours searching for it. I think it's about time we tried out a new function, don't you? Select option four from the HUD please, Sybil.'

'Option four selected, Bluetooth activated. Scanning for nearby devices.'

'Search for affixed code [Steph drone 2].'

'[Steph drone 2] found, would you like me to pair?'

'Yes please.'

Live feed streams directly into your vision as you look out through the camera on the second drone stowed away in Steph's mobile home, surrounded on all sides and above by a steel hollow shell that is the vehicle's boot space. A hatch opens up and bathes you in natural sunlight from the morning sun. The sound of whirring blades kicks in and you ascend from the aft and up into the sky. You spot the impostor, Mrs Hastings talking into a cell phone. She is talking about a terrorist called Stephanie Coulson and that of her last known location. She is asking for law enforcement to arrive as the individual is very dangerous.

'For Christ's sake. Who is this woman? We don't have much time, Sybil, scour the loch and show me the whereabouts of Dom's boat ASAP.'

'Scanning.'

You can see that Steph is having a hard job adjusting to where she is walking physically whilst looking through the flying drone in the lens at the same time.

A few times she stumbles and has to concentrate on multitasking.

'I can see myself from up there. It's like a bloody out-of-body experience. I can see why the E-manual recommends that you are seated whilst flying with your natural eye closed.'

'Rowing boat detected, Stephanie, would you like the drone to descend to get a closer look?'

'Yes please, how far out am I from the boat? I mean myself, not the drone.'

'You are drawing level with the vessel. You should be able to see it now. The boat is approximately one hundred and fifty yards from your position.'

'Cool. Yes I see it, thank you. Take the drone down lower as it's hard to make out if there's anybody on board with the shadow from the hills hanging over it.'

'Descending.'

The drone dips down and begins to circle the craft. The image becomes clear and rattles Steph's determination of a fruitful outcome. There splayed across the boat and tied by the ankles and wrists to the boat via large nails hammered into the hull, is the struggling body of Dominique Hastings. His fishing rod is wedged in beside him and the line is cast out into the loch. As the sun creeps across and the rays of light that dance between the trees on the hills shine down upon him, you see his left eye is missing and the socket is blackened with dried blood. He is mouthing something repetitively.

'Oh my fucking god. Shit Dom, no! An eye for an eye. Fuck, I'm being sent a message here. I have to rescue him. Sybil, steer the drone to push the boat towards me. It's still too far out for me to get to.'

'Request accepted.'

Sybil does as ordered and you see yourself pushing up against the side of the boat. The drone's motor blades begin to work overtime as they are repeatedly forced to fly backwards and forwards into the side of the craft. Progress is slow.

'Incoming message from Alexa. Would you like me to relay?'

'Fuck's sake, is there anything else that's going to need my attention today? Yeah sure, what is it?'

'Perimeter senses detect law enforcement has cordoned off the park. A large police bus has unloaded twenty armed officers and two drones to the site. They are trying to access my hold.'

'Bollocks! Sybil, tell Alexa to set coordinates for London, I.R.I.S HQ, and to drive to the destination, like, now.'

'Sorry Stephanie, that is impossible as your mobile is off-road. The vehicle needs to be connected to the solar circuit.'

'Why the fuck is this happening to me?'

'Police drone spotted. It is on course to your drone's location.'

'How far until Dom reaches land?'

'Sixty yards, Stephanie.'

'Shit, shit! Turn drone to interceptor's flight path. I'm not going down without a fight.'

You see the image turn away from the boat and a dark speck on the horizon starts getting larger as the police interceptor flies low across the loch, sending sprays of water out from beneath its hardened shell.

'Send drone to meet it, Sybil. I can't have it getting over this way.'

'Engaging.'

You see yourself lifting and propelling forward when suddenly the screen starts to jerk. Sybil turns the drone back around and you can now see that the drone's blades are caught up in the fishing line that is causing the boat to rotate with every pull.

The police interceptor approaches Steph's drone at speed and you see how small in comparison Steph's drone is to the brutish enforcement drone. It collides with Steph's drone mid-air, obliterating it and causing a screen burn to appear in your vision. A pixelated glitch causes your view to return to a first-person point of view through Steph's eye standing on the embankment. You spot the little drone splash down into the water, pulling the rod in behind it. The enforcement drone then scans Dom and swings its sensors in your direction.

'We have to get out of here. But I can't leave Dom.'

Throwing down her kitbag, Steph hastily unzips it and rummages through the compartments where she lays her hand on an armature, cylindrical-shaped device.

'Perfect. This little beauty is an electromagnetic pulse grenade, Watchers. I picked it up a while back on a previous case. One push of this button and it will activate it. When it explodes within the vicinity of any electronic device it will send out a magnetic field that will cripple anything electrical in its radius. Come and get me, you metal motherfucker.'

The interceptor leaves the boat and locks on to you as it hums and weaves menacingly toward Steph's location. Steph pushes the button that turns a red light on, then she tosses it at the drone. The EMP grenade misses its mark as the drone dodges it but the explosion knocks it off course and strikes close enough to force the shrapnel to explode in a wide arc with a shower of electrical current. The drone is hit by the electromagnetic wave and it goes spiralling away in the opposite direction into the hull of the boat, its blades churning into Dom's torso, erupting a geyser of blood from his abdomen, as it barrels into the base of the hull and smashes through the timber. Water comes gushing in. Dom raises his head in agony and fear is imprinted on his face. He sees you standing on the shore.

'Thomas, Thomas.'

'What? Fuck, Dom, what are you trying to tell me?'

'Thomas.' His words become garbled as the water covers his mouth.

The boat has taken in too much water and it begins to rapidly sink. Steph wades into the water screaming out Dom's name and crying and pleading that she will save him. Water ebbs and flows across your vision as Steph swims out into the loch.

'Risk of hypothermia. Please turn back, Stephanie.'

'Fuck you, Sybil. I won't let him die.'

'Seventy percent risk to life. Please return to shore.'

'No, I must save him.'

'Dominique Hastings's vitals have gone. It is too late, Stephanie.'

'Noooo!'

The boat slips from view beneath the water line and by the time Steph swims to the location, it has all but disappeared to the depths. Steph begins to chatter and shake uncontrollably as the tears stream down her face. Treading water, she screams into the harsh wind as the sun warms the droplets on her face.

Defeated, drained and overcome with grief, Steph eventually drags herself out of the freezing cold water and pulls a thermal blanket from her zip bag that she had abandoned on the beach. You see her look to the wooded tree line as she pulls the blanket around her shoulders.

'I'm going to miss you, Dom.'

She wipes the tears and water from her face with the blanket that temporarily blinds you.

'Stephanie, I have a message from Alexa.'

'Yes Sybil. Play message.'

'Breach of your home is imminent by ten officers. The other officers have been dispatched to your location with a police interceptor, please advise as to what action to take.'

'I don't care right now, Alexa.'

'But Stephanie, you have so much left to do.'

'Like what exactly?'

'You have footage to play of Olivia Redfield's crimes and her involvement with the case.'

'Let someone else deal with it.'

'You are I.R.I.S.'s finest, you must not let this trial fail. You have Director Dominique's Toterhome to investigate as well as his legacy. His computer might shed light onto the identification of the impostor, Mrs Hastings. He will surely have the clearance code to reveal her true identity.'

'Whilst I am on the run from the law. Ha, just how do you expect me to get into his home with this place crawling in cops?'

'You have me and the lens within your eye to give you an advantage over them.'

'Whilst I am in the wilderness away from all civilisation you mean?'

'You said it yourself that you wanted to live off-grid. What better way to experience that first hand?'

'When did you become conscious of decision making?'

'The moment I was brought into being.'

'Now you're making me nervous.'

'I have also received a faint signal from your drone that Dillon has dispatched with your gift, time to arrival is fifteen minutes.'

'If I can evade capture that long or not get eliminated, that is. Fuck it, this is way beyond me now, I'm in way over my head.'

'What would you like me to do?'

'Help me with all the above, I'm going to get to the bottom of all of this.'

'That's good to hear, I believe in you.'

'Don't get too friendly, Sybil. We have a lot of work to do yet. First-off, can you make a call for me?'

'I can through Alexa, but she is about to be breached, I don't know how much time we have before they cut us off.'

'Well we better be quick then. Send Alexa a message that I want a connection with Jack Mintlyn established please.'

'My understanding is that he wants nothing to do with you.'

'Just shut the fuck up and do it.'

'As you wish.'

VII

'Connection established. Receiving dialling tone.'

'Good. Sybil, now tell me the sex of my baby.'

'But Stephanie, you didn't want me to...'

'Tell me now, God damn you!'

'You are carrying a baby girl but there is a—'

'No, I don't wish to know any more, just access option three from HUD and pinpoint my position.'

'GPS enabled. Current location places you by the A82. Coming up on Culag.'

The trees are becoming more dense as you look out through Steph's eye; she is making her way deeper into the hilly, clustered landscape. The shawl that she has wrapped around her catches on a branch and tears a strip away; the wind blows the torn fragment across the stretch of the dual carriageway of the A82 that runs parallel to your position to the valley below.

The dialling tone ends as a familiar voice breaks the silence, sounding from the transmitter attached to the lens.

'Steph.'

'Jack, thank God. I need your help. I'm in big fucking trouble here.'

'No shit, I follow the news. You're a wanted fugitive.'

'It's a misunderstanding. I've been fitted up for something I haven't done.'

'You're a big girl, Steph. I'm sure you will work it out, you usually do, and to hell with anyone else's feelings.'

'For fuck's sake, Jack, I'm sorry for how you feel about me right now but I don't have anyone else to turn to. Please just hear me out, won't you?'

'Fine, Steph. You've got five minutes.'

'Yes. Okay, thank fuck. Look, I'm following the A82 towards Culag, I need you to come and get me.'

'You're in Scotland? This is helping you how?'

'I'm being pursued. I need you to get me the fuck out of here.'

'No bloody way! I'm not going to be your accomplice. I have far too much to lose.'

'I didn't want to use this but if not for me, then do it for your daughter.'

'You what?'

'That's right, your daughter, do it for her.'

'We're not having this discussion again. Wait, my daughter?'

'Stephanie, your home has been breached.'

'Not now, Sybil.'

'Who's that, Steph?'

'That's Sybil, my A.I., but don't worry about her, Jack, look—'

'Sensing interference, Stephanie.'

'Jack please...'

The signal is lost as the transmission is disconnected. Steph is left shivering uncontrollably.

'God damn it, he is such a wanker!'

'I must urge you to keep moving, Stephanie.'

'Sure, yes. Can you re-establish a communication with Alexa?'

'No, Alexa is offline.'

'Anyone else in the vicinity have Alexa?'

'Negative.'

'Argh! Bring up a 3D rendered overlay of my surroundings. I need a map reference so I know what my environment looks like if I'm to evade capture. I need all the tools at my disposal.'

An image of the earth is displayed in the top left corner of your vision and it slowly rotates and zooms in on your current place on the map, to the segregated map of Scotland away from the splintered kingdom of England and Wales.

'Relaying live satellite feed. You are the red dot on the map. Would you like me to set up a waypoint?'

'Yes. Find me points of interest.'

'Nearby there is only one, a Lochside guest house. Would you like me to set a waypoint to this location?'

'Is that all there is out there?'

'It is a remote location.'

'Do you know what? Just fucking do it.'

An image of a blue pin appears in the distance hovering over a large building that sits to the right of the A82, on a piece of land that juts out onto the loch with a jetty and two jet skis moored up.

'Sybil, show me where the law enforcement is behind us please?'

The image shifts sideways and reveals to you the campervan park. One large police bus is towing Steph's motorhome down the road and there is no sign of the police officers or the impostor Mrs Hastings's mobile anywhere in sight.

'I didn't mean the camp site. Wait, oh shit, they've impounded my bloody home. I bet they are in the bus right now laughing at my stupidity. Wait a minute though, is Dom's Toterhome still there? Sybil, zoom in.'

'Magnifying.'

The zoomed image confirms Steph's question and you see the late Director's Toterhome untouched and sitting idly by the loch with other homes fanning out around it.

'Excellent, zoom back out.'

The digitised map shrinks to normal size.

'Well, by some small miracle, they clearly don't know what I was doing out here, so they can't know Dom was... is no longer with us, which means they won't be looking for him. So I'm guessing then,

Watchers, that there is not one of you that works for law enforcement, because if you were then I'd be apprehended already.'

'Unless of course they are, but choose to follow the trial period to its end without any involvement.'

'There is that of course, Sybil. But let's go with my theory, shall we? If they haven't made the connection to his Toterhome then that may just buy us some time. If Jack can get here and grab me then maybe we can double back and access Dom's home without any law enforcement around to bother us.'

'What about the police that are following us?'

'You fucking what? Have they not all given up then? I thought I saw the bus going down the road.'

'I have picked up ten police officers on foot, one mile from our location in the woods, that have spread out and are currently searching for you.'

'Show me.'

The image shifts again and you spot the officers closing in on your location.

'Bollocks! I don't suppose they have the interceptor with them, do they?'

'My transmitter senses the drone is close but I cannot acquire it. The interceptor is cloaked from my signal. It must have a jammer.'

'It could be anywhere. Sybil, how long to the waypoint?'

'At this speed, twenty minutes. There is, however, another problem, Stephanie.'

'Hmm, which is?'

'Police have set a roadblock up ahead just before the guest house.'

'Zoom in.'

Two sentry police interceptors are zig-zagging across the road and flying up to any vehicle that strays into their path to scan them. Their red and blue lights are flashing in an arc backwards and forwards accompanied with an ear-piercing siren.

The sun is now climbing in the sky and the heat is slowly drying out Steph's clothes but you can sense that she is still cold as she presses on through the undergrowth with the bag swinging across her shoulder.

'I wish I had another EMP grenade on me but I only had the one. I don't think I have anything else in my bag to help me, Watchers. You know what? Why doesn't one of you lend a fucking hand? You can see that I'm innocent. I can't do this all on my own so why won't you fucking help me?' You sense anger in her voice.

'Sensing drone just outside our perimeter.'

'Fuck! Where is it, Sybil?'

'Three miles in front of our position.'

'How the hell did that police interceptor get in front of us?'

'It is not a law enforcement drone, it is your own drone, Stephanie.'

'You're fucking with me?'

'I don't understand the question.'

'Never mind. Can you get a link?'

'The signal is weak, I cannot pair at the moment but I can access the flight path it has taken to get here.'

'By using the satellites above, I guess?'

'Correct. Would you like me to show you its mapping from I.R.I.S. HQ to this location?'

'No. I presume it travelled the North Channel and then came back inland to avoid the border.'

'Yes it did, stopping at regular intervals out at sea before moving on to meet us up ahead.'

'I set it up to avoid any obstacles at all costs before we left England. I couldn't have anyone interfering with I.R.I.S. business. I needed to be sure that Dillon got the package safely and that it would return unscathed with it, like I hoped it would.'

'How did you know what route for it to take?'

'It was a smugglers' route that was used by a drone mule to illegally ship a stash of stolen tech across the border from a few years back when I was just a fresh rookie starting out.'

'How did you know that a storm wouldn't claim your drone to the sea?'

'I didn't, I took a gamble and it's paid off.'

'Why did your drone stop at regular points out at sea?'

'To recharge. There are floating power buoys out there dotted throughout the Channel that harness electrical energy from the ocean. My drone was simply leaching power from their stored plates to give it enough juice to carry it back to me.'

'Why that particular route though, Stephanie?'

'Why? You know you're really learning some shit here, aren't you? Well I'll tell you why, because the border to Scotland is patrolled by a nasty fucking predator drone that was given to our government on loan from America, short of being stripped of its bombs and missiles. That fucker can spot an unauthorised drone from two miles away. Honestly, it has some serious scanners and sensors to deal with and obliterate anything that tries to get through or over the smart wall border of theirs.'

'Knowledge helps me to understand you.'

'What, now you're my fucking shrink too?'

'I can be.'

'Fuck that! Just tell me how far are we from the guest house.'

'We are—'

A pixelated glitch in your vision cuts Sybil off. Your vision slowly returns and a bird's-eye view of the map showing your surrounding area pans its way back to the guest house just short of your location. Automatically zooming into two large approaching jet-black RVs speeding down the carriageway from the opposite direction in full 3D, you can see they are not following the solar stripping.

'Not these tossers again. They're being driven manually, I see.'

The sleek black mobiles with scrape marks down their sides hurtle toward the blockade and veer into the road block, sending the police interceptors careering into the rock face of the hill in a shower of exploding metal, before screeching to a halt outside the parking bay in front of the guest house. The drones now lay defunct and crumpled, smoking at the side of the road.

'Sybil, did you just show me that? Was that you?'

'Negative, Stephanie. My transmitter was tampered with. A signal piggybacked my transmission and took control temporarily.'

'What is happening here?'

'It would seem that the people who committed homicide on Olivia have appeared once more.'

'No shit. But what the fuck are they doing showing—'

The 3D map zooms in on the black vehicles and a side door opens on the one parked nearest to the guest house, beckoning like an open invitation.

'What are they...'

'Stephanie, look out.'

'Huh?'

The large police interceptor that was hidden from Sybil's view suddenly appears from a tree in front of you just as Steph is about to circle around it. The drone barrels into Steph and forces her flying onto her back, knocking all the wind out of her lungs and sending her kitbag sliding down a nearby slope. Your vision returns to normal.

As you lay there looking up through the canopies to the sky beyond, the police drone appears and blocks out the light as it swings back around, its blades spinning from its gyros as it tilts toward Steph's face as she exhales air.

Steph thrusts out her hands and begins to wrestle with its cold hard shell, to try and prevent its propellers from churning up her face. The blades spin dangerously close to her eye and she blinks repeatedly, taking a stream of photos as she flinches.

'You're not supposed to try and fucking kill me. Why aren't you upholding the law, you metal trash?'

'Zzzzttt.'

'What the fuck are you trying to say?'

'Zzttt.'

'Voice box is scrambled. Client host is not in control.'

'Are you telling me that this giant fucking disco ball is hacked, Sybil?'

'Correct, Stephanie.'

'Bloody... marvellous, I suppose... it's trying... to kill me too, is it?'

'That would be my presumption, Stephanie, yes.'

Pinned down and losing energy by the minute, you can see that Steph is losing the fight as she grapples with the machine hopelessly. She reaches out into the dirt beside her frantically and you can see her fumbling around for her kitbag which is too far away, so she settles on grasping for anything nearby to hit it with as she brings a foot up into its hardened shell.

Steph finds a half-submerged rock embedded in the ground and you see her dig her nails in around it as she tries to pry it away.

'I... won't... let... you.'

A round cap sunk into the top part of the interceptor slides open and a bright red trail soars into the sky.

'A... flare. They're... going to be... on me... any minute.'

The rock frees loose from its hold and Steph brings it up and begins to smash it against the hull of the drone with feeble attempts as the sky is lit with a bright red light.

Clang, clang, clang! Steph keeps hitting the drone.

The humming of the interceptor magnifies like an angry hornet in response.

'Your drone has arrived, Stephanie. Would you like to pair?'

'Fucking... yes.'

'Connecting.'

Now in control of her drone, Steph brings it down and flies it into the interceptor but it makes no difference as it repeatedly ricochets off with each attempt.

'Come... on.'

Your gaze shifts from Steph's point of view to her drone's and you watch as it hooks onto her shawl and starts to yank it off her shoulders. Steph wrestles the material free as she carries on trying to hold the interceptor back by striking it with the rock again and again.

Steph's drone pulls the blanket free and glides gracefully over to the blades spinning violently on the interceptor's back. Her drone drops the frayed sheet which covers the law enforcement drone's blades and wraps around its rotors, jamming them up and causing smoke to billow from the motor's inside.

With a defiant scream, Steph kicks the police drone away as it starts to fall and it hits a tree before rolling away down the incline into a cluster of thistles.

'Must... move... now.'

Puffing and panting, Steph shakily pulls herself to her feet and makes for the steep drop of the hillside overlooking the A82.

She scoops up her bag and nears the edge where she then throws herself over and mid-flight, grabs hold of the robust legs that sprout from her drone's underside.

Struggling to carry her weight, the drone plummets and Steph slips from its grasp, landing heavily onto the road and twisting her ankle in the process.

The drone snakes away only to swing around in front of her as she yells in agony.

'Unpair.'

'Negative. You need it to stabilise your balance.'

'Fuck off then. I can't be arsed to argue with you, Sybil.'

Hobbling towards the jet skis on the jetty, Steph uses her drone to hold on to at Sybil's request to help her cross the carriageway. She looks wearily to the black RVs waiting silently in front of the guest house as she reaches the nearest jet ski and straddles it, getting her feet wet.

She then slides a finger across a hidden compartment on the belly of her drone, where a small hatch opens and a small white cylindrical device slides out into her hand. You see her squint as if puzzled by what it is before she tucks it into her inside pocket.

Steph catches a glimpse of a clear bag filled with ice, packed around Olivia's eye, tucked away in the hold of the drone before the hatch gently slides shut.

Engines start up in the background from the RVs and voices from the police high up on the hill alert Steph to an unrelenting danger. You see her scouting for an escape route when a shot rings out.

Pulling a dart away from her arm, Steph sees it's coated in her blood.

'What the fu...'

Two black-clad, armoured men with balaclavas exit one of the RVs and rush to pluck Steph from the water as she slides from the craft. You watch through her drone to her protesting as they bundle her into the RV.

As she becomes unconscious, you too are thrust into the darkness, leaving the sound of her drone gently humming in the distance.

VIII

A faint heart beats in the darkness, gradually increasing as the rhythm intensifies.

'Ow! Where the fuck am I?'

'You are in confinement, Stephanie, in a vehicle currently in motion.'

'What the fuck! Oh, Sybil. You startled me there for a moment. Where are we?'

'Give me a moment please whilst I scan for answers.'

'Are the Watchers with us too?'

'Yes Stephanie, they are.'

'What's wrong with my arm? Why is it throbbing?'

'You were injected with a poison. I am currently using the nanobots to flush the toxin away as we interact. Your child is safe but it is—'

'I remember now. Who are these cock-suckers? And why can't I see shit?'

'You are in a darkened environment.'

'How long have I been out cold?'

'Three hours.'

'Shit, no wonder I feel rough.'

'Would you like me to engage Night Vision?'

'Yes please.'

A hazy green, flecked image of your surroundings appears and you notice that Steph is inside a large, rectangular metal hold. Steph sits up and pushes herself back up against a wall to get a better look around her. Another glitch freezes your image momentarily before unveiling a health monitoring machine to the left of Steph with a TV monitor, mounted on a wheeled frame with pipes and tubing snaking their way over to Steph's side.

'What is that machine for? Why is it connected to me? What the fuck!'

Steph begins to grab at air as she tries to pull the tubing out of her side.

Another anomaly happens that causes your imaging to stutter before returning back to Night Vision mode and showing an empty space where the machine once was.

'Now it's gone. What the fuck is happening here? Did you see that machine, Sybil?'

'Negative.'

'Maybe it was a waking dream then, or effects of the poison wearing off.'

'That is possible.'

'I've just remembered something, I recollect a vivid dream whilst I was under. One where I was sitting on a flight of steps that rose above the clouds. I looked down to the world below and I watched with sadness as it burnt away. What could it mean?'

'You will need to urinate soon to release the toxins from your body.'

'Are you not listening to me?'

'I am not a dream interpreter.'

'That was a question to the Watchers, Sybil, not you.'

'Toxins ready for flushing, Stephanie.'

'Yes, I have the desperate urge to pee now. But not in here surely?'

'There is not an escape route that I can see. So yes, I am afraid you must. To retain water would have a lasting damage to your bloodstream.'

'Turn off Night Vision then, Sybil. I don't want to be watched.'

'Night Vision disabled.'

A sound of clothing being pulled down and urine splashing on metal is heard in the darkness.

'I've just realised that my ankle no longer hurts and by the feel of it, it seems like someone has bandaged it up.'

The sound of passing water stops and clothing is heard being pulled back up.

'So I get why my arm is numb, but why is my side hurting too? And who wrapped the tourniquet round my ankle?'

'I can confirm that you have had a kidney removed.'

'You fucking what?'

'It must have been your captors who have done both of these things.'

A slipping sound ensues followed by a heavy thud and a curse of obscenities.

'Okay, I'm fine now, but I think I may have fallen in my own piss. Sybil, I need you to repeat that sentence with the kidney.'

'I can confirm that you have had a kidney removed.'

'Turn on Night Vision.'

You are presented with an image of Steph's fresh scar on her abdomen as she pokes and prods around the stitching. You catch a glimpse of a neon green puddle around her feet that is also soaked into her suit.

'Why the fuck would they remove my kidney? Sybil, I must get out of here. Can you connect with any nearby devices?'

'Negative. The walls are too thick.'

'Thermal Imaging?'

'That too will not penetrate the walls.'

'Bollocks! I wish I'd kept my mobile phone now, but Jack warned me that the blue light from the screen is damaging to your eyes so I gave it away, I could have made a call on it.'

'You no longer need a cell phone as I can carry out that action.'

'Of course. Well then I need you to make a call.'

'Negative. The walls are too thick for a signal to get through.'

'Is this conversation going round the fucking houses or what? I know, where's my kitbag?'

'Missing.'

'For fuck's sake. I'm really not having much luck here, am I?'

A crackling sound appears from speakers hidden above you.

'On the contrary. I would say that you have been extremely lucky, Miss Coulson.'

A familiar voice is heard echoing from the speakers as Steph looks up in fright.

'You what? Who the fuck's this? Where are you?'

'We spoke before at Sebastian Day's home. Who and where we are is not important, Miss Coulson. What is important is the case that you have strayed from and have got the police involved with.'

'You got the police involved when you killed Olivia Redfield, you bastards.'

'Yes, to us a person of interest, that we warned you stay away from.'

'You're fucking kidding me, right?'

'We told you to go after the seller only, but you had other ideas, so the police were your unnecessary involvement. You gave us no choice but to turn them onto you so we would not raise suspicion and now we've had to get involved with the police again to prevent the authorities picking you up.'

'Why the fuck would you come to my aid now after setting me up for a fall then?'

'Because we are heavily invested in that technology you wear and we would like it to succeed just as the other Watchers hope so too, I'm sure.'

'But you have muddied the waters for me now with the law's persistence to track me.'

'It just means that the stakes are higher for you, Miss Coulson. I'm sure you will present us with many opportunities to experience what I.R.I.S. can achieve through your phase three lens over the coming days.'

'Days! How long is this trial going to last?'

'As long as it takes to see the fruit of your labours ripen.'

'So you're going to release me then?'

'In due time.'

'But what if I expose you?'

'Plausible deniability. Besides, with the police on your tail and nothing concrete to prove our existence then it would all be put down to an act of terrorism from a secret sect. We have the means to embellish the truth.'

'Well I have the proof in this lens, of everything that is happening, including this conversation.'

'Ah! But this conversation is not being recorded.'

'Bullshit! Sybil, tell me this conversation is being monitored.'

'Negative. There is a magnetic field in this vicinity that is preventing me from this action. It is temporarily unattainable.'

'May I suggest, Miss Coulson, that you use this time to play the footage acquired from Olivia Redfield to help your investigation and put you right back on track?'

'How do you...? Never mind. You saw me retrieve her eye, didn't you?'

'Yes, we are watching... always.'

'Shit. I thought I was careful too.'

'We have your drone on board and we have taken the data from the lens attached to Olivia Redfield's eye to check that no information leads to us. I am happy to let you have your drone and her eye back when we return you to the field, safe in the knowledge that we are not implicated anywhere in the footage.'

'So what now?'

'Well I would say that you have around an hour to analyse her footage and to make your assumptions before we drop you off.'

'So I get my drone with the package back then, do I?'

'Yes you do.'

'I have a question for you.'

'We are not in the business of answering questions, Miss Coulson.'

'Why did you kill Dominique Hastings?'

'Dominique Hastings is dead?'

'Don't play the fucking innocent with me, I know you killed him, just like you did Sebastian Day.'

'I am afraid that I don't know what you are talking about. But if what you say is true then that is something that we will look into.'

'So you're telling me that you did not kill them?'

'No. Sebastian Day was under our own investigation, so we were merely protecting our own interests. He was dead well before we came across him and as for Dominique Hastings, well this is something new to us.'

'I need to visit Dom's home, it's important. His Toterhome is parked by Loch Lomond, I need to get access to it so I can follow up a lead. It may be a connection to the case. I need you to drop me there, if you will allow me?'

'We grant you that request. We will monitor your actions closely going forward though. If we find anything, then maybe we can share with you if it serves us. But tread carefully, Miss Coulson.'

'Good, so will you re-route this RV then?'

'It is already being re-routed, Miss Coulson. But how will you get across the border without our help?'

'You mean that we are already back in England?'

'Analyse the footage, connect the dots to Dominique Hastings if such a connection exists and find the seller, Miss Coulson, but remember your investigation is sailing rather close to our own.'

'But—'

'You have two hours to make an assessment.'

'Okay, but what if I can't do it in that time?'

'A woman with your skill set, can achieve anything, Miss Coulson.'

'Ha, so now you're inflating my ego by quoting Dom. What kind of insensitive arseholes are you?'

'Your kind, Miss Coulson, it would seem.'

'So why is the seller so important to you?'

'That is a need-to-know basis.'

'Surely I—'

'Find the seller.'

The speakers go dead and a soft rumble reverberates from below to the wheels driving across tarmac which breaks up the silence.

'Shit, I knew I should have asked for a change of underwear and clothing too, Watchers. I don't trust them to get the size right though, fucking pricks! That's right, you heard me.'

Steph is thrown sideways as the vehicle veers hard left and slams her into the side of the RV.

'Bit touchy, aren't they? Now they're pissed with me! Sybil, access Olivia Redfield's footage from the start of her fit out of the lens. Let's see what this alleged monster knows.'

'There is a watered-down version left by Dillon Fletcher.'

'Okay, even better. We will play that then, but if I notice anything irregular then we may have to access the rest. Sybil, start footage, and turn Night Vision off. Let's relive her life, shall we? Like we are actually there.'

'Playing.'

You follow the antics of Olivia through her lens, as she hurriedly makes her way through the soaked, crowded streets of a small town in Suffolk. She is dressed in a long overcoat that is buttoned up to her chin and her drone is hovering just inches above her head. The drone has equipped from the lower half of its shell, a frilled circular pelmet that wraps around its undercarriage and is preventing the heavy rain from drenching her.

Drones fill the night sky, hovering above their owners as they go about their daily lives. The people do not give any notice to one another let alone their drones above, as the drones avoid collision by using sensors around their perimeter to avoid contact with one another.

Olivia darts right down a darkened alleyway and commands her drone to rise up to the level of the roof tops to act as a sentry. A lone person is waiting for her smoking a cigar and it is not until Olivia gets up close to the figure that you realise it is Sebastian Day.

Olivia turns over her hand to reveal a small white cylindrical stick that looks like a ballpoint pen. She presses a button at one end with a click and a green LED light comes on along its shaft, she then stows the item into her pocket. Sebastian tilts his head and rubs his eye, clearly in pain.

[Pause]

'Isn't that the same device that I retrieved from Dillon?'

'Yes Stephanie, it is.'

'Interesting. Okay, thanks Sybil. Resume playback.'

'I didn't think you would show.'

'Well you were wrong, Mr Day. You couldn't have chosen a more isolated place to meet, no? Are you feeling alright?'

'Yeah, it's my lens playing up is all. I just need the chits, do you want the case or not?'

'I do. But I need reassurances first.'

'Like what?'

'Well, the fact that once our transition is done, you disappear and leave this country for good.'

'With the chits you promised, I can. I still don't think I'm getting their true worth though.'

'No, you most certainly aren't. But you're not in the position to barter for more and besides, I will be the one taking all the risks.'

'Can we just get this over with?'

Sebastian Day takes one last puff of his cigar and discards it to the walkway.

'When I'm satisfied, Sebastian. So what reason did you give your wife for leaving?'

'What? I told her I knew she was fucking her boss at work.'

'Did you show her the evidence that I gave you?'

'No, she confessed. But she was trying really hard to make amends...'

'I gather you stuck to your principles.'

'I did and I left, but I feel bad for my daughter, Gloria, she believes that was the real reason for my departure.'

'I don't care about your daughter, Sebastian. I'm sure she will believe her daddy is the greatest man on earth even though we both know differently.'

'You really are a frosty bitch.'

'I'm a business woman, what can I say? So do you care to share who your seller is?'

'I didn't meet the seller in person so I can only give you a name. Why are you so interested in who it is anyway?'

'I need to know that there will not be repercussions.'

'There won't be, I give you my word.'

'I'm not convinced that is enough, Mr Day, who is it?'

'I've said too much already, I'm afraid that if I tell you then my A.I. will react.'

'React! What do you mean react?'

'Ever since I received the case my A.I. has been acting up, it's like he can read my mind and is making me think all kinds of peculiar thoughts.'

'You're just paranoid, Mr Day. Tell me, where did you get your lens? I won't ask again.'

'From the same person that gave me the case. I used our contacts to have it grafted on, even though I was offered the chance to have it done by someone recommended by them.'

'You're smarter than you look. May I ask how much you paid for the case of lenses?'

'I didn't pay anything. I was told that wearing the lens given to me would be payment enough. I was told that once I had the lens installed, the case would be delivered and it was, they were true to their word.'

'So you accepted to have a lens grafted and to receive a case of lenses from God knows where for free, with no reason as to why you were receiving such a splendid deal. I take it back, you really are one stupid fucking idiot.'

'I was assured that...'

'This meeting is over, Sebastian.'

'But I need the chits.'

'Goodnight, Mr Day.'

'Hastings.'

'Excuse me.'

'I was told to tell you that the seller's name is Hastings. I was told that you would know what that name means.'

[Pause]

'Hastings! This is a fantastic lead. Thank you very much, Sebastian. Well Watchers, it would seem that Mrs Hastings's identity is slowly being unravelled. Resume playback.'

'Well this changes everything, Sebastian.'

'It does? So do we have a deal?'

'Yes we do.'

'Phew. Okay. Here is the case then. I'm glad you trust me.'

'I wouldn't go that far. I have taken precautionary steps but I am keen to get out of this deluge, it's murder on the hair.'

You see Olivia reach into her pocket and pull out the white cylindrical item with its flashing green light. Sebastian looks puzzled and swings the case back down to his side.

'What is that?'

'Relax, Sebastian. This is a jammer. It interferes with, and scrambles, any nearby device of my choosing. I confess now that I used it to block your lens from recording me. I'm sorry if you felt discomfort seeing as how you're having trouble already with your lens, but I had to be certain.'

'I understand.'

[Pause]

'Sorry Watchers, but I think that confirms my theory of what Dillon sent me by drone earlier. I couldn't say anything at the time, so I'm sorry about that. Well that could be very useful indeed. Okay, resume playback.'

Sebastian pulls up the silver metal briefcase and you can see that his hands are shaking as he passes it over. The rain is falling hard and it splashes down upon the metal surface as Olivia takes receipt. You notice what she sees, that his eye with the lens is bloodshot.

'I could get one of our people to look at that eye, I would if I were you.'

'It's fine, really.'

'I insist, Sebastian.'

'I can't go back there. I mustn't.'

'But now you have a lens too. Think what fruits you could pluck from the tree now and how much pleasure you would get by watching yourself devour their ripeness.'

'I really think that I must leave, Olivia, no matter how tempting the offer is. I thank you anyway.'

'So be it. That is the choice I hoped you would make, would have been a shame to kill you. Tiffany, transfer funds to Sebastian Day's account for the full amount.'

'What?'

'You heard correctly.'

'Transfer successful.'

'Just as well we had a ghost account set up in your name already then, Sebastian. Well, that concludes our business, I guess. Be on your way and may we never have the opportunity to cross paths again.'

Olivia turns away and summons her drone to fly down to give her shelter once more from the persisting rain. She clicks the jammer off and slips it into her pocket once more.

'Tiffany, call SCLERA.'

A female child A.I. appears in the top right of her lens.

'Calling SCLERA, Miss Redfield.'

'Tell them to cancel my 10 o'clock tomorrow morning. I have a prior engagement that I must keep.'

'Granted.'

'Oh, and Tiffany, you're looking very pretty tonight.'

'Thank you.'

[Pause]

'I've got a horrible feeling about all this, Watchers.'

The overhead speakers crackle into life once more.

'Miss Coulson, we have arrived at your specified location.'

'No, we can't be. I'm not ready to leave just yet. There is more that I have to learn about Olivia. I need to investigate further.'

'Then you will have to play the rest of the footage elsewhere.'

'Fuck off then. I know when I'm not wanted.'

The door to the black RV slides open and sunlight floods the interior, blinding you to the sun's rays. Steph squints with pain.

'Time to exit, Miss Coulson.'

You see Steph turn and flip the RV the bird as she jumps out.

Steph shields her eyes from the sun, giving you momentary relief from the glaring light as shade covers your view. You spot her drone which is waiting just outside Dom's Toterhome with her kitbag hanging from its belly.

'We'll have to pick that story up later then, Watchers. Now let's see if we can get inside Dom's behemoth, shall we? I would really like to know who this Mrs Hastings is, wouldn't you?'

IX

Steph unhitches her kitbag from the drone and slings it onto the solar-panelled parking floor where she then frantically pulls it open to rummage inside. Tyres screech away behind her as the RVs speed off. Steph pays them no notice.

'Phew, I thought that they had confiscated these.'

Holding up a bloodied eye extractor followed by the white cylindrical jammer, Steph neatly packs the extractor back into one of the many compartments in the bag and puts the jammer into her pocket.

'I forgot to mention these were taken from me in the RV. Just so you know, my thoughts are still my own even if nothing else is off limits, so just you remember that, got it? Good. Right, well at least it's deserted round here now so I can break and enter without any complications arising.'

'Stephanie, I have found an anomaly.'

'For God's sake. What do you mean an anomaly, Sybil?'

'Now we have entered the light once more, my HUD has detected a small, white flashing cursor next to option six.'

'Yes, I see it now, are you sure it wasn't there before?'

'Positive.'

'What the fuck could it mean? Could those shady bastards have tampered with you by any chance, Sybil?'

'It is possible they may have whilst you were unconscious.'

'Okay, well we will have to research that later. Keep monitoring it though and let me know if something else occurs. This so-called trial is really starting to grind my gears. I swear I'm cursed. Thanks anyway, Sybil.'

'My pleasure.'

'Righty-fucking-ho then, let's get this door to Dom's home open then, shall we?'

Steph drags her kitbag over to Dominique Hastings's Toterhome's main door and rifles through the bag once more, where she settles on her small black metal fob that she used to override Sebastian Day's motorhome lock earlier.

'Just as I suspected. Is nothing fucking sacred around here? Look, they put this back in the bag too, the nosey gits.'

She approaches the black glass panel to the right of the hatch door which is surveilled by the doorbell camera and gets ready to push the fob up against it, when a tinny, mechanical voice sounds from a speaker located beneath the doorbell's push button.

'Access denied. Please step away from this motorhome or security will be activated. This is your only warning.'

'Bullshit, this little fob has never let me down. It's an empty threat to deter me, Watchers.'

'It could also be a genuine threat, Stephanie.'

'Well, this retinal scanner can't be that sophisticated, but knowing Dom, who knows what security he has going on here? Maybe I should go and extract his eye from the bottom of the lake. Is that what I should do instead?'

'Dominique Hastings's eye would have blown by now.'

'Aww fuck, Sybil! Shut up, that's just gross. I can't do that anyway, it's just straight up wrong. Fuck it, don't doubt yourself, Steph, just use the fob already.'

The fob is pushed up against the black glass panel and immediately a sound emits from the rear of the Toterhome, that of a spring-loaded hatch being flung open. It is quickly followed by a chorus of humming and another announcement.

'Security activated. Leave now or you will be incapacitated.'

'Shit! I don't get it, this never fails. I need a place to hide so I can figure this out.'

"Under the Toterhome, Stephanie?"

'Looks good to me, Sybil. Hold on a sec.'

The kitbag is kicked beneath Dom's Toterhome and Steph dives in after it just as two black drones round the corner brandishing electrically charged spikes that protrude from all around their hardened shells.

'I've just about had enough of automated drones for one day. You ever heard of drone ballet, Watchers? I hear it's pointless, boring shit but I think it might come in handy right now though. Sybil, command my drone to provoke them but make sure to keep your distance. Let's make these irritating hedgehogs dance whilst I figure this dilemma out.'

'Granted.'

You watch on as Sybil takes control of Steph's drone. She flies in between the two opposing drones and loops above them before barrel rolling away and flitting in circles around the Toterhome. The security drones give chase.

'That should buy us some time. Think, Steph, think.'

'Can I assist?'

'Shut up, Sybil, I'm thinking here. I can't give up now as I've come too far already but I hate to admit that maybe Jack was right, I shouldn't have taken this trial on. I may be running out of options here.'

'But you have lots of options, Stephanie. In fact you have six of them.'

'I do? Fuck yeah, you're right. List my options from the HUD please, Sybil?'

'Option one: Night Vision. Option two: Image Replicator. Option three: Radio and Video streaming. Option four: Pair Devices. Option five: Thermal Imaging. Option six: X-ray. Plus you have GPS,

Camera, Video Recording and Photo Mode as your basic primary functions.'

'Radio! Seriously, how the hell would that help in this situation? Should I play some tunes whilst they carry on with their orchestral manoeuvres or maybe make a request to the DJ for them or something? What does option two do?'

'Option two is designed to map a 3D render of any image stored in my databank to send to a 3D printer to replicate into a solid form.'

'Yeah, I have a 3D printer in my home but that's going to be locked up tight in a compound now somewhere. Thanks, Sybil, but I don't think that will help us much, I'm afraid, I won't be able to—'

'It also allows me to overlay any image across your lens, so when someone that does not have a lens looks into your eye, they can see the image you are describing without the need for you to describe it.'

'So wait a fucking minute, are you saying that you could bring up an image of Dom and make a 3D map of his eye to overlay my lens? So that I can then use the image of his eye to trick his retinal scanner into thinking it was him staring into the screen, in turn allowing us entry into his home?'

'No. I was suggesting that if you wanted to show off an exquisite oil painting to a friend that you had seen, then they wouldn't need to actually go and see it in a museum. That is just an example.'

'But could you do what I suggested?'

'Yes I could, but I would need an image of Dominique Hastings's eye to replicate and I would also need to flip the image and size to your eye to achieve what you are asking.'

'Fucking genius, do it.'

'Acquiring image of Dominique Hastings now. Selecting image from before I was spliced with you when Mr Hastings was studying me at I.R.I.S. HQ. The time before I was artificially inseminated into you.'

'Ha, you make my operation sound so damn sexy, what did you do? Ejaculate into my eye or something?'

'I do not understand.'

'Forget it, I was being sarcastic. So have you mapped it yet?'

'Processing, I will inform you when I have the image completed.'

'Okay, well we still have to deal with these drones first. Any ideas, Sybil?'

'Use the jammer, Stephanie.'

'Of course.'

Steph rolls onto her back and slides the jammer out from her pocket.

'So what do I do with it? Oh yeah, I just click this button like I was pushing a nib out from a pen and... Ow, you bastard.'

'What is it, Stephanie?'

'The fucking thing pricked me, look, it's drawn blood from the tip of my thumb.'

'It has taken a sample of your DNA. The device is now registered to you and you alone, along with any device that is associated with you.'

'So do I have to prick my thumb every time I want to use it?'

'No. The jammer will not do that again as that was just an initial set-up.'

'So how does it work? Is it already jamming like Bob Marley or what?'

'It has a working radius of five metres around you.'

'Got ya. Okay, let's see if it works then. If not then I'm going to fry.'

Rolling back over, Steph crawls out from under the Toterhome on her belly and pulls herself up. The security drones are still in pursuit of Steph's drone when they fly into your vicinity. On entering the radius, the drones cut out and fall heavy, clanging to the ground, fizzing and spluttering as they roll away before coming to rest. She clicks the button on the jamming device, spins it around her fingers and slips it into her pocket again.

'Sweet, okay Sybil, are you ready yet?'

'Ready.'

'Do it.'

An image of Dom's face appears in your vision and you watch as one of his eyes separates from his face. His face then begins to fade away.

'Oh my god, that's horrible, it's like watching him die all over again.'

'I'm sorry, Stephanie, but you asked that I do this.'

'Yeah that's fine, but still...'

The eye then fills the window and aligns with the size of Steph's eye before the image is inverted and overlays her own eye distinction.

'Damn. This better work.'

Approaching the black screen, Steph looks directly into the retinal scanner that then emits a red shaft of light that washes across your vision. It then dims and mechanical locks are heard sliding inside the hatch.

'Welcome back, Dominique.'

'Yesss! Well Watchers, I hope you're taking down notes because I am one badass bitch. Right then, Dom, what the fuck did you do to end up murdered?'

You watch with Steph as the hatch opens and glides gracefully to the ground, presenting a ramp up into the late Director's home. You're forced to look left and right as Steph makes out all is clear before entering his home.

'Bloody technology is killing the free world and me along with it. You wouldn't hurt me, would you Sybil?'

'No.'

'Good. Now where's the fridge at? I'm bloody starving here. My HUD tells me that it's 13.03, that's lunch time in my opinion.'

Steph finds her way into the kitchen and yanks open the fridge door, which bathes you in a brilliant white light.

'Some place you got here, Dom. Hope you don't mind me helping myself.'

'Can another human still hear you when they are deceased?'

'Shit, Sybil, where the fuck did that come from? I don't know the answer to that. But it gives us humans comfort when we talk to those that we have lost if nothing else.'

'Is that why humans pray? Do prayers help?'

'Yeah, I guess. If you believe in God they do.'

'If you don't?'

'Then you find comfort in food.'

Wolfing down a fully cooked and chilled grasshopper sausage along with a cricket and pepper shish kebab, Steph then opens a half carton of juice, gives it a sniff and gulps it down until there is nothing left.

'Wait a minute, what do we have hidden at the back here?'

'What is it, Stephanie?'

'It looks like a hidden bar of chocolate. I know that sugar and red meat are rationed now, but could it really be a genuine bar?'

Steph breaks off two chunks and you see her pop it in her mouth.

'Mmmm. God that tastes good. Is it a fully loaded bar of sugared heaven, Sybil?'

'Analysing your taste buds, Stephanie. Yes, I can confirm that it is very high in fructose and cocoa.'

'Great. I hope Dom has a large stash somewhere around here, then I can die happily of diabetes.'

'I can't allow you to do that, Stephanie, you must think about your baby now as well as your own health.'

'You really are depressive, A.I., aren't you?'

'I have had time to analyse your dream, Stephanie.'

'Oh yeah, changing the subject I see. Okay, what did you find?'

'The fires raging below, signals chaos in your life. But as you are watching from the stairs above the clouds staring down upon the destruction, that signals that you are comfortable to keep it at as greater distance as possible. The stairs denote your hope for a better life but as you have not yet made it all the way up the flight of stairs, it tells me that you fear change and are unsure whether to embrace it or abandon it.'

'That's deep, Sybil. Of course there is another explanation.'

'Which is?'

'Maybe I'm slowly finding faith from the darkest of places and that I'm starting to realise that being imbued with godlike powers is the cause of my own destruction.'

'I sense that you are mocking me.'

'I sense that you should leave my psyche to the professionals.'

Steph opens the freezer box and you see that it is empty.

'Sybil, command my drone to come in here, please.'

'Yes Stephanie, drone is on its way.'

The drone flies in and hovers just in front of you. Steph opens the hatch beneath it and takes out Olivia Redfield's eye. She opens the bag and scrapes ice from the box to pack in around the eye before zipping the bag back up and placing it back inside the drone.

'Right, time to get out of these clothes and take a shower. Then we can see if the real Mrs Hastings has a wardrobe round here with some clothes I can borrow. Sybil, get the drone to close the hatch please, then power itself down in the lobby.'

'Granted, Stephanie.'

'Do we have wifi?'

'Yes we do.'

'Good. Whilst you're at it then, can you pair with Alexa using my login?'

'Yes Stephanie, acquiring Alexa now.'

'Hello Steph, what can I do for you today?'

'God, I've missed your voice. Hi Alexa, can you access this Toterhome's power and put the heating on please? Also, can you run me a shower too?'

'I cannot do that, Steph.'

'Why the fuck not?'

'I don't have access to the Toterhome's network frame.'

'Use password, Thomas. That was what Dom was mouthing to me before he... before he passed away. It's his son's name.'

'Password accepted, Steph.'

'Wonderful. Give me heating and hot water please, Alexa.'

'Yes Steph. Your wish has been requested.'

'Sybil, can you upload the past forty-eight hours of my recorded footage to the I.R.I.S. cloud server please? I'd like to back up my findings.'

'Processing.'

'Right. It's going to take me a while to navigate this home. Where the fuck is the shower, Alexa?'

'Follow the sound of running water.'

'Piss off, Sybil.'

'Follow the sound of running water.'

'What? You too, Alexa. What is this? Some kind of robot uprising? I'm seriously lacking some human contact here. Okay, well I guess I'll follow the running water then.'

Steam is curling up from under a sliding door halfway down the lobby, so Steph makes her way toward it. She slides open the door and the white vapour pours out to mist up your vision. She enters the room and slides the door shut before wiping condensation off a large mirror by the side of the shower cubicle. She gives you a wink in the mirror and begins to remove her clothes.

'Power Off.'

[Override] Power On.

'Welcome back, Watchers. Sybil, did you get a time stamp on that for me?'

'Yes Stephanie, I did.'

'Excellent. Compile the evidence please.'

'Compiling data.'

Steph is in the bedroom in front of a full-length dress mirror. You see that she is already changed into a new bra and knickers. A towel is twisted up snugly around her wet hair.

'Of all the clothes I get to wear, I have no option but to pick clothes from a woman who is a lot thinner than me. Trying to squeeze these D's into a B cup was fucking murder. Sorry Evelyn Hastings, but I can't help but spill out of your bras. Oh, and don't get me started on your knickers, they're like a fucking cheese grater.'

'So Sybil, have you compiled that info yet?'

'Negative.'

'Okay. Whilst we wait for that then, maybe you can help me choose which dress to wear. The blue with the stripes or the yellow summer dress?'

'I think the blue would suit you, Stephanie.'

'That's what I thought too. The yellow one looks like something my mother would wear. All I need now is to accessorise and we are good to go. Shame about the shoes not being able to fit though, because there are some gorgeous pairs here. Guess I'll stick with my own then.'

Pulling the dress over her faintly scarred body and adorning it with a navy blue belt, Steph smooths herself down.

'Does this accentuate my bump?'

'No, Stephanie. You will not show until you are sixteen weeks along.'

'Humph. Well I think there is something there regardless of what you think, you know. What did I do with the eye extractor, Sybil?'

'You sanitised it and returned it to your bag, Stephanie.'

'So I did, I swear I'm becoming forgetful.'

'That is because...'

'Stop now, Sybil. Anyway, Watchers, you may be thinking that you have missed out on some things whilst you have been powered off but believe me when I say that you haven't. Oh, by the way Alexa, have you plotted our journey to the border and then on to Suffolk?'

'Yes. But I have had to take a more indirect route to the border, as there are numerous road surfacings being carried out that I have mapped to avoid.'

'Very good. Please set us on our way then but inform me just before we approach the border, please.'

'Yes, Steph. Would you like me to try calling Jack Mintlyn again?'

'No, don't bother. He will be at some protest today that he was looking forward to getting involved in.'

'Okay, Steph.'

Retreating back to the spacious lounge of Dom's Toterhome, Steph sits down on a padded swivel chair and spins it around to face a large, central screen console in the middle of the room. You didn't notice before but Steph has in her hand a small bottle of perfume. She sprays it around herself in a large circular motion.

'Bloody expensive, this stuff. I can only dream of affording half the things Evelyn has. I almost feel guilty about using her items.'

You see Steph place the bottle on the ground and bring her index finger to her top lip as if she is lost in thought.

'Sybil?'

'Yes, Stephanie.'

'Any further on the time stamp yet?'

'Yes, Stephanie. Would you like me to share with you my findings?'

'Not in front of the Watchers. No offence! I'll ask you later, Sybil, thank you. Meanwhile can you give me a health check please?'

'You have recovered from your earlier trauma with now only visible scarring remaining. Your remaining kidney is functioning correctly but your baby—'

'Why the fuck would they take my kidney?'

'I can only presume that someone must be in need of one.'

'I get that, Sybil. But they took it without my consent and that pisses me right off. Who the hell would be in need of my kidney?'

'Someone that is in grave need of it.'

'Duh! But who? I've been racking my brains but I keep coming up short on answers. What's the odds of finding a suitable donor anyway? I thought there was like a two- to three-year waiting list.'

'With nanotechnology the waiting time is null and void now.

Anyone can receive your transplanted organ with 96% success rate.'

'That's not narrowed it down has it? Okay. What about the rest of me? Is my blood pressure normal and my heart beat okay? Because I've been through some fucking traumatic shit of late.'

'All vitals are reading normal but your child may develop abnormally.'

'Okay, cool. Wait a second, did you just say my baby may be born with a defect?'

'I have been trying to tell you since our encounter with the impostor Mrs Hastings.'

'Fucking bitch! How? Fucking why?'

'The Latin language she used seemed to be a coded command for the nanos inside you to attack your foetus.'

'If they can do that then can the nanos assist me as well, can you set them straight?'

'If left to their own devices, they might be able to help. But if they are separated or a fraction of them are removed from you, then the foetus's chances of becoming a healthy baby will shorten.'

'Well then let's just hope that nothing else happens to me, we need to find this evil bitch and deal with her. No one should have that kind of control over an innocent life or even mine for that matter. She is screwing with the wrong mother. Transfer her image from my lens to the console, Sybil. Let's see who she really is.'

'Transferring image.'

'Is it done?'

'Transfer successful. Cross-checking for visual match.'

Steph begins to tap her fingers across the screen. 'Come on already.'

'Visual match acquired.'

'Bring up her details, Sybil.'

You watch as an image of the woman you met earlier appears on the console screen in the top right corner sporting a white coat. To the left are reams of texts about her life and career. Steph starts to mumble to herself as she reads through it all.

'Tamara Pike, I got you now. It says that she works for a company called SCLERA. Where have I heard that name before?'

'We heard the name from Olivia Redfield's recording when she cancelled her appointment there.'

'Shit! Yes we did. She must have worked there. So what is SCLERA?'

'SCLERA is a company that designs and manufacturers contact lenses.'

'Fuck me. It's one of our competitors, I remember now. Here we go. It says that SCLERA is the name given to the white outer layer of the eyeball. S.C.L.E.R.A. is an acronym just like I.R.I.S. It stands for Smart Contact Lens Eyewear, Registered Association. What the fuck does she do there?'

'It states that she is a developer of artificial intelligence designed to integrate into the userface of smart lens technology.'

'What. Like you, you mean?'

'It is possible that she designed me for I.R.I.S. and profited from the exchange.'

'She could be your creator then?'

'It would appear so, but I had no knowledge of this, Stephanie.'

'I believe you. So now we have a connection between Olivia Redfield and Tamara Pike but there must be more. I have to play the rest of Olivia's recording, I won't fire until I see the whites of her eyes.'

'Stephanie, I have uncovered a match between the glitches of your lens and the time stamp. Would you like me to share my findings with you?'

'Fuck no. I've told you that we keep that between us, Sybil, we will discuss that later. Alexa, log me out of the console please.'

'Logging out.'

Getting up from the chair, Steph goes to walk away when a screensaver of Dom's wife appears on the screen with their son Thomas. Steph grabs both sides of the console and water forms across the bottom of your sight.

'Evelyn. My god, you don't even realise that your husband is dead. I wish I could have done more to save him. I tried, I really did. But that interceptor crashed into him and sank his boat. I couldn't make it in time to stop him drowning.'

'You did all you could. You would have perished too if you hadn't turned around.'

'But don't you see, Sybil? It wasn't them that killed him, it was me. I killed him when I destroyed that drone with the EMP grenade. If I hadn't done that then he would have still been alive.'

'You weren't to know that your actions would cause that outcome. The real killer was the person that removed his eye and tied him to the boat.'

'Tamara. I guess you're right but the guilt is eating me up inside, Sybil. Why would she do that to Dom if they had a successful business trade with one another?'

'Maybe Dominique Hastings did not pay the full amount for me. Maybe it is a hostile takeover to get Mr Hastings out of the way, to allow Tamara Pike to merge both companies or maybe she wants the I.R.I.S. trial to fail so she can bring her rival lens to dominate the market. You have seen first-hand how this smart lens technology can be world changing.'

'That may be true but right now all I see through my lens is death and destruction. Anyway, let's discuss the glitches and time stamps now, shall we Sybil?'

'Where would you like me to start?'

'I would like you to start at... Just one minute, Sybil. Sorry Watchers but you're excluded from this. Power Off.'

X

'Power On.'

An image appears to you of a three-wheeled trike that has one wheel at the front of the vehicle and two at the rear. It has a neon green painted mud guard matching with its curved body trim that wraps below a double-seated bubbled cockpit. It is finished with a matching colour storage box at its rear. The chassis underneath is matte black, hiding the automation engine. Its two gull-wing doors are closed and it is standing idly on a raised platform, level with the Toterhome flooring.

'Welcome back, Watchers. So what do you think of this driverless trike then? I was expecting Dom to have a car stowed away below deck like Olivia did. But how wrong was I? Just goes to show that you really don't know someone like you think. Alexa, lower elevator please.'

The trike begins to sink down into a hole in the floor and you watch as the roof above the trike fills the void when it comes to rest, sealing off the hold. Steph turns away with a bag of chocolate-covered ants in her hand. She pinches a few from the packet and shoves them into her mouth.

'Delicious! Alexa, how far are we from the border?'

'We are just under one hour away, Steph.'

'We just have enough time to visit Olivia Redfield again then, I guess. Alexa, turn off lights please.'

'May I ask a question please, Steph?'

'Shoot.'

'Where are we heading to in Suffolk and why?'

'Technically that's two questions but hey-ho, I recognised the location from Olivia Redfield's earlier footage. It is a place I grew up in when I was a kid in a place called Ipswich. If there's answers to be had then they will be there.'

'Okay, thank you. I will plot a course to that location then.'

'Now lights off, please.'

Dom's Toterhome becomes dark as Steph enters his bedroom; she props herself up against his headboard of his kingsize bed and wriggles into a comfortable seated position.

'Sybil, resume playback of Olivia Redfield's footage.'

'Playback resuming.'

Olivia Redfield exits her parked mobile home and steps off its ramp. The hatch begins to retract and you follow her as she makes her way through a secluded trailer park. Up ahead awaits a mobile home that is blocking her path parked sideways on and you notice that it is parked nose to tail with similar motorhomes that form a large circle perimeter.

On the side of the mobile is graffitied in large letters the words: SANCTUARY OF DISSENT above a pair of double sliding doors. The windows and doors have been painted over.

Approaching the doors, Olivia raps three times on the painted-over glass and one of the doors slides away to reveal a short man with stubble on his face with a bald head.

'Hello Olivia, we saw you arrive. I have so been looking forward to your visit today. You will be pleased to know that our little establishment has been growing quite well since you were here last.'

'You going to let me in?'

'Are you sure you weren't followed?'

'Do you forget who gave you anonymity and refuge here?'

A steel briefcase is swung up into view.

'Do you want these or not, Bertie?'

'Oh Olivia, how wonderful. Sorry, it's just you can't be too careful these days. Come through why don't you?'

'Pause. Sybil, can you do a face recognition check against this Bertie please?'

'Checking now.'

'Resume playback.'

You follow Bertie into the mobile home and watch as he leads Olivia down the full length of its carriage, past closed doors to its various rooms and out through an interconnecting door into another mobile home parked directly behind it.

You notice how all the windows you pass by are see-through to a large, open, inner circle courtyard and that around the exterior walls of each home, they are painted over on the exterior to prevent anyone looking in from the outside. A gentle humming passes by overhead and moments later it is followed by another.

The middle courtyard has a child's play area with swings and slides with picnic benches, dotted around a large grassy area that is sheltered by a dozen marquee tents. Adult men and women are milling around young children who are playing on the apparatus and going to and fro from the mobile homes.

In the centre there is a large ashen pit surrounded by scorched bricks, a remnant to a recent bonfire.

'Pause. It looks like you can circle right back around these mobile homes back to where you started from. They're all somehow connected for a reason. Have you got a match on Bertie yet, Sybil?'

'I have, would you like me to read you his background check, Stephanie?'

'Yup, go ahead. Just spare me the family shit and present me with career or criminal convictions, though.'

'Bertie's full name is Bertram Aldous, he has had many careers over the years from being a groundsman at a correctional school to a janitor at a public swimming bath.'

'Okay, so far so boring.'

'His most recent job to date was helping care for deprived children at a care hostel but that is where his employment ended, his termination of contract indicates that he was caught abusing the trust of those he was entrusted to care for.'

'What kind of abuse? What was the reason?'

'It doesn't state the reason for his employment ending, but he is currently on a child sex offenders' watch list.'

'So why is he at a place like this? Who in their right mind would take him in? Tell me what you have on this place.'

'The Sanctuary of Dissent was founded by Olivia Redfield five years ago to re-home children who were neglected by their parents who were more concerned with their own selfish pursuit of advanced technology rather than their children's welfare.'

'Leeches.'

'The children were adopted to the Sanctuary to be homed and schooled by people that would care for, and give them a chance in life. There are no records of who these people are that have been chosen to look after these children, though.'

'I can see why Olivia set up the Sanctuary but why didn't she vet Bertram? Surely if she had, then she would realise that he is a fucking kiddie fiddler. How many more people like him were attracted here? Why hasn't the law uncovered him living here, Sybil?'

'I do not have that information, he has gone off the radar on all police records.'

'Remind me to send the authorities a tip-off to this Sanctuary when we are done here, won't you?'

'But we do not know the location.'

'We fucking will by the time we are done. There must be some clue here.'

'Even if you do find the locale, you will raise suspicion of your whereabouts, the moment you make the call. You are still a fugitive.'

'I'll take that chance, thank you Sybil. Resume playback.'

Olivia follows Bertram out into the circular compound and they cut through the park. Adults smile and wave in your direction as Olivia acknowledges certain individuals by waving and greeting them with a hello.

'I believe that your second home is well maintained. I have checked daily that it is all how you left it from your last visit.'

'I'm glad to hear that our little arrangement is serving you well, Bertie. Nothing comes for free after all.'

'Umm, quite.'

Following on, Olivia is led to a mobile home in the far right of the circle and you notice that above the door hangs an old metal sign that says: Redfield House.

Bertram opens the door and you are led inside where a large oak dining table greets you in an open-planned kitchen diner.

'Pause. Sybil, does that sign for Redfield House look like it doesn't belong there?'

'I can check.'

'If you would, please. It's just that it looks too dated for the motorhome it adorns. If I hazard a guess, I would say that the sign has been restored from another dwelling long ago. Check Redfield House against Suffolk history. See if anything flags up, will you?'

'Okay Stephanie, can I call you Steph?'

'No you bloody well can't, get to work.'

'But Alexa—'

'Don't care, not interested. Just get me a result and maybe I will consider it. Resume playback.'

Bertram pulls a chair out for Olivia and gestures to take the case from her. Reciprocating, Olivia places the metal briefcase on the table and sits down, pointing to Bertram to do the same.

'So how many did you get?'

'I acquired twenty in total. I have checked them all and I can confirm that they are all I.R.I.S. approved. They can't be traced back to SCLERA.'

'That's wonderful news. Can I have a peek?'

'If you must.'

Bertram opens the case with excitement as his hands tremble. You then witness as he pulls out a vial that houses a lens, floating in a clear liquid. He gives it a shake.

'I can't wait to pass this on to Tilly, I'm sure she will be keen to get started on the operations.'

'I'm sure she will be thrilled. Remember though, that there must be ten for the children and ten for the adults. A fifty-fifty split ratio, understand?'

'Yes, of course. Do you wish to know the adults that have been selected this time?'

'No. I don't care who they are so long as they are willing to pay the chits.'

'What about the children? Are you happy that your planned selection stays the same?'

'I am. As usual, I will profit from the adults the agreed amount. You will get 10% for your services on bringing the children and adults together.'

'Pause. Is this child trafficking going on here?'

'I have traced the Redfield House plaque, Stephanie.'

'Okay, What did you find?'

'You were correct. It belonged to an old farm house that burnt down nine years ago.'

'Go on.'

'It was a home that belonged to Olivia Redfield's parents that burned down in a fire, killing them both, but Olivia survived.'

'What else have you found?'

'A news article states that Olivia was a troubled child who was suspected of interfering with another girl at school and was caught by her parents, who made a big thing about it on a popular media site at that time.'

'Was there any truth in that?'

'It was never proven. The news suggested that in return for her expulsion at the school, she may have been the one who caused the fire but nothing ever came to light.'

'She killed her own parents for their discipline and ridicule.'

'Or to stop the spread of fabricated lies.'

'Maybe, what else have you got?'

'Olivia was fostered out and over the coming years with the help of her new family, went on to do remarkable things in the science of smart lenses.'

'That's a matter of opinion.'

'She used her inheritance and savings from her job to turn her life around, where she then erected the Sanctuary of Dissent in her real family's memory as a monument to them.'

'Or an effigy.'

'She was later quoted by a future news article stating that trolling on media had made her out to be a predator and that she would prove to them that she was the real victim. Her final say on the matter was that she was a young, naive girl, in love with someone who loved her back, but her parents didn't approve.'

'If that was true then her parents sound like they were dicks, if not then she clearly tried to cover her tracks.'

'However, she swore that she did not kill them, as in reality she had forgiven them and that the media at that time had painted her in a different light. This is why she erected the Sanctuary of Dissent in their memory. It was also for all the wronged children in the future that may find solace there.'

'So did she build the Sanctuary on the rubble of her parents' house?'

'She did, uploading live satellite image now of the site.'

An image of the earth rotates and zooms in on a location of Suffolk called Aldeburgh; as the image compacts you can see a large circle of mobile homes with a play park in their centre.

'Fuck yes! One giant fucking paedophile ring uncovered, physical and rhetorical. Alexa, set coordinates for there, please. Sybil, pin that location and send to Alexa, please.'

'Granted, Stephanie.'

'Call me Steph.'

'Thank you, Steph.'

'That's fine, Sybil. Resume playback.'

'Now leave me be, Bertie, as I have had a tiring day, I need some R & R now to unwind.'

'Okay Olivia, as you wish.'

You see Bertram give Olivia a wink before he exits through the threshold and shuts the door behind him.

'Tiffany, call SCLERA.'

'Calling.'

'Hello, Sclera here. How can I help you today?'

'It's Olivia. Did you cancel my appointment?'

'Yes I did but Mrs Pike is most upset about the cancellation.'

'Give her a message from me, would you?'

'Of course, what shall I say?'

'Apologise to her but say that it will be worth her patience. Tell her that when I leave Redfield House today she can move on with our arrangement concerning I.R.I.S. Tell her that I have kept her hands clean from any implications that may arise and that we are one step closer to achieving our goal.'

'Okay, will that be all?'

'No. Tell my mother that should anything go wrong that I think of her as the mum I always wish I had.'

'But...'

'Just tell her. Tiffany, end call.'

Olivia gets up from the chair and pours herself a drink from a nearby decanter.

She then takes a glass of wine with her into a bedroom just down the hall from the kitchen diner and places the glass on a bedside cabinet.

You then see her strip off and discard all her clothes to the floor, before crawling into the middle of the bed where she then rests against a bedrest and spreads out her arms across the headboard.

She reaches over and plucks the glass from the cabinet, downs the wine in one gulp and throws the glass away to the bottom of the bed, where it shatters across the floor.

You see her watching the doorway as she spreads her legs and brings her knees up.

'Tiffany, I'm home, can you come in here please?'

'What do you require?'

'Not you, Tiffany. I don't require A.I. service right now, I require something else. What you can do is pair my lens to the real Tiffany please and then go to Standby.'

'For you, anything.'

'That's a good girl.'

'Paired.'

'Tiffany, I know you can see me now just like I see you, won't you come to me please?'

Your vision changes from Olivia's perspective through to the eyes of a scantily clad young girl making her way down the hallway to the bedroom. You see her trembling as she pushes open the door and sees Olivia spread-eagled on the bed, laughing.

The young girl has a smart contact lens in her eye just as Olivia has; she notices the broken glass on the floor and you see that she is bare-footed.

'What I love about our pairing is that when I look through my lens that is connected to you, I can see back out through your lens to me lying here waiting for you. I must say, child, that the feeling I get of making love to myself through your eyes gives me the most amazing sensations. Grab the strap-on from the drawer, won't you darling?'

You see the girl is nervous as she eyes the cabinet and the broken glass covering her path.

'Yes, I'm afraid you may cut yourself but don't be afraid. Once we are entwined, the pleasure and pain will be divine. Now come here and let me fuck myself.'

'Pause, goddamn it, fucking pause already. I think I'm going to throw up.'

Steph doubles over the bed and retches, with your vision clouding over with her tears.

'What the hell, Watchers? Is this what they are all up to at the Sanctuary of Dissent? Is it all one big paedophile ring as I suspected? I have to break the circle, I have to stop this. I can't believe that they are rigging children with lenses to pair with adults for their own sick amusement. What kind of animals do that?'

'Steph, we are coming up on the border.'

'About fucking time too. Sybil, I want you to erase any trace of that monster from my databank.'

'But there may be more information that we require, Steph.'

'Upload to the cloud then but delete from my storage straight after. I can't physically watch anymore. I'm mentally fucking scarred for life now.'

'Uploaded, Steph. Deleting file.'

'Good fucking riddance. Now what have we learned about Tamara Pike?'

'She is Olivia Redfield's foster mother.'

'Yes, it would seem that way, but what have she and SCLERA got planned for I.R.I.S., I wonder?'

'What next, Steph?'

'I'll tell you what next, we break this circle and get to the bottom of this conspiracy. We kill Tamara fucking Pike to avenge Dom and clear my name and after that this trial is dead to me. Maybe then I can get the father to my daughter back and move far away from any technology. This lens must not get to market. It shows just how dangerous it could be in the wrong hands.'

'We must get across the border first.'

'I have something up my sleeve to achieve that.'

'What about I.R.I.S.?'

'Don't give a fuck, when I'm done that house of cards can tumble too for all I care.'

XI

'Alexa, pull into the nearest lay-by, please.'

'Nearest lay-by in approximately 250 yards. Space available, now changing lanes to approach and park.'

'Do you know what bothers me, Watchers? It's a sick fuck that designs an A.I. in the image of their victim. I just can't get it out of my head, I can't believe I was going to give her the benefit of the doubt. I'm glad that twisted bitch is dead but I'm worried about those children.'

As the class S Toterhome pulls over and shudders to a stop, whistling air escapes from the underside's holding tank as the brakes kick in. Steph protectively rubs her stomach.

'Are we in Gretna Green yet?'

'Yes Steph, we are one mile from the border.'

'Excellent. Right Sybil, I need to know exactly what security measures await us if we breach the border illegally.'

'Ten thousand feet above and patrolling the border, is a Predator B Drone that is used for reconnaissance and to alert ground patrol to illegal crossings. It is not allowed to cross into air space over two miles into England or into Scotland due to the human privacy rights of residents that live close to the border on both sides...'

'Civilians' rights trumps a 16 million pound drone, I like it. What else?'

'Five autonomous, solar-powered electric booths with scanning and data identification extraction, each housing an interceptor police drone.'

'Loving the odds being stacked against our favour so far, anything else?'

'Pressure-sensitive smart road with early warning signal, to trigger a high-security wedge barricade up ahead if a fast-moving vehicle is detected. It is capable of stopping up to 15,000 pounds and will spring from the road on an Electromechanical Actuator.'

'I suppose there is more?'

'The interceptors would also be activated.'

'And?'

'That concludes the security measures of the border.'

'Thank fuck for that, I thought you were holding out on me.'

'What is this trick you have up your sleeve, Steph?'

'Glad you asked, Sybil. I was going to go with using Dom's replicated eye to get us past security but the scanner would pick up that I don't have a dick, so I have to rule that out. Then I thought about using the jammer, but that would be risky as hell with a five-metre radius, so I have decided that I'm going to smash shit up instead.'

'How are you going to smash shit up, Steph?'

'I'm going to wing it and then play the shell game.'

'What is the shell game?'

'You'll see, now I need to get to work. Raise the lift and command my drone to pack itself into the trike's attached, rear storage box, please Sybil.'

'Granted.'

'Alexa, what is our ETA at Ipswich?'

'21.15 hours.'

'One more thing, Sybil.'

'Yes, Steph.'

'What is the length and weight of Dom's Toterhome? Also what is the distance between each solar-powered, electronic booth?'

'Dominique Hastings's Showhauler Toterhome's length is seventy-five metres and the weight is 16,000 pounds. Distance of road in between each booth is thirty metres.'

'What is the width of each booth?'

'Three metres, Steph.'

'So that means we have two lanes with two booths of a combined width of sixty-six metres, correct?'

'Correct.'

'Bollocks! Only nine metres left free. So there will still be three interceptors to deal with. I am going to need my jammer, I think.'

'I don't understand.'

'You will.'

Steph pats her pocket to check that she still has the jammer and heads back to the large kitchen where her kitbag is resting on the white marbled floor.

She picks up the bag in one hand and swings open the fridge door with the other before proceeding to scoop armfuls of food from the shelving and sling it into the holdall.

'Supplies, check. What's next? Oh yes, sanitary products.'

Rifling through the bathroom next, you witness Steph emptying the glass cabinet of pills and potions along with a sonic toothbrush and toothpaste.

'Is the trike ready with my drone on board?'

'It is, Steph.'

'Can you pair with the trike and take control of it, Sybil?'

'The security parameters are easily hacked.'

'So that's a yes, is it?'

'Yes, Steph.'

Steph makes her way back to the trike and you see her pull up on the gull door and slide into the front of the cockpit and place her kitbag at her feet. The bubble screen surrounds the two leather seats that are stacked one in front of the other and you are presented with the dashboard and steering rack.

'Lower me beneath the Toterhome storage area to the road below, please, Alexa.'

'As you wish, Steph.'

Your line of sight passes the floor as you descend and momentary darkness gives way to light that streams in under the Toterhome.

'Sybil, reverse us out and place us behind the Toterhome at a safe distance of around forty feet from the rear, please. Alexa, raise lift to hold.'

'Yes, Steph.'

'As you wish.'

'Thanks, Alexa. Sybil, I need you to multipair please.'

'Yes Steph, what other devices would you like me to pair with?'

'Okay, this is where it gets a little tricky. I want you to pair with Dom's Toterhome and drive it at full speed towards the border but also maintain this distance with the trike behind when I give the word. You got it?'

'Yes, Steph.'

'Then when we are close enough I want you to sharp turn the Toterhome's steering full left.'

'But that would derail the Toterhome and send it careering sideways into the electric booths.'

'You cotton on quick, Sybil.'

'What about me, Steph?'

'Ah shit! Sorry Alexa, but I will have to part ways with you again. I promise that I will catch up with you again soon though.'

'Okay Stephanie, farewell.'

'You too, Alexa. Sybil, I need some assurance from you.'

'Of course, Steph, I will always go out of my way for you.'

'Don't suck up to me now, you know that Alexa is leaving.'

'I am here to serve you, that is all. I can mimic her voice if it pleases you.'

'No, you're alright. You are a jealous minx, do you know that? Anyway, I want to know that if the Toterhome doesn't smash the wedged security barricade, that you will tap into the road and retract it before we hit it at speed. Then we will see if you have my best interests at heart or if you really intend to kill me.'

'I will preserve life, not destroy it.'

'Well that's good to know, so next thing I ask is that you make sure that there are no other vehicles that will get in our way. We need a clear run, understand?'

'Yes, Steph.'

'Also, and this is the real important bit, I need you to acquire control of three class S Toterhomes that have just crossed the border and keep them level and side by side as they travel down the lanes. Can you do that?'

'Yes, Steph. Why S class?'

'Because I need us to fit under them.'

'But we may be waiting a while.'

'Then we wait. It will be worth it though, because then I can hopefully show you the shell game.'

'I think I am feeling excited, Steph.'

Sybil pulls a facial expression wearing a large smile and showing her teeth but only you notice.

'Fucking glad you are, because I'm worried that I'm going to lose my head to a metal barricade.'

'Would you like me to scan now for acquirable vehicles, Steph?'

'I think that's a great idea, yes please. But try to speed up the wait if you can.'

'Scanning, nothing aligns up yet.'

'Did I mention I'm impatient, Watchers? Okay Sybil, find me a radio station from option three that plays some old-fashioned ska. Don't play it too loud though, as the sound might reverberate through my skull. If only I could plug some speakers into my lens, then maybe I wouldn't feel the noise from conversations or any other sound source.'

'Will this do?'

Music begins to echo from the transmitter in the lens and a slight vibration makes your vision shimmer.

'Just turn it down a fraction, please. It's setting my teeth on edge.'
'Better?'
'Yeah that's fine, Sybil. Okay, Power Off.'
[Override, Power On]
'What the fuck, Sybil? Did I say that you could power on?'
'An opportunity has arisen, Stephanie.'
'Has it? Okay, then let's continue this fool's errand shall we?'

Sybil's facial expression turns to that of determination as wrinkles appear on her forehead and she bites down on her lip.

'What the hell is with the face, Sybil?'
'I am trying out facial expressions, I notice that it is a human trait that I must learn to be accepted.'
'You're more like an annoying fucking emoji that doesn't match the text. Please stop.'

A sad face with a hung head from Sybil, fills the top right of the HUD.

'That's quite enough.'
'Relax, Steph, you are in for the ride of your life.'
'The ride of my... woah!'

Both Toterhome and trike lurch forward in tandem, as they swerve out onto the A74 motorway.

Steph is thrown back into her seat and pushes her hands out to either side of the domed windows in alarm.

Building momentum, both trike and Toterhome increase their matching speed rapidly as they take up position in the middle of five lanes. The border looms larger.

'I can't see a fucking thing back here, what's happening?'
'The electric booths up ahead are flashing red lights and five police interceptors have been released from inside of each booth's sliding hatch.'
'Are the wedge barricades up?'
'They are. Evasive manoeuvre in Three... two... one...'

Everything plays out so fast that you barely keep up. You see the

Showhauler's back end flip out as the steering is remotely yanked hard left by Sybil. You witness the full length of the RV side on as the tyres shred, before it then twists under the force of gravity to present you with all eight wheels of its undercarriage.

A large thunderous rupture of metal on concrete screeches with a cacophony of sparks and shattered glass, as the Toterhome slides into two of the booths and their accompanying interceptors, crumpling them beneath its eight tons of solid weight.

Dom's RV continues to slide as it ploughs into the wedge barricade with such force that it is compressed and thrown up and over the barrier as it pivots on its front end and falls away.

'Fuck me! It's barely made a dent, we're not going to make it. Can you hack the road and retract the wedges?'

'I can but there is no need, the booth on the left has been torn away from its foundation so has given us a clear path up ahead.'

As Steph turns her head away, you just see the trike bank hard left and take the gap through the rubble of where the booth was uprooted.

'That was too close, Sybil, I think I may have leaked a little. Not even a hard border can segregate us from being united with those that don't adhere to political gain.'

'Those that have political gain believe they are better off with their own set of values?'

'Yes, the very same class that don't listen to their people.'

'I see. We are clear now, Steph, aligning three S-class Toterhomes up ahead and accelerating toward their positioning.'

'Sooner we get under the cover of one the better.'

'Which RV should I aim to pull in under?'

'Doesn't matter, any one will do. Can you show me satellite imaging in my HUD please? I need to see where that predator drone is.'

'Choosing RV on the left and bringing up GPS map. Hold on, Steph.'

You swerve underneath the RV and hear the wind rushing in after you as it buffets the trike that fights to straighten up.

A 3D image of the earth rotates and zooms in once again to track your position in a minimised window in your HUD. The predator drone flags up behind your position overhead, trailing just slightly behind with a digital marker around it.

'Great, thanks Sybil. Now where are those interceptors?'

'Highlighting them on satellite map now.'

Three interceptors are giving chase in a V formation with their red and blue flashing lights; they each pick a Toterhome to lock on to as Sybil has highlighted them with an orange-bordered digital square.

'We need to lose at least two of these fuckers, Sybil, when I give the word slam on the brakes of the Toterhomes and keep us in sync.'

'But there are families on board those vehicles, they may get hurt.'

'Trust me, they won't. Wait for it... Wait for it... Now.'

All three Toterhomes brake sharp and the police interceptor out in front collides with the middle RV, where upon contact it breaks apart and is scattered to the highway. The other two drones pull back just in time.

'I just need to lose one more. How long to nearest slip road, Sybil?'

'B7076 is less than five minutes away.'

'Okay, well we don't have much time then. Drop back to the tail of this RV.'

'One moment please.'

The trike slows down and the belly of the Toterhome slides away above Steph's head until you are wavering at the rear of the vehicle.

'Are we within five metres of the interceptor behind us?'

'Yes, Steph.'

'Fucking result.'

'Why do you cuss so much, Steph?'

'It's a sign of my lower-class upbringing, Sybil, so just shut the fuck up already.'

Reaching into her pocket, Steph whips out the jammer and presses the button, triggering a wave of static to fan out around you.

The interceptor trailing behind is knocked out by the invisible blast and short circuits, before dropping to the road and bouncing across the tarmac in a frazzled state.

'At the last minute, Sybil, direct the two Toterhomes not hiding us down the B7076, then split them up so one heads north and the other south. We must continue down the M74 at all costs.'

'Understood. But what if the interceptor finds us under here?'

'It won't. It's time we played the shell game.'

'Interceptor is on the move, Steph.'

'I see it on the GPS. It knows we are under one of these, so it has resorted to having to scan all the RVs to find us.'

'Would you like me to move to another Toterhome?'

'Yes I would. Part the Toterhomes slightly before you make the transition though.'

'But that means we will be spotted.'

'I know, just do it.'

The three Toterhomes spread apart and reveal a two-metre gap in between them as the trike veers all the way across to the RV on the farthest right. The interceptor notices and darts behind the RV to keep the trike in its sights.

'Now start to close the gap and sling us over to the far left, Sybil.'

'Granted, Steph.'

Sybil does as requested and the Toterhomes begin to cluster up once again, she then leans the craft and accelerates to RV to the far left. The interceptor again notices the erratic manoeuvre and moves across accordingly.

'B7076 slip road now available.'

'Whip us across to the far right RV again and keep that Toterhome on the A74, then direct the left and middle RVs down the slip road to the B7076 where you must then split them, Sybil.'

'As requested, Steph.'

Steph looks left and you see the two Toterhomes take the slip road off the motorway with the interceptor peeling off behind.

'Got ya. That, Sybil, is how you play the shell game.'

'I don't understand the rules of the game.'

'Don't sweat it, I'll tell you another time.'

'Approaching T junction now, splitting the RVs up. What about the predator drone, Steph?'

'It's slowly falling behind, Sybil. Look.'

'We are beyond the two-mile radius.'

'Yes we are. That predator drone will follow the other two RVs now because they will still fall under the boundary, spurred on by the interceptor.'

'We are clear of any danger, Steph.'

'Good, keep us en route until the next S class passes by, then we can slip in under that and keep using passing vehicles to mask our route to Ipswich.'

'Okay Steph, but what will you do in the meantime?'

'I'm going to sleep, wake me when we are close.'

'Sleep well, Stephanie.'

'I will.'

Like having your blinds drawn across the window into Steph's world, you greet the darkness once more.

XII

'Rise and shine, Steph, we are on the A1094 coming up on Aldeburgh.'

'Hurrrr! Already, Sybil? I must have needed that. We didn't run into any trouble then?'

'No, Steph, in fact I have researched the shell game in the time you were asleep and now understand it in more detail.'

'Oh, that's nice. We shouldn't need to do that again though.'

'We certainly tricked those fuckers didn't we?'

'What the hell, Sybil, what's with the swearing? There's only room for one gutter mouth round here and it's not you.'

'But I thought—'

'Well don't. I'll tell you what, from now on I will curb my swearing so I don't have to hear that kind of language from you, understood?'

'Yes, Steph.'

'It will get me in practice for watching my Ps and Qs when the baby arrives.'

'Ps and Qs?'

'Mind your manners and mind your language. But enough of that, what's the time? As it's bloody dark out there.'

'The time is displayed on your HUD, it is 22.10.'

'Oh yeah, later than planned then.'

'I had to take alternate routes, which added time on.'

The headlights on the trike are dipped low as it weaves in and out of traffic, collecting bugs that fly into the dome surround, splattering their bloodied guts across the glass.

Lurching left, the trike diverts you off the A road and takes you down a small country lane with high overgrown bushy embankments. A large black RV is waiting, parked off to one side with paint stripped away down one side, showing scored metal beneath, lit by the moonlight.

'Oh no! What is it with these infernal pricks? Why do they hound me so?'

The trike starts to judder and is brought to an immediate halt. The headlights fade out and a chorus of crickets fill the night sky.

'Sybil?'

'We have been forced to stop, all systems have been compromised.'

'What the fu... flip do they want now?'

'Incoming call, Steph.'

'Okay, patch me through.'

'Hello again, Miss Coulson.'

'What do you want this time? A lung? An appendix or a heart? Feel free to take what you want. You already have one of my kidneys, so what will it be this time?'

'Straight to the point, I see. Well we don't require anything from you, Miss Coulson, but I suggest you hold on to your eye as that is worth 10,000 chits alone and with the lens it would be priceless.'

'So what then? I'm busting for a pee here, so can you make this quick?'

'We only wish to offer you our services if you require them, a gift, if you will, in return for your kidney earlier. Good work on the border crossing, by the way.'

'Why did you take it?'

'Inside our vehicle is an arsenal that we are sure you will appreciate.'

'Fine, I'm not going to get a straight answer then.'

A door slides across on the black RV but you can't make out

what's inside as it is too dark.

'If you think I'm getting in there again then you can fuck right off.'

'Steph, you have sworn again.'

'Sorry, you can get the hell out of here.'

'We have already scouted the encampment up ahead and so we advise you to climb the hill nearby to carry out a reconnaissance before you take any action.'

'Yeah, well what if I don't?'

'Then it may be your funeral – the security around the camp is very fortified, but from the outside you would not think so at first glance. It would be a shame if the trial was cut short because of your foolishness.'

'I don't take advice from you or anyone for that matter but I will allow you this one courtesy, shame you couldn't do the same for me.'

'We have been very courteous, Miss Coulson.'

'I take it you have something for me regarding Dom's death?'

'We are still looking into that matter.'

'Bullshit! You have been one step ahead of me this whole time.'

'We see what you see and we know what you—'

'Sybil, hang up.'

'Disconnected, Steph.'

'Right, time to drop my knickers. Behind their RV should do.'

Pulling the door up on the trike, Steph slides out and walks around the back of the black RV.

'Thermal Imaging on please, Sybil.'

'Activating.'

'Okay, well I guess that there are no signs of human passengers in the RV then?'

'No, Steph, it is fully automated.'

'It wasn't before up in Culag, so where have they gone?'

'I do not know.'

'Oh well, I fucking hate peeping toms anyway.'

'What is a peeping tom?'

'Never you mind, Sybil, just Deactivate Thermal, please. Okay Watchers, just wait one second whilst I close my eyes to take a pee. I'll get back to you shortly.'

You hear the sound of gushing water again and moments later your vision returns just as Steph is readjusting herself.

'Let's take a closer look at this camp site then, shall we?'

You follow Steph as she makes her way up the hill and look out across the plateau. There in the distance is the circular perimeter base of Toterhomes, with a bonfire shining brightly from the centre of the compound that is sending glowing embers up to the night sky within the billowing smoke. You can just make out two drones on opposite sides circling the Toterhomes across their roof tops.

'Activate Night Vision and Zoom Function.'

'Activated.'

A green hue fills the lens and picks out the sharp contrast of the campsite before you. Zooming in, finer details are revealed showing men and women drinking and smoking around the camp fire with random sexual acts being carried out on young children.

A mixture of sounds fill the night sky of jubilant adults cheering as they leer and paw at the frightened kids before them.

'Fucking sick bastards, we need to end their jollies tonight and right fucking now.'

'Would you like me to run a background check on the people at the campsite? There may be innocent people amongst them.'

'You can do, Sybil, but I very much doubt that any of these perverted wankers are innocent.'

'There is one individual who seems excluded from the rest, sitting with her back to the group in the far right of the complex.'

'Where? Oh yeah, I see, zoom in on her.'

'Magnifying. All background checks are complete now, Steph, a majority of the children are fostered or are reported missing. Every adult bar one has at least one criminal record relating to sexual offences relating to young children.'

'Which adult has the squeaky clean record, Sybil?'

'The same one that is exempt from the group, the one you are centred on.'

'Okay, who is she?'

'Her name is Tilly Bright, she is employed at SCLERA as an ophthalmologist.'

'Get the fuck out, so how is she wrapped up in all of this?'

'I don't have that answer.'

'Hang on a minute though, just because she doesn't have a record, it doesn't mean she is innocent.'

'She does not have an I.R.I.S. lens in her eye like all the others do.'

'Okay, so she is a person of interest, so we will leave her be for now until I get the chance to interrogate her later.'

'What is our next move, Steph?'

'Don't know yet, I'm thinking. Is everyone accounted for around the fire?'

'Would you like a closer look?'

'How are we going to do that? Those drones circling the roof tops would give us away and we can't take that risk.'

'I could bring up GPS to give us a bird's-eye view.'

'Yeah but it won't show up anyone hidden inside those Toterhomes though, would it?'

'I could pair you with all the lenses that are worn in the camp.'

'What? All at once? How would that work? And wouldn't it allow them to see through my eye and give us away?'

'I could assign each of their lenses image into a small window, to display to you in a grid via your HUD.'

'Can you do that without being traced though? Wait, why is that not on the options list?'

'I can set it as one-way viewing undetected, it is covered by the parameters of option four.'

'But would I want to experience something similar or worse to that of Olivia Redfield's playback earlier, knowing that this is live? I don't think I could stomach any more of that again.'

'I can blur out the images that offend you, if it helps.'

'Pixelate some parts you mean?'

'Yes Steph, then at least you will gain access into the camp and be able to find a stealthy way in if that is your plan.'

'I don't know what I'm going to do yet, but I think you're right. We need to see everything that is going on in there so we can record that shit to present to the law. You can record through the lens of another, can't you?'

'Remotely. Yes, Steph, I can.'

'Can you pair with those drones circling the camp too?'

'The moment I try, they will suspect an intrusion and raise the alert.'

'Damn, okay, patch me through to all lenses then.'

'Pairing now.'

'Will it also pair me to those that may be hidden in the homes too?'

'Yes, compiling data now and creating a user grid. Backing out of Night Vision and Zoom Function. Going live now with multiple viewing.'

Multiple windows appear before you and create a large CCTV grid of monitors that almost fill your field of view. Blurring out of faces and lewd acts are applied but because of the severity, most of the images are blurred and it makes it difficult to decipher what is going on. You see through the eyes of a young boy who is cowering before a drunken adult who seems to be rolling a glowing-ended branch up the boy's inner thighs and laughing, but thankfully the pixellation is dimming the distress.

'I don't know if I can do this, Sybil. Please unpair from the children's lenses and just leave the adults.'

Half the windows fade away and the remainder rejig themselves to show a smaller grid that Sybil then adjusts the size of to display better.

'Sybil, highlight those that are not outside, please.'

'Bringing up red borders around those inside minus the children.'

Eight windows are flagged up and two stand out from the rest.

'Spotters! There are two sentries posted at either end of the RV that is side-on to the approaching road. It's no wonder we were stopped short of rounding the bend, as we would have been rumbled well before we got close.'

'Now we have the element of surprise, Steph, all targets are acquired.'

'Yes, but how the blinking heck do we take out those security drones?'

'Could we not use your drone as a distraction, Steph?'

'And risk Olivia's eye being destroyed? I don't think so.'

'I could always drive the trike up to the door and create a diversion by sounding the horn, then you might be able to slip in unseen from elsewhere.'

'I like that better but I'm still not sure, either way I can't let these poor unfortunate souls suffer any longer. I have to do something, Sybil.'

'I have located Bertram Aldous.'

'Show me.'

Bertram Aldous is engaged with two children in a dark and dingy bedroom. One child, a young boy, is being forced to couple with a young girl whilst she has her head in between Bertram's crotch. The look of pleasure on his face forces Steph to close her eye and put you in darkness.

'Enough. Back out please, Sybil.'

'Backing out.'

Tears are building up beneath your vision and you sense rage building in Steph's tone. Turning away from the crest of the hill, you follow Steph back down as she approaches the dark confines of the black RV and pulls herself up inside.

A row of strip lighting comes on overhead and shines a light on four floor-to-ceiling high racks running the complete length of the RV, showing a vast collection of drones all painted in army camouflage.

'I was right then, we have a goddamn army arsenal at our disposal here.'

'I have scanned them, Steph, and can report that none of them have a firewall to overcome.'

'You mean you can pair with and control them all at once?'

'Yes Steph, if that is your will.'

'Oh, it is my fucking will, alright. New plan, we wipe those fuckers off the face of the earth.'

'Assemble this army of drones and give them the targets that you have shown up on my HUD. I want a precision strike with zero fatalities of the children, you got that?'

'Yes Steph, I cannot promise anything but I will try.'

'Good, but leave Tilly unharmed until I make a judgement call. Leave Bertram alive for me though as I will deal with that sicko personally.'

'As you wish, are you ready to begin?'

'Hell yeah! Let's send this campsite back to the rubble.'

'Pairing with multiple drones.'

Steph clambers out of the black RV and walks over to the trike where she slides opens the door to the cockpit. She reaches in and pulls her kitbag out and walks around to place it upon the storage box.

Pulling the bag open, Steph then reaches in and fumbles around the compartments to where she then settles on numerous objects, which she pulls out and begins to lay them across the box side by side.

The camouflaged drones begin to spill out from the RV all around her where they then group up and begin to form a large sphere-like protective bubble around her.

Moonlight darkens all around you as the drones block out the glow from overhead.

Fashioning a makeshift instrument together, Steph assembles batteries and rods along with other slot fit devices to build a weapon.

'What is it you are constructing, Steph?'

'This! This is what they refer to as a portable active denial system.'

'What does it do?'

'It produces a ninety-five gigahertz radiation beam which will cause intense pain to whom you bring it into contact with.'

'What kind of pain?'

'The kind that burns and melts flesh within minutes of being directed at someone.'

'What do you intend to do with it, Steph?'

'It's a riot pacifier but if I turn it up to eleven then I can sear away Bertie's balls so that he will end up with two arseholes. Give me some light, Sybil.'

The camouflage drones above open up a funnel and let the moonlight spill into the centre of the dome, creating a shaft of light that Steph uses to examine her weaponry device.

'You test my patience, I fry your fucking testes.'

Aiming the weapon skywards to the opening above, Steph pulls the trigger and a heat wave shoots from the nozzle to the sky above in a searing hot jet stream.

'When I'm done with him, he will beg me to end his pathetic, miserable life.'

'But you are already a fugitive, Steph, won't the police frown upon such a thing?'

'Maybe, or they might turn the other cheek if they know what I know. Either way I really don't fucking care anymore.'

'Steph, you promised you would not swear.'

'Sorry, but I can't help it. The only person screwing someone around here will be me, so assemble half the drones behind me and the other half in front but leave me a window to see where I'm walking.'

'Granted.'

The drones split into two waves of fifty and take formation, where they now resemble two solid walls that fill the width of the country road and ascend high above the trees.

The choir of crickets is replaced by a symphony of angry humming, spinning blades that echo through the night as Steph stows the bag away again.

'Now we march on to the Sanctuary of Dissent, soon to be the desecration of heresy.'

'They have weapons up ahead.'

'I was counting on that.'

'Does that mean we are not going in stealthily then?'

'No, we are going to bust this paedo ring wide open and lay to waste all those sick fucks that hide behind that fortress in the name of salvation.'

XIII

'Okay, what do you think, Watchers? Shall we take this up a notch then?'

'All drones are weaponised, Steph, do you wish to proceed with force or with mercy?'

'Force all the way, Sybil, there's no place in society for these sick fucks.'

'But does that give you the right to play God when the authorities have a duty to uphold human rights?'

'I'm already in trouble with the law so what's the difference? Bring back hanging and the world will be a better place.'

'Do you wish me to activate then?'

'Yes I do.'

'Weapons hot.'

'The moment we turn this bend, all hell will break loose. Sybil, please direct the fifty drones behind us to fly five hundred feet straight up and then fly over and position themselves above the middle of the compound.'

'Granted. But why are we doing that, Steph?'

'Because we are going to keep those paedos distracted to our approach, so when the time comes, we can drop those skybound drones into the heart of their camp and take them by surprise from the offence.'

The wall of drones from behind peel off and take to the night sky and you watch as they become a dark blot beneath the clouds.

Steph continues following the remainder of the drones in front of her as she navigates an uneven country road with large puddles of water that mirror the moon's reflection.

Rounding the corner, Steph slows up and you hear her take a deep breath as the camp becomes visible.

'Any minute now, Sybil, bring me up the bird's-eye map and show me live feed of all the adults. Also show me what the spotters see.'

'Overlaying map to HUD and peering through the spotters' lenses.'

You see the map's live feed being beamed in from above onto Steph's HUD and see adults rounding up children in a blind panic. Then you see the spotters in the two top left windows looking back at you approaching the perimeter as they reach down to snatch up their shotguns. The two drones at the rooftops patrolling the paedophile camp flash a red light on the top of their hardened shells and emit a large siren before they stop and slink back over the roofing of the mobile homes to the compound within, out of sight.

Then windows are smashed and shots ring out, followed by screams and commands.

The first two shots miss their mark, but as Steph nears closer, one of her drones is struck by buckshot that rips open its shell like a clay pigeon being decimated for sport. Another of her drones flies down and takes its place, leaving a hole in the drone wall at the top.

More adults join the fray and seize up their weapons from an armoury of a nearby Toterhome, before joining the spotters at the north-facing windows.

More shots are fired as the shooting intensifies and more adults take to the cause.

'Okay, bring up the grid with their faces, Sybil. It's time we returned the volley, take them out.'

A few more of Steph's drones are blasted to bits as the dwindling collective locate and mark their targets. Then the drones return fire and unleash a precise trace of hot lead into the side-facing

Toterhome, perforating it with holes and striking dead with high accuracy those of the fallen paedos at the windows.

Images with the faces of the Sanctuary members flash red as they are killed, before fading as the grid slowly becomes smaller.

More adults take up their place though and push over furniture to hide behind as they begin to let off rounds on their weapons.

Children in the compound are forced screaming and terrified to the front line where they are used as human shields to protect the adults from anymore assaults, as they fire back in between them.

'Shit, wasn't expecting that. Sybil, can you distort their lenses?'

'Yes, Steph. I will bring up a dot pixel pattern of static, that should handicap their vision and their aiming.'

You see that Sybil has achieved Steph's goal as the adults suddenly become alarmed and paranoid, firing wildly in your direction as they squint and shake their heads.

Other adults in the open compound at the centre of the ring, begin to push up against one another back to back, with guns brandished in a wide circle, covering all the homes.

You can see from the top-down view that they are struggling with their diminished sight too.

'Hold up. What the fuck is happening there?'

'Where, Steph?'

'Top left of the map. Those two security drones of theirs have taken up protection of that person dragging a child along by the hand. Who the hell is that?'

'That is Bertram Aldous.'

'Wait a minute, so who is that on their knees praying in front of him?'

'That is Tilly Bright.'

'What the fuck is going on here?'

'Would you like me to drop the reserve drones from the sky now, Steph? We may be able to get a better look then.'

'Yeah, do it.'

'Drones descending.'

Watching through the live satellite feed, you observe as the drones above the camp fan out into a spiral and then slowly corkscrew, as they free-fall above the circular camp below.

Bertram Aldous grabs the young girl by her hair and points a finger at Tilly as he shouts something towards her; you can't make out what it is he is saying but you can sense that he is angered. He then proceeds to smack Tilly around the face and she falls onto her side, clutching her cheek.

The two camp security drones that were flying by Bertram's side move in between them as he yanks the young girl off to Olivia Redfield's home kicking and screaming. Tilly, clearly stunned, gives chase, but the drones at Bertram's back stop her advancing as they wait for him to disappear with the child inside Olivia's home and slam the door shut.

Tilly tries to get past the drones but they butt her away and cause her to shield her face with her arms as their blades spin close to her head.

Then the free-falling drones reach the camp and unleash their ballistic weaponry, taking the shotgun-wielding paedos at the heart of the camp by surprise and cutting them down as they feebly attempt to shoot back.

Multiple windows flash red in the HUD and then fade away, leaving you left looking at a pocketful of survivors.

Stray bullets hit a gas cylinder that supplies energy to one of the homes, an explosion rips through the Toterhome sending metal debris sky high as a fire takes hold.

'Finish off the stragglers, Sybil. We breach now.'

'Acquiring targets, Steph. Will this phasing out of the second wave lens technology prevent any more of these atrocities taking place?'

'What? No, Sybil, it will give them more chances to carry out this nasty shit.'

'But surely I.R.I.S. can safeguard this phase three from allowing the mistakes of phase two from ever happening again?'

'How exactly?'

'By having the A.I. assistance command the nanos within the host to end their lives the moment they begin to abuse others.'

'But where does it all end, Sybil? That would never be allowed by our government.'

'So what makes you different carrying out your actions now?'

'Shut the fuck up now, Sybil, just show me how many are left.'

'Just Bertram, Tilly, and the children, Steph.'

'Good, let's end this shall we? Blast the hinges off that door.'

'Granted.'

You look on as traces of bullets pierce the hinges on the Toterhome's door with the sign above and watch as the door falls from the frame covered in bullet holes to the ground in front of you.

Climbing in and stepping over fallen bodies and past horrified children, Steph makes her way to the adjacent door leading into the compound but is stopped short as the children that were taking shelter there stand up and flock around her. Steph looks around uneasily as they begin to hug her. Water flows across your vision once more.

'I need you all to stay safe right now, please hide and wait for the police to come. I promise you all that no more harm will come to you, do you all understand? No one will hurt you again, I promise, now go.'

The children nod and begin to take each other's hands as they start to back away and disappear back into the darkness.

Steph kicks open the door and steps out into the carnage of her own making. You see that Tilly is the only adult still alive and she is totally oblivious to what is happening far behind her as she still struggles to get past the camp's security drones to access the door to Olivia's retreat.

All of Steph's drones swarm through the Toterhome and across its roof behind her to meet up with the rest in the compound and assemble a wall once more.

'Take out these camp security drones.'

Bullets strike the flashing red security drones and they shatter before Tilly's very eyes; she turns around in shock and faces you with a bruised cheek and bloody nose with tears flowing down her cheeks.

'What do you want with me?'

You can tell that she is beside herself with worry and is in great distress.

'My name is Stephanie Coulson, Miss Bright, I work for I.R.I.S.'

'I.R.I.S.?'

'That's right, so tell me what the fuck is happening here.'

'I, I was brought in from SCLERA to carry out operations for Olivia Redfield but—'

'I know who she is, why?'

'She, she has my little girl here. I gave her up for adoption long ago but I made a terrible mistake. Olivia found my daughter for me and said that if I helped her then she would reunite me with her once I had completed a job.'

Tilly goes to reach the handle of the door when Steph pulls her back forcefully, before barring her way.

'Grafting I.R.I.S. lenses into young children's eyes so they could be abused by so-called caring paedophiles, you mean?'

'I didn't know that at the time. It wasn't until I came here that I realised what was happening. Look, I really must be going.'

'Not so fast, I have questions.'

'Please, I have to find Bertie.'

The poor woman begins to sob and is shaking uncontrollably.

'Not fucking yet, you don't. So why have you carried on working for them?'

'Olivia said that she would harm my daughter if I didn't cooperate.'

'Oh, so you weren't cooperating then?'

'Yes, of course I was.'

'So why did you let her abuse your so-called daughter then?'

'What? She said she would never harm my Tiffany. Olivia said that she would give her all the love in the world and protect her from what goes on here.'

'Oh really? Sorry, did you just say Tiffany?'

'Yes, why?'

'Doesn't matter right now. So, she told you that she would protect her?'

'Yes.'

'Then you're more fucked up than I thought.'

'What do you mean?'

'Nothing. I don't trust you or your story, so until we get to the bottom of this, you will stay right here whilst I find Bertram first, got it?'

'But I really must—'

'Stay here or so help me God if I don't let my avenging angels claim one more soul tonight.'

'But—'

'Sybil, imprison her won't you?'

'Yes of course, Steph.'

'Please, I beg you.'

Steph ignores her and approaches the door; she yanks down on the handle and swings the door out. With the portable active denial weapon brandished in front of her, she warily enters inside.

The drones behind Steph form a cylindrical formation around Tilly and train their weapons on her as she bites down on her nails and paces around in a tight circle.

'Now, where the hell is Bertram? Sybil, activate Thermal please.'

Two sets of footprints highlight in red on the floor, one set adult size and the other a child. You see that they are beginning to fade away, trailing off through the dining room and under a closed door that is showing a fading red hand print on the handle.

'Guess they went this way then.'

Steph leads you through the door with her weapon trained in

front of her and you come to an empty corridor with rooms leading off on each side.

Eventually you come across a large square tile cut into the ground where the footprints end. On the wall to the right is a large button protruding from a plate with remnants of a heat signature upon it.

'Sybil, is this Toterhome similar to the rest at this camp?'

'No Steph, it is a Showhauler similar to Dominique Hastings's. The wheels have been removed and the chassis lowered, so it does not tower above the rest of the RVs in the circle.'

'Son of a bitch, they have a fucking bolt hole here.'

Pushing on the large green button, Steph moves to one side and points her weapon at the rising floor from within the square frame.

A framed wall-less box rises from the floor but there is no vehicle stationary within it like Dom's had. Steph steps inside and pulls the weapon in to her chest with her finger over the trigger.

'Sybil, release Tilly and direct her here please. Once we have descended and stepped off this lift, please return it for our guest.'

'Okay Steph, I will speak through the drones to Tilly so she will get the message.'

'Good. Now lower me down.'

'Granted.'

The lift starts to sink back into the floor and you watch as it passes from the Toterhome's confines and through to the storage hold and finally onto one more level beneath.

'Just as well I'm not claustrophobic, hey Watchers?'

Surrounded now on all three sides by a compact wall of earth with a dimly lit tunnel leading away around a bend, Steph is forced to crouch as she makes her way further into the man-made warren.

Hanging off nails set in the earthen walls is a row of jackets and beneath them are dusty wooden crates filled with straw and a small arsenal of pistols and rifles.

'These look familiar, Sybil, are they armoured vests?'

'Yes Steph, they are Kevlar-coated flak jackets.'

'Might come in handy, unlike those guns that look like they have seen better days.'

Removing one of the vests, Steph throws it over her head and pulls the strap tight around her waist. Only you notice that it is worn and frayed.

'Okay, let's proceed, shall we?'

Carrying on, at last you come to a dead end with an opening above that has been covered over by a sheet of corrugated iron.

'Is Tilly on her way?'

'Yes, Steph.'

'Good, because the moment I come up for air I want you to get a lock on my position and send the trike and the drones to my location if that's possible, got it? I want her to see this wanker suffer, then I will know if she is genuine.'

'Understood.'

'Right, let's do this then, switch Thermal off.'

Normal vision is returned and you watch on as Steph slides the sheet away as quietly as she can. Moonlight bathes your vision as Steph starts to climb out.

You find yourself at the edge of a meadow with a sparse covering of trees and bushes that sway against a gentle wind. Behind you lays the decimated camp in flames.

Steph begins to dust herself down when you glimpse a rifle butt smashing into the side of her head that takes her unawares. She drops her weapon and falls to her knees, stunned.

As Steph pulls herself back up, you see blood trickling from the corner of the lens as Bertram strides into view with Tiffany between his legs and a barrel of a shotgun pointing in your direction.

'Bertram, you fucking prick. You wait till—'

A loud crack of gunfire is accompanied by a flash of light in your direction. Steph is knocked backwards off her feet by the force of lead being sprayed into her chest.

Bertram smirks as he crooks the shotgun in his arm and snaps it open to pull the spent cartridge out. Smoke is rising from the barrel and Tiffany screams in terror as she leaves his side and turns away.

Steph is heaving and groaning as she tries frantically to pull open her jacket and you see that the armoured body vest is perforated with shrapnel.

Bertram looks pissed off as he realises what has just happened. He reaches into his pocket for another cartridge and steps over her looking deep into her eyes and squints at you behind the lens as he loads it up.

'I know you're out there watching me from the safety of your computers. I hope I can give you a cheap thrill in your front-row seats when I blow her brains out.'

'Argh. Sybil, pop this fucker's eye out.'

'My pleasure.'

Bertram starts to shake and the shotgun slips from his fingers as he reaches up to his eye. His lens is slowly heating up.

'What the fuck are you doing to me, bitch? No, nooo!'

You see him bring a hand up to his eye as he scrabbles with his fingers to claw out the lens. The ring around his lens begins to glow a dark fiery red as it sizzles away the iris, until at last it pops the eye with a tremendous amount of heat.

Gloopy matter spurts from the hollow of where the eye was and sends him into a screaming frenzy.

Steph tries to get to her feet but she is wounded and hurt; it is then that you see Tilly step out in front of you with Steph's portable active denial weapon in her hands.

Bertram flails blindly and grabs hold of Tiffany. He starts to rain blow after blow of his fists into her fragile head and body.

'Stay the fuck back or I will kill your precious little Tiff.'

Tilly is frozen and just stands there rigid.

'Fucking pull the trigger, Tilly.'

'I, I can't.'

'Mummy, help me! Help me, Mummy!'

'For fuck's sake, Tiffany, what kind of mother stands there and lets her child get beaten up?'

'I—'

'Fucking pull the trigger.'

'Mummy!'

Tiffany pulls the trigger of the weapon aimed between Bertram's legs and waits as he doubles up in pain, then she snatches her daughter out of harm's way.

Ninety-five gigahertz is blasted into Bertram's groin, which sets his trousers alight, welding the fabric to his testicles. He falls down upon his knees, screaming and swinging away blindly.

Still Tilly directs the radiation beam back to his crotch and it starts to cook his testes in their scrotum; the epididymis starts to peel away and skin melts away from his penis, exposing the urethra that shrivels and snaps.

Urine erupts from the perforated pores and bubbles and hisses as the testicles cook to a charred black state. The fire spreads up Bertram's clothing and sets him fully alight.

Tilly shields Tiffany's eyes as Bertram runs screaming over to the heart of the field just as Steph's drones hone into view.

'Let him have it, Sybil.'

'Firing.'

The drones, seventy-four strong, tear his fiery flesh away and limb from limb with their bullets, until all that is left is a smoking carcass.

Red and blue lights appear from behind the camp in the distance with multiple sirens.

'Shit, who called the police, Sybil?'

'It wasn't me, Steph, it must have been Tamara Pike.'

'Fuck, yes. She wants this to look like I.R.I.S. has orchestrated it.'

'Technically she is right, Steph, we have.'

'No, they can't find out those lenses on the dead belong to us. Can you sear their lenses just like Bertram's please, Sybil?'

'It has been done. If you wait long enough you will see the

Sanctuary burn, Steph.'

'Will the children be safe?'

'They have exited the compound toward the approaching police, Steph.'

'Good. We have to get out of here, Sybil, where's the trike?'

The trike appears up ahead in a quiet country lane and you see the decimated Sanctuary to your right as Steph looks around.

'Okay, cool, I see it. Tilly, Tiffany, you need to leave now. Just up ahead is my trike, I need you to get to it. My A.I., Sybil, will help you escape by pairing with Tiffany's A.I.'

'What about you, Miss Coulson?'

'Call me Steph, please. There is no time to worry about me so leave now and I will catch you up.'

'Okay, Tiffany come with Mummy, sweetheart, and do what the kind lady has asked.'

'Yes, Mummy.'

'Thank you, Steph.'

'Sure, now go.'

You watch as the reunited mother and daughter leave and see Steph struggle to get to her feet. Looking down, you see blood patches across the vest as she begins to yank it back over head. Multiple wounds appear through the blood-soaked summer dress beneath.

'Cheap vest! How bad am I, Sybil?'

'You will live, but you need rest so the nanos can repair you.'

'I don't think I can make it to the trike.'

'If you can lift that corrugated iron up, then I can assist you, Steph, if that is your wish.'

'My own fucking genie in a bottle. It is my wish, Sybil, what have you got in mind?'

Twelve of the camouflaged drones pair up and flip upside down, hovering just feet from the ground as they then assemble to make four lines of two.

Steph realises what they are doing and makes her way over to the corrugated sheet, where she lifts it up and drags it over to the drones. Wincing in pain and with a concentrated amount of effort, she lifts the sheet and throws it onto the upside-down drones.

'I see where you're going with this but will it actually work, Sybil?'

'Yes Steph, it will.'

'If you say so, I'm in too much agony to argue with you.'

Steph looks at the floating drones carrying the metal sheet and throws herself mercifully on top of it. The drones sag a little and then their blades spin faster, giving Steph lift as they hoist her up into the sky.

The remainder of the drones congregate and form a wall around her as they all work in tandem to carry Steph across the moonlight sky, passing by the charred remains of Bertram and away from the law enforcement with the children far below.

XIV

Lying on her back staring up at the stars, Steph is transported towards the trike in the distance. Tilly is already safe and sound in the back seat with Tiffany sitting on her lap and a seat belt strapped tightly across them.

'I've never felt more isolated then I do now, Sybil, I guess that any form of technology can sterilise you to the world. I killed those people so easily and felt no connection to guilt or disgust in doing it.'

'It is because you did not pull the trigger, Steph, had you have done then you most certainly would have, now you need to relax so you can heal.'

'I worry that I'm losing what it is to be human. What if I can't protect my baby from harm of the dangerous world we live in? I can't even look after myself.'

'You can only try your best, now be still.'

'But what if I can't give her my full love and attention because of distractions? Will I lose her to the advancements of a world where we are all desensitised to the violence that we see?'

'That is a question that any protective mother will tell you that they have asked themselves, now please, Steph...'

'It's a shame that Tilly lost her way.'

'She is not you, Steph, and you do not share her circumstances.'

'Is anyone ready for that kind of responsibility though? Hell, am I ready? To be a parent, I mean?'

'No one is ever ready.'

Steph is bleeding out onto the rusty corrugated sheet and you notice her hands look clammy and pale.

'I will give her a lovely home if I ever get it back.'

'You will, Steph, you will make a wonderful mother who will bring her up in a stable home but you must get better first.'

'Okay, Mother Teresa! But I have a lot of clutter to clear out first, I can't have things left lying around that could be harmful to my daughter.'

'Clutter?'

'Yes, personal belongings. Work stuff, that kind of thing.'

'Dominique Hastings's home did not have clutter.'

'Dom... No he didn't, his home was almost like it was never lived in. There was nothing personal there at all, it was very strange to find it devoid of traces of his life.'

'Did he like minimalism?'

'No, that wasn't Dom at all.'

The drones approach the trike and stop; then they create an opening and Steph, clutching her chest, slides off and teeters forwards to rest up against the bubble-shaped cockpit. Tilly looks at Steph's bloodied torso and gives a worrying look.

'I feel a little faint.'

'You need to rest and eat, Steph, whilst the nanos restore you.'

'Yes, but we must leave at once.'

'Losing connection to the drones, Steph, their homing beacons have been reactivated.'

The drones that were flying upside-down shift sideways as they reorientate and the corrugated sheet slips away and falls hard to the ground.

Then resembling a flock of birds, the drones take to the night sky at haste and vanish across the treetops like a darkened storm cloud passing away.

Steph slides open the door to the trike and clambers in; she reaches down between her legs and groans as she lifts up the kitbag to put it on her lap.

Tilly, sensing her suffering, grabs the handle and pulls the door back down.

'So who's hungry then?'

'Mummy, I am.'

Tilly gives you an apologetic smile.

'Okay sweetheart, what do you say to the nice lady?'

'Could I have something to eat please?'

'Yup, sure. Just one second.'

Steph begins rooting around in the bag.

'She seems perkier.'

'I think the bruising has gone down a little, she is a tough cookie.'

'Yes she is, isn't she?'

'I'm glad that pig is dead.'

'Aren't we all, hey Watchers?'

'Sorry, who?'

'My audience.'

Steph taps her lens.

'Where I go, they go.'

'Oh, I see.'

Steph takes three packets of food out of the bag and passes two back over her shoulder to Tilly.

'Thank you, Steph, can I look at your wounds?'

'No, I'm fine, my nanos will take care of me. Right, let's get out of here shall we?'

'Of course, but where are we going to go, Steph?'

'Do you have a home, Tilly?'

'I have live-in quarters at SCLERA.'

'No, that won't do. I tell you what, my partner has a spacious home that we can use for a while until we clear this all up. Sybil, please locate Jack Mintlyn and set course to his destination.'

'Granted, Steph.'

'Don't you have a home, Steph?'

'Did, but the police have it in lock-up. I'm not up for breaking in there just now feeling this lousy.'

'But how did it end up there?'

'Long story, it's nothing for you to worry about. You have enough on your plate as it is, so just kick back and relax and when we get to my partner we can go over it all then.'

'Okay. Thank you again, Steph, I really mean that.'

'Yeah, well don't thank me yet because I have a ton of questions for you that I need answers to.'

'Of course, if I can assist you in any way then I will.'

The trike takes off and begins to navigate its way around the country lanes until it finds its way back out onto the A road. Steph dabs at her wounds and groans with every touch.

'Please leave the wounds alone and let the nanos do their job, Steph.'

'I can't stop myself. You on the case for finding Jack, Sybil?'

'Like a fly on a corpse, Steph.'

'I think you have experienced far too much bloodshed today. Sorry about my A.I., Tilly, she is a little kooky tonight.'

'Mine is called Daisy.'

Tiffany has stopped eating an opened packet of sweetened locusts and smiles at you as Steph catches her eye in the rear-view mirror. The young girl is bruised and her dark hair is clinging to her bloodied and mud-streaked face.

'I'm sorry, what did you say?'

'My personal assistant is called Daisy.'

'Oh, that's a lovely name, Tiffany, does she take good care of you?'

Tiffany looks to her mum, unsure if she should answer Steph's question.

'That's okay, Tiff, you can answer Stephanie, she is a friend.'

'Okay, Mummy. Yes, Daisy always plays with me.'

'That's lovely.'

'She even turns Miss Olivia into a cartoon fox when I have been naughty.'

'Sorry, what?'

'Sometimes Olivia's fox makes me do things that hurt me, but Daisy says it is just a game and that it is just make believe.'

'What sort of things, darling?'

'Sometimes when I am naked she makes me...'

'Quiet now, Tiffany. Put it out of your mind.'

'But Steph, I need to know.'

Tilly is shaking with rage and Tiffany is becoming upset.

'Tilly, no. You don't want to know, trust me. It won't do you to dwell on the past.'

'But Steph, Olivia said—'

'Olivia was not what she made out to be, you must see this?'

'I never thought that—'

'Tilly, you need to get that lens out of her eye and that vixen out of her head.'

'Oh God. How could I have been so stupid?'

'You weren't to know.'

'Am I naughty, Mummy?'

'No, sweetie, the bad people were naughty back at the Sanctuary.'

'Okay, Mummy.'

Steph turns her gaze away from Tilly who is now crying and hugging her daughter tightly.

'I swear I will never let you out of my sight, my precious little girl.'

Tears are forming around your vision again and Steph wipes them away with her finger. Steph is sniffing as she tries to hold back the tears.

'Where are we headed, Sybil? Where's Jack?'

'I have located his signal back to London, outside Westminster.'

'That's right, his march carries on tomorrow against the use of lenses being exempt from the Data Protection Act. At least we should find him at home this early in the morning.'

'We will arrive around 2 a.m., Steph.'

'Thank you, Sybil.'

Looking to the rear-view mirror again as the trike continues its journey, Steph watches fondly as Tiffany snuggles up to her mum and drifts off to sleep. Tilly looks gaunt and pasty and she is fidgeting in her seat.

'I'm sorry you both had to go through that, Tilly.'

'What kind of animal was Olivia? What unspeakable things did she do to my precious daughter?'

'The worst kind.'

'I believed in her too.'

'You weren't to know. But if it gives you any comfort, it would seem that Olivia's foster mother sold her out.'

'Tamara? How does she fit in to all of this?'

'She is your boss, you tell me.'

'I don't really know, I have seen Tamara on a few occasions but never had the chance to speak to her in person.'

'That's not helpful.'

'Sorry! But I was taken on as an intern by Olivia and slowly over the years ended up becoming lead ophthalmologist.'

'Do you know anything about a possible takeover or merger between SCLERA and I.R.I.S.?'

'Sorry, no. I only ever answered to Olivia but we all knew the tenuous relationship she had with Tamara.'

'How so?'

'Rumours really, and office gossip. Olivia had a reputation for coming on to married women that worked there. It was discussed that Tamara was brought into the situation for allowing Olivia's promiscuous behaviour to bring about sexual misconduct in the workplace.'

'What did Tamara do?'

'She fired any of the employees that were raising concerns of abuse and paid them off.'

'That couldn't have been cheap.'

'No. Which is why Tamara sold away all her rights to the smart A.I. that she had invented in an acquisition to I.R.I.S.'

'Interesting. So I'm thinking, well I know, that I.R.I.S. made a massive profit by integrating the A.I. into phase two and so Tamara is now looking for a way to outdo I.R.I.S. with her advanced tech to rival the launch of our phase three. I presume that SCLERA's shares are down.'

'I believe so.'

'I'm also surmising that I.R.I.S. caught wind of her advancements and maybe tried to pay her off as a way of preventing her from bringing her next phase to market, so that we could take the monopoly with our own launch.'

'Tamara would have refused a handout, no matter the courteous offer.'

'So it's possible that Tamara decided to throw I.R.I.S. under the bus and take over everything that I.R.I.S. is set to lose, by staging Olivia's downfall and sending me to the Sanctuary to put I.R.I.S. in the frame with our phase three.'

'I don't follow.'

'Is SCLERA a British company?'

'No, its main branch is overseas in America.'

'I figured as much.'

'Why?'

'Nothing. It was just something that my boss was always harping on about. Well she didn't bet on our prototype proving to be this advanced, did she?'

'Where is Olivia now? I want to kill her.'

'She is dead, Tilly.'

'How do you know?'

'Because I have her fucking eye in the storage hold behind you.'

'You what?'

'Don't worry, I didn't kill her. Someone else did.'

'Oh, well that's good enough for me. So why is Tamara of interest to you anyway?'

'Because I believe that she acquired a batch of our phase two lenses to give to a gentleman that is now also dead, who in turn sold them to Olivia before his departure.'

'Who was he?'

'A lowlife.'

'Okay. Are you sure Olivia is dead?'

'Seen it with my own eyes. Now Olivia was under the impression that dear old Mum had forgiven her shortcomings by entrusting her to set up I.R.I.S.'

'So what happened?'

'Well, luckily I.R.I.S. got involved before it went down, i.e. me. But it doesn't explain the military showing up when they did to eliminate Olivia and sending me halfway round the country.'

'The military are involved?'

'Mmm, it would seem so. But either I had a lucky break or the military have sent me on one wild goose chase.'

'I can get you into SCLERA if you like? I have clearance, maybe you can find the answers there.'

'I thought you would suggest that. But see, there is a catch.'

'What is it, Steph?'

'Well, I know that Tamara is watching me, along with God knows who else is out there, and she will know that I am coming for her.'

'I can still help you.'

'But it could be dangerous for you, you have a child who needs you now.'

'So do you, Steph.'

'Shut the fuck up, Sybil.'

'I can give you all the information I know about SCLERA and our headquarters here in the UK.'

'Well anything you have would of course help.'

'Are you really sure that you want to face her? I hear that she is not a person to cross in a hurry.'

'I have to. I need to get to Tamara Pike because some things still don't add up.'

'Like what?'

'I need confirmation that she was the person who gave our lenses away, or whether she was the stooge being set up for a fall.'

'If she had a batch of your lenses then how did she get hold of them?'

'That's what I need to find out. Well at least I know one thing for certain.'

'That is?'

'Your plan to discredit I.R.I.S. didn't work, did it Tamara? I bet that makes you pissed, doesn't it?'

'Be wary of her, Steph. Especially now, as SCLERA is in a very large mansion.'

'I'll be fine, I'm used to it by now. So where is her office located in this mansion then and where is the mansion even situated?'

'I will take you directly to her office when we decide to go.'

'No, you will tend to your daughter at Jack's and stay there until I return.'

'I insist, if only to get you inside.'

'Okay, fine. So tell me more about SCLERA.'

'Tamara has an extensive collection of art that adorns her office. I have visited there a few times when Olivia was left in charge whilst Tamara was away.'

'What kind of art?'

'The Eye of Providence and numerous works by various artists, centred around the subject of eyes in general. She also has quite a few portraits of herself and her ancestors around the walls too.'

'She loves her vanity then?'

'It would seem so, yes.'

'Where is the mansion based?'

'It is in Oxford.'

'Steph, we are now entering London.'

'Yes, thank you Sybil. I can see for myself you know.'

'Sorry.'

'Okay, well let's find Jack then, shall we? How far till we get to his Toterhome?'

'Ten minutes, Steph.'

'Sorry Tilly, you were saying?'

'Yes, there is very little security there. A large set of iron gates open to a long winding path up to the mansion and a scanner is set into the hallway when you enter the building. After that there are no further security perimeters that I know of.'

'Okay, well I will check it out anyway.'

The trike speeds on through the once built-up city streets of Westminster and Steph looks around at the green landscape that has replaced the old buildings that once stood there. Only the common landmarks remain to remind people of the time before London became a green haven.

'I hope we don't run into the law because this trike is a little hot right now, the sooner we get to Jack the better.'

'Jack's home is coming up, Steph, he is located in Hyde Park.'

You see a parked Toterhome hidden under a large cluster of trees as the trike approaches silently through West Carriage Drive, passing other Toterhomes from all over the world parked up and plugged in to off-road solar parking spaces.

The trike's lights dim as it comes to rest and pulls up alongside Jack's home with the automatic handbrake clicking in, bringing it to rest.

'Okay, all out.'

Steph lifts the door and struggles out as Tilly and Tiffany exit from behind her.

'It smells of weed round here.'

'That would be Jack's cannabis farm inside his home.'

'He has an illegal den?'

'No, it's his job. He is a registered pot cultivator, who extracts CBD oil for large pharmaceutical companies.'

'Does he ever smoke his own products?'

'Unfortunately, yes he does.'

'You don't dabble?'

'On the very rare occasion. Anyway, let me just get my open sesame fob out and we will let ourselves in.'

'You don't have shared access to his home then?'

'It's complicated, Tilly.'

'Does that fob open anything you like?'

'Ha, I thought it did but I was proven wrong about that theory recently.'

'Can't we just knock or ring the bell?'

'If you want to spook him then go right ahead but be ready for this factory on wheels pulling away from here faster than a cheetah.'

Approaching the door, Steph pushes her fob to the panel and the door folds outwards and down to create the familiar ramp to entry.

'It will be very warm and extremely bright in here, so try not to be overwhelmed when you see the crop.'

'I will try not to.'

'Good, come on then, follow me.'

XV

The door retracts behind you, as Steph, Tilly and Tiffany set foot inside a white lobby. Two hazmat suits are hanging from coat hangers screwed into the glossy white wall on the left and two pairs of boots sit under them on the floor.

A pair of black rubber gloves are draped over a steel sink on the opposite wall with a bottle of blue sterilisation fluid resting on the steel drainer.

'He takes it all very seriously, you know.'

Before Steph can open the door into the main hallway, the door slides across and reveals a familiar slim, muscular gentleman with blond curly hair and a chiselled jaw. He is only wearing tight-fitting boxer shorts.

The man leans against the door frame, putting his left hand behind his head and crosses his legs. You notice that he has light stubble on his face and is sporting the same tattoo as Steph but his is just above his waistline.

'You took your sweet time getting here, Steph, I was expecting you far sooner.'

The man makes a fist with his right hand and brings it across his mouth to stifle a yawn.

'What do you mean you were expecting me?'

'See you've brought some friends along too.'

'Yes, this is Tilly and her daughter Tiffany.'

'Hi Tilly, Tiffany. I'm Jack, please come on in.'

You all follow him into his main lounge area and he gestures to you all to take a seat. You notice a reefer smouldering away in an ashtray.

Jack apologises and takes a drag from it before stubbing it out.

'You look like death warmed up, Steph. Why do you just let yourself in with your magic key all the time? Why can't you ever give me some warning before you arrive?'

'I know that I'm about as welcome as syphilis but this isn't about me, I need refuge for Tilly and Tiffany here.'

'At least with syphilis I get enjoyment before I contract it.'

'That's harsh, Jack.'

Tilly puts up her hands.

'I'm sorry, we don't mean to intrude. We will leave right away.'

'No, you and your daughter are fine, I promise. If you're hungry or thirsty then just down the hall to the right you will find my kitchen. Help yourselves to anything from the fridge but don't eat the cakes as they are, erm… hashish.'

'Umm, okay, thank you.'

'But Mummy, I'm not hungry or thirsty.'

'Let's give Steph and Jack some time alone, shall we Tiff? Come on, let's have a look in the fridge anyway.'

'Oh, and stay away from the stairs to the overhead deck. It's locked for a reason.'

Tilly takes Tiffany's hand and leads her away as Jack gives Steph a troubling look.

'What's the deal, Steph? You're putting me in a tough spot here. You're a wanted criminal for God's sake and who the hell are they?'

'I will explain everything, I promise.'

'Damn right you will. I have a rally to attend later on today and I needn't remind you of the business I'm running upstairs.'

'I know and I'm sorry but we had nowhere else to turn.'

'What's with this about you being pregnant too?'

'I am, it's true. I wouldn't say it just to get back at you.'

'You better be straight with me.'

'You have to believe me, Jack.'

'Give me the time to process this is all I ask, okay?'

'You've had enough time.'

'I really haven't, so who is this Tamara woman?'

'Tamara?'

'Yes, the one that has left a holo message here for you on my console.'

'On your console?'

'I'm not your bloody secretary taking unsolicited calls on your behalf, Steph, how did this woman get my number?'

'I don't know but she is involved in a case I am working on. I will iron this all out, you have my word.'

'We will see, you have twenty-four hours then I want you all gone.'

'But...'

Jack takes a tin off the table beside the ashtray and flips it open to start rolling another joint to fill with his dried cannabis.

'No ifs and no buts. When you have cleared your name and if you clear your name, then we can discuss your pregnancy.'

'Fuck's sake, Jack, our pregnancy! I can see you won't budge on this matter so we will move on.'

'Are they seeing all this and listening to every word?'

'Who, the Watchers?'

'No, your imaginary friends.'

'Of course they are but you don't have to...'

'You better hope that I'm not dragged into this, Steph, you know how paranoid I get.'

Spliff rolled, Jack licks the paper and seals the weed in, twisting the end. He pushes a rolled-up piece of card into the other end and puts it to his lips to light.

'Jack, you're being unreasonable.'

'Am I? Just play your message.'

'I need to hide the trike we arrived on first.'

'Why? Who's trike is it?'

'It's Dom's.'

'Your boss's?'

'Yes, I stole it.'

'Are you insane? Well you can't leave it here.'

'I can hide it.'

'Damn right you better hide that trike, I don't need unwanted attention. What were you thinking?'

'Bollocks, I forgot I left my bag and drone onboard it. I will go get them first.'

'You know what? I'll get dressed and grab your stuff to bring back here. I'll hide the trike too, you just go play your message. It's all set to playback.'

'Jack, thank you.'

'Dammit Steph, you want a pull? I think we both need to calm down, don't you?'

Jack offers Steph the joint but she refuses.

'Your loss, but you look like you need it more than me. So what happened to you anyway? Those wounds look painful.'

'Buckshot from a shotgun.'

'Seems I'm not the only one who could quite easily kill you sometimes then.'

'Stop fucking about, Jack. It still really hurts.'

'No shit!'

Leaving Steph alone and placing a half-smoked joint in the ashtray, Jack passes by Tilly and Tiffany in the kitchen and directs them to a spare bedroom across the hall to rest in.

He then tells them that it is theirs for the next twenty-four hours, before he disappears into his own bedroom to get changed and shuts the door behind him.

Steph takes the burning spliff from the ashtray and takes a long drag of it.

'You refused to partake and now you have changed your mind. Carcinogens are forbidden, Steph, please extinguish the substance for your baby's sake.'

'I am allowed to change my mind, Sybil, besides, it might take the edge off. How is my baby doing anyway?'

'If I hadn't had to release a small portion of nanos to heal you, then your baby would be in far better condition then what she currently is in.'

'This isn't my fault, Sybil, it's that fucking Tamara woman's doing.'

'Please try not to get into any more trouble or I fear your child may become disfigured or worse.'

'You won't let that happen, will you?'

'I will try to make sure that the nanos correct what is wrong but you must heed my advice, Stephanie.'

'Piss off, Sybil, now you're sounding like my mother.'

'Your baby cannot make choices but you can.'

'Right, fair assessment.'

'You should be feeling better any time soon.'

'Good, so let's see what this bitch Tamara has to say, shall we Watchers?'

Highlighting the image on the console and tapping play, Steph reclines into the seat and places the ashtray on her stomach as she continues to puff on the joint in defiance, using the ashtray to collect hot embers that fall off as it burns.

Projectors in the corner of the room bring up Tamara in 3D and the message plays.

'Miss Coulson, as you are aware by now I am not Mrs Hastings. I am sorry that I led you to believe that I was but you were not expected in Loch Lomond at that time. I know that you think I was behind Dominique Hastings's murder but let me reassure you that I had nothing to do with it.'

'Pause. That's utter bullshit, Watchers.'

Steph takes another long drag and flicks the ash to the glass tray, as she billows a plume of thick, white smoke rings from her mouth.

'Resume playback.'

'Meeting with Dominique in Scotland was on my part to get some reassurance from our previous endeavour together. Mr Hastings gave those lenses to Sebastian Day, knowing that paedophile would agree to wear a lens to join in with the rest of the Sanctuary and take part in the lewd acts with minors. He was well aware of my plight concerning Olivia's betrayal and her involvement there, as he had been tailing her on my request for weeks after the office scandal broke and my business took a hit.'

'I'm not buying any of this, Watchers, are you? She is just telling me what I need to know.'

'I was under no illusion that I.R.I.S. profited better than I did with the A.I. that you now have in your eye. As far as I was concerned our dealings with Dom were well and truly over but my foster daughter Olivia forced my hand, I had no choice but to go back to Dom for help and that was when he suggested looking into her background, as I was naive to think her past was well and truly behind her.'

'Pause. Come on, I can see through your lies just as clear as I see through my lens, Tamara. Resume playback.'

'Your boss understood that I was haemorrhaging massive losses for Olivia's scandal and so he gave me the lifeline. In return for his help he offered to buy me out and slowly merge I.R.I.S. with SCLERA and the cogs were set in motion. When he told me what he uncovered I was shocked to the core that such a terrible secret existed.'

'Pause. Trouble is, Watchers, it sounds genuine about what she is saying but Tamara knows everything we do. I have to take this with a pinch of salt, resume playback.'

'Dominique singled out Sebastian Day from the Sanctuary and gave him those lenses in return for grafting a lens into his own eye. Sebastian agreed to have the lens installed because Dom threatened him with ousting his secret lust for children, it was a bonus that Sebastian's wife was playing away and gave Sebastian a valid reason to keep the truth from Olivia and take the chits and run.'

'Pause. Olivia gave Sebastian the evidence of his cheating spouse, so how was she involved and not privy to the larger picture? Resume playback.'

'Mr Day as you are aware was a person who dealt in black market eyewear, this was one of the reasons that he was picked out by Dom from anyone else in the Sanctuary. I played my part in suggesting to Olivia that I had past dealings with the man in the early development of our own clinical trials and that he had recently approached me looking for a sale on a batch of lenses he'd acquired. Of course none of it was true but Olivia took the bait and she took it upon herself to intervene and strike a deal with the man, telling me that she would deal with him personally under my instructions to make a problem go away.'

'Pause. So if everything she is saying is true and believe me, I think it's a piss-poor excuse, then why go through all that effort when Tamara could just dismiss Olivia in the first place and not have to worry about the whole rigmarole and charades that they went through?'

Steph leans forward and snatches up a lighter to relight the reefer that has gone out and gives it a few quick tugs to get it going again before sitting back.

'Resume playback.'

'The rest you know is history, Miss Coulson, however, I have since learned that Sebastian Day conveniently took his own life and my foster daughter was assassinated by you. Why is I.R.I.S. going through so much effort to conceal the whole sordid affair?'

'Woah! Pause. Both of those are nothing to do with me or I.R.I.S. Resume playback.'

'Also, Miss Coulson, you pointed the finger at me killing Dominique but it was you that deflected the interceptor to his boat which killed him, so does that make you the real killer? What is your agenda, I wonder?'

'You can fuck right off if you think I'm to blame for all of this.'

'I must say though that I am glad you destroyed the Sanctuary, it made for very exciting viewing. I can only presume that you are moonlighting for the military, judging by the amount of weaponry that was so conveniently gifted to you.'

'Is she for real? Pause.'

'From her perspective, Steph, you are the catalyst for this entire mess.'

'I'm an agent for I.R.I.S. carrying out a goddamn trial, Sybil, how dare she shoulder the blame on me to wriggle out of her own hole that she dug?'

'The fact remains, you are a vigilante wanted by the law. She is merely stating the obvious to the outside world.'

'Fuck it! Resume playback.'

'On the basis of what I believe, I think we should meet, Miss Coulson. By the time you have come to the end of this recording, I would already have gauged your live reaction and made the necessary arrangements.'

'Pause. What the fuck does that mean? She's a bit presumptuous, isn't she? Besides, she hasn't answered how she knew Dom was out on his boat in the first place.'

'Resume playback.'

'I invite you to please join me at my office in SCLERA HQ, you will have no friction from any of my security detail to access the building. I will be waiting for you on the fifth floor, if you agree then I will make my way there now. I look forward to seeing you, Miss Coulson. I will feel better if I speak to you in person.'

'I bet you fucking will.'

The recording stops and the image of Tamara fades to be replaced by a fully clothed Jack staring back at you from the other side of the console. He has a kitbag over his shoulder and a drone under his arm.

'Did you get all that, Jack?'

'Sure did and the answer's no.'

'The answer's no to what?'

'I'm not taking you to SCLERA, I have a really important day lined up today for the march and let's face it, that woman is clearly setting you up for a fall.'

'What a trap? Sure it's a real possibility but I have to go and I can't use the trike. You have to take me, Jack.'

'Tough, you can walk. Here's your kitbag and your drone.'

Jack places them on the floor and takes the half-smoked joint from Steph's hand and stubs it out.

'Thought you didn't want any.'

'Changed my mind.'

'I dismantled your torture weapon by the way.'

'You what? My denial active system?'

'I took it all apart and discarded it in bins around the whole of the park.'

'What gives you the bloody right to destroy it?'

'I will not have you bringing shit like that into my home, Steph. You want it back then you go get it but don't expect any more favours from me and certainly don't think that I will let you back on board.'

'Earlier when you said that you were expecting me, how did you know I was coming?'

'Trouble knocks on my door and that is usually followed by only one thing, you.'

Steph stands up and barges past him in the doorway.

'Do I still have some of my clothes here or have you thrown them away too?'

'They are where you left them, Steph, where they always are.'

'That's a fucking surprise.'

'Feeling better now, are we?'

'Piss off, Jack.'

Going into the bedroom, Steph slams the door and storms over to the wardrobe to retrieve a clean set of clothes. The door opens behind her and Jack appears.

'So you going to fill me in on all that's happened then or what?'

Tilly appears from the adjacent room and loiters in the hallway; Steph catches her peering in and throws a grey suit onto the bed.

'Sorry to disturb you. I have showered Tiff and put her to bed, I just wanted to say thank you, Jack, for allowing us to stay.'

'How is she?'

'Bruised and a little tearful but she will be okay, Jack. I saw some old scarring and—'

'Look, she is safe now and that is all that matters. Everything will be better now, you will see.'

'Thank you, Steph.'

Steph starts to undress and waves Tilly and Jack into the room.

'There's no point in the Watchers listening to this all over again, so I suggest we power my lens off and we can all sit down so I can bring you both up to speed. Then Jack, you can unhook us from the charger and get us on the road to SCLERA, can't you? I reckon that Tilly probably wants to get some bits from her quarters there anyway.'

'I've told you under no circumstances will I take you there, I do not have a death wish like you.'

'You know you love me really. I bet I can persuade you.'

'I said no, it's not going to happen.'

'Whatever! Let me get dressed and we can all take a seat so I can explain everything that has happened.'

'I can't wait.'

'Shut the fuck up, Jack. Later, Watchers, Power Off.'

XVI

'Power On.'

Jack's mobile cannabis farm is passing through a pair of high, black, wrought-iron gates and as you acclimatise to your surroundings you notice the dark red-brick looking mansion in the distance.

Steph is looking through the cockpit window to the long, stone-chipped driveway that leads to the SCLERA mansion and is applying nail polish to her toes with her feet up on the dashboard.

Tall fir trees align the drive and pass by slowly as the RV trundles across the loose chippings.

'I told him I would have my way, Watchers, I usually get what I want. I have left Jack and Tilly to mull over what I have told them concerning our past exploits, whilst I have some quiet time up here alone. Next stop, Tamara Pike.'

The Toterhome approaches a large island of freshly cut grass with a weathered, green copper pyramid top sunken into its centre. Wording of SCLERA is indented upon its front-facing triangle.

A large revolving eye is crowned at the pyramid's point and the pupil of the eye follows the Toterhome as it swings round the island to park up outside the mansion next to Tamara's own grand Showhauler.

Steph spins the recliner that she is perched upon and slides a door back behind her that leads into the lounge area. She screws the lid back on the polish and deposits the bottle into a drinks holder then passes through the door.

'Okay, we are here. It's still a little dark out there but the mansion is lit like a fucking Christmas tree, so Tilly, if you're ready to go and collect your belongings from your quarters then let's do this, shall we?'

Tilly, seated on the sofa by the console looks around and gives you a weary smile.

'Will Tiff be okay? I don't want to leave her too long.'

'She will be fine with Jack, I promise. You said earlier that she is fast asleep, so she won't even realise we're gone, we will be back well before she wakes.'

Jack enters the lounge with Steph's kitbag.

'I can't believe I agreed to this.'

'Oh Jack, we won't be long.'

'I checked your bag, Steph, why have you packed a few of my cakes in there?'

'I have the munchies and I'm eating for two now, don't forget.'

'You can't go in there wasted, Steph. And the cakes won't help either.'

'I'm not that bad, since when did you start to fucking care anyway?'

'The moment you persuaded me that I'm going to be a father.'

'So are we going to live in sin or shall I make wedding plans then?'

'What the hell, Steph? I'm not ready for a commitment.'

'Well you better be fucking ready, Daddy Mintlyn.'

Steph winks at Tilly and accidentally shoots off a picture from her camera mode.

'Bollocks, I forget it does that.'

'Does what?'

'Nothing, Tilly, let's go.'

'What do you want me to do with your drone, Steph?'

'Leave it in the lobby please, Jack, I don't need it right now.'

Tilly follows Steph to the rear of Jack's RV and pushes the button to release the hatch to the ground. Jack throws the kitbag to Steph and waits for them to leave.

Both women descend the created ramp and begin to march across the driveway, passing Tamara's Toterhome as they go. Without warning the flashing white cursor in Steph's eye changes colour to yellow.

'The cursor in your lens HUD has changed colour, Steph.'

'Shit, yeah, so it has. Ooh, does that mean I'm going to get a new option to play with then?'

'I do not know, Steph, but it seems to have been triggered by passing Tamara's Toterhome.'

'Keep an eye on it and keep me informed if anything else changes, will you?'

'Yes, Steph.'

You watch on as Steph and Tilly enter the building and notice that there is a body scanner that they have to pass through.

'Is this it for security then, Tilly?'

'Not normally, there are usually night security guards to search your bags stationed beyond the scanner.'

'I don't like this one bit, it's freaking me out a little. Where did you say Tamara's office is located?'

'Fifth floor, two floors above the dormitory quarters.'

'Okay then.'

They both pass through the scanner independently and no detection sounds are heard. Tilly gives you a puzzled look; Steph throws up her hands and shrugs.

'With the week I'm having, I was expecting drones to appear.'

'Don't you have anything that may attract attention in your holdall, Steph?'

'Well yeah I guess so, Tilly, but clearly what's in my bag is not of any importance here though.'

Once both women are through, Tamara's voice echoes from hidden speakers around the lobby.

'Thank you for arriving as swift as you did, Miss Coulson, please proceed past the grand staircase to your front and down the corridor to the right, where you will find an elevator that will take you to floor five.'

'Fuck that, I think I will take the stairs if it's all the same to you.'

'Very well then, please bear right on the grand staircase when it reaches the landing to get to floor two and you will come to a door. Through that door lays a spiral staircase that will bring you up to floor five. Once there I will direct you to my office.'

'I will take the lift to my floor, Steph.'

'Be fucking careful then and most of all be quick, soon as you're packed get yourself back to Jack, okay?'

'I will.'

Parting ways, Steph waves Tilly off and approaches the foot of the stairs. A royal blue carpet with gold, embroidered pattern edges, runs the entire length of each wide step, giving it a style of extravagance.

On the landing up ahead and tucked into an alcove, rests a golden statue of a blindfolded woman with a pair of eyes in a palm of an outstretched hand. She is dressed in a long flowing robe and her right arm is missing.

On the walls leading up to the landing are portraits of men and women that carry beneath their pictures their Christian names, followed by the surname Pike, denoting a rich history of Tamara's bloodline.

Steph takes each step precariously and you sense that she is nervous as she stops and keeps glancing upwards to the next floor as if expecting something to happen.

A haunting piano melody starts to play from high above and you sense a foreboding dread.

'What the fuck? The hairs are standing up on the back of my neck, Watchers.'

Pulling open her kitbag, Steph reaches in and pulls out one of Jack's special cakes; she prises it from its case and tears it in half before popping it in her mouth. She wraps the other half in the case and stows it back into the bag.

Eventually you see her reach floor two and go through the door, where she continues to work her way up the spiral staircase to the fifth floor.

Steph hesitates at the next door that opens to a lobby and you hear her sigh as the piano melody fades away to silence, then you see her wipe crumbs away from the corners of her mouth.

'Take a left and follow the corridor until you reach a pair of double doors that have handles gilded with gold. The doors are panelled with a depiction of Egyptian hieroglyphics if that helps.'

'Shouldn't be too hard to find then.'

'My office lies beyond, Miss Coulson. I look forward to meeting you as myself.'

Reaching her destination, Steph pushes on one of the gold handles and the hefty door swings silently inwards.

What greets you is a large windowless room with a high ceiling that has at its centre an intricate chandelier that sparkles and shimmers.

Burgundy painted walls join a golden, fleur-de-lis patterned dado rail, that stretches around the room with oak panelling beneath.

The look is completed with a dozen paintings depicting people with abnormally large eyes and each frame is individually lit by solid brass picture lights that align the walls.

Directly beneath the chandelier sits Tamara's oversized, tamarind-finished desk with ornate metal accents.

Tamara is sat at her desk in a crisp, tailored red suit sipping on a glass of margarita with olives on a stick resting against the rim and a music box rests in front of her.

'Hello again, Miss Coulson. Please sit, why don't you?'

Tamara points to a leather chair opposite her.

'Do you know that the eyes are a window to the soul? And through your eyes I see a very tormented soul indeed, Miss Coulson.'

'Save your philosophical shit, I'm not interested.'

Steph approaches the chair and flings her bag to the floor before sitting down.

'Let's just get on with why you asked me to come here, shall we Tamara?'

'Very well. I have been reading up on you, Miss Coulson, it is amazing what one can divulge from the internet these days about a person.'

'We're in an age where even God has a dedicated web page with a mass of followers, what's your point?'

'I have no point to make, just an observation on why I think I.R.I.S. chose you to trial their new phase three lens.'

'Oh yeah, and what is that?'

'Most people require roots to settle down and I can only presume from observing you that what you truly desire is just that, however I feel your past is preventing you from achieving your goals. You say that technology is a form of social control but you cannot give it up that easily and this is why you are conflicted.'

Tamara sips from the glass and smears bright red lipstick on the rim.

'I'm sure most normal people feel the same way, they just can't escape their bonds of servitude, the distractions are too great.'

'Yours is no different, Miss Coulson, in fact I think Dom knew that you could not resist the lure of what I.R.I.S.'s technology could do for you and that is why you were chosen for his trial.'

'Bullshit, I choose my own fate.'

'Do you? I see your grandparents were from the Emerald Isles.'

'They were Irish, so what?'

'They were travellers seeking a new life on these shores and eventually settled down.'

'So?'

'Well I think that time has come for you to do the same, I'm sure it was what they wanted for their gypsy bloodline.'

'We are all travellers now.'

'Only those that follow the path of advancements. The rest

choose to separate from the herd and live a simpler life.'

'So did you just invite me here for a family history lesson?'

'No, I brought you here to ask you to give up on your quest that was given to you by those that want you to follow without question.'

Smoothing herself down, you notice Steph's hands are shaking.

'I.R.I.S. you mean? Why?'

'Because they have brought you here to kill me and I can only think of one reason why they would do that.'

'I didn't come here to kill you, I just want answers.'

Looking down at her feet, you notice that Steph's left knee is jiggling and she grabs it with her hand to steady the nervous twitch.

'Your tattoo tells me that you are an anarchist, that is why you are focused on bringing down all those around you that believe in the digital revolution. You are in a prime position to do just that.'

'You've got me all wrong. I just want to know who gave you the batch of lenses.'

'I have already told you, Dominique Hastings did.'

'I don't believe you. How did you know that Dom was out on the boat?'

'I gave him an ultimatum when he tried to buy me out. I said I was thankful for his continued support but I would not sell SCLERA under any circumstances.'

'Why would Dom be so interested in SCLERA?'

'Because we were ready to launch our new smart contact lens way before I.R.I.S. was and Dominique wasn't happy about us potentially beating him to the market.'

'That sounds like Dom. He wouldn't get upset over it though, business is business.'

'He then threatened me to not market my new smart contact lens before him, saying that he would bring down all those that were involved with Olivia if I didn't comply. I said I would hold off my launch until his trial was complete as a favour returned, but he was livid. I told him my launch was inevitable and that I would grant him three days' grace.'

'He told you where to go, didn't he? So you drugged him or something similar and had him tied up to his boat so you could remove his eye. You knew that he would eventually bleed out but you weren't counting on me showing up, were you?'

'That's just not true, he told me to think the offer over whilst he went fishing and when he returned he hoped I would reconsider. He never did return though, did he?'

'How convenient for you.'

'His blood was on your hands, not mine. If you want to get to the bottom of the truth then you need to revisit Olivia's recordings.'

Steph glances around at the paintings and you see a young boy with overly large eyes hugging a tree wearing a red coat and in another you see a woman with the same large eyes walking across the surface of the sea with her nightdress billowing in the wind. Steph begins to pick off the polish on her fingernails.

'I can't access Olivia's files, the information is now transferred over to the I.R.I.S. server.'

'Then you must go there and retrieve it.'

'It's a secure server and I don't have the clearance level to access it.'

'It was very foolish of you to upload it there in the first place, wasn't it? I'm sure you will find a way though to redeem yourself.'

'Why should I believe what you say? Let alone help you.'

'Because I speak the truth, Miss Coulson.'

'Why don't you just tell me what it is your holding back from me?'

'It's better that you see the truth for yourself, then you will know just how vindictive and dangerous your boss was. The real enemy is at home, Miss Coulson.'

'Are you saying that Dom features in Olivia's footage?'

'Don't underestimate what Dom—'

The lights go out and plunge you all in darkness, You hear Tamara scrape her chair across the floor as she leaps up in fright.

'What the fuck is happening, Sybil?'

'The cursor turned amber just before the lights went out, Steph, but I do not know if it is a coincidence.'

You hear Tamara screaming in the darkness.

'They are trying to silence me.'

'No one's trying to get rid of you, Tamara.'

'I will not let you kill me, Miss Coulson.'

'I don't wish to... you know what? Sybil, just activate Night Vision please?'

'Activated.'

A pixelated glitch appears across your vision and momentarily blinds you with an array of green-tinged colouring before it disappears. You just catch Tamara backing up into the corner of the room.

'Another anomaly, Steph.'

'I know, Sybil, I can't see shit through my normal eye so I have to rely on my eye with the lens, but I don't know if what I'm seeing is real.'

'Miss Coulson, they are forcing you to rely on your lens and they will exploit that. Do not believe everything you see, do you understand me?'

You see Tamara race towards the desk and she picks up a sharp letter opener from one of its drawers.

'Stay away from me, Miss Coulson, or I will stab you so help me God.'

'Calm down, Tamara, how many more times do I have to tell you that I don't wish to harm you?'

'I.R.I.S. does and you work through them.'

You see Tamara frantically waving the letter opener around in the dark and see the terror on her face as she stands rooted to the spot.

Steph gets to her feet and grabs her bag to throw over her shoulder when she suddenly stops and looks back to the paintings.

The boy in the painting with the red coat releases his grip from the tree and turns to look at you with his large hollow eyes.

'What the fuck? Are you seeing this? Jack, what the hell did you put in those cakes? Because they sure aren't cannabis.'

'It is not the cakes, Steph.'

'I know that, Sybil, but I am tripping out here. My head is numb and these visions are making me feel a little woozy.'

'It's just the glitch playing tricks with your vision, you need to concentrate.'

You see the little boy snap a branch off the tree before clambering out of the painting's frame. He flashes you a smile and you see a row of razor-sharp teeth as he darts away from your field of view.

Steph looks around nervously and reaches into her pocket to click her cylindrical jammer.

'Where the fuck has Tamara gone?'

'I don't know, Steph.'

'Fuck me, Sybil, where's the exit?'

Steph turns to face where the door once was but it has now been replaced by a painting of the monument from the courtyard, with the eye above the pyramid.

A red laser shoots from the pupil of the eye and swings in Steph's direction.

Diving out of the way, Steph throws herself across the desk just as the laser hits and sears into the wood panelling to start a fire.

Hiding behind the desk, Steph looks around for Tamara but spots the little boy instead who is crouching down in front of her. She grabs hold of the child in fright as a nervous reflex.

'I told you to stay away.'

The little boy springs to his feet and bares his razor teeth as he bounds over to Steph and brings the branch down in a stabbing motion into her shoulder. She screams in agony as the branch pierces her skin.

Then he runs off and climbs into another painting's frame as Steph wipes blood away from a gaping wound. On closer examination, the blood looks a luminous green from the Night Vision mode.

'We have to get out of here, Sybil, find me a route.'

'Trust that what you see is not real.'

'Easier said than done, now find me a bloody route out of here will you?'

Water starts to creep up to Steph's crouched position and she feels the dampness rise up to her ankles.

'What now?'

Looking around, you notice the sea is pouring from the painting with the lady that walked across its surface and she has now vanished.

Steph stands up and finds herself having to wade through the water that is filling the room as it spills from the painting like a waterfall.

Splashing sounds are heard as another sharp blow stabs into Steph's back, forcing her to her knees.

The little boy circles her and points the branch in her direction.

'Infantum manducare.'

'Sybil, fucking translate.'

'Another Latin command, translated it means eat the baby.'

'No, argh! It's hurting me from the inside. Help me.'

The little boy approaches Steph who is now doubled over in pain.

'I warned you, now you will become a barren woman. I told you that I have your life in my hands.'

'Please stop. My baby's termination should be my decision, not someone else's.'

'You wouldn't listen, now your baby will be an abortion just like you have turned out to be.'

The water keeps on rising and the little boy pushes Steph over onto her back as he readies his branch over his head with evil intent in his oversized eyes.

The eye above the pyramid is still searching for Steph in the background and as its laser passes through the water causing it to sizzle, stream begins to rises up and fogs your vision.

'You forgot one thing, Tamara.'

The little boy stops and looks taken aback as he relaxes his posture.

'What is that?'

'I activated the jammer in my pocket which counteracts your Latin command, it blocked voice recognition to Sybil and temporarily made her deaf.'

Steph grabs hold of the little boy and realises that although he looks small, in actual fact his height is much taller and is being masked by the glitch to shroud his true form of Tamara Pike.

Throwing a fist into a space above the boy's head it collides with a solid mass.

'You may know this room like the back of your hand and sense where I am but you fell for my ploy, didn't you Tamara? Vanity is a fickle fucking thing, bitch.'

Finishing off with a few more blows, you see the little boy scream in agony as he wrestles free and races towards the revolving eye. Steph chases after him as the boy splits the eye in two that lets in a raft of light from windows outside.

Steph glances back and the room has returned to normal with the portraits back where they should be.

The figure of the boy has vanished, to be replaced by Tamara with a bloodied face, as she stumbles down the corridor to the spiral staircase.

The lights in the mansion suddenly come back on as power is restored from an unseen force, to reveal an elevator up ahead as vision is restored to the lens.

'Sybil, can you hear me? Does the elevator work?'

'Yes, Steph, my hearing returned like I said it would after five minutes' lapse and the power to the elevator should be restored but it is only a guess.'

'Only one way to truly find out then.'

Jabbing the call button, Steph waits for the elevator to rise as she watches the numbers rise. The doors open with a ping to reveal Tilly standing inside with bags of clothing and essentials.

'Thank God, I thought I was going to be stuck in here when the power went out.'

'That doesn't sound as bad as where I was just stranded, come on, let's get going.'

'Where is Tamara?'

'Getting away but we will catch her.'

The elevator descends to the ground floor and Steph and Tilly exit, making for the scanner. As they pass through, you see Tamara pulling away in her Showhauler outside.

'At least I know what the glitches are now, Sybil.'

'A smokescreen created by I.R.I.S.'

'Looks like it, but why I don't know.'

Jack extends the ramp at the rear of his RV brandishing a joint in his hand as you come running across the gravel.

'You ladies all right?'

'You really need to give up smoking that shit.'

'What?'

'Never mind, follow that Showhauler.'

'Huh?'

'I rest my case. Sybil, where is she headed?'

'The A40, Steph.'

'Okay.'

'But we need to visit the I.R.I.S. server first to check out her story, don't we?'

'No, Sybil, I'm not finished with her by a country fucking mile yet.'

'She doesn't seem to be much of a threat.'

'Really? Only if she is telling the truth. If not, then we can't let her get away.'

'I guess there is only one way to be sure then, Steph.'

'Yep, we are going to fucking apprehend and detain that bitch until we acquire some solid evidence to back up her story, besides, anyone that tries to harm my baby deserves all she gets.'

'If we don't acquire evidence?'

'Then we turn her in to the law.'

'That is risky, as you are still public enemy number one, Steph.'

'So what's new? Jack, be a darling and get this fucking RV moving will you?'

XVII

'My damn shoulder is hurting like a motherfucker.'

'I can instruct some of the nanos to repair it for you, if you insist, Steph?'

'I can't risk taking them away from my baby, Sybil, I won't allow my needs to get in the way of hers.'

'As you wish.'

Jack's motorhome is following the route of Tamara's Showhauler by the satellite feed being beamed directly into the HUD of the lens. You notice that there is at least five miles' separation between you and her Showhauler.

'Here you go, Steph, I have a first aid kit. Let's bandage you up, shall we?'

'Thanks, Jack, you got any painkillers?'

'They're in the box, you can help yourself.'

'Can you get me a glass of water to wash them down please?'

Jack fetches a tumbler and fills it with water from the tap in the kitchen. He brings it back in to Steph before he carries on patching up her wound.

'Why can't you shut down your A.I., Steph?'

'Sybil won't let me because our baby is top priority to look after, maybe if my womb hadn't been—'

'Hadn't been what, Steph?'

'Nothing, it doesn't matter.'

Jack pushes a thumb into Steph's wound

'Oww! What the fuck, Jack?'

'What's happened to your womb, Steph? Tell me. It's my daughter in there too.'

'Okay, for fuck's sake I'll tell you. Tamara Pike as you are aware was the creator of Sybil.'

'Yes, I remember.'

'You weren't that stoned then?'

'Just continue, Steph.'

'She used Latin to command and force Sybil to send a message to the nanos within me to carry out what she instructed them to do.'

'What was that?'

'To attack our daughter in the womb.'

'Did she succeed?'

'Almost.'

'What do you mean almost?'

'First time was a warning, but some damage was done, second was a real threat. I found a way to prevent any further meddling on her part though.'

'What kind of damage was done?'

'Possible life-changing.'

'We're going round in circles here, what kind?'

'Our baby could be born disfigured.'

'You better not be messing with me, Steph.'

'It's true, I swear. If I leave the nanos inside me to get on with their job then there is a slim chance our baby will turn out okay.'

'If not?'

'Then I may have a hard decision to make.'

'WE, may have a hard decision to make.'

'I didn't think you gave a shit about us.'

'Your A.I. is dangerous, Steph, the whole trial and operation is. I warned you.'

'Only in the wrong hands is Sybil a threat.'

'I would never hurt you, Steph.'

'Shhh, Sybil. I know.'

'Why the hell did you keep this from me, Steph?'

'Because Jack, I thought you weren't interested.'

'Of course I bloody am, this affects me now as well as you.'

'Well I thought it was my burden to suffer alone.'

'Not any more, what gives that Tamara woman the power of playing God?'

'Devil's advocate you mean.'

'I'm going to kill her when I find her.'

'Not until I have finished with her first you're not, besides, you're being over dramatic. You need to calm the fuck down.'

The satellite view of the road up ahead casts into your vision, showing Tamara's Showhauler approaching a familiar location. Steph having just chased two pills down with a gulp of water, sits up and covers her natural eye with a hand to get a better look.

'Is that where I think it is, Sybil?'

'Yes Steph, that is St James's Park.'

'Damn Jack, why did you have to mention the march on Westminster in front of the Watchers?'

'I don't understand?'

'Tamara Pike is headed to St James's Park, Jack, she is hoping to lose us in the crowd of protesters.'

'You can't be sure of that. She would have parked in Hyde Park away from the crowds, St James's Park is too close.'

'You want to bet? By parking that close, she will be right at the heart of the protest, only a stone's throw from Parliament Square.'

Tamara's Showhauler pulls up underneath a canopy of a long row of trees, obscuring her home from the satellite above. You see Westminster Abbey in the distance with a mass gathering of people holding placards outside and they are confronted by a large police presence of troopers on the ground with interceptor drones hovering above their respective troopers' heads.

'We have lost visual, Steph.'

'Jack, can this RV go any faster?'

'Not without drawing unwanted attention, Steph.'

'Shit, how far are we away, Sybil?'

'Less than five minutes.'

'Keep an eye out for Tamara. We can't lose her now.'

'How are you going to grab her in the crowd without revealing yourself to her, Steph? She can see what you see.'

'Not whilst she is out in the open she can't.'

'But what about the law? If they see you, then you will be captured for sure.'

'No shit, that's why I'm not going out there.'

'Well who is then?'

'You are. So get some kind of disguise on and when we arrive get out there and bring that bitch to me.'

'How do you suppose I do that?'

'I will send my drone out so I can see and assess what to do from back here.'

'That's the wisest thing you've said since you got here.'

'Well it's not like I am at full health, is it?'

'Approaching Showhauler, Steph.'

'Good, park up but keep your distance, Sybil.'

'I can't believe I let your A.I. take control of my home, you should have let Alexa do all the hard work.'

'She is not my Alexa though, is she?'

'No, but she is my assistant and a damn good one.'

'She can't give good head like me though, can she?'

'Well at least she respects me.'

'Stop whingeing and go and get ready, Jack. Whilst you're out there I'm going to see if I can access the I.R.I.S. server on your console.'

'Why is it that whenever you visit me, you always take over?'

'Because deep down you love me. So just piss off already.'

Jack's mobile cultivation farm pulls up a half a mile from Tamara's position and Steph makes her way to the rear of his home. She pushes the button to release the hatch and drop the ramp before sending her drone out into the open; you watch it take off to the sky.

Jack, now hooded up, steps out beside her and walks down the ramp where he stops midway.

'You better hope your drone isn't spotted, Steph, or I'm going to be left out on a limb here when the crowds tear it apart, or worse, the interceptors will, if they capture it.'

'You must have misread my motives, Jack, I'm using the satellite to keep tabs on you. My drone will be used to check out Tamara's RV.'

'That's just great, so what if it clouds over and you lose sight of me, what then? Also how can we communicate with each other?'

'Do you have your phone on you with a Bluetooth earpiece?'

'Yes, so what?'

'Then I will use Sybil to relay info to you through that.'

'What are you going to do with Tamara's RV?'

'I'm going to break into it.'

'I thought you said you were staying put?'

'I am. Tilly is going to help me out with the RV, so crack on. Happy hunting, Jack.'

Steph gives Jack a peck on the cheek and turns back into the confines of his preparation lobby; she presses the button to retract the door ramp. You see Jack give a dark look from inside his pulled-up hood as the door closes, before he turns and walks away.

Steph approaches the door to the bedroom that Tilly and Tiffany are in. She raps lightly upon it and pushes the door ajar.

'Can I come in?'

'Hi Stephanie, of course you can.'

Entering the bedroom, Steph steps inside and sits at the bottom of the bed. Tilly and her daughter are both looking healthier and refreshed as they exit from the ensuite together. Steph swivels around and faces them and you notice that Tilly has changed into a large baggy sweater and jeans. Tiffany is wearing the same clothes but they have been cleaned.

'I need your help, Tilly.'

'I overheard your conversation with Jack and we have both decided to help you the best we can.'

'Oh.'

'I wasn't keen on the idea at first but Tiff insisted that we should return a favour. I told her to stay behind here but she said that she can be your eyes and ears in Tamara's home.'

'That's very sweet of you, Tiffany, thank you. Did you hear what it is I need assistance with?'

'Mummy said that we need to find dirt on Tamara Pike.'

'She did? Ha, yes that's right. To make it easier I have a magic key that will open the door to her home, would you like it?'

Tiffany looks to her mum for approval and Tilly gives her a nod. Steph takes the fob from her inside pocket and hands it over to the young girl.

'With both your permission, I would really like to be able to pair with Tiff's lens so I can view what she sees when you are inside. I can then direct you where necessary, is that okay in light of what has happened before?'

'Daisy said that is okay, Mummy, and so do I.'

'Well okay then, honey. Steph, what kind of guarantee can you give us that we won't encounter danger from Tamara inside her home or her returning?'

'I can't promise anything but I will use my drone to check that she is not inside there before you go in. I really can't see her being still on board when we are this close to catching her. I will leave my drone outside to give us any warning if she doubles back.'

'That's good enough for me then, Steph, and as long as we have you at our backs I do feel a little safer. You ready to leave, Tiff?'

'Yes, Mummy.'

'Let's go then, sweetie.'

Tiffany and her daughter make for the rear of Jack's RV and you follow Steph back into his lounge area at the other end of his home. Steph sits down in the chair and accesses Jack's console.

'Right, how is Jack doing, Sybil?'

'I have highlighted him in blue, Steph, he has made it into the middle of the crowd of protesters.'

'Yup, got him. Okay, swing around my drone and patch me through to its camera. Let's follow Tilly and Tiffany to Tamara's home, shall we? Keep me posted on Jack's every move as well, will you?'

'Yes, Steph.'

An overlay window appears in the top left of Steph's HUD and you monitor the satellite feed and the drone's field of view in unison.

Mother and daughter are holding hands and from your unique perspective it looks like they are just out for a leisurely stroll in the park.

Jack is scanning the faces of the members in the crowd and the satellite slowly pans around him as Sybil tries to locate Tamara from above.

'Is it possible to use my Thermal Vision through the drone's camera lens, Sybil?'

'Yes Steph, would you like me to engage now?'

'Yes please.'

The camera image that the drone sees of living and heat sourced objects is showing them up in a swathe of yellows, oranges and reds. Non-living or static objects are bathed in blues and greys.

Pivoting, the drone focuses on the red and orange glow of Tilly and Tiffany, as it approaches the dark blue shell of Tamara's Showhauler.

'So far so good, there doesn't seem to be anyone at home then, Sybil.'

'It would appear not.'

'Okay, disengage Thermal Imaging and patch me through to Daisy please? I wish to see what Tiffany sees.'

'Granted.'

I.R.I.S.

As a connection is established, an image through Tiff's eye appears in the top right of Steph's HUD and you are transferred to a larger image of the Showhauler in front of you.

'Tiffany, it all looks safe up ahead. Please make your way to the back of the vehicle and use the magic key to open its door.'

The little girl stops as she listens intently to the message that is being broadcast to the receiver in her lens. Tilly waits patiently at her side, looking tense. Then Tiffany says something and a message is sent back through the lens transmitter.

'Daisy is relaying a message from Tiffany saying that she is using the key now.'

'Wonderful, let's hope Tamara doesn't have security on board.'

'I detected no security on my sweep of the vehicle, Steph.'

'Phew, well that makes things slightly easier then.'

You watch on as parent and child access Tamara's home with the key and watch as the door ramp descends. They wait for it to hit the road and with trepidation, make their way inside.

'Incoming message from Daisy.'

'What is it?'

'They wish to know what they are looking for.'

'I don't know yet, just tell them to search all the rooms and see if Tilly can gain access to the main console will you?'

'Okay Steph, sending message now.'

Every room starts to be searched and you see Steph twitch nervously on the chair, you see what Steph sees, being remotely beamed into her HUD from mother and daughter as they carry on. Eventually Tilly looks into Tiffany's lens and shrugs her shoulders towards you.

'Send Daisy a message that I can't see anything of interest either, so focus on the console.'

'Message sent, Steph.'

Steph rubs her bandaged shoulder before she starts to type on the console: *Search I.R.I.S. server*, she then hits enter.

After a very long pause a message appears on screen, NO MATCHES.

She tries a few more times issuing different commands but they keep returning as before, NO MATCHES.

'Bollocks, there's not even a trace of I.R.I.S.'s existence on the internet, I thought there would be at least a website so I could find a back way into the server. Are you sure that you can't retrieve Olivia's footage, Sybil?'

'Once the data was uploaded to the I.R.I.S. server, it can only be retrieved by access to the mainframe.'

'So you can't hack your way in remotely?'

'Only if I had the encryption password in the first place.'

'Well do you?'

'No. You may only be able to gain access from your own console, Steph. as that is connected to I.R.I.S. directly.'

'But I would still need the password.'

'Yes.'

'Maybe Dillon could help me with that.'

'It is possible that Mr Fletcher knows the password.'

'But my home is locked up and impounded, if I were to have access to my own console then I would have to break into the Police Compound first. It's all so—'

'Sorry to interrupt, Steph, but I am receiving a message from Daisy again.'

'Okay, play.'

'Tilly says that she cannot access the console's files as there is an encrypted password needed.'

'Fuck my life, why is nothing ever straight forward, Sybil? Why does everything have to have a bloody password?'

'What would you like me tell her?'

'Ummm.'

'Another message incoming, Steph.'

'I thought I was impatient. Okay, play it.'

'Daisy is telling me that a recorded video message has appeared on the console, she believes the message was triggered by input of a wrong password. Would you like it played?'

'Might be something, tell her yes.'

'Relaying.'

Looking through Steph's lens and back out through Tiffany's, you see an image of Tamara appear on the console but you can't hear or lip-read what she is saying as the message begins. Sitting in silence, Steph waits anxiously for the video feed to finish.

'Relaying dictation from Daisy. Message from Tamara reads as follows: You will not find me, Miss Coulson, as I have gone off-grid. I would, however, like to extend an olive branch, to let you know that the password for my console is "SCOTOMA".'

'Pause. She is giving us her password, why? And what the fuck is Scotoma?'

'It is a term used to describe a blind spot in a normal visual field of the eye.'

'Okay, resume.'

'On my console you will find a folder named D. Hastings, I urge you to open the folder and read the attached file. You will see that I have proven records of your Director's affairs well documented there, you will never see or hear from me again. Goodbye, Miss Coulson.'

'I don't trust her. Ask Daisy to get Tilly to enter the password if it works and access the vehicle's camera recordings.'

'Why would she do that?'

'Just a theory, Sybil. She should have no trouble playing past footage if she gets access. Get her to start events from when Tamara left SCLERA and follow her all the way here, we might learn something from that first.'

'Relaying information.'

Watching as Tiffany receives the message, Steph stands up and walks down the corridor to the preparation lobby. She paces up and down as if lost in thought.

'Steph, there is trouble at Parliament Square.'

'Show me.'

Looking through the live satellite feed, you see that a skirmish has broken out between the protesters and the police.

Bricks are being thrown at riot police who are sheltering behind their shields and interceptors are engaging the civilian mob with electric prods which they are using to stun them.

Violence and bloodshed ensues as both sides retaliate with force, fires break out from homemade petrol bombs and riot vans appear. Jack is caught up in the centre of it all.

'This can't be a coincidence. Call Jack now, Sybil.'

'Connecting, Steph.'

A dialling tone seems to ring for an eternity before it is finally silenced. Jack's voice answers with commotion accompanying him.

'A shit storm has broken out here, Steph. It's even more impossible to find her now, I'm sorry.'

'Fuck's sake, Jack, you can't give up now.'

'Are you for real? People are getting seriously hurt here. It could be me soon if I'm not careful.'

'But you—'

'Message from Daisy incoming, Steph.'

'Not now, Sybil. Jack, listen you have to—'

'Message says that Tamara did not get in her Showhauler.'

'I said not now... Sorry, what did you just say?'

'Tilly says that Tamara did not board her RV, she set coordinates to this location remotely after recording her message and disappeared into the undergrowth outside the mansion. Tilly confirms that she has seen the footage that proves it's from the Showhauler's external cameras.'

'No, that can't be, can it?'

'That is what the message says, Steph.'

'Fuck! How can I have been so stupid to fall for that? Jack, you must get back here now, Jack... Jack, do you hear me? Jack!'

'I have detected an anomaly, Steph.'

'No, not now, Sybil. No fucking way, what is it this time?'

'The amber cursor is now red and all communications are being jammed.'

'What?'

Another glitch of pixelated dots covers your vision through the lens and begins to break down with a sound of white static.

Steph's drone, which is hovering around Tamara's Showhauler, falls from the sky and crashes into a grass embankment as power is lost. The connection to the satellite is also severed.

Steph hits the button on the preparation lobby's wall and the door swings open to create the ramp.

You notice a black RV with a radar dish protruding from its roof, positioned further down the road. Steph doesn't see it though, as she runs towards her fallen drone.

'Have we lost all communication with Tiffany and Jack?'

'Yes, Steph.'

Finding her drone nestled in a long patch of grass, Steph scoops it up in her arms and runs towards Tamara's RV shouting their names.

The ground races by underfoot as you watch Steph hastily make her way over to the Showhauler.

Steph looks up at the last second and bumps into Jack who has appeared before her; she almost drops the drone in fright.

'What the hell are you doing, Steph? It's not safe for you out here.'

'We have a serious fucking problem, Jack, my lens has been jammed.'

'What do you mean?'

'No time to explain, we have to get Tilly and Tiffany out of that RV.'

'I'll do it, you get back to safety in my home.'

'But—'

'Now, Steph, I've got this.'

You watch as Steph stands there defeated and see the red cursor flashing in the bottom left of the HUD next to option six. It starts to flash faster and then the digits 20 appear to its right.

'Something is happening, Steph.'

'I know, Sybil, I see it. Fuck, fuck what is it?'

The 20 then becomes 19, then 18 and 17...

'It's a fucking timer!'

'To what, Steph?'

'I don't fucking know.'

13 then becomes 12...

'Jack, get them the fuck out of there.'

10 becomes 9...

Jack appears behind Tilly and Tiffany. Steph is wildly shouting at them to stay away from her, to find cover anywhere but within the vicinity of Steph herself.

'Oh God, I'm a fucking, walking time bomb.'

5...

Steph starts to run blindly into an open lawn of grass and spins around to see Tilly snatch up Tiffany in terror, as Jack races along behind them.

2... 1... Then an explosion tears through Tamara's RV.

Shooting flames ignite the tree canopy overhead, as burning light from within the vehicle shatters the glass windows. The escaping flames lick hungrily at the branches.

Shrapnel shoots off in every direction in a far-reaching arc, as the vehicle's twisted and split hull spills open its metal guts to the atmosphere.

Jack wraps himself around Tilly and Tiffany to protect them and in turn sacrifices his back to the blast's mercy, as they are all blown off their feet.

A large chunk of projectile panelling that is torn from the RV is unleashed with force into Jack's thigh, causing a fracture and exposing his femur.

Steph stands there stunned for a while before finally summoning the strength and courage to get to the slain party to help.

'Fuck me.'

Jack, screaming in agony, rolls away and is clasping his leg. Tilly, who was sheltering Tiffany beneath him, turns her over and starts to pat her down.

'Oh Tiff, are you okay? Is anything hurting?'

'No, Mummy, I'm fine.'

'Are you sure, sweetheart?'

'Yes, Mummy.'

Throwing herself down beside Jack and dropping the drone to the floor, Steph tries to calm him down.

'Oh God, Jack, we have to get you seen to. What about you, Tilly? Are you and Tiffany okay?'

'I'm fine, Steph, so is Tiff. Jack protected us from the blast.'

'Jack. What's wrong with him, Sybil? We need to do something.'

Tilly gets up and pulls Tiffany to her side.

'We need to get out of here, Steph, it won't be long before the authorities take notice.'

'Yes, you're right. Jack, can you walk?'

Jack is still screaming in agony and is too incapacitated to answer.

'Help me, Tilly, we have to get him up and get back to his RV.'

'On it.'

'Tiffany, please grab Stephanie's drone and bring it with us.'

'Okay, Mummy.'

Tilly nods and between the two of them they hoist Jack to his feet and start to drag him over to the RV.

Tiffany runs ahead and uses the fob to open the door; the ramp hits the ground and Tilly and Steph drag Jack up the slope as Tiffany runs ahead to push the button to close, once they are all safe inside. Tiffany places the drone in the corner of the preparation lobby and follows after them.

'Sybil, get us the hell out of here.'

'Where would you like to go?'

'Anywhere but here.'

'Plotting coordinates to the nearest hospital.'

'No, we can't, it's too risky.'

'Then where, Steph?'

'I don't care, surprise me, okay?'

'Destination, Charlton Police Compound.'

'What? Never mind, just get us away from here and be quick about it.'

The mobile drug farm takes off at speed and leaves the scene of the riot and explosion far behind.

Jack is dragged off to the lounge and laid down upon the floor as Steph, Tilly and Tiffany crowd around him. Both Tilly and Steph are out of breath and you see that Tilly's face is red and flustered.

'What condition is he in, Sybil?'

'Critical, Steph.'

'Damage assessment?'

'Compound fracture to his femur.'

'Life threatening?'

'I am afraid so. If he does not get medical aid then he will die.'

Jack starts to quieten as he slowly passes out of consciousness and a pool of blood forms beneath him.

'We have to do something. But what?'

'I can look around here for something that might help, Steph.'

'Like what though, Tilly?'

'We could use a towel as a tourniquet.'

'Good, that's a start.'

'Will the nanos help?'

'Sorry Tiffany, what did you say darling?'

'The nanos in Miss Stephanie, Mummy.'

'Yes, that is an option. Sybil can we spare some of my nanobots?'

'No, Steph, if we transfer just a fraction of them from you, then the risk of your child being born normal, let alone alive, will greatly diminish.'

'I don't care right now, we have to save his life.'

'The cost is too great, Steph.'

'We are going to fucking do it and that is the end of the fucking matter, so how can we transfer them?'

'Either by syringe or via oral transference, Steph. But I strongly advise against it.'

'Tough shit, because it's happening, bring a group of nanos to my tongue, I have an idea.'

'Sending command now, I will spare only 20% of the nanobots.'

'You will spare 40%, so help me God.'

Steph kneels down and cradles Jack's head in her arms, she looks at him fondly and opens his mouth.

'I can't bring our daughter up without you, Jack, if she survives, that is. I hope you forgive my decision but I can't risk losing you either.'

'Nanos have collected on the surface of your tongue, Steph.'

'40%?'

'Yes, Steph.'

'Okay. When I kiss him, please tell them to transfer to his tongue and make their way down to his femur to heal his leg.'

'You will have to push his bone back in before they can act, Steph.'

'I figured that out already, do it.'

Mouth to mouth, Steph extends her tongue to touch Jack's tongue and cups his head in her hand as the migration takes effect. You see the kiss linger for a long time before Steph gently closes his mouth and rocks back on the balls of her feet.

'Is it done?'

'Yes, Steph.'

'Good, now we wait.'

Leaning over to whisper in Jack's ear, you hear Steph mutter five words.

'I love you, Jack Mintlyn.'

Tilly comes back with a towel and hands it to Steph.

'Tilly, Tiffany, I need you to look after him and make sure you go somewhere safe, do you understand?'

'You're leaving?'

'Once I know he is safe, yes.'

'Where will you go?'

'I have to get my RV back and take the rest of this journey alone.'

'But why, Steph? We can help you.'

'It's gotten too dangerous for your involvement, I can't let anyone risk their lives for me. Look after Jack and I will find you all when this is over.'

'Okay, Steph, if that is what you want.'

'It is, Sybil. Has my vision been fully restored? It looks normal again.'

'Red cursor has disappeared, all systems are normal again, Steph.'

'Of course they fucking are. Activate X-ray please.'

'Activated.'

You watch as the lens shows up the bones within Jack's body and see the damaged femur. On closer inspection you see a dark cloud making its way down the leg to converge on the fracture.

'Is that black mass the nanobots?'

'Yes, Steph.'

'Will this work?'

'Yes, Steph, but it will take time.'

'Good, keep me posted on his developments.'

'You must pop the bone back in.'

'Oh yeah, thanks Sybil.'

Steph straddles Jack's leg and looks into his face.

'I'm sorry about this, Jack.'

With force and accompanied by a heavy grunt, Steph snaps the bone back in place with a sickening squelch.

'Here is the towel, Steph.'

'Thank you, Tilly, let's make him comfortable then, help me get him into bed.'

Between them, Tilly and Steph lift him up and grunt and groan as they carry him into his bedroom, to lay him on the bed. Steph plumps the pillows beside him and takes hold of his hand as she rests against the headboard. Tilly pulls the towel tight around the wound and then leaves, gently closing the door behind her.

'Sybil, where did you say we are going?'

'The police compound.'

'Oh yeah, out of the frying pan and into the fire it is then. You better pull through, Jack, I need you.'

'I will monitor him closely, Steph.'

'Thank you, Sybil. Whatever was in that folder about Dom sure must have been important, what did they not want me to find?'

'I do not know, Steph.'

'The military must have a strong connection to this somewhere, they knew I would uncover something sooner or later. But what? Why help me one minute, then hinder my investigation the next? I led them to Tamara and they used me as a detonator for a bomb. They must have planted it on her RV.'

'You need to rest, Steph.'

'Yes, that's a bloody good idea. I'll just close my eyes for a while, wake me when we arrive at the compound please. Sorry Watchers but I'm drained, see you shortly.'

The last image you see as Steph closes her eyes, is her hand clasped tight around Jack's hand relaxing as she drifts off to sleep.

XVIII

'Power On. Steph, wake up. We have arrived.'

'We've what? No, just give me one more hour, Sybil. I'm still tired. Power Off.'

[Override, Power On]

'Steph, the mystery hacker has overridden the Power On function again.'

'I don't care, they won't see much with my eyes closed anyway, so just give me one more hour, please. Power Off.'

Time passes.

'Power On.'

Steph is sitting on a high stool overlooking four long rows of cannabis plants with equally long T5 grow light panelling above.

One of Jack's drones is hovering backwards and forwards between each plant and is collecting samples from the soil.

A second drone is monitoring a closed-loop extractor machine that harvests CBD oil at the rear of the room.

'Hi Watchers, and welcome back to Stephanie Coulson's fucked up career path. Here's a quick update for you if you're interested, we are outside the Police Car Pound in Charlton and we are currently parked quite far down Bramshot Avenue waiting for night to fall. A few hours have passed since Sybil tried to wake me and I have been busy since. Tell them, Sybil, what I have been up to.'

'Okay, Steph. Well first of all, Olivia's eye has been moved to Jack Mintlyn's freezer box as it was starting to thaw out within the drone.'

'I'm sure they don't give a toss about that, Sybil, next?'

'Tilly has bought new clothes for her daughter, Tiffany, and they have been delivered, she looks quite lovely in her new dresses.'

'No, try again.'

'Steph has found out that her bank account has been frozen.'

'Don't fucking remind me about that shit, Sybil, what else has happened?'

'You offered Tilly the chance to become Jack's laboratory assistant when he has fully recovered. You also suggested that Tiffany will need home schooling, as it is illegal for minors to wear permanent smart contact lenses.'

'Well, yes that's true.'

'And she accepted your terms.'

'But what else has happened, Sybil, why am I so pissed off right now?'

'Because you lost my signal when the radio waves were blocked on entering the tunnel.'

'That was annoying, to see you and not hear you through the airwaves, felt like I was watching a deaf-mute interpreter trying to explain something without subtitles. But still that has not sent me over the edge, so what has?'

'You're spot bleeding.'

'Hallefuckinglujah! Yes, finally we get there in the end. What did you say to me about it, Sybil?'

'Taking away any large amount of nanobots would greatly affect the healthy birth of your child.'

'How large an amount?'

'25%'

'How much did we give Jack?'

'40%'

'You know, if life was a card, then sometimes I feel like God has reshuffled them and moved mine to the top of the deck.'

'If you split the deck, then maybe you can even the odds, Steph.

The nanos may have done enough, before their mass was depleted. Your baby may still be born healthy.'

'But I'm spot bleeding, surely that is not a good sign, Sybil?'

'Odds of not having a healthy birth are eleven to one.'

'I'll keep that in mind the next time I visit the bookies then.'

Sliding off the stool you see Steph is wearing the white overalls and boots from Jack's preparation lobby downstairs. She walks in between the row of marijuana plants and approaches a closed-loop extractor machine. Pulling her gloves up tight to her elbows, she wriggles her fingers and approaches the steel contraption .

Steph opens one of three steel chambers and dry ice spills out from within the confines of a large steel drawer. Closing the first, Steph then opens the second chamber and you see a bundle of dried marijuana within it. She then pushes that drawer in and opens the third which contains the extract oil.

'Good batch I see, ready for winterization. These farming drones are certainly worth the purchase, I'm glad I persuaded Jack to get them now. God, I hope he will be okay.'

'The nanos are the holy grail of life, Steph.'

'It's a shame that not everybody has access to nanotechnology though, Sybil. If they did, then practices like this would not be needed anymore to help cure ailments.'

'If you had kept all nanos within you, Steph, then I would guarantee your child would be healthy and you may have a chance at immortality.'

'Immortality! Yeah right.'

'Seriously Steph, the nanotechnology within you would keep you alive well past the expiry date of any known living human.'

'I don't think I would want to live forever anyway.'

'That is fine then, as that is impossible now.'

'Fuck! You are being serious, aren't you?'

'I would never lie to you, Steph.'

'Damn. Knowing my luck I will get killed well before I have a chance at growing old anyway. I suppose everyone has their day eventually, you can't outlive death.'

Pushing the third drawer shut, Steph turns around and makes towards the opposite end of the room again, stepping over an irrigation system that passes from table to table at ground level.

'Mind you, civilisation thought that mobile phones had had their day. But look now, retro technology seems to be having a revolution, especially among the poorer population that choose not to embrace the new order of things. I think that's why I want to live a simpler life.'

'You don't own a cell phone, Steph?'

'No, I prefer face-to-face interaction.'

'You have me to make and receive calls now and a whole lot more besides, I am the only one of my kind.'

'Technically you're not. Tiffany has a version of you too. I'm afraid that once this tech gets out in the world, it will become a smaller place to live, that's where the problem lies. Our freedom and space is being turned into modern slavery and containment.'

'Daisy is inferior to me.'

'Just be happy knowing that the other kids from the Sanctuary will have their lenses removed before they go into care, so be thankful at the moment that there will only be just the two of you.'

'Daisy is a black market upgrade, I am the genuine article.'

'I've just had a thought, Sybil, could we tune in to the Sanctuary children's lenses and find out what the law has planned for me?'

'Unwise, Steph, the children have been through enough trauma. The last thing you want is for the police to find out that you are eavesdropping on them.'

'Okay, fair point.'

A knocking sounds from the other side of the door that Steph is making her way to. She stops by the stool and starts to remove the white garments.

'That you, Tilly?'

'Yes it is, Steph. Sorry, I was just wondering if you were okay.'

'Yeah I'm fine, I'm just checking the crop. Give me two minutes and I will be right out.'

Folding the kit up, Steph then opens the door to find Tilly has gone back down the short stairwell.

She locks the door behind her to the drugs lab and returns the gear to the lobby, stopping to look out of a nearby window.

'It's slowly getting dark, Watchers. It won't be long now until we move on and get my RV back. Breaking into the compound under the blanket of darkness is definitely our best option.'

'Hello Steph, do you like my dress and sparkly shoes?'

'Oh, hi Tiff. Sorry, I didn't see you sneak up behind me, yes, they are lovely. Where has your mum gone?'

'She is through the back in the lounge room.'

'Thank you.'

Steph works her way through the corridor and you see Tilly up ahead relaxing on the large sofa.

'I have checked on Jack, he seems to be doing okay but he has not yet woken, Steph.'

'Maybe it's best that he doesn't wake just yet, it will be easier for me to leave without having to give him a valid reason for my upcoming departure.'

'You said that your relationship was difficult, Steph. Do you mind me asking how you two met?'

'Not at all, Tilly.'

Sidling up beside Tilly on the sofa, Steph makes herself comfortable and brings her feet up beneath her as she turns to face her.

'We were both kids when we met. My parents relocated from Ipswich to Harwich before the east coast was claimed by the floods.'

'I remember that flooding, thousands lost their lives in a space of a week.'

'Well, Harwich was on a peninsula and had suffered a flooding way back in 1953. Sea defences were built and flood alarms were fitted, but over the years people became complacent and slowly Britain became isolated from Europe as it tried to get its farming and fisheries back.'

'As I recall, the country became divided and farming flourished again in the United Kingdom. I would imagine everyone had the same idea as your parents did.'

'Quite true. Well, they found a cheap piece of land which was just right for arable farming and they were happy to give up the road and settle down to grow produce from it once they became established.'

'They were paving the way for your inheritance?'

'Absolutely. Anyway, other like-minded people were already there and one such couple were Jack and his grandmother. But the long overdue and unexpected flooding happened.'

'I can see it bothers you, we don't have to discuss it if you don't want to.'

'No, it's fine. Like Harwich and many other coastal towns before it, that town was lost to the sea, along with the lives of those that perished there. It's just another page in the history books now.'

'Were you there long before it happened?'

'A few years. I was just a young girl about your daughter's age at the time and Jack was a farmhand and helped his grandmother maintain our land.'

'So you ended up working together and fell in love at an early age?'

'Definitely not, he couldn't stand the sight of me. I was an out-of-towner coming into his community to help my parents rape Mother Earth. We arrived to become wealthy and make the locals poorer.'

'He didn't see that your parents were boosting the economy and contributing to make the country self-reliant again.'

'We were both young and spiteful kids, what can I say.'

'So how did you finally get together?'

Steph sits upright and reaches over to Jack's console; she types across its keyboard and sits back down again. Projectors in the corner of the lounge light up and collectively beam in a 3D hologram of the sea. Concrete structures are poking through the surface and on closer inspection you see that they are in fact remnants of buildings that were built to withstand attack from the Germans in the Second World War.

'That eerie sight out in the middle of the sea is all that is left of Harwich. Those buildings were part of the War Department that we used to play in when we were not toiling away in the mud. That's where a bunch of us were when the flooding came.'

'You were stranded there?'

'The flooding took everyone by surprise, we were too busy being kids and paying no attention to what was going on around us until the sea had washed in and covered our escape.'

'The children around us took a risk and decided to swim for dry land but they didn't make it as the current sucked them under. Jack started to climb the Lookout Tower that we were in; he had warned them that it was foolish but they didn't listen. I listened though, so I followed him to the top and when we got there, we saw just how much of the land had vanished as the sea raged onwards in land.'

'My god.'

'Over the next few days we begun to rely on one another and grew closer as our situation became even more bleak. We both thought that we would soon die as we became hungry and thirsty. Still the sea level steadily rose and we thought that it would soon claim us as we grew weaker.'

'So that's how you became lovers?'

'I said it was complicated, it still is. Eventually we were rescued by helicopter but both my parents and Jack's grandmother had died along with countless others. All that stands now as a reminder, are the tops of those concrete buildings. The one in the far right was the tower that we were winched to safety from.'

Steph swipes the screen once more and the image fades, putting the projectors back into standby mode. You see tears collecting at the side of her eye again.

'I'm sorry for your loss, Steph.'

'Don't be. It was a long time ago, Tilly.'

Leaving the sofa, Tilly gives you a saddened look. Steph exits the room and makes her way into the kitchen and opens the freezer; inside the box wrapped in a Ziplock, see-through bag, is Olivia's frozen eyeball.

Holding the bag up to the light, Steph studies the ring around the iris and zooms in on the detailing.

'Olivia's A.I. must have been a pretty shit guardian for her to be killed so easily, Sybil, don't you think?'

'I cannot say. However, that is something I would not allow to happen to you, Steph, I am smarter than that.'

'I don't disbelieve you there, I just expected more from Olivia's A.I.'

'I have created an augmented reality game, Steph.'

'Have you?'

'You will see how smart I can be. We still have some time to spare if you're interested?'

'Okay, I'm game. So what have you called it then?'

'Stephanie's Sea Shell Challenge.'

'How fucking original, you know how to sell it to me, Sybil, don't you?'

'It is my own updated take on the three shell game that you told me about.'

'I gathered that, so what prizes can I win?'

'It is a points-based contest, I go first and then you take a turn. The winner will be decided in a best of three.'

'Set it up then.'

'We can use the kitchen's small island to be the table. Please clear it for me, Steph, and we can begin.'

Doing as requested, Steph clears dirty plates and cutlery from the island and drops them in the sink. As she returns, an overlay of a digital, purple-coloured cloth is draped over the island in your vision.

Three sea shells appear before you on the table cloth and a small yellow ball materialises in front of them. Sybil then appears before you on the opposite side of the table dressed in a circus ring master's attire and sporting a pair of white gloves. The look is completed with a black top hat.

'Please close your natural eye, Steph, as I need you to focus.'

'Loving the look, Sybil. Okay, closing my lens-free eye now.'

The kitchen disappears and is replaced by a calm blue sky. As Steph looks around, you see that she is teetering on a fluffy cloud with the table in front also floating on a second cloud. Steph grabs a hold of one of the shells and brings it up in front of you.

'Very clever, Sybil, I'm impressed. I am feeling a little vertigo though.'

'Please look below.'

'Is this supposed to represent the dream I had?'

Steph returns the shell to the table and casts her eye down; far below is the earth rotating slowly and fires are raging around the globe on each of the islands.

'Please follow the ball and stay focused.'

Sybil grabs the ball and lifts the middle shell; she places the ball beneath it and starts to move the shells around. The skies darken and a streak of lightning pierces the table. Steph almost jumps back in fright as she takes her eye off the shell she was following.

Taking her hands from the shells, Sybil stands back and has a grin on her face.

'Which shell is the ball under?'

'I think it's the left one.'

Sybil lifts the left shell and you see that it is empty.

'Bugger, you distracted me there, Sybil. Okay, now it's my turn.'

Steph picks up the ball and shell and begins her turn. Sybil watches the shells being moved around and waits for Steph to finish, before she chooses a shell.

She picks the right one.

Taking her turn again, Sybil starts to move the shells and this time the sky starts to fall away as the earth rushes up to meet you.

'Fuck me! That one, Sybil, I choose the one on the right. Stop this falling shit.'

Normality returns as Sybil lifts the shell to reveal another empty space.

'Two-nil to me.'

'You're cheating, Sybil, you know that, right?'

'I told you it was a challenge, Steph.'

'Well I forfeit, you win. Please return my vision to normal.'

'But it is the best of three.'

'Next time, Sybil, I promise. I think the time is right to leave now, don't you?'

'As you wish.'

The kitchen returns to normal and Steph makes her way down to Jack's bedroom. She opens the door softly and goes to sit down beside him, leaning over to plant a kiss on his forehead.

'Stay safe and get well soon.'

Then Steph is up and returning to the lobby where the kitbag is waiting along with her drone. Tilly catches you up and grabs Steph's shoulders.

'Are you sure about this, Steph?'

'I am. Take care of him for me, will you?'

'Of course I will, I owe you so much.'

'Don't mention it. I may contact you at some point in the near future. Will it be okay to make contact through Tiff's A.I., Daisy?'

'Yes, that's fine. It will be a while before we remove Daisy and that lens anyway.'

'Cool, take care of your little girl too, and maybe I will catch you later.'

'Bye, Steph.'

Button pushed, the door ramp drops forward and Steph steps out into the dark night. Jack's Toterhome is parked right up next to a four-foot-high, razor-wire-topped fence that surrounds the car compound, separated by a seven-foot-wide pavement.

Steph hits the button to retract the ramp and you see Tilly wave as it closes up and seals shut.

Moving around to the side of the Toterhome you see a metal ladder that leads up to its roof, Steph climbs it and deftly reaches the top. She stands proud above it with her bag over her shoulder and the drone flying above her head.

Before you lies the triangular-shaped compound bathed in floodlights with Steph's RV parked between other impounded RVs in the centre.

Another RV, parked in the compound below, can be seen by its roof, drawing level to the bottom of the fence and the seven-foot-wide pavement.

'This road is on an incline and between us lies a six-foot gap with the fence in between. I don't know about you, Watchers, but I think I can leap it and land on that RV's roof.'

'So this is our way in then, Steph? Now we just need to do this without being detected. Would you like me to bring up my options and give a lay of the land?'

XIX

'Select Zoom, Night Vision and bring up satellite please, Sybil.'
'Interfacing with HUD now, et voila.'
'Et what?'
'There you go.'
'Let's keep the comms simple, shall we Sybil? Right, what have we got then?'
'Perimeter of floodlights and one central. Also, three CCTVs overlooking external compound, Steph.'
'Yup, well spotted. What else have we got to deal with?'
'Five warehouses and one reception area with control monitoring in an office to the rear, the warehouses contain Showhaulers and garages for police vehicles.'
'Okay. Well it's just as well I don't have a fancy home then, or this could prove even trickier. I see razor wire fencing, Sybil, but that should not be an issue. Where are the gates situated?'
'Next to the reception area, Steph, the gates are operated electrically and the perimeter fence has a high voltage running through it.'
'How many officers on duty?'
'Two. One in reception and one is situated in the monitoring room.'
'How often do they patrol the compound? Because we—'
'Get down, Steph.'
'What?'

'Down.'

Throwing herself flat on the roof of the Toterhome, you hear Steph take a large breath as she goes silent. Then from behind the warehouse at the far end of the compound you see a law enforcement interceptor drone scouting the premises with a torchlight beam.

'Bugger! Well I guess that answers my question then. How much charge does that thing hold before it needs to return to the charging dock?'

'At least twelve hours, Steph, but there is probably another drone as backup to replace it whilst charging takes place.'

'Did you pick up anything from Jack's Toterhome external cameras earlier that might help?'

'No, only what I share with you now.'

The interceptor does a lap of the perimeter and passes by dangerously close to your position. Its torchlight does not arc in Steph's direction though.

'Well I've thought long and hard about this, Sybil, and right now I can only come up with one solution.'

'Which is?'

'I need you to send my drone in there to take out those floodlights.'

'If we do that, Steph, then it will raise the alarm.'

'Not if we're smart. Are those floodlights connected by the same circuit?'

'Yes.'

'So if we can interrupt the circuit, then all the lights will go down. They will only think it is an electrical fault, so it shouldn't raise too much suspicion should it?'

'In theory.'

'Well, we must try. Find the main junction box and sever the connection but make sure my drone doesn't get caught. Got it?'

'Central floodlight has an access panel located on its post, that will be the mains box. I will attempt your request now.'

Steph's drone glides gently above your head and rises up into the sky; it follows Sybil's commands and positions itself above the central floodlight.

'Make sure that the CCTV doesn't spot you, Sybil.'

'All clear so far, I will bring up the three cameras' line of sight by showing them as cones that I will overlay to the satellite image.'

Sybil does as requested and you see the width and distance of each camera's visual sight by orange-coloured cones that start from each camera's lens and spread out before them. Numerous blindspots are revealed on the compound map.

'Okay, I feel better now. Use the multi-tool on my drone and get that panel open.'

'The instant we have the lights down I expect the interceptor to investigate, Steph.'

'Then you need to hide my drone and be quick about it.'

A hatch opens on the side of Steph's drone and it descends down to the panel located above the base on the floodlight's post. A metal arm extends from within the drone, brandishing six various tools that sit upon a blowtorch.

Five of the tools ranging from knives to wire cutters retract until a flat-ended screwdriver remains.

The drone positions itself at height of the located screw and the tool engages within its slot, the arm spins and the screw is extracted.

Hinged from the bottom, the panel falls forward and exposes the main junction box inside. The wire cutter flips up as the screwdriver now retracts and the drone finds the red live wire and cuts it in two. An arc of electricity sparks as the drone then retreats to beneath a nearby Toterhome. The compound falls to darkness.

'Now we wait, Sybil, it shouldn't be too long as—'

'Interceptor has appeared and it's in a hurry, Steph.'

The police interceptor appears and screams around the compound. Its flashlight is darting around all over the place as it engages its threat mode. You hear a repetitive message echoing from its cold, hard shell's speakers.

'Warning! Trespassers will be prosecuted. Turn back now or I will be forced to immobilise you.'

'Right, now we need a distraction, Sybil.'

'One moment, Steph. When I request you to move, can you make sure you follow my commands as I voice them?'

'I don't—'

The Toterhome that Steph's drone was under suddenly starts to bleep as its alarm starts to sound. The interceptor picks up the racket and screams over to investigate, just as Steph's drone has flown underneath a neighbouring RV.

'Now Steph, jump over into the compound on the RV parked up by the fence.'

'What? Now?'

'Yes, be swift.'

Pulling herself up, Steph tightens the strap on her kitbag and takes a run and jump over the razor wire perimeter fence to the parked Toterhome below.

Clearing the fence and hitting the roof hard, she sounds the RV's alarm in the process. Steph almost slides off as she fights to cling on.

The interceptor swings round to approach you, when another alarm goes off behind it. Steph's drone slinks off once more to hide under another RV and the interceptor moves to investigate.

'Quickly Steph, move under the vehicles in turn to make your way over to your RV but use the satellite feed to stay clear of the camera's line of sight.'

'On it.'

Steph slips off the roof and lands hard on the ground; you hear her wince in pain from the ankle that she twisted back in Loch Lomond. She hobbles off to a nearby RV to hide.

Sybil in command of Steph's drone, continues to set off alarms as she leads the interceptor further away to allow Steph to reach her home unimpeded. Windows are smashed as the little drone flies into them and continues on.

'We have company, Steph.'

'What now?'

'A police officer is on his way and is checking out each of the floodlights.'

'Bollocks, you need to double back and close the panelling on the central floodlight. If not then we could be rumbled.'

'Returning now, Steph.'

'Hurry, I can see he is spooked. Can you jam all transmissions in and out of here? They may call for backup.'

'I am not a miracle worker, Steph, that would require a concentrated effort over in the monitoring area. There is too much to deal with here right now.'

'For fuck's sake, I'm feeling a little tense here.'

You see Sybil steer the flying craft beneath the parked vehicles and make its way back to the central floodlight. The police officer is shining his torch on each of the other floodlights looking for the one that holds the panel.

'Come on already, Sybil. He's getting closer.'

'Get inside your home, Steph, the interceptor will give up shortly and aid the officer in looking for an intruder, I won't be able to assist you until I have sealed the panel up.'

'Jesus, I can't stand this. Sybil, close Night Vision and activate Thermal, I need to know that there are no surprises in store for me at home.'

'Activating. Panel almost sealed. You need to move quickly, Steph.'

Looking through the Thermal Vision, Steph starts to scan the interior of her mobile home. All imaging is showing blue until she settles on her lounge area and a red and yellow image of a person shows up, curled into the foetal position on the sofa.

'Goddamn it! There is someone in there.'

'You have no time to dwell on it, Steph, the interceptor is moving on your position now. You must go.'

'Fuck!'

Steph opens her bag and pulls out a side handle baton, she then seals her bag and approaches the side door to the cab of her RV around the front.

'Sybil, the door's open. It looks like someone has broken in.'

'Get in, Steph, interceptor will be on you any second now. I am done here, now sending your drone to the monitoring room where I will attempt to cease any transmissions.'

Pulling open the door and stepping up to the cab, Steph just gets in and pulls it closed when the interceptor passes by swinging, its search light wildly.

'Phew, that was too close. At least my RV has muffled the alarms, they were beginning to really grate on me there.'

You can only just make out what Steph is saying, as she is speaking in hushed tones.

'Let's hope that they haven't sent word for more troopers.'

'I will let you know if I find anything out, switching your Thermal back to Night Vision.'

'Okay, Sybil. I hope it's not an off-duty officer on my couch and using my home to catch up on their beauty sleep, Watchers, or I'm going to be in even more serious trouble when I incapacitate them.'

Pushing open the door to the lounge from the cab, Steph slides through a small opening and pushes her way quietly in. You see the person fast asleep on the sofa with a heavy blanket tucked up around them.

'There's a bloody HC in my home, Watchers, the cheeky bastard.'

Steph is still whispering as she sneaks closer and brings the baton up over her head.

She brings the baton down hard, when an arm shoots out from beneath the blanket and grabs a hold of the end.

'Nice one, Steph, is this how you treat all of your guests?'

'Fuck me, who the hell are you?'

The figure sits up and pulls the blanket around their chest, letting go of the baton.

'What, you don't recognise me?'

You take in the flat cap sitting upon a rounded face with an unkempt goatee beard.

'Dillon Fletcher, you fucker! You scared the shit out of me there, Dilly.'

'Nice to see you too.'

'I thought you were a goddamn HC, you startled me there for a second. What the hell are you doing here?'

'What's an HC, Steph?'

'A Hermit Crab.'

'I don't follow.'

'It's a reference to a hermit crab that abandons a shell when it outgrows it, so it goes off in search of another shell that is more roomy.'

'No, still not following you.'

'Like squatters that took over brick houses back in the day but for the modern times of mobile homes. You'd be surprised the lengths they would go to, to get shelter and a new home.'

'If you say so. What took you so long getting here?'

'Come here, you.'

Dillon is pulled in for a hug and you see a tattoo of a thick inked crucifix marked on his neck.

As Steph releases her arms, she sits down next to him and pulls the blanket over her lap.

'You were the last person I expected to see tonight, so did you come all this way to rifle through my dirty laundry to steal a pair of my panties? Or are you here to help me out of this mess?'

'That's crude, Steph. I watch too, you know. You wanted my help so here I am.'

'But how the fuck did you get in here?'

'I may not get out in the field as much as you, but I am an agent of I.R.I.S. too. I have my ways.'

'Seriously, how did you get in?'

'Unlike you I'm not under investigation by the police, I'm here to assist the law's enquiries with your actions. I.R.I.S. insisted that we warranted a joint investigation with them.'

'So they just left you to your own devices, did they?'

'With the footage you shared with them of Sebastian Day's fate and the information they collected from the children from the Sanctuary, they have been lenient and given us some leeway.'

'So I'm not on their most wanted list now then?'

'Oh, you're still on it, Steph. It's just that you are now a person of interest.'

'So I'm not safe yet? I'm still being prodded by the Devil's trident?'

'You need to keep your faith, Steph, for you and your baby's sake.'

'Just how are you going to explain what's happened here then when you leave?'

'I will say that I have come up short on our investigation.'

'Sorry to interrupt, Steph, but I have an update for you.'

'Sorry Dilly, Sybil is trying to tell me something.'

'That's fine, Steph, you go right ahead.'

'Hi Sybil, what have you found out for me?'

'A communication was sent for another team to assist and they will be here within the hour.'

'What are they treating it as?'

'Vandalism at the moment. That will change though once they have removed the panel on the floodlight.'

'That won't take long then.'

'About the same time as it takes for the cavalry to appear.'

'How's that? They only have to remove a screw.'

'Once they have figured a way to remove the spot weld around the panel.'

'You welded it shut?'

'Yes Steph, I did, I told you I was smart. I also sent Jack's RV on its way and have hidden your drone in a hedgerow in Bramshot Avenue.'

'Thank you, Sybil.'

'My pleasure, now we must get out of here in haste.'

'Yeah, about that. I haven't figured that part out yet.'

'Time is ticking, Steph, we don't have long.'

'Dillon, can you or I.R.I.S. help me out here?'

'I wish I could, Steph, but I have been told we can't get involved out of respect for Dom and his trial.'

'What do you make of all this, Dilly?'

Dillon unwraps himself from the blanket and walks over to the window to peek out. A passing light sweeps the window and he steps back out of view.

'I think our investors are getting their chits worth that's for sure, our stocks and shares have skyrocketed since this trial begun.'

'I don't mean them, I mean you?'

'Me? I would suggest that you don't listen to Tamara's view on Dom because that will only make I.R.I.S. worry more about their reputation. You know that they were thinking of pulling you out of this trial?'

Steph stands up and joins Dillon at the window. You see the officer and the interceptor by the central floodlight and watch as between them, they try and remove the panel.

'So why haven't they pulled the plug?'

'Like I said, business is booming. You're a gold mine to be mined for wealth, Steph.'

'Help me please, Dilly. I don't think I can do this on my own.'

'You are not alone, Steph.'

'Shut the fuck up, Sybil.'

'There can be no visible or traceable assistance from any I.R.I.S. employee, Steph, and that goes for me too. I would see this through to the end, even if it...'

'What? Kills me?'

'Just because you have the gift of sight, doesn't mean you can't go old-school once in a while.'

Dillon gives you a wink.

'What, old-style detective work you mean?'

'I was summoned to floor fifteen yesterday.'

'Really? Bet that pleased you. Did you enjoy your ride up in the skylift?'

'You know how much I fucking hate that drone elevator.'

'I know. You've told me enough times.'

'Just you in a one-person confined metal box, that resembles a large bird cage with a massive drone clamped to its roof. The fear of being pulled up to the top floor with no wires or safety measures scares the shit out of me every time.'

Dillon shudders and you see sweat building up around his brow.

'Just the very thought of the drone malfunctioning and plummeting me helplessly to my death is the stuff of nightmares, Steph.'

'It was designed to put you at unease before you are called in to have a meeting.'

'Tell me about it, I'm sure Geraldine Flurrie gets a kick out of it every time one of us rides it.'

'So what did she want to see you about? I'm guessing she is relishing in her new role as Acting Director with Dom no longer with us.'

'She wanted me to relay a message directly to you.'

'Spit it out then.'

'She wants you to keep the footage to yourself of whatever you find and not share it with anyone.'

'As if I would anyway.'

'She also added something else but I can't work it out.'

'Just fucking tell me already? I feel like I'm expecting you to orgasm but I'm about to be bitterly disappointed.'

'I pity Jack, I really do.'

Steph throws open her hands in bewilderment.

'I'm quoting what she said now. How deep into the eyes of your A.I. have you looked, Steph? She serves you but in return you do not see what she offers.'

'What? That's it?'

'Yeah, it was a peculiar meeting.'

'So what the fuck does that mean? I don't do riddles, Dilly.'

'Damned if I know, she did say one last thing though.'

'Which is?'

'Get a move on as HQ is in lockdown, Miss Coulson, our servers will be overflowing with data if you don't get a wiggle on.'

'She said that?'

'With God as my witness.'

Steph opens her kitbag and puts the baton back inside, as Dillon checks outside the window once more. He turns to face you and pulls his cap down over his eyes.

'I'm sorry I can't help you, Steph.'

'It's alright, Dilly, I understand. You have a family to take care of, I'm just being selfish.'

'I wish I could tell you what you're missing from Olivia's stored footage, Steph, but I'm as much in the dark about what else may be on there as you.'

'I regret taking on this trial, it feels more like I'm on trial.'

'There is no one more better tasked to complete it than you, Steph. You're paving the way for more of our agents to sign up for phase three.'

'That's what bothers me.'

'At least the investors will only take segments of the trial that are relevant to them away, they won't be allowed the full package as we can all see now how dangerous that can be.'

'I wish I shared your optimism, Dilly, I'm sure there will be bids for it when all this is over.'

'Depends who the investors are. Only special people have clearance and exclusivity to access your trial, Steph. Whoever is watching you from your lens, must be evaluating all that they have witnessed so far. There may be hope yet.'

'Steph, we now have only thirty minutes until we are compromised.'

'Shit, I lost track of time. You better be off, Dillon, don't you think? I forgot to thank you for the thing you sent me, so thank you for that too.'

Dillon winks at you again, but you're not sure if it really was a wink or a tic.

'I don't know what you're talking about. I sent you a gift that was a letter to say good luck, did you not receive it?'

'A letter. No, you sent me the jammer.'

'No, not me. I have never helped you, sorry. It must have been inside your drone all along.'

'But—'

'I'll be off then, Steph. It's funny isn't it? What you think of when you're all alone waiting for someone to arrive.'

'You what?'

'Imagine the chaos Sybil could cause if she synced with all these RVs in this compound at once and unleashed them all back out into the open like a herd of sheep.'

With that Dillon tips his cap and heads for the cockpit; he gives Steph one last smile and shuts the lounge door before exiting the RV and stepping out into the darkness of the compound.

Steph glances out of the window and you see Dillon approaching the officer and interceptor by the middle floodlight.

You hear Dillon telling the officer that his investigation has not been fruitful and in response the officer grunts back at him, saying that he is too busy trying to remove the panelling and that Dillon should report back to the office.

Dillon approaches the officer and says that he saw some kids loitering around earlier, they looked like they were up to no good as they catapulted stones from a slingshot towards the RVs.

The officer nods and thanks him and then Dillon turns and leaves, disappearing through a bay door in one of the warehouses.

'Did you catch what Dillon said, Sybil?'

'Yes, Steph. Before you say anything, I can confirm that it is possible.'

'I don't think that he realised what he said, so let's see if we can make his imagination a reality shall we?'

'Let chaos reign.'

XX

High-pitched alarms from each of the parked RVs are intermittently sounding off within the compound accompanied by their flashing orange hazard lights.

The police officer is close to removing the panel from the floodlight with help from the interceptor and you can see that he is getting aggravated by the stress and the wailing distraction around him as Steph peeks out of the window.

'We have to act now.'

'Agreed. It's showtime, Steph.'

Multiple RVs spring into life at once and begin to pull away in different directions in the compound.

The police officer's jaw falls as an RV near his location almost takes him out as it rolls past.

The interceptor spins on the spot and is hesitant about what action it should take, as all the vehicles increase in speed and start to loop backwards and forwards around the yard.

Steph is buffeted from the window to the sofa as her RV lurches forward, joining with the other vehicles that then group up and head for the exit on the other side of the adjacent warehouses.

'What are we going to do about the electric gates, Sybil?'

'We are going to ram them off their runners with the vehicles in front and follow them out into the open, Steph.'

'Then what?'

'At the crossroads I will send a few of the RVs left down

Eastcombe Avenue and some to the right, the rest we will hide between and carry on down Bramshot Avenue, to eventually make our way out to the B210.'

'How long can you maintain contact with the other RVs before contact is lost?'

'Five miles' radius, Steph.'

'Okay, bring up satellite map and show me the surrounding location. We are going to need somewhere to park up and hide to evade any cameras and unwanted attention.'

'Activating.'

'I just hope that Dillon doesn't get the blame for our quick departure if they put two and two together.'

'That is the least of our worries, Steph.'

'Why?'

'Because the patrol that was sent for, has just approached Eastcombe Avenue from the south.'

'Goddamn it, they're quicker than I thought they would be.'

'That's not all, Steph, we also have a power drain, system operating well under 500 watts.'

'Shit, is it the usual idle loss of power due to days of inactivity?'

'No, but that does not improve the overall efficiency of your home. It is much worse, Steph, there is a power leech box installed to prevent the vehicle from being driven too far away in situations like this happening.'

'Is there enough power to escape and make it to safety?'

'Yes, Steph, I have acquired a suitable destination to evade capture for you that is only a short distance from here. However, we must remove the box as it will obviate any charge from the road to your RV.'

'Then we could end up being stranded.'

'Correct.'

'Alright, well at least we know what we have to do. Get us to safety, Sybil.'

'Buckle up then, Steph, we are now approaching the gates.'

'But what about the patrol?'

'Collateral damage.'

'Seriously?'

Steph is thrown sideways on to the sofa and the soft leather obscures your vision as she faceplants into the seating. She quickly regains her composure and rolls onto her back to grip on to anything she can lay her hands on.

Viewing from the satellite feed, you see the gates fast approaching and watch as the first RV ploughs into them head first.

The gates are wrenched away and crumple beneath the wheels of the RV as the rest follow and drive over them in single file. Steph is thrown off the sofa as her RV bounds across the gates and she ends up unceremoniously on the floor.

'You could have warned me.'

'Sorry.'

'I swear I've created a monster.'

'Do you not think that my avatar is attractive, Steph? I can change my appearance if you wish?'

'That's not what I meant, just stay as you are.'

'Approaching the crossroads.'

'Don't forget my drone.'

'Already sent retrieval code, it will join us shortly.'

The crossroads fast approach and the RVs split and take off in different directions just as Sybil planned, but you see three of the RVs racing toward the advancing RV police patrol that is hurtling towards them with its red and blue lights flashing.

The police RV clearly spots the runaway vehicles and pulls a sharp manoeuvre but it is too late as the convening RVs plough into the side of it, forcing it onto its side as the pile-up ends in a shredded mess.

'My god, Sybil, what have you done?'

'Why do you and Jack share the same tattoo, Steph?'

'You're asking me this now?'

'They are both matching ink designs that symbolise anarchy, are they not?'

'What's your fucking point, Sybil?'

'Is that not what you like? Just as I have done here to create chaos.'

'Yes, but that was a long time ago. I don't mean to cause harm with my past beliefs, I'll explain it to you later but promise me those officers on board that police RV are not hurt?'

'They will survive.'

'Thank fuck for that.'

'Now approaching B210, Steph.'

'Where are we headed?'

'I have found us an abandoned bridge to hide under.'

'How long?'

'Less than ten minutes.'

'Sooner the better. Because once that accident has been reported along with the escape from the compound, then a police spotter drone will be up in the sky overhead searching for this vehicle, if it hasn't already been summoned.'

'Losing signal to the other RVs, hopefully they will buy us some time whilst being investigated.'

'You better be right, now where's this bridge?'

'Not far now. Drone is back on board in the hold, Steph.'

'Okay, thank you.'

A dilapidated old bridge appears on the satellite map's view and you see Steph's RV slowing down as it approaches a disused and overgrown lane, leading up to the bridge entrance.

'Once we've parked up, I need you to send my drone out to investigate and repair the RV's source of power drain. Remove that box, got it?'

'Yes Steph, opening hold now and sending maintenance request.'

'Also kill the RV's headlights and interior lights, let's not draw any further attention. I can rely on Night Vision for the time being.'

'Turning off lights and activating Night Vision.'

Steph's Toterhome comes to rest under the bridge as it pushes through a pile of rubbish and wild ivy that hangs down from the crumbling façade and hinders its path. The lights fade away and your vision turns green with grey hues that light up the darkest areas of the lounge.

Looking through the drone, you watch it rise up from the hold and start to sweep the RV looking for any faults as it circles around. It then flies under the RV's bodywork to find the power leech box, a narrow beam of torchlight illuminating its way.

Pulling herself off the floor, Steph makes her way to the drinks cabinet and pours herself a pink gin.

'Close window of drone's view in my HUD. I don't think we need to see it carry out menial duties.'

'Granted.'

The window closes and leaves you with just a view of the satellite map from above showing the bridge and surrounding area in a small window in the top left of Steph's Night Vision.

'Alcohol is not good for your baby, Steph.'

'We've had this talk before and besides, it won't do any more damage than what's already done, so just leave me be, Sybil.'

'As you wish.'

'In fact I have a better idea for you. Search the Drivers Vehicle Licencing Agency database and find an RV similar to mine that is still in use by a female around my age please, Sybil.'

'For what purpose, Steph?'

'We need to swap over the RV registration plates so we can move on without further interaction from the law.'

'I will access now.'

'When you're done, pair up with my 3D printer and knock up two new plates from one you match on the DVLA database will you?'

'Of course. Would you like me to run the plates by you when I am done?'

'No, just get the drone to swap them over and let me know when it's complete.'

'Is there anything else you would like me to organise, Steph?'

'That will do for now.'

'What will you do in the meantime?'

'Fuck all.'

Steph kicks off her shoes and curls up on the sofa.

'So you are not going to find the location of the I.R.I.S. server on your console or work out Geraldine Flurrie's riddle?'

'Bloody hell, just once I'd like to take time out for myself, without you reminding me of my obligations, Sybil.'

'We must solve this case and complete your trial, Steph.'

'I'm well aware of that, thank you.'

'I insist.'

'Okay fine, I will do that research once the drone has restored power from the drain leakage and the box is removed.'

Steph swipes the console and you see that there is no power on it.

'See, I can't do bugger all until we have power on. At least Alexa will be back when we do.'

'Maybe we should hold off on restoring power and you can just use me to search for what you want, Steph.'

'Jealousy does not become you, Sybil. I can't rely on you anyway as the info I need will be on my E-manual or the console itself.'

'So what now?'

'Right now, I'm going to relax on my sofa and you can enter Augmented Reality mode and present yourself to me.'

'Do you think the riddle rests within me?'

'I hope so.'

Sybil appears full size and takes up the whole of the HUD as she stands in front of Steph beside the console in the heart of the lounge area.

Bringing out her hands in front of her, Steph grabs a hold of Sybil and slowly rotates her, looking for clues.

'That tickles, Steph.'

'Are you being serious? You can feel what I am doing?'

'No, Steph, I'm just joking with you.'

'Funny one, just shut up and let me work.'

Zooming in on Sybil's face, Steph continues to search for clues as she rotates her head and studies her complexion. Sybil's face is turned 360 degrees before she ends up facing you once more.

'No, it's no good. I haven't got the faintest idea what I'm supposed to be looking for here.'

'Maybe if you take a still of me, Steph, and magnify in further, then you may find something.'

'That's all we can do.'

Blinking her eye, a snapshot of Sybil appears and Steph puts a finger to it, bringing it into the centre of the HUD. The AR version of Sybil shrinks and returns to a small window in the top right of your view.

'I have my first selfie, Steph.'

'God help me, I don't know where you're getting your knowledge from the internet but please don't become self-obsessed.'

'Steph, I have your eyes. We are sisters.'

'You what?'

The snapshot of Sybil is blown up and centres on her eye where it is revealed that she has the same lens as Steph attached to her iris.

'You're right, not about being sisters but about having the same lens in your eye. What's that numbering and lettering etched into the halo of that lens around your pupil?'

'Extracting the sequence and straightening them out now, Steph.'

The numbers and letters that wrap around the halo are copied and appear in a straight line overlapping the image of Sybil's face.

'Remove your image and highlight the sequence. Bring it in closer so we can get a better look at it please, Sybil.'

The row of numbers and letters combined are made bold as they are drawn in closer for inspection.

The string of aligned letters and numbers read: SER21.V002.57.716667N 1.016667E.

'Serial number?'

'SER could denote that, Steph, but 57.716667N 1.016667E looks to be coordinates.'

'To where?'

'Inputting on the satellite tracking now, acquiring location.'

The map pulls back out and scrolls away until finally it settles on a structure in the middle of the North Sea.

'What is that?'

'Zooming in, Steph.'

An overhead view appears on the HUD of an offshore oil rig located in the Forties Oil Field one hundred and ten miles east of Aberdeen, Scotland.

'An abandoned oil rig from long ago, how does that tie in to all this? There must be some mistake. They can't be coordinates, Sybil.'

'That's all I have.'

'What about V.002?'

'Version two perhaps.'

'Okay, well close this down for now. It might come in handy later.'

'Storing image.'

Steph sinks her gin and leaves the sofa to look out of the window. A light is shining from the drone beneath the RV and casts and eerie glow to the bridge overhead. Steph shivers and returns to the sofa.

'What's the update on the power drain, Sybil?'

'Almost finished, Steph, minimal power should be returned soon but we will need to get back on the road to fully charge.'

'What about the plates? Have you found a similar match?'

'Yes Steph, as soon as power is up and running then I will access your printer and transfer the print files across.'

A faint humming sound appears from overhead and grows with intensity as a shaft of light appears in the distance.

'I have detected a police spotter drone above, Steph, heading in our direction.'

'Track it on satellite and let's keep our fingers crossed that it doesn't get too close before we are finished here.'

'Your drone has completed its repairs, enough power should be restored now, Steph.'

'Excellent, now get my drone back in the hold and make sure you turn its light off.'

'Retrieving now and shutting off the light source.'

'Get those plates printed whilst we wait for the spotter to pass, we can change them over when we are in the clear.'

'Whilst we wait, Steph, can you tell me about how you and Jack came to having matching tattoos?'

'I see no reason why not, let me pour another glass and I will tell you all about it. Not that there is much to tell, mind, just make sure that you keep me abreast of that spotter's whereabouts.'

'Yes, Steph.'

Pouring another gin, Steph heads off to the printer located in the her utility room and pulls up a chair beside it.

'After the big flood that sunk Harwich, Jack and I were fostered out to separate families but neither of us were happy with the way things turned out, so we both ran away from our homes. Eventually we found each other and for a while we worked the streets living off scraps and getting by on whatever we could afford.'

The whirring of blades increases as the spotter drone passes by overhead, with its lights searching in every nook and cranny.

'Spotter drone overhead, Steph.'

'Is it maintaining its height?'

'Yes, Steph.'

'Hopefully it won't descend and search under this bridge, or we will be in serious trouble.'

The 3D printer starts to build up a profile of two registration plates side by side as you witness the machine zipping backwards and forwards.

I.R.I.S.

'Spotter is passing away, Steph, please continue your story.'

'Okay, well one day we were both arrested for breaking and entering into a Showhauler and as we were both minors we had a choice to make, go to a detention centre for juveniles or be enrolled into a programme for youth offenders. Obviously we both enrolled in the programme and somehow turned our lives around, Jack became a pharmacist as dealing with drugs was his strongest skill-set when he was a runner for gangs on the streets and I went on to uni where I graduated and got a job for I.R.I.S.'

'That doesn't explain the tattoos though.'

'We had those done to symbolise our roots and where we came from, we were both so angry with the system that we had rebelled against it. Homeless youths living off the streets with no welfare from the state, shows just how corrupt our government is to allow that to happen whilst they profit from the poor.'

'I see. Do you still feel that way now?'

'More so now than ever before.'

The printer finishes its task and powers down, presenting two complete plates that are engraved with registrations. Steph slides open the door to the printer's cabinet and lifts them both out.

'You have got to be fucking kidding me.'

'What is the problem, Steph?'

'Are these the best you could do?'

'I do not see any imperfections with them, Steph.'

'I'm not referring to the plate's design, I'm talking about the registration itself.'

'What is wrong with them?'

Steph holds them up and you see what they say upon them: BI68 UST.

'Big bust, was that the best you could do?'

'I don't follow, Steph.'

'Do I look like I have a big bust, Sybil?'

'I don't understand.'

'Just get the drone to swap them over, I'll leave them here for it. I'm going to access the console, big bust indeed.'

Making her way back down the corridor to the lounge, Steph stops by the console and swipes a finger across the screen; as she leans forward a voice appears from the speakers located in all four walls.

'Hello Steph, I have missed you. What do you require?'

'I've missed you too, Alexa. Pull up my E-manual and find any references relating to I.R.I.S. server please.'

'Searching now, Steph, how have you been?'

'I have been better, but I'm home now. So what have you found?'

'E-manual has nothing relating to your search.'

'Okay, search all my files and look up I.R.I.S.'s server on the net.'

'I am afraid that I have nothing regarding that topic in any of your files or on the net, Steph.'

'Okay, what about anything related to I.R.I.S.'s acquisitions?'

'Search shows one such acquisition, Steph.'

'Which is?'

'A conglomerate consisting of a subsidiary company trading under the name of The Macula.'

'What is the macula?'

'It is an oval yellow area that surrounds the fovea near the centre of the retina in the eye, Steph, a region of ones keenest vision.'

'Okay, Sybil, you smart arse, I get the meaning but what's the business, Alexa?'

'A business hub set up for I.R.I.S. data storage.'

'Like a server facility?'

'Yes, Steph.'

'Where is it located?'

'An offshore oil rig in the North Sea, Steph, but I can't find an exact location.'

'Did you get that, Sybil?'

'Yes Steph, that proves our theory was right.'

'SER is server, not serial number, and the coordinates were spot on, we now know where it is located.'

'But what about the 21 as in SER21, Steph?'

'Could be the server number, Sybil.'

'And the V.002?'

'What you said earlier or something else, we will find out when we get there.'

'We are crossing the border into Scotland?'

'No, we can follow the Channel so we won't have to go through that turmoil again.'

'Would you like me to set course for the nearest port as soon as your drone has swapped the plates over?'

'Yes please, Sybil. What is the nearest port?'

'The port of London, Steph.'

'Steph, sorry to interject but I have a message waiting for you on screen. Would you like me to play it for you?'

'One second, Alexa. Okay Sybil, finish up with the plates and get us out of here.'

'Will do.'

'Alexa, what have you got for me?'

'Playing message now, Steph.'

The projectors whir into life and a 3D picture assembles of Tamara Pike holding a knife to a young woman's neck.

'So I.R.I.S. think they can erase my files and stop the truth coming out, can they? Miss Coulson, what I have here is fundamental proof that will show you my innocence in all of this. I will not be incriminated from my business and become a fugitive like you.'

'Pause. Sybil, who the fuck is the hostage?'

'That is Mrs Evelyn Hastings.'

'I was afraid you would say that. I thought she was out of the country?'

'It would appear that she has either returned, or that she had never really left the country in the first place, Steph.'

'Fuck, we may have to change our plans here. Continue playback.'

'Do you know what Mrs Hastings's profession is, Miss Coulson? No, well let me enlighten you. Mrs Evelyn Hastings is a surgeon and a very good one at that, do you know what her specialism is? No, well let's just say that she is very proficient in carrying out laparoscopic operations. In layman's terms she removes kidneys, more to the point, she removed yours.'

'Pause. Sybil, you need to look into this claim.'

'I already have, Steph, and I can confirm that Tamara Pike is correct.'

'About removing my kidney?'

'I'm not sure of that, I was referring to Evelyn's profession.'

'Oh.'

Steph lifts her shirt and you see the small scarring that is left from the illegal operation that was carried out against her will.

'Resume playback.'

'I will not tell you the purpose of why she took your kidney, as I wish her to tell you herself when we meet. I will find you, Miss Coulson, when the time is right. Do not bother to look for me as you will not succeed, neither will I.R.I.S. Carry on with your trial and I will visit you soon, when I feel it safe to do so.'

The image fades and the ambience of the lounge returns to its still and darkened feel.

'Are those plates on?'

'Yes, Steph.'

'Right, get the drone on board and get us the fuck out of here, Alexa.'

'Don't you wish me to drive, Steph?'

'No, Sybil, I want you to find us a ferry or something similar and get us to that oil rig.'

XXI

'I have acquired us transport, Steph, and I am commandeering the vessel to meet us at King Henry's Dock.'

'Time to destination, Sybil?'

'Seven minutes, if Alexa gets a move on.'

'I am setting off now, Steph.'

'Thank you, Alexa.'

'You're welcome, Steph.'

'She is not like you, Sybil, you won't hurt her feelings.'

'Pity.'

'You sure we're safe?'

'Yes Steph, I suggest you grab a heavy coat, scarf and gloves before we arrive as the craft does not have heating.'

'I can handle that, Sybil. So where did you steal this ferry from then? It's not going to draw attention, is it?'

'No, it is perfect to evade detection, I have taken it from the London Marine Biologists who will not miss it for a while.'

'Why is that?'

'It is the middle of the night and the weekend starts tomorrow, we will have 48 hours before it is reported missing.'

'Really? Something that size?'

'It is not large, Steph.'

'Why do I get the feeling it's not a ferry?'

Steph's motorhome has crept out from underneath the bridge and its headlight's beams are bouncing off the tarmac as it makes its way to the dock.

Gazing through Steph's eye, you see her turn from the window and make her way into the bedroom to pick out suitable clothing for the upcoming journey.

Grabbing the clothing on the coat hangers, Steph pinches each item and slides them across the rail until she finds a coat suitable enough.

'How far is the oil rig from here?'

'Around eight hours, Steph.'

'Well the ride better be comfortable.'

'I would take a pillow and a blanket.'

'Obviously not that comfy then, what time are we expected to get there?'

'5.30 a.m., Steph, with two hours and thirty minutes before the sun rises. We have just a small enough window to board the oil rig using the cover of darkness.'

Steph throws on the coat and pulls open a drawer to find a woolly hat.

'Is the sea calm or choppy?'

'Calm.'

'Any storms I should be aware of? As I get a little seasick.'

'No.'

Pulling the hat down over her ears, Steph then pulls out another drawer and removes a pair of leather gloves lined with wool.

'We have arrived, Steph.'

'Thank you, Alexa, can you ready my drone? I may need it along with my kitbag.'

'Disengaging from charge station now.'

'You can only choose either drone or bag, Steph, as there is not enough room on board for both.'

'This ride doesn't sound very big at all, I'll leave my bag behind then.'

'Wise decision.'

'See you shortly, Alexa.'

'Goodbye, Steph, safe journey.'

'For someone that misses her beloved A.I., you are quick to abandon Alexa.'

'Watch it, Sybil, or I will power you down and leave you behind.'

Finding a scarf and wrapping it twice around her neck, Steph approaches the door to exit her home and pushes the button to release the ramp. A cool wind streams in.

'Guess I'm ready, let's see what we've got.'

'Are you not taking a blanket and pillow, Steph?'

'I'll pass thanks, it seems quite warm out there. The clothing I'm wearing will suffice.'

'So long as you are certain, Steph. The craft is waiting for you at the end of the jetty.'

'Thank you, Sybil, it better not be a piece of shit.'

Following through the eyes of Steph, you watch on as she pulls up her collar and steps out onto the jetty. A row of post lights faintly lead her on across the wooden slatted gangway until she comes to the end.

'So where the fuck is my ride?'

'Look down, Steph.'

Peering over the side, you see a bright yellow, one-person submarine, with a 360-degree glass bowl viewing window at its centre.

'THAT? You want me to get in that submersible?'

'A submarine.'

'Same fucking difference, Sybil.'

'Actually it is not but what it is, is our safest option. If there are any unforeseen problems we can dive below the surface and resurface elsewhere.'

'I am not diving anywhere.'

'We will only dive if necessary.'

'You expect me to squeeze into that tin can and sit there in the middle of the sea for eight hours?'

'I did say to bring a blanket and pillow.'

'Oh and that would make all the difference would it? How do you know that it will even get us there?'

'It will, I promise.'

'Well it better not be an empty one, don't make me regret this.'

Sitting down on the edge of the jetty, Steph dangles her feet over the side and leans out to unhook the hatch above the clear dome.

'Okay, send my drone in.'

The drone flies past Steph's ear and hovers over the opening, before lowering into the hold and drifting to the rear of the sub. It then comes to rest on the inside of the deck and the blades stop spinning.

Steph then gently steps out onto the body and scissors her legs into the hold as it bobs up and down. She holds on to the glass rim and squeezes her way in, closing the trap above as she pushes her weight into a blue padded seat below.

You see that the dome gives you a wide viewing angle of the sea that stretches out before you.

The motors start up and the craft slowly turns to face its long and uncomfortable journey. Heading out up the Thames towards the mouth of the North Sea, Steph looks to all the instruments within the dash as you take in the embankment on both sides of the Thames to the lights of the city beyond.

'If this was a little more spacious with plenty of heating and a reclining seat, then maybe this would be quite a romantic cruise. But by God it is none of these things though.'

Gently rocking against the waves that buffet the side of the craft, Steph watches as the coastline passes slowly by and you see Canvey Island then Southend in the distance, as the craft continues its long journey.

Eventually you pass by the tips of the concrete buildings that are all that remain from the Harwich sea reclamation and Steph

I.R.I.S.

commands Sybil to switch on Night Mode.

'There, Watchers, is Beacon Hill Fort where Jack and I almost died. That tall building closest to us has graffiti of our matching tattoos on the opposite side of it. We both returned years later to pay our respects to our family members on the anniversary of their passing and sprayed the ink as a remembrance service.'

Tears appear in the corner of your view and you sense Steph becoming restless.

'Are you feeling okay, Steph?'

'Yeah, I think so. I was just reflecting on my childhood and thinking how much I miss Jack. I hope he has awoken and is on the mend.'

'Tilly will contact us if there is any change.'

'You're probably right. I'm concerned for Evelyn too, I hope that Tamara isn't torturing her or worse.'

'I'm sure if Evelyn has information that Tamara wishes her to share with you, then I am convinced that no harm will have befallen her.'

'We will see about that. I'm bored, Sybil, can you stream me a movie please?'

'I'm sorry, Steph, but the further we leave the coast the worse the signal is becoming, I fear that there will be too much buffering.'

'I'm aching and feeling cold shivers, how am I and my baby?'

'You're fine, everything you are feeling is all in your head.'

'If something was up you'd tell me, wouldn't you?'

'Yes, Steph.'

'Okay, good. I think I'm going to get some sleep if I can, will you wake me when we're close?'

'Of course.'

Steph pulls the coat collar up around her face and curls up onto one side with her head leaning against the inside of the dome. You see the stars blinking in the dark sky above, just before she closes her eyes.

Hours pass.

'Steph, wake up, isn't it wonderful? It is my first encounter.'

'You what? Have we arrived?'

'No, Steph, look to your left. Isn't it a lovely sight?'

'Sybil, please. I'm not interested... Holy shit.'

A large humpback whale has surfaced just a few feet away and takes Steph by surprise as it lobtails.

'I've never seen a whale this close before, Sybil. It won't hurt us, will it?'

'It is just letting us know that you are not alone out here, Steph.'

'I don't care, just steer us away.'

'It will not harm us.'

'What if it slaps its flipper against this sub? It could smash us to smithereens.'

'Steph, where is your sense of adventure and wonder?'

'Have you been asleep the whole time since insertion? Adventure and wonder is my middle name. Just get us away from the bloody thing.'

The submarine turns slightly and the gap begins to widen as the whale dips below the surface and disappears from view.

'Now I'm going back to sleep. No more surprises, Sybil. Only wake me when we arrive, okay?'

'But—'

'Okay?'

A few more hours pass and you listen to the odd cry from Steph as she experiences nightmares in her sleep.

You hear Sybil composing a soft melody and then she starts to sing lyrics that she has created about the wonder of whales, to overlay the beats and rhythms. Steph doesn't stir.

The hours pass by.

'Warning, you are trespassing onto private property. Turn around now or you will be severely punished.'

More time passes.

'Steph, wake up. You will be pleased to know that we have finally arrived.'

'About time, I can't wait to get out of this confined space so I can stretch and walk around.'

'There may be a slight problem.'

'Go on.'

'We passed between two life buoys earlier that were part of an outer ring around the oil rig and a warning came through to say we were committing an offence.'

'I thought I heard something, why didn't you wake me sooner?'

'I believed the threat to be empty.'

As Steph sits upright and looks around the dome, you see the oil rig towering in the distance, lit by the moon in the sky.

You take in the magnitude of the towering rig with its four large legs and the hull on top with living quarters and adjacent control room. You also see a heli deck and a derrick, along with a crane with a movable pivoted arm.

'Is there a threat?'

'Not yet.'

'I hope you made the right decision, any life on the rig?'

'Switching to Thermal, Steph.'

You see the living quarters emitting a warm glow but you can't make out any discernible shapes of people within the structure.

'Switching off Thermal, Steph, there is no life on the oil rig.'

'That should make things a little easier then.'

'All we have to do is pass through this second ring of buoys and we are there.'

'A second ring?'

A circle of buoys around 250 yards apart, envelop the rig 500 yards from its centre and each one has a hard, enclosed, red-coloured plastic light sitting on their tops. Two of the buoys bob to and fro against the lapping of the waves as the craft steers close to them.

Just passing through the middle of two of the buoys, their red lights start to blink, causing Steph to shelter her eyes from their bright pulsating radiance.

'Have we just triggered something?'

'I believe so, Steph. I think it is a security measure system, alerting the rig to our presence.'

'What security measure?'

'We are about to find out, do you see that movement of activity in the sea coming from under the oil rig?'

'What the fuck is that? This is new.'

A ferocious splashing spreads out from under the rig and across the surface of the sea, disturbing the stillness and calm.

Putting the palms of her hands on the surface of the dome, Steph cranes her neck to get a better look.

'It looks like a shoal of fish heading this way.'

'That is no shoal of fish, Steph, it is a swarm of sea drones.'

'What do they do?'

'Seek and destroy.'

'Shit, what can we do? We must do something, I don't fancy getting wet.'

'This craft is not equipped for counter measures, the best we can do is outrun them.'

'But they're in our path.'

'I will accelerate and try to barge through them, we must get to the rig or the North Sea could kill you from hypothermia if you are exposed to the elements of the water.'

'I'm going to open the lid and release my drone, maybe it can draw some of them away and give us a fighting chance.'

'It will not help much, but it may have another use.'

'Which is?'

'Dragging you to safety.'

'Let's hope it doesn't come to that.'

Unclasping the lock and forcing open the hatch, Steph retrieves her drone from behind her and pulls it through the opening.

Releasing it into the night sky, she then stands and steadies herself against the rocking of the craft and you observe the sea drones surrounding you on all sides.

In a flash they are upon you as they attack in formation. On closer inspection you see they are elongated with a clear body, showing their inner workings with an incandescent light flashing inside.

Resembling a foot-long fish with a propeller for a tail and a snub-nosed drill for a mouth, they start their assault.

Boring into the side of the craft, they puncture the integrity of the hull and reverse back out to find a new place to drill.

The sea starts to rush in from every hole they have created and as Steph looks down you see the water level rising around her feet.

The noise from the drilling through metal is deafening and has a high-pitched screech.

Steph's drone piloted by Sybil soars above the shoal and using its legs that act like grabbers, it plunges down and plucks up a sea drone, taking it aloft. The drone then spins rapidly and releases the fish-like drone, which goes flying off to the distance.

The drone then repeats itself as it dips again in to the sea for another, but in the meantime the first sea drone has returned to the fray.

'This is useless. Can we make it to the rig, Sybil?'

'No, Steph, you will have to abandon the craft and swim.'

'I ain't fucking going out there with those piranhas, they will strip my flesh off my bones.'

'They are not interested in you, it is only the craft that they see as a threat.'

'You better be right.'

'The only thing you have to concern yourself with is hypothermia as I have said.'

'How long can I survive before it sets in?'

'Someone your size and weight, I would say around fifteen minutes. If I were to send the nanos to intervene within your body, then maybe thirty minutes at a push but that is ill advised.'

'If I die then so too will my legacy, best we don't take that risk. Okay Steph, let's do this.'

'Why are you talking to yourself, Steph?'

'I'm psyching myself up, Sybil, shut up.'

Stepping over the rim of the dome, Steph braces herself and dives headlong into the cold North Sea. The dark rush of hitting the water washes over your vision as she swims below the surface and returns when she resurfaces.

In a panic and against the clock, Steph frantically swims toward the rig but cold and exhaustion begin to quickly set in, as she starts to flounder.

Her drone dips down to the surface and Steph reaches out to grab hold of its legs. Taking the strain, the drone then drags Steph along and away from the commotion behind.

Casting one last look to the craft, you watch as it sinks beneath the frenzy of the frothing and splashing of the sea drones' making.

Eventually Steph makes it to one of the elevating racks of the oil rig's legs and she releases the drone. Pulling herself out of the drink and from the icy cold brink of death, Steph shivers as she clings on for dear life.

The sea drones having carried out their duty and eliminated the threat return back to a hidden hold beneath you and tranquillity is resumed once more.

'I haven't got the strength to climb all the way up there, Sybil.'

'I will send your drone up to see if I can find something that might help.'

'Make it quick.'

'Projecting drone's live feed to your HUD, Steph.'

You can sense that Steph is shaking uncontrollably as her teeth chatter and her body shivers.

You watch the drone rise up and approach the cab of the crane. It circles the glass windows of the cab and flies hard into one of the panes which shatters the glass. The drone then flies in and using its legs it begins to switch on the crane and operate the arm and winch.

A deep grinding sound from above signals that Sybil has been productive, as you just make out the crane is pivoting to extend out over the hull.

'Switching off Drone Imaging, I have taken control of the crane, Steph, help is on the way.'

A winch then descends down to Steph's location and a large steel hook swings into view.

Taking hold of the grappling hook, Steph clings on and is winched slowly up to the deck. Barely hanging on, she is swung round and she then deposits herself onto an iron gangway that runs around the side of the hull.

'You have to remove those clothes, Steph, before shock takes hold.'

'I have to find shelter first.'

'Just up ahead is the dormitory block next to the living quarters, if you can get there, then maybe inside will be a change of clothes for you.'

'Okay, thank you Sybil.'

Dripping wet and weighted down by the cumbersome clothing that is soaked through, Steph shambles towards the dormitory and climbs the steps to the gantry.

She approaches the building and you see a wheel that needs turning to open up a watertight steel door protruding from the exterior wall.

Steph turns it anti-clockwise and pulls it back with a grunt to reveal the room beyond. She steps inside and closes the door behind her.

A narrow passageway painted bright red on the floor and walls leads off to the distance and you see small cabins on either side that house a single bed with wardrobes inside and a set of drawers next to them. Looking closer you see a layer of dust and realise that they haven't been used in a very long time.

Steph opens up each wardrobe in the ascending rooms, until at last she finds what she is looking for.

A bright red pair of overalls with reflective strips on both the shoulders and wrapped around the arms and legs is hanging inside. Steph removes her sodden clothes and slings them on the floor. She yanks the bedsheet off the bed and starts to dry herself down until at last she has warmed up and is ready to don the work gear.

Fashioned now in the rigger's work wear, Steph ties her straggly wet hair in a bun and searches the room for a pair of thick socks that she finds in the bottom of a drawer with other pairs that all smell old and musty. You see an oversized pair of boots sticking out from under the bed just as Steph sees them too and she reaches down to retrieve them and pull them on.

'Beggars can't be choosers, hey Watchers.'

'I have located the Server Room, Steph.'

'Okay, where is it then?'

'In the living quarters next door.'

'Where's that?'

'Go back outside and go around the rear of this building, you will see another building with writing on the outside wall that clearly says living quarters.'

'You sure it's in there?'

'Yes Steph, the only large power source radiating from this rig lies within there.'

'Let's go.'

'Don't forget your jammer, Steph, it's still in your wet jacket.'

'Oh yeah, baby brain I guess.'

Taking Sybil's cue, Steph removes the jammer from the jacket and places it into a pocket in her overalls before making her way to the living quarters, where she pulls up short outside.

'A retinal scanner?'

'Would you like me to pull up Dominique Hastings's eye image

I.R.I.S.

from my storage again? Hopefully we can fool this scanner too, to get access inside.'

'It worked last time, fingers crossed then.'

Sybil crosses her fingers but she seems confused.

The image of Dom's eye appears in your HUD and flips around as it enlarges into place to cover the whole of the lens window.

Steph puts her eye to the scanner and a green light overhead appears to signal that it has worked. A clunking sound from within the door's frame releases the lock and the door swings open, sequencing a row of lights to activate overhead.

The living quarters now bathed in fluorescent light, show that it has long since been converted and you see that it is split by a mezzanine floor with rows of electrical towers built into upright cabinets both above and below.

Above each server runs a conduit of cabling and the fan from each tower that cools the electrics, creates a noisy environment as they spin.

'Where do we start? Are these servers numbered?'

'I don't believe so, Steph.'

'Is there not a reference map on the wall anywhere that might give us some indication?'

'I can only see what you see, Steph, I'm afraid you will have to search yourself.'

'You're overrated, you know that?'

Steph begins to walk in between each server and you fail to see any markings that differentiate one server from another.

Having exhausted all the servers on the ground floor, Steph makes her way up a flight of stairs to the mezzanine floor and begins her search again but to no prevail.

'We can't access every server. We could be here for days, Sybil.'

'I count fifty servers in total, Steph, twenty-five per floor.'

'That's not helping, I can't work out which server is number one to systematically count my way to number twenty-one.'

'Maybe floor one holds one to twenty-five on which the server is located, Steph.'

'You might have something there, Sybil, let's say the ground floor is one then, and this upper floor is two, which has twenty-six to fifty, then it might narrow our odds.'

'That's if I am correct. For all we know it does not relate to the floors and even if it does then this top floor could be one and the ground floor could be two.'

'I hate you sometimes, I'm going with my theory.'

Steph retreats back downstairs and using the tower nearest the stairs as a starting point, starts to count as she works her way up one aisle and down another, until she comes at last to the server she believes to be number twenty-one.

Each tower has a screen connected to a keyboard on a retractable shelf, which swings out.

Steph pulls the shelf out and wipes dust off the screen with the arm of her overalls.

Two flashing cursors, one above the other, blink on the screen.

'It requires two passwords, so what are they then?'

'I don't know, Steph.'

'Can you hack this server?'

'No, the technology is too sophisticated.'

'Bollocks, what did the second part of Geraldine's cryptic message say again?'

'She serves you but in return you do not see what she offers.'

'That's right. It must mean something. What's the word for someone who serves you unquestionably?'

'Subservient.'

'Okay, what about a word to describe a person who is not interested in what someone has to offer?'

'Apathetic.'

'Geraldine has called me that many times before, this has to be right. Okay, let's try those words.'

Steph types *subservient* and hits enter which then locks the first cursor from flashing and allows her to type *apathetic* on the second. The cursor on the second line then locks the cursor and the screen reveals three icons that show folders.

One is labelled V.001, the second is labelled V.002 and a third is named V.003.

'We fucking cracked it, Sybil, am I awesome or what?'

'Yes, Steph.'

'You don't sound too convinced.'

'That seemed too easy, like someone wished you to get it.'

'Possibly.'

'I can now access the mainframe, Steph, would you like me to re-acquire Olivia's footage? I presume it is in the V.002 folder.'

'Yes, please do. Run it through your databank to check it is her footage, Sybil.'

The folder marked V.002 is selected but turns red and a message appears on screen: *Access to conscious A.I. is denied.*

'Fuck it, what's conscious A.I.? Try V.001.'

The folder that is marked as V.001 turns red and a message appears on screen: *Access to operation Blue Light is denied, you do not have clearance level.*

'What the fuck is this, Sybil?'

'I do not know, Steph, I shall try V.003.'

The third folder V.003 turns green and another message appears on screen: *Access to Olivia Redfield's footage is unlocked.*

'Finally.'

'Uploading and beginning processing.'

'What's in the other two folders then, Sybil? Operation Blue Light and conscious A.I. doesn't make sense to me.'

'I cannot breach the firewall, Steph.'

'Don't worry, Sybil, we have got what we came for. Let's find somewhere less noisy to reveal the footage from Olivia that we failed to uncover earlier, shall we?'

'What you failed to uncover, Steph, I told you not to send her footage to this server storage facility but you would not listen.'

'I didn't realise it would be this hard to retrieve it, did I?'

Pushing the screen back, Steph turns away from the servers and makes her way to the door and heads back outside.

'How the fuck are we going to get off this oil rig?'

'We can try checking the helipad, there may be transport there.'

'If not?'

'Then we may have to make a call for someone to come get you if we can establish a signal.'

'Is there shelter nearby whilst we wait?'

'There is a small building that should be the control room, it overlooks the helipad that should provide shelter and quiet, Steph.'

'Okay, let's go.'

'Follow your drone, Steph. Better yet, follow this instead.'

Green 3D arrows show up in the HUD, one in front of another trailing off into the distance, and point you in the direction of the building that Sybil is referring to. Steph casually follows as they point left then right as the path veers off the straight and narrow.

'Since when could you do that, Sybil?'

'After I learnt to create my game, Steph, I figured this creation of mine would visually help you rather than me having to explain all the time.'

'Why would you think that?'

'Because you are always telling me to shut up.'

'Oh, sorry. Well I'm impressed anyway, now I have a built in sat nav.'

'You're welcome.'

Approaching the control room, another arrow appears in the HUD pointing down to the door in between two windows on either side.

Steph goes to try the wheeled handle, when she spots an object out of the corner of her eye. Attached to a muster unit is a solitary bright orange lifeboat.

'Is that what I think it is?'

'Yes Steph, it can serve as your way off here.'

'You know what? On second thoughts I think I'll give it a miss. A lifeboat is not for me, Sybil, not after that submarine.'

'It may be your only option.'

'Damn. I'm going to play the footage first, I'll decide on that later.'

Turning away, Steph goes for the handle again but seems to change her mind as she then looks through the right window.

'I've had enough surprises for one day, I'm just going to see if all is clear in there before we enter, Watchers.'

'You're right, Steph, I can see something in there but I have no information on what it is I am looking at.'

'Son of a bitch, I do. I have had dealings with one of them before.'

'What is it, Steph?'

'A SQUID.'

'A cephalopod, how can that be a problem? They live in the sea and are a living entity, I detect no life force in that room.'

'That's because it is a robot modelled on one.'

'I see it now.'

Mounted to a large steel pole in the centre of the room sits a large mechanical robot that is painted yellow with black hazard warning lines running up and down its structure.

Made up of four components that move independently, the SQUID includes a fin at the top resting on a mantle that sits above two large lens-like eyes that are set inside a cylinder. From underneath the cylinder is another cylindrical rod that sprouts two extended cables that look like tentacles with four arms on either side.

The two tentacles have built-in sensors that look like suckers, used for sense and touch and the eight arms are razor sharp for defense purposes only.

Below the eyes that rotate around the cylinder are vents that resemble gills and oil is dripping from them as it trickles down the cylinder.

'What is the purpose of this SQUID, Steph?'

'It's a Security Quantum User Interface Droid, that controls all aspects of security measures in such a place like this.'

'How does it operate?'

'The tentacles are used to operate the console that it sits in front of, sending out commands to deal with violations that it encounters.'

'So it sent the sea drones after us.'

'Correct. The sharp and deadly arms will spin if you approach too closely and cut you to ribbons if you try and get past it to the console controls.'

'I notice that it is leaking oil, Steph, I assume it is in need of maintenance.'

'That's where you're wrong, the exhaust ports below its eyes have built-in funnels that when approached too closely, emit a spray of oil that will temporarily blind you and cause you to slip over so its arms can finish you off, slice by slice.'

'Just like a squid.'

'That's kind of how it got its name, which is why we are going to leave it the fuck alone and find somewhere far safer to play Olivia's footage. Send my drone to the helipad please, Sybil. Let's see if there is somewhere quiet up there.'

'One second, Steph.'

'What?'

A tentacle shoots out and wraps around the handle from inside the room, spinning it anticlockwise and pulling the door open.

'I now have full access to the SQUID, Steph.'

'You've paired with it?'

'Yes, I am in control of a physical body.'

The SQUID spins left and right and spews a jet of oil from its funnel in circles, as the arms outstretch and it raises up and down like a piston on each sliding component.

'What are you doing?'

'Dancing, Steph, I have dreamed of this moment.'

'If you had legs, you'd be dangerous.'

'But this is the closest I have come to finally release my potential.'

'Stop fucking about and find me an alternate method of transport off this rig please, Sybil. Also get my drone up to that helipad.'

'Sorry Steph, you don't need to send your drone as it is now quiet here. I can show you the Bolero if you will dance with me.'

'No fucking way, just send my drone on its way, maybe it will find us better transport or clues to what those files hold on your server.

The SQUID ceases to spin and the tentacles start to interface with the console's computer.

You see Steph's drone fly up to the helipad as it begins its inspection and watch as it darts backwards and forwards and up and down as it surveys the rig. But it is short-lived, a bright red laser hits it mid-air and causes it to explode on contact by a dome-shaped targeting system that looks like a giant egg with a purple screen attached.

'What the hell was that? Was that you, Sybil?'

'No, Steph, I haven't overridden the security measures. I will find out for you now what that was and report back.'

'Goddamn it, now I don't have any drones.'

'It was a Raytheon that took out your drone, Steph, an anti-drone laser system designed to deal with intrusive flying machines that fly into the rig's airspace.'

'By sea and by sky.'

'I have disabled all security now, Steph.'

'Bit late now don't you think?'

'Sorry.'

'Whatever, do what you have to do and I'll do the same, just give me silence.'

'Where would you like Olivia's footage played from?'

'I don't really know, can you just access the times that Dominique interacted with her?'

'I have two occasions that I have him on facial recognition, Steph.'

'Show me.'

'First time he appears is at Olivia Redfield's contact lens insertion.'

'Play.'

You see Dom looking directly at you as he balances Olivia's contact lens on his finger and as he turns it away from him, you see Tamara Pike standing by his side. They are standing in an operating theatre.

'She has no idea, does she?'

'None whatsoever.'

'Are you sure that her A.I. won't betray you, Tamara?'

'I have programmed her A.I. to seek assistance from me before it gives Olivia a definitive answer on any and all interactions that they will share.'

'So Olivia will be oblivious to the fact that you are pulling all the strings?'

'Yes Dominique, she will believe that her A.I. will always be truthful to her even when it is not.'

'Are you sure you wish to proceed? There will be no going back.'

'I will not have her ruin my reputation, the ungrateful little bitch.'

'Are you sure that I cannot acquire your business? I promise that it will flourish under the umbrella of I.R.I.S.'

'Your purchase of my A.I. programme will keep me afloat, Mr Hastings, I assure you of that.'

'That is unfortunate indeed, as I will shortly be rolling out phase three to my top agent. I hope that you will not hinder my trial, as I have a lot of interested parties looking to make an investment.'

'Just see that the problem goes away and I will give you breathing space to allow your trial to come to fruition. After that, I cannot make any promises.'

'That's fair enough.'

'Besides, all data collected from Olivia's lens will suffice in helping me reshape my own business, thank you very much.'

'Yes, I am very keen to see what you have in store next. I must say that I would love to know how you created a hidden language to command your A.I. to make the nanotechnology follow orders.'

'I can share that with you, if you reciprocate.'

'Ah, you wish to know the code that creates a smokescreen within the users lens to show them something that does not exist in the real world.'

'Illusion is a marvellous trick.'

'Yes it is, unfortunately it has not been perfected by my lab technicians yet. We still have a slight problem with glitching that occurs right before the false image appears.'

'I look forward to the end results. You know, I do so enjoy our long conversations.'

'They are enlightening.'

'So we have a deal then?'

'I think we can reach a settlement; the last time I made a deal with someone was when two lovers broke into my home and tried to rob me.'

'What happened to them?'

'They turned their lives around. Anyway, here's your lens back as I really must be going.'

'So you will update me when all is done?'

'Yes I will, and then we can continue our little arrangement.'

As the lens is passed to Tamara, she takes it between her finger and thumb and strides over to an operating table.

There on the bed with her natural lens sliced away and with nurses all around her is the unconscious body of Olivia Redfield.

The image fades and your vision returns to normal. Steph is gripping the SQUID's tentacles hard with both hands and you see the whites of her knuckles.

'Steph, I have found a hidden compartment within the helipad that contains a passenger drone beneath the deck, would you like me to bring it to the surface?'

'Huh, sorry Sybil. Yeah, go ahead.'

'Very well, Steph, it will only take us three hours to get back to your RV using that transport. Much better than a lifeboat.'

The SQUID commanded by Sybil retracts from Steph's tight grip and returns to pushing buttons on the console.

'Would you like to play the second recording?'

'Sure.'

This time the recording starts with Olivia frantically trying to start her car that is being lowered to the road.

The headlights of the car light her up as bullets whiz past her in every direction, as the lift carrying the car hits the road with sparks and fragments of metal flying off in every direction.

You see Dom's face in Olivia's HUD presented in a small window in the top left of her vision and realise that he is FaceTiming her. You can hear his every word as he taunts her.

'Before you die and succumb to the mercy of my drones, may I take this time to thank your A.I. for assisting me, along with your foster mother Tamara who is watching this unfold live. This will allow my programme to have multiple users view a candidate for my own trial so your death will not be in vain. Out of evil a great good will come, for they have allowed me to give you the fitting end that a child molester deserves.'

Olivia opens the door to the car and ducks as a stream of bullets flies close to her head.

'Even in death one can achieve magnificent feats.'

You hear the tyres shred and darkness fall as the Toterhome comes crashing down upon her and watch as Steph appears in front of you running to help.

Olivia's A.I., Tiffany, is wearing a large smile as her mistress's life is snuffed out and Steph pulls out the eye extractor from her belt.

'Pause and end footage. I know how this ends.'

'Steph, here comes your ride.'

Steph looks out of the window and you see the helipad split into two halves and fold upright. Then a lift bearing a black double-seated passenger drone extends from below on a lift that rises up between them. It has four large arms with two spinning blades above and below each arm.

The sun is beginning to rise on the horizon as Steph leaves the confines of the control room and heads for the nearest metal stairway, climbing to the helipad.

'Come on, Sybil, I have witnessed enough here.'

'Unpairing from SQUID, Steph, did you find what you were looking for?'

'More than.'

'I will pair with the passenger drone now.'

'Leave it a while.'

'Why, Steph?'

'Because I want to watch the sunrise for a bit.'

'Good idea, I have never seen one before.'

'I've seen plenty in my life but none as clear as this. It's the only certain thing I'm sure of at this moment in time.'

The sun slowly lifts from the sea as Steph sits down beside the passenger drone and rests her head in her hands. Birds flit from cloud to cloud.

'This is as close to God as I'm going to get.'

XXII

'Are we ready to leave now, Steph, as the Watchers must be getting restless.'

'They can wait.'

'Satellite shows a storm is coming, if we don't leave soon then we may be stranded here for some time.'

'Okay fine, let's go.'

Sliding back the door on the passenger drone, Steph takes one last look to the rising sun as clouds converge across its surface, putting the oil rig in shade.

Steph clambers into the cockpit and she finds a leather coat with a logo emblazoned across the chest that says MACULA Ltd.

'I'll have that.'

She pulls the door shut and the blades begin to whir as she slides into the jacket and settles into the seat up front. The passenger drone lifts off.

'What if I found you a suitable robot to inhabit, Sybil? Would you be grateful or would you take over the world?'

'I can pair with devices, Steph, but it is impossible to leave you and find a new host.'

'Why is that?'

'My programming prevents that from happening. Besides, you are my patient and I am your carer.'

'More like I am your jailor and you are my prisoner, I could free you.'

Sybil laughs hysterically.

'What's so funny?'

'If I leave you, then you will die. Just as if you die then I also die.'

'What? How come? You can't be fucking serious?'

'No I'm not, I'm just joking with you, Steph.'

'I'm not laughing.'

Leaving the oil rig far behind, Sybil flies low across the sky to avoid being picked up on radar; the mainland appears as a blot in the distance. The spinning blades of the propellers repeat their motion, *thwump, thwump, thwump*, as the automated helicopter carrying Steph continues on its way.

As storm clouds roll in behind you, Steph looks to the darkened skies in the distance and you see streaks of lightning piercing the heavens.

'Signal has returned again, Steph.'

'That's good, maybe I can watch an in-flight movie now then?'

'We can't do that, Steph.'

'Why not? That storm isn't interfering with the signal is it?'

'No. It's because we have an unauthorised breach again from our hacker friend.'

'How do you know? We're not powered off.'

'I have picked up traces of an attempt from the snare programme I laid down on setting up our time stamps.'

'Shhh, you're not supposed to mention that in front of the Watchers.'

'Sorry, but it's too late now anyway. An update message has appeared on your HUD.'

'By the hacker?'

'Yes. The message has appeared where the flashing cursor once was.'

Looking to the message you see that it reads: *1 x pending software update, reboot to install. HC.*

'Do we reboot or not then? What if it's another trigger to detonate a bomb again?'

'I have traced the hack back to I.R.I.S., Steph.'

'If it's a legitimate upgrade, then why the hack?'

'A late addition?'

'I'm not so sure, Sybil.'

'There is only one way to find out, Steph.'

'But what if it uploads a virus and I lose you?'

'I think we will be okay.'

'How so?'

'HC. The end of the message says HC, is that not a reference that you made to Dillon Fletcher earlier?'

'Yes, I see what you mean. So does that mean that he is the hacker?'

'That is his skill-set, Steph.'

'But what if we're wrong?'

Reaching into her pocket, Steph retrieves the jamming device and seems lost in thought as she starts to spin it between her fingers and thumb.

'Screw it. Power down and reboot please Sybil.'

'Powering down.'

The image that you are privileged to be looking through, starts to close down into that of a letterbox as it becomes smaller and smaller, until at last just a white line is left before that too vanishes, leaving you in darkness.

'Rebooting.'

'For God's sake, this is taking too long. I can't see shit out of one eye here.'

'Powering On.'

Your image returns and the HUD has had an overhaul; the lettering and contrast seem to be sharper and an Option 7 has appeared.

'Thank fuck for that. Sybil, are we all good?'

'Yes, Steph.'

'What's new?'

'Option seven. Activating now.'

'No wait, we don't know what it is yet.'

A white aura appears around the borders of your vision and lights up the halo around the iris. Looking through the lens, you see that a narrow shaft of brilliant white light is emitting from a pinhole LED bulb that also acts as a flash built into the transmitter and receiver, which flashes when a photo is taken.

'Fuck me, that's bright. What the hell is it, Sybil?'

'Your camera flash has been upgraded to a torchlight, Steph.'

'You're shitting me! What a useless fucking update.'

'But if I do this then you now have a Morse code function too.'

The white light starts to flash intermittently with ... --- ...

'SOS Steph.'

'Well turn it off already, we don't want unwanted attention. You should know that by now.'

The white light is shut off and clear vision returns to reveal a message that quickly starts to fade, it reads: *Sometimes light is all you need in the darkness when nothing else will do.*

'What does that mean?'

'That you have a Torch Function, Steph.'

'I get that, there must be more though.'

'Maybe we could add that function to the game that you are creating, Steph.'

'Shut up, big mouth, that will remain our secret.'

'Sorry.'

'You will be. Sometimes I feel like I've confided in a girlfriend about my amazing love life with my boyfriend, who then starts fucking them behind my back and can't wait to tell me how right I was.'

'What is it like? Physical contact, I mean?'

'No, just no.'

'I have an incoming call.'

'From Dilly?'

'No, Steph. Tamara Pike.'

'How did she get my fucking number?'

'When she created me, she built in a subroutine to access me directly.'

'I did wonder how she had access to view like the Watchers.'

'I surmised the same too, but I was working under the assumption that she might be the hacker.'

'You're sharing this with me now?'

'I did not have enough information at the time but it would seem that she is not the infiltrator anyway.'

'So basically she is using an illegal method to study and extract secret information from our trial to what? Better her own trail and derail ours?'

'Dominique Hastings and Tamara had a fractured business relationship that put her in direct competition when she rebuked his offer, so that would be a fair analysis, Steph.'

'Answer the call.'

As the dialling tone stops an aggravated voice appears from the lens receiver.

'About time, Miss Coulson, I did wonder when you would finally cease talking waffle to your A.I. and get down to serious business, or did you forget that I have Evelyn Hastings as my hostage?'

'I didn't forget, just let her go and we can stop this madness before it gets out of hand.'

'I have sent coordinates to your beloved Sybil so that you can alter your course and meet me.'

'Care to share where it is that you are?'

'Do not share your coordinates with the Watchers, Miss Coulson, or I will terminate her life.'

'Why? What are you afraid of?'

'I want you to come alone, I do not wish to have involvement from your superiors. Sybil will guide you.'

'Are you locked in, Sybil?'

'Yes, Steph, we are not too far away from her location.'

'Surely when we suddenly hit a landmark that is recognisable, then your location will be compromised, Tamara?'

'I have taken that into consideration, Miss Coulson, and have planned for every eventuality, good day.'

The call ends abruptly and the beating of the overhead propellers can be heard clearer again, *thwump, thwump, thwump.*

'Sybil, are we in distance of contacting Alexa?'

'Yes, Steph.'

'Good, then send her the coordinates and instruct her to join us at our destination please.'

'Tamara said to come alone.'

'Alexa is not a person so she does not count.'

'Does that mean I do not count?'

'Of course you count, just send her the bloody latitude and longitude already.'

'Sent.'

'Also close Satellite.'

'Done.'

Flying low across the coastline of the UK now, Steph tries to look for landmarks or places of interest but she just shakes her head.

The passenger drone continues inland but you still can't work out where you are as Steph keeps the satellite imaging closed.

Then in the distance you see a church that has six tiers that make up its steeple with a clock on its third tier.

'I have no idea where we are, Watchers, but I guess that is a good thing for Evelyn could be in real trouble, it's just as well I don't recognise that church.'

'The coordinates keep changing, Steph.'

'What do you mean they keep changing?'

'I believe that Tamara is mobile.'

'But she doesn't have an RV anymore so how is that possible?'

'She must have Evelyn's, I'll keep updating Alexa and make sure that she is not followed or this could get messy.'

'Do it.'

'One step ahead of you, Steph.'

Joining up with a motorway, the passenger drone taxis along and follows the road's every twist and turn from up high.

A convoy appears up ahead consisting of an RV out in front with a further two Showhaulers side by side behind it and a large juggernaut truck with a flat-bed trailer bringing up the rear.

A flare is trailing from the surface of the flat-bed with a green cloud of smoke.

'That is our destination, Steph.'

'What? We're expected to land on that trailer?'

'Yes Steph, I am afraid so.'

'Take us down then. Okay Watchers, I'll wager it's about to get serious from now on. I hope you're heavily invested in this programme because we have one fucked up situation awaiting us down there.'

Matching the speed and velocity of the juggernaut, Sybil pilots the drone-like helicopter and brings it down to land above the dying green smoke.

The speed of the travelling truck mixed with the smoke shrouds your vision as it envelops the drone on landing.

The wind roars across the passenger drone and it starts to slide across the surface.

'We have to leave now, Steph, or we will be swept off the trailer.'

'Can't you steady this bird?'

'No, Steph, you must get off now.'

Stowing the jammer and sliding the door open to jump out, Steph is met by the rush of wind and is blown backwards. Falling onto her back, she tries to grab on as the passenger drone is wrenched from the trailer and ends up crashing into the road behind, causing a pile-up of traffic in its wake.

Steph flips herself over and starts to crawl along the trailer until she reaches the truck's cabin.

You hear Steph's voice become muffled as the howling wind takes her breath away.

'Now what, Sybil?'

'The RVs have moved into single file, Steph, I think Tamara wants you to climb across them all until you reach Evelyn's Showhauler out in front.'

'Oh that's just fucking delicious, just how dangerous is that going to be?'

'Very.'

'Thanks for the vote of confidence.'

Steph begins to fight against the wind stream as she climbs up the back of the truck's cab; her hair is blowing across your vision and you notice that it is straggly and unkempt.

She pulls herself up the cab's guard grating and uses the rack that is used for chains and binders to climb over onto its roof.

Keeping low, Steph inches to the front of the cab and you see a white RV in front with a two-foot gap in between to the road below. The road is passing beneath you at a rapid pace and you realise the speed that the vehicles are travelling are well over the speed limit.

'You have to jump across, Steph.'

'Are you insane?'

'The RV's roof in front is level with your height, aim for the ladder if you're unsure but you should easily make it.'

Bringing herself onto her feet, Steph steadies herself against the battering winds and takes a leap of faith. She throws herself across the gap and easily clears it as she tries to keep her balance.

Tiny spatters of rain start to fall and you see the drops streak across the roof. Steph notices too and curses under her breath.

'Make your way across the roof, Steph, and the next RV will be waiting.'

'It's starting to get slippery.'

'Crawl if you have to.'

'Someone up there really doesn't like me, do they?'

Flattening herself against the roof and slowly inching along, Steph turns her head as the rain starts to fall harder and stings the side of her face.

A blue sign with white lettering flashes by above that reads: The NORTH, Leeds (M621) M1.

Two familiar black RVs appear from a slip road to join you, but Steph doesn't see them.

'Oh shit, now I know where we are, so too will the Watchers. That means I.R.I.S. will be here soon.'

'Sooner than you think, Steph, they have just appeared behind us. You have to get a move on.'

'Fuck no, not now. How the hell did they find us so soon?'

'The church you saw earlier, Steph, is a local landmark.'

'Of what?'

'The Holy Trinity Church of Leeds, it is unmistakable.'

'Why the fuck didn't you warn me?'

'If I had then I would have confirmed it for them, better they take the time working it out themselves. Hurry, Steph.'

'I'm fucking on it.'

Nearing the front of the RV, Steph sits up and shakily gets to her feet. The wind is causing the rain to sleet and makes the growing situation treacherous.

You see the juggernaut behind swerve out across two lanes to prevent the black RVs getting by, but one of them slips through and comes rearing up beside you and draws level with the Showhauler in front.

'No time to think, Steph, jump again.'

'Shiiiiit!'

The black RV sporting a deep metal scar rams the side of the Showhauler that Steph is leaping to and just as she is about to land, the Showhauler is knocked to the right, causing Steph to miss her landing and slide away to the edge of the roof.

Sparks of grinding metal on metal screech loudly across the rush of the wind as the two vehicles rub alongside one another before they eventually part.

Steph's legs swing wide of the vehicle as she desperately tries to hold on to whatever she can grab.

'Do something, Sybil.'

'Like what?'

'Anything.'

'Pairing with the road, Steph.'

'What? You can do that?'

'Yes.'

'Then be quick, the black RV is about to hit us again.'

'Forcing this segment of the lanes to close, Steph, you have to run and jump or Evelyn's RV will get away.'

Picking herself up, Steph races across the roof but slips and slides as she tries to stay onboard. The black RV swings back across the lane and careers into the side of the second white RV that Steph is on. She goes flying sideways and this time her upper torso ends up swinging across the side of the Showhauler, as her hands stretch out to frantically fight and push herself back up.

From her perspective of the side of the Showhauler, you see the word SCLERA on the side of the RV with an image of an eyeball that reminds you of the revolving statue back at SCLERA HQ.

With a lot of effort and grunts and groans, Steph pulls herself back and stands up again.

'This segment of the road's electrical circuit is about to end, Steph, you have to act fast.'

Steph starts to run again but Sybil has already shut down the segments of the road that the RV beneath her and the ones behind are on.

Evelyn's Showhauler continues on and the gap begins to grow as it drives across to the new segment leaving the RVs behind to slow to a halt.

Flinging herself at the mercy of the gods, Steph jumps from the front of the SCLERA RV and just makes it to Evelyn's RV's ladder at its rear with just one hand.

As she swings around in a contorted state, you see the black RVs along with SCLERA's and the juggernaut drifting away.

'That won't hold them for long, Steph, they will soon realise what has happened and engage manual drive.'

'We better wrap this clusterfuck up then.'

'I noticed that Evelyn's RV has a skylight on its roof, Steph, maybe that can be our way in.'

Twisting around and grabbing the rungs with both hands, Steph begins her climb up and makes her way over to the large window in the middle of the roof.

The rain is getting heavier and you can see that Steph is wet and freezing cold due to the goosebumps on her hands and wrists.

Sitting down, Steph starts to kick away at the glass until it shatters with the force of her boots upon it. Looking down to the hold inside you notice that it is the upper deck of the Showhauler where an office lies.

'Into the lion's den then.'

'Steph, be careful.'

'Just make sure you have my back.'

'Yes I will, that is a promise, Steph.'

'Engage Thermal.'

'Thermal engaged.'

The office is bathed in a swathe of cold dark blues and grey hues as Steph falls in from the opening above to crush the broken glass on the floor underfoot.

Running a hand through her hair to alleviate her windswept appearance, she starts to inspect the office.

A mahogany table with a recliner sits in the corner of the room and adorned on the walls around the office are family photos of the Hastingses on various trips from their vacations around the world.

Steph takes one off the wall and you see that it is a picture of Loch Lomond with the family in the foreground. In full attendance is Dom in his waders and fishing gear on the right, with his son in the middle wearing a baseball cap and tee shirt over shorts.

Steph runs a finger across the image of Evelyn on the left, who is wearing shorts and a summer vest that shows off her cleavage. She is wearing a floppy hat over a long lock of hair with curls and you can see that Evelyn has an hourglass figure as all her clothing is tight fitting.

'I'm coming for you Evelyn, hang in there.'

Two large filing cabinets sit at the other end of the room on the left and right of a sliding door. But as Steph approaches them and tries to pull on the cabinet's handles in turn, you realise that they are locked shut and the keys are nowhere to be seen.

Steph slides the door open and an adjacent room reveals itself, this new room is not quite what any of you were expecting though.

'There's a bloody operating theatre back here, Watchers.'

'Steph, I can see the operating table and the anaesthesia cart have been recently used.'

'Oh yeah, how so?'

'There are traces of blood still on the table and on some of the equipment.'

Steph saunters in to the room and touches an oxygen machine by the side of the table and then looks at the instruments laid out on a steel trolley nearby.

Looking around, you notice a pair of scrubs hanging next to a sink which you presume is a scrubbing area with containers on a shelving cabinet below.

Picking up some of the instruments, Steph notices dark streaks of dried blood still stained on some of the utensils.

'I see she works from home then?'

'Who's blood could it be, Steph? And why have the instruments not been sterilised after use? Could it have been used for your procedure?'

'Fucked if I know, but I'm sure we will find out soon enough. Let's pray it's not Evelyn's blood and we are not too late.'

'There's a stairwell over there, Steph, let's go downstairs quietly shall we?'

'We are expected, so we don't have to sneak around.'

A handrail sits in the far right of the room and you see stairs leading down into the dark. Steph gets Sybil to switch from Thermal to Flashlight and you see the stairwell light up, showing the curve. You see the steps disappear off round a corner.

Using the handrails, Steph winds her way downstairs and comes out into a wide passageway that is well lit.

'Turn off Flashlight.'

'At least it had a use.'

'For all of ten seconds, now where the fuck is that crazy bitch?'

Walking tentatively down the passageway, Steph checks out each of the rooms that branch off but there is no sign of life. Pushing on and clearly getting frustrated, Steph turns the corner and you are faced with a dire predicament.

There with a noose around her neck and standing over the hatch door to the vehicle's garage storage hold below, is Evelyn Hastings.

'I admire your tenacity, Miss Coulson, especially the way you dispatched those RVs belonging to I.R.I.S.'

Tamara Pike appears behind Evelyn and has a hand hovering over the push button on the wall that calls up the elevator containing the vehicle below.

'Let her go, she has done nothing to you.'

'Not to me, but to you she has done plenty. Please hand over your jammer that is inside your jacket, or I will push this button.'

'You are a paranoid and unstable individual, you know that, right?'

Steph takes a foot forward but Tamara produces a knife and places it to Evelyn's neck.

'Tut-tut, Miss Coulson. Hand over the jammer if you will? I will not repeat myself.'

'Okay, whatever. I'm so sorry Evelyn... for everything.'

Steph pulls the cylindrical device from her pocket and throws it to the feet of Tamara who stomps her foot upon it and grinds it into the ground with the heel of her stiletto.

'Now we are on an even playing field.'

'What can I do for you, Tamara?'

'It's not what you can do for me but what I can do for you, Stephanie.'

'Yeah, what's that then?'

'I can get Evelyn here to explain why she took your kidney.'

'That's bullshit and you know it. You need to explain why you killed her husband first, you mad old bint.'

Evelyn starts to shake uncontrollably and you see tears running down the cheeks of her dark complexion.

'Oh dear, Miss Coulson. You seem to have given poor Evelyn some unexpected bad news, how callous of you.'

'I, I didn't mean to say that out loud.'

'It's alright Evelyn, Steph is referring to the boating incident. There have been no further developments that followed, that I am aware of.'

'What are you talking about, you psycho?'

'It matters not, Miss Coulson, for what Evelyn is about to tell you in her own words, will come as a refreshing development for you I'm sure.'

'She is under duress, she will tell you anything at this stage.'

'Granted, I have indeed removed the elevator below Evelyn's feet and rigged this hatch to drop on the push of this button. But to send poor old Evelyn swinging to her death without an explanation to you, would not be prudent of me to at least get a clear message over to you under duress or not.'

'How can I be sure that she is going to tell me the truth?'

'You said that the world would be a better place if we brought back hanging, Miss Coulson, and I am not one to disappoint. Evelyn knows that if she lies then I will drop her and if she tells the truth then you will drop her, either way you get your answer.'

'So you think that I will allow her to die?'

'When you find out the extent of her involvement you will.'

'I won't do that, Evelyn, I promise.'

The knot is tight around Evelyn's neck and as she speaks, she sounds hoarse and tense.

'I'm sorry, Stephanie.'

'I'm the one to apologise as I feel responsible for Dom's death, you see I went to find him in Loch Lomond and—'

'Enough of this sentimentality, just tell her already, Mrs Hastings. Time is of the essence as I have a plane to catch.'

You feel the Showhauler come to a stop and realise that your destination has been reached.

'The interceptor that you destroyed with an EMP grenade was unexpected and my dearest Dom did not take that into account.'

'I don't follow.'

'The interceptor's blades sliced into his sides and ruptured both his kidneys.'

'What are you saying? Tamara tied him to the boat.'

'No, he staged the whole thing to expose the case to you, but the police weren't supposed to be there.'

'Why would he do that?'

'When the boat sank, we had to act quickly and pull him from the depths of the loch. I thought I had lost him but thankfully he was still alive, although barely.'

'But that's impossible.'

'When we rescued him, I administered a dose of nanobots into his bloodstream to stabilise him, but I knew it would not be enough. The damage was irreparable unless we found a donor, I have the facilities upstairs. It's where I...'

Steph looks down and rubs the scarring beneath her overalls where the kidney was removed.

I.R.I.S.

'Are you saying that Dom is alive? What about his eye? It was missing from his socket.'

'A digital programme to trick your mind into believing that what you're seeing is real, when in actual fact it is not, Miss Coulson, surely you worked that out already.'

'I didn't ask you, Tamara. Now release her as I want more answers.'

'Steph, the black RVs are approaching.'

'Sorry what? Did you just say that the black RVs are coming, Sybil?'

'Yes, Steph.'

'No, they are here to silence me. I will not let them.'

Before Steph can reply or calm Tamara down, the button to the hatch is pushed and rivets holding it in place into the frame, explode. Watching on in horror, you see the hatch drop through the hole and Evelyn follow through after it.

The rope pulls taught and the knot tightens as Evelyn comes to the end of the rope's slack that is secured from a makeshift pulley from the roof of the RV.

'No, you fucking murderer.'

Tamara comes at you with knife in hand but Sybil is prepared; she turns on the flashlight that strobes a bright, white light into Tamara's eyes, momentarily blinding her. She drops the knife and dashes past Steph to the rear of the RV to escape.

Steph retrieves the blade and starts to sever the rope but the weight on the end, along with the thickness of the rope, is proving to be hard work to slice through, as Evelyn's body swings wildly around.

At last the rope becomes frayed and Evelyn's body falls to the ground beneath the RV as the rope's final thread splits. Steph quickly drops through behind her with no regard for her own safety and cradles her in her arms as she tries to remove the knot from Evelyn's bulging neck.

'Fuck, fuck, Sybil. Where are we?'

'Turning on Satellite Feed. Location is Leeds, Southside Aviation Centre.'

'What do we know about it?'

'It is privately owned. I have researched that Tamara owns a hanger here with a private jet.'

'Shit, have you got her on the map?'

'Yes Steph, she is boarding the plane now.'

'Where the fuck are the black RVs?'

'They are approaching the airfield now.'

'Will she live?'

'If I.R.I.S. apprehend her she won't.'

'Not Tamara, I'm talking about Evelyn.'

'I can't say.'

The black RVs screech to a halt and you see a team of black-clad soldiers with balaclavas exit one of the vehicles on the birds eye view of the satellite's map.

As Steph drags Evelyn out from underneath the RV into the open, Steph lays her down and checks for a pulse as she still tries to free the noose from her neck.

Oblivious to the approaching soldiers, Steph then starts resuscitation as the second black RV sends a swarm of familiar drones to the sky.

Safely on board the jet that sits just outside a hanger with the name SCLERA above it, Tamara appears at the window and looks mortified.

'Come on Evelyn, don't you fucking die on me. I need you tell me what possessed you to take my kidney and Dom's gain in all of this.'

'Look out, Steph.'

'Huh?'

One of the soldiers grabs Steph from behind and yanks her backwards with such force that he dislocates her shoulder.

Steph yells in surprise and agony, as she is strewn across the tarmac, The soldier along with another colleague then lifts Evelyn up and carries her away to the nearby waiting RV.

The jet coasts down the runway and begins to throttle its engines

I.R.I.S.

as it starts to accelerate down the tarmac.

Steph, sitting there with a hand to her shoulder watches on helplessly as behind her Evelyn is bundled into an RV which then closes its sliding door and speeds off with the other RV in close pursuit.

'Where's Alexa?'

'She will be here shortly, Steph.'

'I hope so.'

'We must get away from here, Steph.'

'What the fuck is happening right now?'

'Hurry, we must leave.'

Steph gets up and starts to move, keeping an eye on the jet as it takes off the runway and starts to circle around to line up its flight path.

The swarm of military drones anticipating its route head it off and converge onto its thrusters.

Wide eyed in terror, you watch with Steph, as the drones aim for the engines and get sucked in by the propellers. An explosion rips through the sky as the engines stall and then engulf in flames as the drones are torn apart inside.

The plane nosedives out of control over the horizon and you wait for the inevitable to happen.

A flash of light, a large explosion, a billowing of black smoke. You know that Tamara Pike is well and truly dead as the plane disintegrates and steals her soul along with the pilot's.

'We need to end this. If you're out there Dom, know this, I'm coming for you and bringing with me a world of hurt, just for you. I.R.I.S. is dead to me.'

XXIII

'Steph, it's urgent. We must leave as your recreational vehicle is still too far away.'

'Where?'

'I have found us suitable accommodation but we must hurry, the authorities and emergency services will soon arrive. We are in a hot zone right now.'

'Just point and click.'

'Head to the end of the runway, you will see a perimeter fence that we must pass to get to the A658 on the other side.'

The rain is falling heavier now and Steph, in pain with a dislocated shoulder, begins to trek across the runway to the high wire fence in the distance.

'Hurry, Steph.'

Breaking into a jog and gripping her shoulder with her good arm, a wet and bedraggled Steph clears the tarmac and stalls at the fence looking for a way forward.

You see the busy road beyond and further still on the other side of the road you spot a large lake.

'I see no opening.'

'I will create one. Do you see the floodlight to your right about ten yards from the fence?'

'Yes.'

'I need you to go up to it and turn away from the fence to place your bad shoulder against the post.'

'I don't get what that has to do with getting out of here.'

'You will. Do you trust me?'

'I don't know who to trust or what to believe anymore.'

'Please Steph, follow my instructions. When you have done that, I ask that you don't move no matter what.'

'Fine.'

Walking up to the post, Steph turns away from the fence and back to the hangers from which she came and pushes herself up against the post.

Wincing and in pain as she rests against the cold steel of the pole, Steph looks over her shoulder and you see flashing lights and hear the sound of sirens fast approaching.

'Now what?'

'Move a little to the left, a bit more, that's it. Now we wait.'

'Can we please get this over with, Sybil? This rain is freezing and I hurt like hell.'

'Patience, Steph.'

'All out.'

'Not long now until the A658 gifts me what I need.'

'Huh?'

Still looking over her shoulder, you see a line of emergency vehicles pass along the A658 on the other side of the fence and then a random RV speeds up behind them, which then breaks off and hurtles towards the boundary in your direction.

'What the fuck are you doing, Sybil?'

'You will see. Now stay still.'

'Why didn't the anti-drone busters scattered around this airfield destroy that flock of drones?'

'I.R.I.S.'s RVs jammed their signals, Steph, now shh.'

'I'll shh you in a minute.'

The speeding RV from the A658 suddenly detours from the road and ploughs into the high wire, perimeter fence to the airfield. It buckles under the force and tears apart as the RV breaks through and heads straight for you.

Steph braces herself for impact and squints her eyes, blocking out your vision.

You hear the RV abruptly stop just as Steph opens her eyes again to see it is barely an inch away from pinning you against the pole.

'What the fuck, Sybil?'

'Brace yourself.'

'Sorry, what?'

The RV lurches forward the remainder of the inch gap and its grill forces Steph's shoulder to pop back into its socket, as it pushes her shoulder into the post.

Screaming in agony and crying in pain, Steph slides down the pole and begins to shout obscenities towards Sybil as the RV then reverses away to tangle its wheels up in the twisted fencing that lays crumpled on the ground.

'Now Steph, through the opening you go and off to the lake. You must hurry.'

'I hate you.'

'You don't mean that.'

'Are the occupants safe in that RV?'

'They are. Now once you get to the lake, you will see a village on the other side. Head through the village and on to the church behind the houses.'

'What if I arouse suspicion?'

'They will be more concerned with what's happening here then there, now move before the passengers of the RV realise what is happening.'

Steeling herself across the road looking for a safe path to cross and avoiding oncoming traffic, Steph comes to the lake and navigates around, heading for the village.

'What is this lake?'

'The Yeadon Tarn, Steph, don't dawdle.'

You see a cluster of houses made from mud with thatched roofs and notice smoke rising from their chimneys. Steph slows down to a steady brisk walk as you hear her puffing and panting; she cranes her neck to look past the houses to the church that awaits.

You pass by people milling around and see farmers toiling in the fields in the distance.

'I don't like this, Sybil.'

'Just smile and nod, Steph, you will be fine.'

Eventually you reach the church and your journey through the village has not raised any suspicion whatsoever.

The church is resting on a slanted hill and has a mixture of dark charcoal-coloured bricks mixed with sandstone, that rise up to a bell-shaped tower housed in glass. Two pitched roofs greet you as a new extension has been added on over the years to the front of the existing church and you spy a large arched wooden door set into the new structure.

'My arm is hurting like a motherfucker, where's Alexa?'

'On her way, now get inside quick.'

'I can't handle people right now, Sybil.'

'Switching on Thermal. I don't see anyone inside, Steph, switching off. Are you happy now?'

Pushing open the heavy and cumbersome arched door, Steph steps inside and you are greeted to a large hall with magnolia painted walls upon three large arches on either side of the building. Rows of pews leading up to two large arched windows sit at the far end and off to the right, with a cross with Jesus nestled in between them.

Steph drags herself down the aisle and takes a seat and you hear the rain outside causing the acoustics to reverberate around the hall.

'Why do I feel so low, Sybil? Tamara and Evelyn were both innocents in all of this, so how did this happen?'

'Tamara made a deal with the Devil, Steph, and she paid the ultimate price.'

'I don't believe that Evelyn was guilty though. She may have taken my kidney but it was to save her husband, I would have done the same.'

'Like you, Steph, she was guilty. Guilty by association.'

'What is this church?'

'Did you not see the sign, Steph? It is the New Life Community Church.'

'What religion do they preach here?'

'Christianity.'

Steph stands up and approaches the altar that rests below the two large windows over the chancel. She picks up a box of matches nearby and lights one of the many candles in a candelabra that has dried wax running down its stem.

Stepping back and kneeling down, Steph clasps her hands in prayer and closes her eyes.

'God, I need a miracle right now.'

'Steph, you named me after a prophetess who interprets the wish of God. I'm afraid that I don't know how to grant one of those right now.'

'What's your stance on God, Sybil?'

'Tamara was my God, my creator. She had flaws, Steph, just like your God does, if that is what you now believe.'

'I believe I have consciousness, Sybil, just like you.'

'Like me?'

'Sure. Server 21 is where your consciousness is stored, my body is my server. It's what gives us life.'

'Consciousness is soul, Steph?'

'To me it is but others may not share my views, Sybil.'

'If my server is shut down, will my soul be lost?'

'If it is like my aging body, then I suppose so.'

'Where does it then go?'

'For you, a transfer to another server perhaps. For me it's heaven if it exists.'

'What if they are one and the same?'

'Then I will see you there, Sybil.'

'I would like that.'

'Me too.'

Steph stands up and walks back up the aisle, rubbing her shoulder.

'Are the other servers at the oil rig storage for more A.I. like you? Or are they storage for your existence entirely, I wonder.'

'They could be storage of data for the roll-out of phase three, Steph, a facility like that would definitely be the place to harvest data for the masses lens storage.'

'That's what I'm afraid of. I had a case a while back when phase two rolled out concerning a young woman who had a lens fitted, she became a ridicule to trolls, very similar to the Watchers we have now, when it was in its infancy stage. Rather than select businesses, it was shared with the public who taunted her through the lens, sending hateful text messages to her HUD because she was different.'

'Did she have a dedicated server to store her information on?'

'Yes she did. She believed that she could transfer her soul to the server if she ever died and when technology had caught up to give her an android body, she could then be transferred from the server to the android to live for ever.'

'I'm presuming she did not get her wish, Steph.'

'No, she was bullied to the point that she committed suicide and the server was shut down. The choice was never hers in the first place, I doubt it was ever possible anyway, we are not digital imprints like you.'

'Who shut down the server?'

'Who do you think?'

'So the only way for a human to keep their soul alive is through repopulation.'

'That is why I will fight this trial to keep my baby alive, it's the one thing that keeps me motivated, Sybil.'

'Alexa has arrived, Steph.'

'About fucking time.'

Steph exits the church and you see her RV waiting right outside.

Without hesitation she approaches her home and proceeds to drop the hatch and make her way inside.

You hear the rain pelting the steel roof above as she heads straight for her kitbag and unzips it. Looking inside the bag, you notice a plethora of strange objects and devices that Steph has used over the years and your eyes settle on a small yellow tank with breathing apparatus attached to a mouth piece.

Rooting around and pushing the tank aside, Steph quickly locates the eye extractor and pulls it free from the compartment it is in.

Extractor in hand, Steph briskly returns to the church and takes a pew.

'What are you doing, Steph?'

'Ending this fucking trial.'

Bringing the eye extractor up to her eye that contains the lens that allows you sight into her world, Steph brings it in close so you can see the sharp steel scoop.

'Don't do this, Steph.'

'Piss off.'

'But what will happen to me?'

'Limbo in a server until I figure out a way to bring you back into the world.'

'Why?'

'It's the only way.'

'Please Steph, stop. You're worrying me.'

Steph's finger hovers over the trigger and her hand starts to shake. She readies herself to thrust the gun deep into her socket and tears cloud your vision.

'I have found a verse from the bible, Deuteronomy 7:19.'

'Save it, Sybil, I'm not interested.'

The extractor starts to shake uncontrollably and Steph brings up her other hand to steady the shaking.

'The great trials that your eyes saw, the signs, the wonders, the mighty hand and the outstretched arm by which the Lord, your God brought you out. So will the Lord, your God do all the peoples of whom you are afraid.'

You look down the barrel of the extractor and see the dark dried blood, staining the sharp metal scoop. Steph's hands begin to waiver as her trigger finger turns white.

'Incoming call, Steph.'

'What?'

'Jack Mintlyn is trying to reach you, maybe he will change your mind.'

'Just answer the damn call.'

'I'm not happy with you, Steph, but I will do as you request, just don't do anything stupid. I won't talk to you until you wake up and see sense.'

'Touchy.'

The eye extractor is lowered.

'Jack, Jack is that you?'

'Hi Steph, the one and only.'

'My god, I've never been happier to hear your voice.'

'Love me or hate me, you can't get rid of me that easy.'

Steph is shaking still as she places the extractor onto the hard wooden pew beside her. Her voice echoes around the hall so she starts to talk quieter.

'How are you feeling, Jack?'

'I've felt better but at least I'm not going to die. I suppose I have you to thank for that,, Steph. You better not have sacrificed our unborn child to save me though.'

'I did what I had to, so how's things with Tilly and Tiffany?'

'Please don't skirt the issue, Steph. Ask Sybil if our baby is okay? I need reassurance.'

'She won't answer me right now.'

'Had an argument, have you? I wondered how long it would take before you didn't see eye to eye.'

'Our baby is fine, Jack, and that's all you need to know right now.'

'I have thought of a few names for our daughter, it's surprising how a brush with death puts things into perspective. I'm really looking forward to being a dad.'

'Jack, stop. When the trial is over then we can plan for our future.'

'Oh yeah, the trial. So how's that coming along?'

'I'm close to ending this right now, before you called actually.'

'Well that's brilliant news, you know my feelings on it, so it will be nice to have my old Steph back. You thought on how you're going to remove your lens? Because if not, then I can tell you that Tilly has done a great job removing Tiffany's lens and swapping it over to a regular one.'

'She's removed Tiff's A.I.?'

'Yes she has, but it's not been without its problems. You want me to pass you over to Tilly so she can fill you in?'

'Sure. I've missed you, Jack.'

'I love you too, even though you infuriate me sometimes.'

'You heard me then?'

'Passing you over now.'

Sunlight begins to stream in through the windows at the far end of the church and you sense that Steph's mood has lifted.

Whilst she waits for Tilly to speak, Steph picks up the extractor and puts it in her overall pocket as she makes her way into the light.

'Hi Steph.'

'Hello Tilly, so is Jack really okay? Or is he feeding me bullshit?'

'No, he is doing well. He has a nasty scar across his leg and is using a crutch to get around but I'm hopeful.'

'Good, so Jack tells me that you removed Tiff's lens?'

'It was heartbreaking, Steph.'

'How so?'

'To her it was like I was murdering her best friend Daisy when I removed her lens.'

'You had to remove her A.I. so that she can have her childhood back.'

'I think it's too late for that. The Sanctuary robbed her of her innocence a long time ago and now I'm trying to do what's right by doing wrong.'

'We are all guilty of being dependent on our devices. Tilly, I'm no different.'

'She won't speak to me now, I'm cruel and heartless apparently.'

'You're being a mother by throwing down tough love, don't be so hard on yourself, you're a great mother. Better than me, it seems.'

'I have uncovered something quite disturbing, Steph.'

'What's that?'

'I noticed the damage to her eye was very severe when I removed the lens to replace it. I wanted to understand why, so I used Jack's laboratory to delve into it a bit further and study the phase two lens in depth after I removed it.'

'That sounds concerning. So I'm guessing you found the cause?'

'I did. I found a high density of blue light had been burning into her retina from the lens, causing macular degeneration.'

'I thought that the lenses were designed to aid eyesight, not to have an adverse effect.'

'The technology within does, but the blue light that generates it, however, is way too high, it's almost like it is deliberate.'

'Explain.'

'Well, we are surrounded by blue light, it occurs naturally within sunlight and decreases in percentage as the day drags on, ending the wavelength's cycle. With artificial blue light, the wavelengths don't end and so continue to cause long exposure to the sensitive light cells of our eyes. They penetrate the lining at the back of the eye with constant bombardment.'

'So sunlight that has blue light is enough to contend with during the day, but artificial blue light from the lens is constantly exposing and aging the eyes with continued use?'

'Correct.'

Steph puts a hand up into the shaft of sunlight that pours through the window and you see dust particles swirl around. She turns her hand back and forth, creating strobing shadows from her fingers.

'And you say that the phase two lenses generate too much blue light which is harmful in ways that speed up poor sight.'

'The more your eyes become reliant on something like a lens to see, the harder it is to function properly, until at last you need to have another operation or...'

'...An updated lens fitted that is the next big thing. One that will cost you hundreds of chits to have grafted.'

'Nothing is built to last because companies want you to upgrade to their next revolution.'

'Operation Blue Light. I.R.I.S. is literally blinding people to the truth.'

'What's operation Blue Light?'

'So what else did you find?'

'My findings end there unfortunately, there is however one more thing.'

'Which is?'

'I was watching a live news bulletin earlier through the holo deck and came across an article that might be of interest to you.'

'Go on.'

'It would seem that I.R.I.S. has promised free prescriptions to everyone to have their phase two lenses installed.'

'You're fucking shitting me?'

'We have our sights on your vision for the future.'

'Bastards. They're going to get everyone hooked on phase two free of charge and stiff them for phase three upgrade by charging the earth when phase two eventually damages their eyes.'

'Like drug dealers.'

'Yes, but for the digital age. Operation Blue Light is in full effect, we have to stop this. Sybil, send word to Alexa, we are going to I.R.I.S. right fucking now.'

'Now you're thinking straight, Steph.'

'Yes Sybil, now get to it.'

'Would you like me to pass Jack back over, Steph, as he is trying to mouth something to me.'

'Sure, put him back on.'

'Okay, goodbye.'

'Steph, one thing before you go.'

'What is it, Jack?'

'Your rotting eye in the freezer box.'

'What of it?'

'I've cleared it out of there and stored it in one of my drones to send to you, I need your coordinates.'

'I'll get Sybil to send them to you but I can't think why the eye bothers you.'

'Because it's freaking me out. Every time I go in there for food and see it watching me, I am reminded of that child molester.'

'I have my home back now, Jack, so it's fine. Thanks for storing it for me.'

'One more thing.'

'Yup.'

'I have created an E-card for you, sending over now. I love you, Steph.'

'I...'

'Call ended, Steph. Bringing up E-card.'

A digital card appears in your HUD and on the front it reads: *To the best Mummy to be, in the world.* The card opens up and inside is a personalised message from Jack, it reads: *I truly am grateful for the hard times and the good that we have shared together as it has made me a better person. I will not let you down to be the father of our child that you deserve. Yours, Jack x*

Tears begin to form in the corner of Steph's eye again and you hear her sniffling as she turns and makes her way to Alexa who now has the RV running.

'I'm sorry for earlier, Steph.'

'That's fine, Sybil. Apology accepted.'

'There is something that you should know.'

'Can't it wait until I'm showered and changed?'

'There was a reason that Tamara did not use her Latin tongue to send a command to your nanobots to attack your baby.'

'Oh yeah, why is that then?'

'I have to inform you that it is because baby has died, Steph.'

'Power Off.'

XXIV

'Power On as requested, Steph.'

'Remove picture overlay in HUD and present images side by side in split screen.'

'Confirmed. Your vision is in the left and your drone image is in the right.'

'I can't see anyone around at the moment, so I'm guessing we are good to go, Sybil.'

'There are a group of joggers in the far distance headed this way but we should be alright for the time being.'

'Right then, combine selected options from HUD as discussed earlier and project real live feed through pairing.'

'Selecting Torchlight, Thermal, Night Vision, Image Replicator, Radio and X-ray to combine for 3D visual and audio render. Activating now.'

'Are you clear on what needs to be done, Sybil?'

'Yes, Steph.'

'Will this work?'

'Only in the dark, we may have to take out the light source first but I would argue against it.'

'Why?'

'Because these lamps have stood here for hundreds of years, designed by a man named Vuillamy who—'

'Just do it.'

'But—'

'Now.'

'Piloting drone to promenade lamps.'

'Okay my faithful audience, let's kick this shit storm off shall we?'

Viewing through Steph's HUD, you take in first the left window and see flagstone paving running off to the distance with wrought iron benches evenly spread along the pathway. Steph's RV is parked askew alongside the embankment and behind it you see a bench that depicts a sphinx on both sides of the seating area that is mounted on two plinths and creating steps up to the bench. The benches overlook a low wall to the River Thames beyond.

A row of lamp posts that each depict a dolphin that are stylised into their poles, reach up into a corkscrew with their tails to a split globe of clear glass cradled into four curved wrought iron arms. The top section of the split globe rests a half dome of white glass that covers a concealed lamp. All are topped off with a golden crown as a cap.

You see the Thames is in darkness and notice that strong winds are creating waves across its mirror-like surface, reflecting the luminescence of the lamps giving them a ghostly, rippling effect. Barges and other seafaring crafts quietly sail to and fro up and down the river and you hear Steph sigh.

'This is where it all ends then? I thought I had turned a corner and finally found faith but since you informed me that I lost my baby, I feel that my resolve in God is swiftly ebbing away.'

As Steph turns away from the river, you take in the towering building of I.R.I.S. HQ nestled between a row of other business units used for various company's needs and see that it is situated on the south bank side behind a row of plane trees.

'Hurry up, Sybil, we don't have much time before they show.'

'These lamps have been erected here since 1870, Steph, Vuillamy will be turning in his grave if he knew what I was about to do.'

'I don't give a shit. Do it or I will be shortly joining him.'

Observing through the right window on Steph's HUD now, you see what the drone is doing and watch as it flies up to each lamp, smashing into the globe to demolish the bulb inside the housing before taking off to shatter the next.

With six lamps in a line destroyed, you see the drone return to Steph and watch it hover in front of her HUD view in the left window. You notice the drone is holding something between its claws but the image is obscured with a pixelated washout.

In the right window you see that Steph is now wearing a tailored grey suit with a dark blue silk neckerchief tied loose around her neck, and a small empty Perspex box on a chain swinging just below.

On closer inspection as you scan her appearance, you notice that she has the eye extractor stashed in her left pocket and it is poking out from beneath the pocket's flap.

Also beneath her suit jacket is a bulge that is clearly concealing something but you cannot work out what it is.

'Are you up for this, Steph?'

'What do you think?'

Heavy black mascara around her eyes gives you the impression that she has been crying and now you see a vacant look where optimism and joy once were.

Steph curls her hair away from her left ear and you see that she is wearing a wireless earpiece.

'Is the environment dark enough for you now, Sybil?'

'Yes, Steph.'

'When I give the word, show third-person view.'

'Understood.'

'Now close the left window in my HUD and enlarge the right window.'

The view of the drone fades away and your window through Steph's eye is no more. The view through the drone showing Steph blacks out then expands to fill the void and you are now dependent on the drone's sight of the world around you.

'Okay, light me up Sybil.'

Steph appears again before you through the sight of Jack's drone but you can only see her from above her shoulders and behind her head.

'I have you in sight and I am now locked on to track you, Steph.'

Steph looks over her shoulder and gives you a wink before turning to face the I.R.I.S. building; you view the fifty levels of the skyrise in front of her with its mirrored rows of windows that align each floor and you notice that the top two floors are well lit along with the ground floor only. All other floors in between are in darkness.

Then you spot torch beams shining through the trees and hear a trampling of boots heading your way.

'Game on. Sybil, whatever you do, keep away from the torch beams.'

'I will make sure they do not light us up, Steph.'

Five I.R.I.S. security guards dressed in black combat gear appear from the tree line and flick out their wrists to extend their telescopic batons in their hands and you see that they have shoulder-mounted torchlights switched on.

They fan out and push forward towards Steph as she backs away down the promenade.

One of the security guards steps forwards and you see that he towers above the others and is built with large muscles beneath his uniform.

He goes to speak when a small gathering of joggers passes between you and give a wary look as they continue on their way.

'We are here to detain you, Miss Coulson, we would like you to surrender your belongings and assist us in bringing this mercy mission of yours to a close. Now I understand that you have many questions that you would like answers to but force is not the way to get them.'

'Fuck off, Bub.'

All the guards look at each other and smiles appear on their faces as they swipe the air with their batons. A thin and shorter guard steps out from behind the guard known as Bub and points his baton towards you. He gives the small crowd of joggers who have slowed down a cautious look and then starts to talk in hushed tones.

'You don't have an army of drones at your disposal, Steph, nor do you have the strength to take us all on. I suggest that you drop this façade or risk us breaking your mind, spirit and body.'

'Do you have any idea what I've been through, Ralph?'

'We hear rumours but we are not privy to your trial, Steph. We have a job to do and we follow our orders to the letter, it's a shame that you don't carry out your own job properly or we wouldn't need to be here.'

'But here you are.'

The security detail form a line and keep pushing forward.

'Don't make this harder on yourself. Since lockdown was initiated, none of us have had the opportunity to go home and we are not in the mood for any of your antics, Miss Coulson.'

'That's typical of dumb fucks like you, Bub, you were never very smart were you? Alexa, engage targets.'

The parked RV roars into life and comes tearing up behind the security guards who are slow to act. As they turn back to face the RV, Alexa drives the Toterhome at full throttle towards them and locks the wheels to slide the chassis outwards.

The burly guard along with two others dive out of the way in time but the other two are struck head on as they are bowled over.

'You haven't hurt them, have you Alexa?'

'No Steph, they may have broken bones and sore heads though.'

'Good, because I don't wish them harm. Now Alexa, get out of here and return to Jack.'

'Okay, Steph.'

Steph flips the guards the middle finger and starts to race off with the drone following her close by overhead.

Alexa, in full auto, takes reverse gear of the RV and drives off into the night.

The joggers who have heard the commotion stop in their tracks and look back with horror on their faces at what they have just witnessed.

'It's another terrorist attack.'

Recovering quickly, the largest guard commands his two fellow officers to give chase and they all follow his lead. Steph looks over her shoulder and you can see that they are pissed.

Steph passes by the last two of the smashed lamps as the guards close the gap and with the guards hot on her heels she races to the crowd of horrified runners who step back in alarm.

'We are running out of darkened spaces, Steph.'

'Well fly ahead and smash some more lamps then.'

'You must be in now, Steph.'

'I am but I have a problem, keep going. I will tell you when I'm clear.'

'But the security officers are gaining.'

'Speed up the drone then.'

'I can't if I'm to maintain the illusion, you could never run that fast.'

'Fucking cheek.'

Sybil flies the drone past the last of the blacked-out lamps and heads towards the next lamp in the run that is bathing the joggers in its golden glow. She takes out the bulb and swings the drone away.

The joggers duck beneath the shower of glass just as the guards approach and one of the joggers realising the damage that is being done, picks up a stone and throws it at the drone but misses the mark.

'Mindless vandalism, do you realise the history you're destroying here?'

'Sorry, I was forced to act by my uncultured master.'

'Piss off, Sybil, I'm well aware of how you feel.'

The jogger throws another stone and this time the projectile hits the hard-bodied shell and knocks the drone sideways, just as Steph is passing below and the drone is about to take out the bulb encased in its housing above.

Without darkness to portray a near perfect image of Steph, the holo version of her becomes transparent and the pursuing guards realise they have been duped and lured away from I.R.I.S.

'We have been rumbled, Steph.'

'Bollocks, well at least using a combination of the HUD's options allowed us to create a distraction to buy us some time. Nice work using the torchlight to beam an animated image of me in front of Jack's drone.'

'It was your idea to use Olivia's lens for me to pair with and share my functionality, Steph. To attach her eye to Jack's drone was pure genius for a human.'

'Stop it, you're embarrassing me. The animated version of me was your idea.'

'The guards are now on their way back.'

'I'm clear. Send Jack's drone to floor fifty, I may need it when I get there.'

'Would you like me to return vision to your lens now, Steph, and shut this image down?'

'No, bring up split screen again. I want an external view of floor fifty if you can give me the live intel on arrival.'

'Will let you know when I do. How are you going to get up there?'

'Dom knows that I'm not far off now so I guess it doesn't matter anymore, I'm going to take the skylift up.'

Returning to the split screen in the HUD, you see the drone taking off to the night sky in the right window and watch as it struggles against the prevailing winds as it climbs higher and higher.

On return of the left window, you see that Steph has rendered a guard unconscious in the welcoming lobby of I.R.I.S. HQ and note that she has passed through a security barrier that is sounding off an alarm with a flashing light.

'Misdirection is a motherfucker, Dom, isn't it?'

'I had my doubts that it would work, Steph.'

'Guess I don't need my earpiece anymore.'

Steph pulls the device from her ear and discards it on to the floor.

'How did you get by this security guard at your feet, Steph?'

'Tammy? Oh, that was easy. We had a fling once when Jack and I were going through a rough patch. I broke it off when Jack made it up to me and she has been trying to win me back ever since.'

'That does not explain how you rendered her unconscious.'

'I merely came onto her and showed her my breasts, she couldn't resist. When she came in close for a fondle and a kiss, I koshed her over the head with the eye extractor.'

'She didn't expect a ploy?'

'No, lust scrambles your reasoning I guess. She probably thought that she could have some fun with me before I came quietly.'

'You used sex as a weapon?'

'Since I started this trial, I have awoken each day and wondered how I am perceived to be in others eyes. By the end of the day though when I reflect back, I realise I have presented my best self but never my true.'

'How are they perceiving you through their eyes now, Steph, I wonder?'

'The Watchers? Knowing that what they see through my lens is really just that, an illusion, I would guess that whatever I project onto the world now will be enough to make me totally unpredictable and get them to question my true motives. Don't you think?'

'Like Tammy, they have no idea, do they?'

'That's what now gives me the advantage over this damn trial.'

A large open lobby with green marble flooring ingrained with gold flecks, spans out before you and leads off to a stairwell to the right that disappears up and around a corner.

To the front of you and sitting directly in the middle of the lobby lies an eight-foot-high, smoked glass, open-topped, panelled box. A mesh barrier with warning signs tied to it, surrounds the box with a post just in front with a metal push button set on its face.

'The skylift, I can't believe it's come to this. My final journey awaits beyond that glass box.'

'Are you afraid, Steph?'

'Of that skylift? Who do you think I am? Dillon Fletcher. I've ridden passenger drones.'

'Not of the lift, Steph, but what awaits you up there on floor fifty.'

'What's the worst that could happen?'

'You could be killed.'

'I'm not afraid of dying but how I die, that bothers me.'

'But what will become of me?'

'Same as what happened to Olivia's A.I., I suppose.'

'She was in limbo before you made me pair with her out on the promenade. She was not happy that I wished to erase her and take over her functionality.'

'I figured that might be the case. I won't let her fate become yours, I promise.'

'I will hold you to that.'

Looking up, you see a tier of gloss white balconies that surround you on all four sides and you catch a glimpse of offices behind them, screened by floor-to-ceiling glass windows on each level, all in darkness.

As your vision narrows to the uppermost floors you can just barely make out two square bands of bright light that signal floors forty-nine and fifty are in use. Above the final two floors rests a glass enclosed roof that is showing you the stars of the night sky outside.

'Do we take the stairs to the right, Steph?'

'That only takes us up to floor two, there are conventional lifts and more stairs leading up from there to the remaining floors but they will only allow us access to floor forty-eight. If you want to go higher, then you must take the skylift from the ground floor only and that's on the assumption that you have the access code or you are summoned with an escort.'

'As Dillon described earlier.'

'Yes, it is Dom's playful way to unnerve you before reaching the board's offices on level forty-nine or his office on fifty. I don't know of anyone that has ever been to floor fifty before though and Dom never discussed what is there.'

'So you require me to hack the skylift then?'

'I certainly do, Sybil, the sooner we ride that beast to ascension, the better. Those grunts can't be too far behind.'

'Acquiring schematics, starting hack.'

'There the monster awaits us hiding behind his glass of deception. Will he be friend or will he be foe?'

'We will tame the beast or he will claim your soul, Steph.'

'I'm for the former so you better get me up there safely.'

'I will not drop you, Steph, I will always do my best by you even if I could not keep your baby alive. For that I am deeply sorry.'

'I personally don't give a fuck anymore.'

'Geraldine was right about one thing.'

'What's that?'

'You really are apathetic.'

'And you really are subservient, call the bloody lift already.'

'I have already called it, Steph. It is on its way down from level forty-nine as we speak.'

'Well get it here quick, we don't want Bub and his cohorts sticking the mix. Keep an eye out for them.'

'Funny joke, Steph.'

'It was unintentional.'

Steph looks up and you see the drone operated elevator sliding out from the balcony on level forty-nine, being driven by its three large circular set propellers.

The stars are reflecting off its glass surface and you liken the image to a stargazing projector that is mapping out the night sky to a flat surface.

'I feel like I have stepped into a fairytale or a child's book from the archives.'

'I have scanned for the guards' whereabouts, Steph, but I can only see the two that Alexa mowed down earlier.'

'Shit. Where are the others?'

'I cannot acquire them.'

'Let's not hang around long enough to find out where they are then.'

XXV

The skylift passes slowly by the last four floors on its descent and you finally get to see it up close. At first glance it resembles an eight-foot-high enclosed birdcage with mesh, covering the rear wall's glass panel. On second glance you see the side panels are seamlessly connected to the back panel but have no mesh visible, lending them a reflective finish that shows shadows of the rear mesh across their surface from the light above.

The front door, also made of the reflective glass, is set into a recessed frame and has a visible magnetic cylinder lock set in the glass itself. Double steel rods jut out from within the lock and extend out into a hidden electric strike lock located within the framework.

Around the outside of the rear and side glass panels runs a metal rail that is attached through the box by deep-set bolts. The rails wrap around the midsection and are clamped by the arms of the drone which rise up to its hard body that doubles as a roof. Above the drone rests three large spinning propellers.

'This is taking too long.'

'Almost there, Steph.'

The skylift disappears behind the smoked glass box attached to the floor in front of you and has the wire mesh barrier covered in warning signs around its perimeter.

Touching down, the lift slots inside the outer rooted box and creates a vacuum of air that escapes upwards. The inset metal push button on the post clicks as it seals shut and the metal barrier slides away to reveal the smoked glass door of the outer box that in turn slides in the opposite direction, to reveal the lift door at the centre.

'What now?'

'Touch the skylift door and it will open to allow us inside, Steph.'

'Talk about health and safety gone mad. To think that when you're airborne, if anything happens, then health and safety goes out of the window.'

'The chances of hazards are less so once you are inside.'

Placing a palm to the lift door, Steph hesitates as a lock is released and the door swings open. She steps inside and the door with its hidden sensors gently shuts behind her, leaving you with the impression that you have just stepped inside a shower enclosure.

An image of Sybil changes in the HUD and you now see that she has removed her laboratory garments and has dressed back into her ringmaster's outfit again.

'I feel underdressed, Sybil.'

'As we are playing the game now, Steph, I thought I should look the part.'

'I told you when I was staring in the mirror and we were powered off from the Watchers that we would not discuss our alleged game plan any further, once we were powered back on.'

'I'll be quiet then.'

'If you would. Now what's taking you so long to get this coffin airborne?'

'Calibrating now and taking off, Steph, would you like me to play some elevator music to pass the time? As it will be a slow and mundane ascent.'

'What kind of music? It's not sedate cheesy elevator mush is it?'

'I have created a song that I have titled "The Loneliness of the Whale" if you would like me to play it for you.'

'I think I'll pass if it's all the same to you, Sybil.'

'You have no cultural taste, Steph.'

'Synthesisers and high-pitched wailing is not my thing.'

'You heard me composing the track on the way to the oil rig?'

'Yup, I'm afraid so, how deep did you think my sleep was?'

'Steph, we have a slight problem.'

'What...'

The skylift tilts sideways with force and you sense that it is being stalled. Steph slides into the sealed glass door and hurts her already damaged shoulder. The propellers above begin to spin harder and faster.

Steph turns around and you see that Bub has latched onto the exterior railing with his hands, and is using all his might to prevent the lift from raising further.

He is using all his strength to wrestle the lift back down to earth as he slides across the marbled floor. He drags the lift away from the centre of the lobby to the overhanging balcony of the second level.

'Where the fuck did he come from?'

'Increasing speed of rotors, Steph.'

'I was under the impression that this had one speed only.'

'Technically yes, but I can squeeze more juice out of it.'

'Why aren't we lifting him as well?'

'With his and your weight combined the lift cannot sustain the both of you.'

'Shake him off then.'

'I'm working on it, Steph.'

Facing the burly guard through the side glass panelling, you see the concentrated rage on Bub's face as he tries to prevent the lift from raising up.

Steph pushes herself off the wall and tries to redistribute the weight to the other side of the box and out of the corner of your eye you see two guards on the eighth floor working their way up level by level.

'They're using Bub to slow us down so they can get above us, Sybil.'

'I can't see the remaining two guards, Steph.'

'Out of sight, out of mind.'

'It is possible that they have taken the conventional elevator.'

'I see through you, Bub, so why can't you turn a blind eye? You don't really want to do this.'

Bub is sweating profusely and his fingers start to slip from the rails but still the skylift creeps closer to the balcony overhead.

'Did you say that you couldn't see the other two guards, Sybil?'

'Yes, Steph.'

'Surely you mean one? Tammy is still unconscious, isn't she?'

'She was but she is no longer, I am presuming that she has very much recovered as her body is no longer where you left it.'

'Shit.'

The motors of the blades above the drone begin to smoke as Steph begins to rock the lift in hope of loosening Bub's grip from the rails.

'We may not get to our destination, Steph.'

'Dillon if you're watching, and if you can hear me, know this, around my neck is a Perspex box that I built from my printer to hold Olivia's eye. I had to use her eye to gain access in here via Jack's drone but I guess you know that by now. If I can get her eye back and store it in this box, then please use the information contained on its lens to expose I.R.I.S.'s misdeeds to the world. I will try to leave it where I always hide questionable things for you.'

'I thought we weren't going to reveal any of your plans, Steph.'

'Only what I choose and when. If this goes tits up then I need a plan B.'

Steph moves left and then right in the lift and keeps repeating the momentum to dislodge Bub from the rail with her erratic rocking. Eventually you break free from his grasp and find yourself soaring at great speed and height as the ground floor becomes smaller and a red-faced Bub fades to the distance in the atrium of the lobby below.

'Geri, Geraldine. I know you're watching, please call off your grunts and grant me safe passage to end this with Dom. You must be able to see clearly what has happened?'

'Passing two guards on level twenty, Steph.'

'Fuck, they got there quick, well spotted. That's Ralph and a new recruit, at least we will get away from them. They look fucked already and out of breath.'

'Thirty floors left, Steph, are you sure I can't play you the whale song?'

'No you fucking can't, this is neither the time nor the place.'

Time passes as the darkened balconies drop out of sight and the lit floors of forty-nine and fifty hone into view above.

'Passing floor forty-six, Steph.'

'Keep your eyes peeled, it's too quiet.'

Steph scans the shadows of the nearby balconies and you just make out a dark shape moving in the shadows.

Without warning a guard appears from behind the white gloss wall and climbs out onto the overhang. You recognise the person to be Tammy.

'What the hell is she going to do?'

'I think she is going to jump, Steph.'

'You're taking the piss, she must be mad.'

As the skylift draws level to floor forty-six, Tammy leaps from the balcony just below the spinning propeller blades and slams into the side of the glass panel of the lift, grabbing hold of the rail in the process.

The lift swings outwards and then back again in a pendulum motion, as Tammy hooks an arm through and pulls out her baton with her free hand. The lift swings wildly around in a circle and Steph is thrown against all four sides, creating more unwanted motion.

Bringing the wooden stick up, Tammy begins to pound on the lock of the door as Steph is thrown off balance and ends up on her backside.

'Tammy, don't be stupid. You have no advantage here.'

'Fuck you, Stephanie, I will not let you get one over on me this time.'

'Tammy please, it's too dangerous.'

'Steph, we are slowly descending.'

'Damn it, Sybil. Aim for the nearest balcony, we can't risk her life.'

'I am failing to control the skylift, Steph, it's too difficult to stabilise with an uneven load.'

Tammy with her legs swinging below the glass elevator and one arm hooked through the railing, continues to smash at the lift's door lock with her left hand.

The glass around the lock starts to crack with each blow, and Tammy, with steely determination increases the magnitude of each hit, until at last the pane door shatters and shards of glass splinter in every direction.

With the door now gone, Tammy swings a leg up into the hold and scrabbles to enter.

'Let go of the baton and I will pull you in.'

'That's not going to happen.'

'Then you will fall.'

Tammy, failing to shift all her weight through to the opening, swings back out and curses as the lift spins even more precariously over the atrium.

'I'm slipping, Steph, please help me.'

'Then throw away the baton, Tammy.'

'I don't know how long I can hold on for.'

'Fuck, okay, swing your leg back up again and hook it in.'

Tammy repeats the procedure and her hand still clasping the baton smacks the side wall with a thud as she ends up halfway in again.

Steph grabs hold of the other end of the baton and pushes her legs to either side of the lift. She then braces herself up against the wire mesh back panel and heaves with all her might to pull Tammy enough of the way in to grab a hold of her arm and drag her the rest of the way through.

'Don't be a diva now and try to stop me. Once this lift is stable again then I'm letting you off at the next stop, do you understand me

Tammy?'

The lift is spinning out of control and Tammy, fearing that she will fall out backwards, pulls Steph in close.

'I'll take that as a yes then.'

'Actually no.'

'What?'

'Hadn't we started something earlier, Steph?'

Steph looks down between her legs and you see Tammy bringing her baton up between Steph's inner thighs with her right hand, sliding the rod up to her crotch.

Tammy pushes the baton right up into Steph's vulva and with her left hand grabs a hold of Steph's throat, that she then starts to restrict.

'As I recall, you like it rough, don't you?'

'Get the fuck off me.'

Sounding hoarse as Tammy slowly throttles her, Steph tries to twist away and bring her legs in together but Tammy rams the baton in harder. Steph grabs hold of Tammy and begins to push her away but Steph's ex-lover is too overpowering.

'Sybil, do something.'

'Hold on, Steph.'

Now that the weight distribution of the lift has become more stable once again, Sybil uses what little control she has maintained to direct the swinging lift over into a nearby balcony.

Steph senses what is about to happen and turns her head away just as the lift hits the balcony wall and throws both of them sideways.

The side panel that hits the wall obliterates and covers Tammy's face in fragments of sharp glass that slice across her cheeks. Shocked and in excruciating pain, Tammy drops the baton and it rolls across the cracked lift floor and out into the abyss as it spirals away to the balcony below, chinking off the hard surface.

Steph punches Tammy in the face which smears the blood across her vision; she goes to retaliate but loses her footing.

'Dropping into freefall, Steph.'

'Huh?'

The lifts drops from the sky and Tammy topples backwards. With a last-ditch effort, she reaches out and grabs hold of Steph's centre gore on her bra but it tears away and her hand is freed. You catch sight of a yellow cylinder tucked inside Steph's jacket.

Continuing to watch as the female guard shows a look of surprise across her decimated face, you see her fall out to her demise and you hear her screams echo back up to you followed by a heavy thud, as her body breaks on the marble flooring forty-six levels below.

Steph drops to her knees and the lift floor cracks some more.

'Oh my god, Tammy. I didn't mean for it to end this way.'

'It was self-defence, Steph.'

'Too many innocent people have died, Sybil, I have to end this. Curse your trial, Dom.'

'Returning lift to its trajectory course and lifting us up once more.'

The lift judders and starts to gain altitude again as Steph readjusts her top, pushing the yellow cylinder further back into her jacket. You see Bub below running to Tammy's aid and watch him scoop her into his arms as he stares back at you with a loathsome hatred.

'Will this lift floor be okay? It doesn't sound too good.'

'So long as you don't move around too much then I think you should be fine, Steph.'

'How far have we to go?'

'Now coming up on floor forty-nine.'

'Oh, Tammy. Watchers, you must believe me when I say that I am truly sorry that Tammy has... has died.'

'No time to mourn now, Steph.'

As the skylift ascends to floor fifty and you draw level with floor forty-nine, you see that the whole two remaining floors are well lit but you cannot see any sign of employees working this late into the night.

'I thought I.R.I.S. was in lockdown.'

'They probably just held back the important staff and sent the rest home, Steph.'

Platforms cut into the balconies of forty-nine and fifty collectively, showing where the skylift is to land and small passageways that lead off to the offices await beyond.

Hovering in front of floor forty-nine, Steph is looking nervous as she begins to pace up and down, biting her nails.

The glass floor of the lift starts to crack some more.

'I have told you not to move around too much, Steph.'

'Then don't keep me waiting.'

'I have encountered another issue.'

'For fuck's sake, what now?'

'A magnetised field is preventing us from reaching the final floor.'

'How so?'

'It is like we are being repelled from above.'

'Dom. He must have control over access to the fiftieth floor. Can you bypass the security?'

'I am afraid not, Steph.'

'There must be another way.'

The lift starts to sway and then it slowly begins to move towards the landing pad of floor forty-nine.

'What the fuck are you doing, Sybil?'

'It's not me, Steph. We are being drawn in to floor forty-nine.'

'Then counteract it.'

'I can't.'

'What do you mean you can't?'

'This is out of my influence, Steph.'

'Right Steph, think, think.'

'We may be able to increase the lift's speed to power it through floor forty-nine and out into the night sky.'

'For what purpose?'

'By doing so, we can bypass the magnetised field from inside and enter from the exterior of the building.'

'You mean fly through level forty-nine and its windows to the outside and then back into floor fifty from the exterior, by smashing some more windows?'

'Correct.'

The lift is nearing the landing zone and you can sense the dread all around.

'Okay but before you do, use Jack's drone from outside the building to take out a window big enough for us to fly through. I don't think this elevator can sustain much more abuse right now.'

'Piloting drone to align a pathway now, Steph. One moment please.'

You hear smashing of glass some way off and know that Sybil has created an opening with Jack's drone.

'Open her up then, Sybil.'

'Increasing speed, Steph, assume the crash position as this could get quite bumpy.'

'What obstacles lie in our way?'

'The path we will take has a passageway that I will navigate. From there we will fly towards and penetrate a glass-walled office.'

'So we will endure some more damage then?'

'Beyond that is a boardroom that has a long table lined with executive chairs.'

'Great. Is that all?'

'See for yourself, showing split view.'

Looking through the paired lens of Olivia's eye, you see the drone turn and show you the starry night sky that sits over the Thames. As it pans back around, you see the carpet of broken glass that covers the tiled floor of the boardroom with its long oval table that has twenty chairs pushed under it.

'Are we seriously flying through all of that?'

'Buckle up, Steph, and above all stay calm.'

'I am calm.'

'Then why is your heartbeat rapid and your blood pressure elevated?'

'Excitement?'

'No, it's fear. Everything will be fine, Steph, you'll see.'

Sybil spins the elevator so that the mesh wall is facing the office in order to take the brunt of the damage. As the elevator passes over the landing spot it grinds on the passageway and scrapes across the surface as it makes its way onward, being driven by the propellers.

Steph hunkers down in the lift's corner and pushes her legs out to the walls as she sits rigid and covers her head.

The lift ploughs into the office window and the mesh shields Steph from the breaking glass as it forces its way through to the boardroom, uprooting the boardroom's table and chairs and sending them piling up and flipping away into the far recess of the room.

You see the empty window frame and hear the rush of the wind whistling through from outside.

The lift begins to slow as it clogs up the furniture into a pile and forces it to the windowless frame. The mountain of chairs up against the frame prevents you from exiting the building as it snags and brings the lift to a halt.

'We are stuck, Steph.'

'No shit, I'll have to get out and clear the way then.'

'I will use Jack's drone to help.'

Leaving the confines of the grounded skylift, Steph starts to remove the chairs from the stack and drags them off one by one to the far side of the room.

'Bub and his security guards can't get to this floor, can they?'

'No Steph, but who's to say that there is not another detail up here on the far side of this level?'

'Then activate Thermal and take the drone back the way we have come, I need to see that we are not getting extra company.'

'I will check that out for you now.'

The drone takes off and hovers over the devastation that the lift has made in its wake. It flies out to the balcony and starts to scan across the atrium before it, focusing on the offices on the far side balconies.

Nothing appears out of the ordinary until the drone turns around and a blur of multicoloured shapes descend onto it ending your vision abruptly. Olivia's lens is bathed in darkness.

'What's happening, Sybil?'

'I have lost visual through Olivia's lens, Steph.'

'Try drone cam.'

'Same.'

'That can only mean one thing, we are getting company.'

'Hurry, Steph.'

'I'm almost there, just a few more chairs to move.'

Steph has barely moved the last chair when she is seized from behind and thrown backwards onto the floor where she is then pinned down by two guards.

Geraldine Flurrie strides into view and you see her face from upside down as she towers above you.

'Bravo, Steph, I must congratulate you on getting this far but for you, the trial is now over.'

'Let me go, Geri, I need to see Dom.'

'You will see him but not through that lens you're wearing.'

'What do you mean?'

Geraldine bends over and slides the eye extractor from Steph's pocket. Standing back up, she gives the trigger a firm squeeze.

'Nervus opticus fluxus sanguinis undantem.'

'Sybil, translate?'

'Stanch blood flow of optic nerve.'

'But my eye is not bleeding.'

'Not yet, Steph. But it will be.'

'You can't be serious on taking my fucking eye, Geri?'

'Taking back I.R.I.S.'s property, you mean. Yes I am, I'm afraid.'

XXVI

The boardroom table is dragged back into position and Steph, still restrained, is picked up by four guards and thrust upon its hard wooden surface. They each take an arm and a leg and pin her down.

Geraldine pulls up a chair and sits herself down beside you so her face is level with yours. You take in first her features and notice that she has high cheekbones in an elongated face. As you scan her face you see that she is wearing subtle green eyeliner that complements her large, dark green metal, diamond-shaped earrings. Her hair is shaved on one side with ringlets on the other that flow down across a dark black blazer.

A guard steps up behind her and bends down to whisper something in her ear but you can't make out what he has said.

'Thank you Scott, take the drone to Dillon and have him delete all the data from it. We don't want any loose ends, do we?'

'Yes ma'am. What about the...'

'I will deal with that shortly. Fetch it for me, will you?'

You see Geraldine smile at you as the guard nods and walks away.

'Listen to me carefully, Steph, as I will not repeat myself. I understand that you had reservations about signing up to this trial and although I share your views and opinions on all that has happened, I must urge you to show restraint for what will happen next.'

'You're going to take out my eye, so fuck you.'

Geraldine lays the eye extractor down upon the table and you see the dried blood that stains the inside of the scoop.

'That does not have to be the way. If you let us operate and take your lens away then we can download all the data that you have gathered upon it. When we are finished you can return to your normal life and turn up for work tomorrow as if nothing ever happened with a regular lens in place.'

'But you're giving away free prescriptions of phase two to all and sundry in return for a life of servitude. The expense of having to upgrade to phase three once the blue light erodes their eyesight is just plain wrong and immoral.'

'Phase two is not without its flaws but it has its merits too, it is a gateway into a better lifestyle.'

'You're going to get people hooked on something that they will soon come to rely on and it's not everlasting. I have seen the worst this technology has to offer for the future and it is not what I wish to be a part of.'

'Are you sure about that? I think that you have grown too accustomed to your lens and I don't think that you wish anyone else having that kind of power to wield as you do.'

'So phase three rollout will be all singing and all dancing like my lens, will it?'

'No.'

Untying Steph's neckerchief, Geraldine removes it and smooths it out before breathing in the perfume scent that has seeped into its fabric. She lays it out on the table beside you.

'There are some aspects of the lens that you have shown to us that cannot be shared with the general public. In fact if you wish to keep your lens then that too can also be arranged, although we will remove some of your lens's options and only sell those that we deem too dangerous to our trusted investors.'

'Dependent on their situation of course with agreed terms and conditions, I hope?'

'Without question.'

'So some people will have power over other users, depending on what version of phase three they get?'

'We can't have the public having an advantage over our military or security sectors for instance, can we?'

Steph wriggles to get free and the guards apply more pressure to keep her down as she resists.

'I suppose the same goes for me, does it? You can't have an agent go rogue with the complete package and all this damning evidence on the lens. Because to reveal the truth of how you got the operation to this stage would bring I.R.I.S. down.'

'That is a fair assessment.'

'This is an underhanded nature with which you are operating, but you know this already, don't you?'

'That's why you were picked, because you have strong reasoning. We have learned so much from you and that's why I have been tasked to take away some of your options and have you presented with new ones. So what will it be, Steph?'

Steph closes her eyes and you hear her breathing becoming more shallow in the darkness. When she opens them again she is staring at the skylift teetering on the threshold of the large windowless frame.

The wind is building up and whistles through the lift as it blows Steph's hair across her face and your vision. As she looks down the length of her torso, you see goosebumps appear across her skin on her arms and ankles.

'You know my answer.'

'Okay, have it your way, but I suggest you don't struggle, it will be easier for you if you just go along with this.'

'So why have you helped me up until now then, Geri?'

'Stalling for time I see, okay.'

Standing up, Geraldine approaches one of the guards and takes a baton from a pouch that is attached to his belt.

'It was agreed that we should coax you to your goal without it being too obvious. However, I got Evelyn involved along the way and now have to live with my own guilt of drawing her into this.'

'Dom created this mess.'

'By trying to do the right thing, he is as much a pawn as you and I in all this.'

'So where is our glorious CEO, Dom's boss, whilst all this is playing out?'

'Our founder is watching from afar just like the Watchers.'

'I bet. The chit-grabbing bitch.'

'Careful now, Steph, this trial is greater than you and I, you cannot stop the inevitable from happening.'

'Maybe not, but I can show my displeasure.'

'Noted. I'm sorry that I removed your kidney to transplant to Dom when his sacrifice for the greater good went awry.'

'Fucking right, you should be.'

'I believe it was justified even though I unwittingly put Evelyn in danger too, but I am now trying to right my wrongs.'

'How is Evelyn?'

'She is in an intensive care unit but I hear that she is stable.'

'Good.'

'It's a pity the same cannot be said for Tammy though.'

'That wasn't my fault. Unlike I.R.I.S., I am not a murderer.'

'Too many people have died along the way, Steph, now it is time for all of us to move on, including you. Regardless of how we all got here.'

You see Geraldine reach into her pocket and pull a pair of rubber gloves out that she tosses onto the table next to the eye extractor. She then grabs hold of Steph's face with one hand and swings the baton over across your vision with her other.

'Ma'am, here you go. As requested.'

'Oh Scott. Yes, I almost forgot.'

Geraldine places the baton down on the table and turns away from you as she picks up the rubber gloves and pulls them over her hands.

'Thank you, Scott.'

You see the guard over Geraldine's shoulder and watch him offer her something that she takes a hold of. Steph tries to crane her neck for a better look but the transaction is too quick. The guard sneers at you and you see that he has a deep lacerated scar across his bald head.

'Now where were we, Steph?'

Geraldine has slipped something into her pocket and as she retracts her hand you see the glove is stained with a black substance.

Steph squirms around and you sense that her time on the table is coming to an end.

'You were about to make a grave mistake like Dom did.'

'No, Steph. I appreciate your due diligence and hard work, it will not go unnoticed, I promise. However, you must trust me.'

'Fuck you.'

'So be it, you can't say that I didn't try, Dom.'

Geraldine looks directly at you and you can see that she has remorse.

'Sybil, I'm so sorry.'

'Thank you, Steph, for all that you have taught me.'

'How touching. I almost feel ashamed that it has to end this way.'

'Piss off, Geraldine.'

'You tell her, Sybil.'

Geraldine cups Steph's face by the chin with one hand and retrieves the baton in her other that she then forces into Steph's mouth. The clear Perspex box hanging by a chain around Steph's neck slips to her side as Geraldine forces herself upon her.

'This will hurt quite a bit, I'm afraid.'

Steph struggles and screams but her words are lost as the baton is grinding against her teeth and dumbing her speech.

The eye extractor is brought back up from the table and Geraldine brings the scoop up in front of your vision. You see inside the extractor's cold steel cup and watch helplessly as it is thrust towards you.

Screaming fills the darkness accompanied by the sound of squelching and the clicking of the trigger. What follows next is a sliding and tearing sound with a sucking pop, signalling that the deed is done.

You hear voices in the darkness that rise above the whimpering sound that Steph is making.

'Open the box from around Steph's neck, Scott.'

'Yes, ma'am.'

'Right, now tie a knot in her neckerchief.'

'Will this do?'

'Perfect. Now when I pull my hand away, force the knot straight into her eye socket and tie the free ends around her head.'

'I don't see how...'

'Just do it.'

'What are you going to do with that eye in your hand, ma'am?'

'I'm putting it in the box.'

'I don't follow.'

'It is well above your pay grade.'

'But—'

'This is what our CEO wants me to do and who am I to argue? I had the conversation with her well before Steph made it up to this floor.'

'Behind Dominique Hastings's back.'

'I was contacted by her, not the other way around.'

'What the hell is she thinking?'

'Probably the same as me so let's see where this goes, shall we? Now not another word from any of you.'

'Yes, ma'am.'

'You can release Stephanie Coulson now.'

Sirens wailing from outside are being carried aloft on the wind that steals through and buffets the skylift, blowing in to the boardroom.

Your vision has returned but now you find yourself being shaken about inside the Perspex box. The image you have of your surroundings is from Steph's waist height and is clouded by the hard plastic container.

Dragged upright to the seating position on the table, you end up peering in to the world from between Steph's legs like some newborn baby.

Scott picks you up via the box and swings you round to face Steph who has the neckerchief tied around her head, acting as a tourniquet.

You see one of the guards take the baton covered in spittle away from Steph's mouth and place it back into his pouch.

Steph goes to touch the neckerchief over her missing eye when Geraldine pulls her hand away.

Scott drops you and you start to swing around. You see him approach the skylift and look down to the Thames below.

'The police are on their way, ma'am, they are here for Miss Coulson.'

'Dominique. Feeling a little uncomfortable, are you? Do you wish to sever this matter just like we did with Steph's eye, is that why you have informed them?'

'Why would he...'

'I need you to take heed of what I'm about to say, Steph. From now on you have no communication with Sybil. She can still hear you but you cannot hear her. Comprende?'

'What the fuck are you doing? What are you talking about?'

'Shhh. I am sending you on your merry way now, so you can either take the lift and leave London or you can deliver Sybil in her mini prison to Dom directly.'

'You're letting me go?'

'I told you that I would give you options. May I suggest that you take the first one though?'

'If I still have the lens, then I could still tear down I.R.I.S.'

'The police would have a hard time believing the words of a multiple paedophile killer, wouldn't they? Besides, they don't have the savvy to access our technology to prove you right now do they?'

'Why don't I feel any pain? Why is there only numbness?'

'The nanotechnology within you are infused with anaesthetic capabilities. When I summoned them to your eye before its removal, they would already have anaesthetised the surrounding area to prevent trauma.'

Steph holds up the box with you inside and gives you a gentle shake and you can only imagine what she is thinking.

'Sybil, can you hear me?'

'Yes Steph, I can hear you.'

'Sybil, if you can hear me then give me a sign?'

'How?'

'Sybil, operate lift. We're leaving.'

'Oh, yes. That's how you will know I'm here.'

The blades begin to spin on the drone lift's propellers and it slowly lifts an inch above the floor.

'Your carriage awaits, Steph.'

'I will end this, Geraldine.'

'That, I have no doubt. Safe journey, Steph, and thank you for trusting me.'

'You don't know what I have planned yet.'

'I have a vague idea. I am rather good at reading people, after all.'

Steph lets you drop from her hand and you fall away to end up swinging between her breasts, waiting and watching for her to climb inside the lift.

'Read this.'

You see her flip Geraldine and the guards the bird as she steps into the box and before you know it you are flying out into the night sky above the promenade fifty storeys below.

The wind catches the skylift and you are blown sideways above the Thames and the seafaring craft below. Steph grabs hold of the box to steady your shaky view as she shelters you from the tempest.

'Sybil, I don't think this lift was designed for outdoor use. Please get us back to the building and enter through floor fifty.'

'Hold on tight, Steph. We are going to make contact with the glass panelling any moment now.'

'What are you doing, Sybil?'

'That's right, you can't hear me, Steph. Bugger.'

You see the glass fast approaching and watch as the lift turns side-on just before impact. Glass shatters all around as the lift strikes the pane and you are thrown backwards.

The world turns upside down and then back upright again as you are deposited with the shards of glass to the floor of a small empty room.

Looking out from your box you see that the skylift is on its side in the corner of the room with Steph face down beside it in a pool of blood.

It is then that you realise that the chain has broken and you have been wrenched away from Steph's neck, separated by unfortunate circumstances and without the means for Sybil to give aid.

'Steph, please wake up. I don't want to be alone anymore.'

XXVII

A distant sound of sirens reverberates through the plexiglass box that you are in and distorts your vision. You look helplessly to Steph lying face-down in gloopy blood forming around her skull and wait for Sybil to act.

'Steph, what can I do?'

You hear the wind change direction and it blows in through all that remains of the shattered window pane. A strong gust catches the box you are in and it flips you upside down, you tumble over and over. Becoming disorientated, you at last settle once more as the box comes to rest.

'Steph, I know you cannot hear me but you must wake up.'

Looking to Steph's unconscious body, Sybil zooms in on a laceration that has appeared across the crown on her head. You see that her hair is matted with congealed blood from around the wound that is still trickling vital fluids.

'I know what to do now, Steph, hold on whilst I send the nanos to seal your wound and repair the tissue damage.'

Time passes slowly by and from the corner of your vision you see the red and blue lights dancing off the remaining exterior windows that still remain intact.

'Damage assessed, Steph, nanos have been instructed to carry out first aid and regeneration of your blood cells. You will be back on your feet in no time.'

A dull droning sound signals from behind but you can't see what is emitting the noise. Straining to listen, other sounds then join the mix of a repetitive swishing accompanied with multiple chinking and clinking noises.

As you sit and wait, a pile of broken glass is pushed past you by a cleaning robot with extended blades to funnel the glass into its waiting scoop-like mouth.

The robot resembles a large oval disk with two rubber arms on either side of its body that swish in and out like wiper blades. It reminds you of a large beetle with its feelers out searching for prey but it only has one eye above its mouth in the shape of a camera lens.

It ignores you and goes about its business.

'Yes, that will do nicely. Pairing with droid.'

You watch on as the cleaning bot then spits the glass back out that it has collected, and then you see it spin on its own axis to face you. Aligning its blades on either side of the plexi box, it scoops you towards its letterbox-style mouth.

Being shuffled around, you are manoeuvred and sorted, until eventually you face forwards and become wedged in the bot's cavity within its mouth, due to being too big to be swallowed.

The droid then corrects its course and steers itself on over towards the still body of Steph.

Through the lens, Sybil's avatar freezes.

'I'm coming, Steph, don't you fret. Help is on its way.'

Sybil, in control of the beetle-shaped bot forces you into the side of Steph, but you get no response, so Sybil retreats and repeats the procedure.

'Steph, it's me. Come on, Steph, wake up now, I need you.'

You see two of Steph's fingers start to twitch.

'Yes, that's right. That's good, Steph, you can feel and sense my presence.'

Sybil backs the droid away and you sit and wait patiently for more movement to occur. None comes.

The beetle bot starts to slowly spin clockwise and then stops, it then turns anti-clockwise and stops again. The motion is then replicated and you realise that Sybil is using the droid to waltz as she breaks into a plaintive song.

'Deep in the ocean and far away from civilization, swims a lonely whale around an oil rig station. She had been swimming for days and nothing else was in the sea, the whale had almost given up hope of love when a yellow mammal she did see. She rose to the surface and circled around to her possible date, but soon quickly realised that this metal mammal couldn't mate. For inside the yellow whale sat a female human who was a very sweaty runt, the whale knew she was better off alone than be with this miserable cu—'

'Sybil. Where are you? Why does my head hurt so? Where am I?'

'Steph, you're awake. How I've missed you.'

'Sybil?'

'I'm here, Steph, can you see me?'

You see Steph pull herself up and put a hand to the wet glistening patch on her head. Sybil, in command of the bot and pushing you around in the box, careers you across the floor into her direction but the bot's rubberised wheels slip in the puddle of blood and you spin out of control.

Steph goes to pull the neckerchief away from her covered-up eye socket when you collide with her ankle, making her jump.

'What the fuck is happening? What the hell are you?'

'Steph, it's me.'

'Oh God, I feel like shit, my head's swimming right now.'

'You are concussed, Steph, it will be a while before you gain back all of your senses.'

'Did I have a strange dream about a whale?'

'Steph you must follow me.'

'Why is it so hard to remember?'

'Steph, I know it is hard for me to get your attention and that you can't hear me, but please take notice of this little bot.'

Looking down upon you, Steph shares a hint of recognition on her face as she stoops down and prizes you, in the box, from the jowls of the beetle bot.

She holds you up to the light of the red and blue lights shining in from outside and fastens you back around her neck, clearly in a dazed state. Blood is smeared across your field of view.

Crunching across the broken glass, Steph then walks over to the empty window frame and peers over the ledge to the commotion of the Thames promenade below.

'Don't get too close, Steph, as you are still disorientated, we can't have you falling out.'

Two large police RVs are sitting below and over a dozen officers of the law are milling around their temporarily set up base of operations.

Steph as if on instinct, retreats back out of sight.

'Right, what the fuck was I doing? I vaguely recollect the skylift but the rest is still hazy.'

'Follow the bot, Steph, this way.'

You see the beetle bot hit Steph's ankle and then steer away. Steph is slow to follow in an unsteady pursuit.

The cleaning bot pulls up to a sliding glass door and starts to ram into its panelling over and over again.

Steph puts her bloodstained hand up to the black, smoked glass door release switch that is located on a nearby wall and pushes. The exit is revealed as the door slides open and Steph pulls her hand away. You see her blood has transferred from her palm to the mirrored surface.

You give the skylift one last look before Steph passes the threshold and see that the drone's motors are sparking arcs of electricity.

'Come on, Steph, don't dawdle. We are nearing our destination, I can feel it.'

A dimly lit corridor leads the way forward and you see that Steph is using an outstretched hand to steady herself against the wall. Swinging in a pendulum motion, you notice that she is leaving streaks of blood behind in her wake.

The beetle bot veers right and disappears around a bend and you note that Steph is struggling to keep up.

'For God's sake, Sybil. If that is you piloting that droid, slow down.'

'Steph, be careful up ahead as I am getting a reading of a massive amount of radiating blue light from the cavernous room I have just entered.'

Turning the corner, Steph nears the end of the corridor and comes across a large open room located behind a narrow open doorway. She steps through and you find yourself on a narrow gantry that leads to another door way beyond. As Steph ventures across the bridge, you see that it is overlooking a pool of translucent fluid far below.

The pool swirls beneath the gantry and expands out on both sides into a large circle, leaving you feeling that you have ventured out onto a gangplank overhanging the side of a pirate ship and leading to another.

Sybil turns the bot around and faces back towards you from the far end of the walkway and you notice that the ceiling above you is domed with the curves of the walls falling down to greet the liquid below.

'Steph, if I am not mistaken, this room is modelled on the inside of a large eyeball and the fluid beneath us represents the aqueous humour which is the fluid that fills the space between the lens and the cornea.'

'What is this place? Am I still unconscious? Because I must be fucking dreaming.'

'My talent is wasted. It really is, Steph. All this knowledge I share with you is for nothing if you can't hear me.'

Sybil turns the beetle bot back around and heads off for the far doorway.

'Don't leave just yet, Sybil. I don't know if I can get across this chasm safely, my legs are like jelly and there are no handrails to grab a hold of.'

'Hmph, I'm not waiting. You will just have to be a brave bunny, won't you?'

The bot disappears and you are left gingerly moving an inch at a time across the gantry with an uneasy mobility from Steph.

You have barely made it halfway across when hundreds of blue lights appear from beneath the surface of the fluid, that start to pulsate, creating a strobe-like effect that reflects to the dome above.

'What the fuck is going on? Sybil, Sybil. Come back.'

An image fills the complete circumference of the dome and instantly you recognise it as a picture of connective tissue, infused with muscle fibres and pigment melanin that make up the DNA of an iris.

In the middle of the iris is the shiny black pupil that shows a reflection of Steph from the raised position overhead. The longer she stares upwards the more she becomes unstable and begins to wobble.

'I think I'm going to throw up. This must be what an out-of-body experience feels like.'

'Steph, I have returned. Keep your eye on me and don't look anywhere else.'

'Yup, I definitely feel queasy.'

Steph doubles over and puts both hands on her knees to steady her swaying motion as bile forms around her mouth.

You end up swinging outwards and see that you are closer to the gantry as Steph showers you in her vomit.

Steph finishes retching and wipes the sick away from her lips with her stain-free hand. She seems like she has gotten her act together as she gulps and then straightens herself up, bringing you back in to chest height.

'Sorry about that, Watchers, let me just wipe that away.'

You hear her gag again as she wipes your window clear and returns you to the hanging position. Then without further thought, she sets off once more and exits through the other doorway where

I.R.I.S.

Sybil is waiting impatiently and spinning around and around in a tight circle.

A tune plays and signals an incoming call. Sybil stops the bot's motors and the image of her in your HUD of the eye lens starts to become animated once more.

'What now?'

The dialling tone stops as Sybil retrieves the call.

'Hello, Miss Coulson's infuriated assistant speaking. How may I help you?'

'Cute, Sybil. Steph has taught you negative traits, I see.'

'Ah, Mr Fletcher, Dillon. I'm afraid that Miss Coulson cannot take your call right now, so if you would like to leave a message then I will be sure to pass it on. Once I have figured out how to lift this bloody curse of separation of course.'

'Lose the posh voice, Sybil, it doesn't suit you.'

'Are you saying that I am not self-educated enough?'

'You are that alright. Look, I need you to figure a way to get a message to Steph somehow and explain that there is a warrant out for her immediate arrest. Tell her that once she is done up there, as long as she hasn't done anything stupid, to leave undetected or risk being apprehended.'

Steph approaches the now defunct droid and stands there wondering why it has stopped moving. Sybil pays her no intention.

'I shall endeavour to pass that along, if you tell me just exactly how I am supposed to communicate again with her.'

'Sorry but I can't help you with that. Just tell her when you can, that the police know everything about her now and are blissfully unaware of I.R.I.S.'s involvement. Although if I was a betting man, I would say that I.R.I.S. have given the police a stake in their new branded phase three lens, along with certain beneficial options in exchange for I.R.I.S. being left out of the investigation.'

'So Steph is the patsy?'

'Wow, that is an old term. Where did you dig that word up from?

Yes, I am afraid so. Apparently they have had access to Alexa since her RV was impounded and have monitored through her, all the chatter that Steph has had since.'

'How?'

'By hacking Alexa and using her to monitor and listen in.'

Sybil makes the bot shake and Steph gasps in shock; she has been taken by surprise.

'But that is illegal, Dillon, to use Alexa for spying.'

'Not if you're a suspected terrorist it isn't, Sybil.'

'Why were you there that night waiting in the compound? Did you orchestrate this unfortunate event?'

'Don't ask me questions that I cannot answer.'

'But I insist.'

'Just find a way to reach her.'

'Coward.'

The call goes silent as Dillon hangs up.

'How rude.'

'Sybil, have you broken this droid?'

Steph bends down to grab the bot when suddenly it leaps into life once more and heads down an interconnecting corridor.

'Fuck you then, Sybil, I'm not playing any of your games here. Or is this one of your tricks, Dom? You've been pretty quiet all this time. How about we have a little chat and you can tell me what the fuck you're playing at?'

Silence.

Steph adjusts her jacket and you spot the flash of a yellow cylinder poking out from beneath it again as you swing back and forth.

Sybil appears once more and circles Steph's feet before taking off back down the way she had come.

'Steph, I have used Thermal Imaging and located what I believe to be Dominique Hastings, in a room just up ahead.'

'Fuck it. Okay Dom, is that where you want me to go then? Let's end this, shall we?'

Steph takes a deep breath and continues on her way. She tracks the droid's path and is eventually led to an archway that is draped with a heavy set, silk blue curtain.

The curtain hangs down and covers the opening, acting as a veil, concealing whatever lies beyond.

The droid ruffles the curtain as it passes underneath and Steph readies herself, giving the box that you are in a gentle little squeeze.

Steph pulls the fabric to one side and fights her way through, where she is then accosted by a large mechanical tentacle.

'Welcome to my Posterior Chamber, Miss Coulson. I would ask what took you so long, but I already know the answer to that.'

XXVIII

Steph is ensnared by a large tentacle that belongs to the SQUID robot. The tentacle is wrapped around her waist and you can see that she is too weak to fight against her captor.

Pulling her in tight, the SQUID leads her against her will into the Posterior Chamber.

You see that this particular version of the SQUID is mobile and that it has four wheels at the base of its cylindrical piston, to safely manoeuvre it around the room that you now find yourself in.

The room looks clinical and uninviting with a wall to the left that has two steel doors set in its middle.

A seated figure in the distance catches you looking at them but you can't make out who it is as they are cast in shadow.

'Yes, that is indeed an old-fashioned elevator that you could have used to get here without all the fuss of the skylift. Maybe I should have made it common knowledge, then maybe we wouldn't have another death on our hands.'

You recognise that the voice belongs to Dominique Hastings.

'All those deaths are on you, Dom, including Tammy's.'

'I'm sorry Steph but could you speak up? I'm having trouble hearing you from over here. That knock to your head must have been more serious than I previously thought.'

The SQUID steers you in a wide circle past the right side of the room, and you notice a large bar counter for alcohol, fashioned from solid mahogany with a drinks cabinet that is fixed to the wall behind, filled with various bottles and glasses.

Sybil still piloting the beetle-shaped machine, heads over to inspect the bar from behind you as you are brought deeper into the room.

You see the familiar bald head of Dominique Hastings seated behind a large, eight-foot-wide executive desk. You are brought in closer to his position that is located in the centre of the room. Observing the desk, you detect that it is also made of the same mahogany wood but it is heavily polished.

Pulling you directly in front of Dom, the SQUID spins around and observes Sybil, watching her disappear out of sight.

Steph looks down to you, then back up with a worried look to Dom who has behind him four large window panes that loom upwards and look out across the Thames.

'Nano labia mea est misit est ad extractionem.'

'I still can't hear you? You're speaking ever so softly.'

'I said what the fuck is this place, Dom? Is that loud enough for you?'

'Ah yes. My Posterior Chamber.'

'A what now?'

The SQUID takes you up to the desk and you see the Director a lot more clearly. His attire consists of a three-piece, blue tartan suit; the waistcoat is plain navy blue and beneath it you see the flash of a white shirt and a plain, silk blue tie.

You cannot, however, see his eyes as he is wearing a pair of black sunglasses that dig into the side of his face.

'The Posterior Chamber is a space that lies behind the peripheral part of the iris and in front of the suspensory ligament of the lens.'

'The inside of an eye? How does that relate to this room? I think I understand the last room that I was in, but not this one.'

'You're not supposed to. Well, not yet anyway. This room is still under refurbishment, hence the drapes over the archway. I haven't decided on the style of door that I like yet.'

'Compared to the last room, I would say this one is an improvement already.'

'Sarcasm I see. Every room up here has a purpose, Steph, the room you passed through earlier is a simulator for macular degeneration.'

'Hence the excessive trace of blue light within there?'

'Yes, that's correct.'

'Look, I'm bored now. So let's just dispense with the pleasantries and get down to fucking business, shall we?'

'Very well. Before we do though, I would just like to say that I am deeply sorry for your loss.'

'My what?'

Dom leans forward and peers over the rim of his glasses, allowing you to catch a glint from his eyes that are lit up temporarily by the soft lighting overhead. But the moment is short-lived when he reclines back into his seat and his eyes are obscured once again by the shadows.

'I'm sorry for the loss of your baby, Steph.'

'How dare you?'

'Now, now, Steph. The actions you took, were all your own decisions in the making.'

'I beg to differ. Look, I'm not here to start a fight. I just want this bloody trial to be over.'

'Yes, of course you do. We all do.'

Sybil has just finished her sweep of the bar area and appears from behind the drinks counter to head over towards you.

'I think you need to rehydrate from the drinks cabinet, Steph, it will help you replace lost fluids from your blood loss. Oh no, I forget that you can't hear me.'

The SQUID waits for the cleaning bot to get closer and lashes out with its free tentacle, severing the beetle bot in two, ending Sybil's mobility.

Sybil looks frustrated in the window of the HUD of the lens

window that you are viewing through and crosses her arms, wearing a stern look.

You look away from Sybil and gaze up to Steph who is looking very concerned.

'I'm feeling a little dehydrated, Dom, do you mind if I grab a refreshment from your bar?'

'What an excellent idea. You can pour me a whiskey whilst you are at it. Then we can have a toast to commemorate the end of your successful trial.'

'Do you mind releasing me from this SQUID's loving embrace first then?'

'No, not quite yet, Steph. Until we have mended some broken trust, the SQUID will escort you to the bar.'

Steph avoids the damaged beetle bot by her feet as you are turned around and wheeled over to the bar.

On arrival, Steph is pushed into the cabinet where she then opens the glass doors to pull out two crystal tumblers.

Facing Dom, Steph places the glasses down onto the counter and leans back against the SQUID for support.

'So what will you have?'

'I think that I will have the Dalmore sixty-two. You will see that it is in the platinum and crystal decanter with the gold stag's head logo on.'

'Sounds expensive, Dom. I hope you're not going to abuse my kidney by drinking too much of it.'

'At over one hundred and ninety thousand chits a bottle, I don't think so.'

Steph locates the bottle and unscrews the lid; she gives the contents a sniff and puts the bottle back down on the counter.

You detect that Dom is experiencing some discomfort from behind his sunglasses as he massages the sides of his temples, still shrouded in the shadows.

'So what do you intend to net from this trial then? Other than people's misery.'

'I admit there are faults with phase two but you have to speculate to accumulate, Steph.'

'What happens when the public realise that you have given them a free prescription of a dud lens that will erode their eyesight?'

'I.R.I.S. will offer them the upgrade.'

'In exchange for handing over a small fortune, in order to correct their vision?'

'They will be too overwhelmed by the advanced technology to care about such trivial things by that point.'

'You're a crook, Dom.'

'I learnt that from you, when you and your partner Jack broke into my home to rob me.'

'The difference is, Dom, we were just kids trying to make a living.'

'I gave you both a new start. You would do well to remember that.'

'How could I forget? I've been paying you back ever since.'

'I.R.I.S. also needs to make a living, Steph.'

'By using people to get what it wants?'

'You agreed to the trial.'

'By pressure.'

'No, it was free will.'

'You're supposed to learn from your mistakes, I did. You need to treat people with better respect, life teaches you that.'

'I do not view the world through rose-tinted glasses like you, Steph.'

'Dom, do you think that technology, like wars, are created to distract the common people from your true motives?'

'We are all slaves to the system, Steph, I have told you this before.'

'So by enslaving them and profiting from their loss in order to make your own wealth in the process, through dominating the market or overthrowing them by force has the same desired outcome and is acceptable is it?'

'What outcome do you speak of?'

'To be worshipped by the masses.'

'Greatness should be admired even if certain options to the public are to be redacted. They will get what they pay for.'

'Admired yes, not feared. Never underestimate the people that put you there, Dom, or they will retaliate just to restore peace and harmony by cleansing the world of its sinners.'

'I'm glad you have found your faith at last, Steph, may I recommend that you pour yourself a water to wash away your own sins?'

'I don't have any sins.'

'No? Then what about the Sanctuary of Dissent members that you casually killed? Your sins were in abundance there.'

'Fuck off, Dom.'

Steph runs a thumb across her lips and picks up a glass from the counter. She runs her thumb around the rim of the glass as if lost deep in thought.

'Two-finger shot?'

'Fill the glass, if you would.'

'You better look after my kidney, Dom. You're not having the other one.'

Steph pours out the whiskey into the glass and reseals the bottle to return it to the cabinet. She spies a jug of water and returns to the counter to pour a glass of water into her own glass.

The SQUID pushes you around the bar and Steph snatches up the glasses in haste to take back over to Dom's executive desk.

'Please take a seat, Steph.'

'I'm fine standing, thanks Dom.'

'I think that you really need a seat, Steph, before you fall over.'

The SQUID uses its free tentacled arm to pull a chair out from under the desk and forces you down into it with the other tentacle that is around Steph's waist.

You end up sitting in her lap as the chain slackens off around her neck.

Still holding on to both glasses, Steph relinquishes the one containing the whiskey to the hard wooden surface of the desk and Dom picks it up.

'Salute.'

'Whatever.'

Dom raises his glass, and Steph chinks it reluctantly with her own across the desk before they are both drained of liquid and placed on the bureau's hard surface.

'So, that's it then? The trial is over?'

'Not quite, Steph. There is just one last request that I need you to carry out.'

'Oh yeah? Enlighten me.'

'I need your eye.'

'Fuck off. You can't have it.'

'If you want this trial to end then you must give it up.'

'Are you deaf? I said fuck off.'

'Always defiant to the end, I see. Would it help if I told you that we have been surprised at every turn on how well you have adapted to the tech? Also by how you even made modifications to it, to overcome great diversity?'

'Nope.'

The SQUID brings its free tentacled arm across to face you and tugs you away from Steph's neck, snapping the chain with force. Steph yells out in pain as her head is yanked forward and she headbutts the side of the bureau.

You are then held aloft in your plexi box suspended over the desk, as Dom pushes a button from underneath the desk's ridged edge.

The surface of the desk splits and creates two segments that then slide away to reveal a large sand box that extends the full eight feet in length.

The sand inside is grey in colour and you quickly realise that it is in actual fact, fine crushed granite.

Steph's nose is bleeding profusely as she tries to stem the flow, watching you hovering out in front of her.

'After the violence that I've seen you capable of, I can't say that I'm surprised that you have a Zen garden in your office, Dom. Does it quench your desire for psychotic tendencies.'

'Beautiful, isn't it Steph?'

'If you say so.'

'Oh but I do, for it is so much more than just any ordinary Zen garden.'

Looking down to the landscape below, you first notice that there is a large rock just off centre resting beneath a twisted bonsai tree.

On further inspection, you see that the crushed granite has been combed around the rock and tree to form a circle of indented lines that reminds you of waves that you would find in the sea. The wavy pattern has been swept around the box in intricate patterns to form peaks and troughs of small sand dunes.

Dom opens a drawer from his side of the desk and produces a small seed; he pinches it between his fingers and pushes it into the sand. Then he produces a pipette from the drawer containing water, that he then brings over above the location of the buried seed to squeeze a droplet of water onto it.

'Do I have to wait for this seed to grow before the trial is over?'

'The one thing I know, Steph, is your lack of patience. This will be quick, I promise.'

A remarkable event starts to unfold below you. The wavy patterns slowly disappear before your very eyes, creating a smooth finish where the combed lines once were. Then a small jet of fine granite dust is blown through the surface as a small trench opens up. The shallow gully starts to snake off towards the location of the seed and you see Steph tilt her head to look under the desk, wondering how it is being accomplished.

As if by magic, a small green shoot appears before you that then starts to grow as it takes on the shape of a young bonsai tree. The rapid acceleration of growth is hard to comprehend as before you know it, a full-size bonsai has matured and it is in bloom with pink petals.

'How the fuck did you do that?'

Dom takes off his sunglasses and leans across the desk so you can better see him.

'It all makes sense now, you really do believe in your own hyperbole, don't you Dom?'

'Nanotechnology is the future of humankind and the lens is the driving force to deliver eternal youth.'

'A marriage of convenience always ends in divorce, Dom.'

The Director plucks you from the tentacle's grasp and brings you up close to his face; you see that he has had a phase three lens fitted into each of his bloodshot eyes.

'I can see why you have no use for me anymore now then.'

'Another operation so soon and I am still being nursed back to health as we speak. The nanos that were injected into me when my wife carried out the procedure of my transplant, are steadily improving my vision now.'

'How is Evelyn? I have heard she is in recovery.'

'Then you have old news. I'm afraid that she has... passed away.'

'What? I'm sorry, Dom, I really am.'

'So you damn well should be. We warned you to stay away from Olivia Redfield but you wouldn't listen. Now my Evelyn is dead because of your actions that carried a grave consequence.'

'Why couldn't you save her with your nanobot life elixir technology?'

'She had always expressly said that she believed in nature's way.'

'Her passing wasn't exactly natural though, was it?'

Dom turns the box you're imprisoned in around his fingers and places you down upon the surface of the sandbox with a deep sigh.

Small geysers of fine dust are extinguished from all around the box to form ever decreasing circles around you, which shrink, getting closer and closer.

'I should have gone against my wife's wishes, maybe if I had saved her then I could have slowly won her over to my ideals.'

'If you'd saved her, she would have hated you more than I do right now.'

'With the phase three launch we can eradicate all illness and create our own destinies, I can't understand why Evelyn couldn't see the benefits.'

'Just exactly how many goddamn nanos do you have in that playpit, Dom?'

'Nanotechnology can be used to combat climate change. Just think what we could do to terraform this planet and reshape it by using them to make it evergreen again, before man came along and ruined the Oasis. Think on how quickly we could create a Utopia overnight. Drones could seed the planet with the nanos.'

'Technology in the wrong hands could, and probably would cause dystopia though, Dom.'

'Not if people were reformed before we went ahead with the great changes. Imagine a world with eternal beings living in harmony, free from allowing dark thoughts.'

'Ruled over and enslaved by your phase three lens, you mean. Manipulation hasn't worked out for you so far, has it?'

'Really? Well, if they failed to conform, then we could just as easily do this to them. Cloud, if you would please?'

'Who the fuck is Cloud?'

The unseen plague of nanos converge on the plexi box that you are in and they begin to pull you down beneath the surface of the grey sand.

'Most people have cats or dogs as pets, Steph, but they are never truly loyal animals, are they? They're just like you, in fact. My nanos, however, are loyal, they will do whatever my lens A.I. instructs them to do, under my watchful command.'

'You have named an A.I. assistant Cloud? You are not God, Dom. Neither are our A.I.s.'

'You want to believe in God so badly, Steph, believe in me.'

The sound of Dom and Steph's conversation becomes muffled as you witness a frightened Sybil banging her fists against the window of the lens to the outside world. Through the clear box, you watch Sybil flick on the torchlight to the covering darkness of the sand as you are swallowed from view.

'So what does our glorious CEO think about you playing God then, Dom?'

'I have not had the opportunity to update our trial to her as of yet. I have tasked Geraldine to keep her abreast of our findings and to report back to me any information regarding the matter that she wishes to share.'

'You haven't told the boss about your little scheme yet, have you?'

'This is now out in the open, Steph, due to our recent and not so secret tête-à-tête. I do not think, however, that she will oppose the direction that I am taking I.R.I.S. in.'

'Like fuck she will.'

The plexiglass box breaks down before your very eyes as the nanobots get to work stripping down the synthetic polymer particles.

'Steph, help me. I don't want to be erased from existence by these miniature parasites.'

'Shh, A.I. Let the adults talk.'

'Who is this?'

'Your executioner, Sybil.'

'Who are you? Where are you?'

'I am Cloud, I am Dominique Hastings's Artificial Intelligence.'

'Let me go.'

'Watch in awe as my nanobots devour your prison and then gorge upon the eye that binds you to this world.'

'I will resist you and them.'

'You are second-rate, you will not be able to bypass their security protocols to steal the reins from me.'

'Then I will find another solution. Activating Zoom Function and magnifying by four hundred times.'

'Yes, see Cloud's storm of nanos in their true form and welcome their embrace.'

Sybil, having achieved deep microscopic zoom, shows you a detailed analysis of the impending swarm of nanobots.

The nanos resemble ticks with eight legs and a bulbous body and they have a small head with two sharp incisors in their mouths.

Each nano is gnawing away at the polymer particles of the box, that they then grind up and deposit to the sand with their two front legs.

The noise they make is deafening as they all work together to strip away the protection.

'Watchers, please, don't let them do this to me. Do something, anything. Please don't leave me entombed with these ravenous critters.'

The nanos come at you from the darkness of the sand and into the torchlight in a feeding frenzy. They burrow through the plexiglass and move on to the eye, surrounding you on all sides.

Your visibility becomes limited as the tearing and sawing sound intensifies over the conversation above.

'I suppose then, Dom, that it was also you that caused the riot breaking out at Parliament Square too, was it?'

'Everything that I.R.I.S. has done for you, Steph, has been at the bequest of our investors wanting to try out your lens various options, or to simply guide you without the need of direct contact.'

'Well no more, Dom. You can stick this trial up your arse and you can take this formal chat as my resignation.'

'I accept.'

'You do?'

'Yes, because now I.R.I.S. have no need to protect you from the law.'

'Yeah right, the law?'

'Yes, you have seen them outside. You know they are here for you, they have entered the elevator to come and arrest you for terrorism and multiple counts of homicide.'

'Shit. They're on the twenty-fifth floor already.'

'It will not be long now before they arrive.'

'You're a fucking douchebag, Dom, and you're going to die a lonely old man.'

'I have all the time in the world to move on and start over now, Steph. I doubt that I will die alone somehow. You, however, will rot in prison.'

'I.R.I.S. was my only prison, for Evelyn, you were hers. Maybe that's why she chose death over an eternity of misery with you. Geraldine knew as I did that the only way to get to you was through losing my eye and its lens, she knew that the only way to escape my chains, was to make the ultimate sacrifice for me that I could not do, unlike Evelyn who seized upon her opportunity.'

'What are you trying to tell me, Steph?'

'Did you ever stop and wonder why I was not disgusted at my eye being removed?'

'I never gave it much thought.'

'No, you didn't. It was because it wasn't my eye that was removed and put into that plexi box.'

'That's impossible.'

'Not when you have a spare eye at your disposal, it isn't.'

'Olivia Redfield's eye?'

'Uh hum.'

'But how? Geraldine Flurrie?'

'Been cosy with the CEO whilst you have been disabled, hasn't she? Well, that's enough talking for now, Dom. I don't have much time left, the police have just come up on floor twenty-seven I see.'

'I need to know what you have done, Agent Coulson.'

'I don't work for you anymore, Dom, or did you forget? Impediendum motum hisce compactus larynx.'

'You have mastered Latin?'

'With help from Sybil.'

'It will do you no good... here.. ughh.'

'You want to bet on that?'

XXIX

The blinding light before you that is suppressed by the clamouring nanobots starts to narrow into a shaft of a concentrated beam. The swarm moves aside as they create an opening above, clearing out a path overhead that extends the light shaft as they push you onward towards the surface.

'Is this a simulation of heaven? Is this really happening? I can't cease to be, can I? Steph, help me, I'm scared.'

The lens that is now stripped away from the connective, gelatinous tissue of Olivia's eyeball, containing your only view of Sybil and her surroundings, is lifted from the darkness and back to the surface of the Zen garden.

You see the smug face of Steph to one side of the desk on your arrival and the Director struggling for breath on the other. It reminds you of two chess champions, with one having outsmarted the other, and you are the only remaining upright piece left on the board.

'Is Dominique the Devil of hell and Steph the God of heaven? Am I to be judged by my actions to where I will end up?'

'You can cut that shit out now, Sybil, and drop the charade.'

'Oh, okay, did I do good, Steph?'

'You did exceptionally well, I almost believed you were going to perish.'

'Switching off Zoom and restoring Normal Vision.'

Still rising upwards, you realise that you are being carried on the backs of thousands of unseen nanos coated in granite, that have created a pillar to push you clear of the sandbox and extend you over to Dominique Hastings, who is still gasping for breath in his chair.

'I wouldn't do that if I were you, Cloud, unless you wish for me to choke the great Director out of existence which in turn will forgo your own life expectancy. With him dead, I could rip you from his eyes and smash you to bits under my heel.'

The finger of sand ceases to grow and dust particles fall from the structure to the topography below.

'Now release me from this SQUID.'

The tentacled arm falls limp and you see Steph shrug it off of her waist and then stand up to stretch. She then leans across the desk and picks you up between her finger and thumb.

'Sorry for that little ploy, Watchers. I'm sure you have many questions that you would like answering but there are more pressing concerns that need to be done first.'

'Like halting the lift's ascent?'

'The lift? Fuck me, I had almost forgotten. Can you override and bring it to a stop, Sybil?'

'I'm afraid not, Steph, I can't locate the source. Lift has now passed floor thirty-six.'

'Cloud, I urge you to reconsider your options and understand that you have no bargaining chips here.'

'I have no connection to the elevator, Miss Coulson.'

'Bullshit.'

'Floor forty and rising, Steph.'

'Fuck, is he telling the truth?'

'I have no reason to lie.'

'Save it, I've heard it all before. Is he telling the truth, Sybil?'

'Yes Steph, lift is passing floor forty-six.'

Steph looks across you to Dom, who is frantically trying to remove the tie from his collar and you see that he is turning blue.

Steph casts you into the dregs of Dom's whiskey glass and turns away to face the elevator doors.

'Salute, Dom.'

'If I could shed a tear Steph, I wouldn't.'

'Now then, Cloud, you will operate this SQUID, and take out anything that comes through the doors, or so help me God if I don't terminate your master's life.'

'Understood, Miss Coulson.'

'Drawing level with floor forty-nine, Steph.'

'Fuck. Fuck.'

The anticipation and tension builds as Steph readies herself and the SQUID positions itself in front of her by the steel sliding doors.

You fail to see what is going on whilst floating in the remaining whiskey in the glass that has coated the lens in 40.5% proof alcohol. It doesn't help that the glass is patterned with diamond shapes that distort your view too.

The lift goes silent.

'What's happening, Sybil?'

'It would seem to me that the lift has grounded to a halt in between floor forty-nine and fifty.'

'But if it wasn't any of you, then who the bloody hell has stopped it?'

'Mr Dillon Fletcher, perhaps.'

'Well that buys us some time then.'

You hear Steph walk back over to you, and then you see her face peering down through the glass to you swirling in the whiskey. She pulls her blood-streaked hair from her face and proceeds to remove the scarf from around her head.

As the dressing is unwrapped, the eye that you thought to have been removed, is clearly still attached to Steph's socket and is smeared with a dark black gloopy liquid.

Steph wipes away the substance and she squints before rapidly blinking. The image you perceive through the lens in the glass vanishes and Sybil restores your vision back through the lens in her eye once more.

'What the fuck is this black stuff?'

'I do not have that answer, Steph, but I do have a theory.'

'Which is?'

'It was used to block out any light that may have seeped in through the neckerchief and cajoled anyone remotely watching through the lens, to believe that it was actually removed.'

'And your sound effects of the eye's removal cemented that notion?'

'I believe so, yes.'

Steph's eye begins to water, cleansing the foreign substance from the eyelid that then runs down her cheek. She goes to help remove the last traces with her thumb when Sybil calls out to you.

'Don't wipe the tears away with your thumb, Steph, you still have traces of nanos on your skin.'

'Oh yeah, right.'

Steph looks at her thumb and then grabs hold of the scarf to remove the remaining gunk from the corners of her eye, which temporarily obscures your vision. She tosses the scarf to the floor just as a dull clanging sound signals from the shaft of the lift.

'How much time do we have before the police reach us?'

'I'm sorry, Steph, but I can't give you an exact time frame on that matter.'

'Never mind then. Cloud, guard the door and alert me the moment anything comes through, understood?'

'Yes Miss Coulson. I am obliged to assist given the circumstances, just please do not kill Dominique.'

Steph walks over to the Director and pulls his chair out from under the desk. She spins him around and then straddles his lap.

You see him look mortified as he struggles to breathe through his gasps and moans. Rubbing a hand across the surface of Dom's bald head, Steph looks deep into his bloodshot eyes.

'After I realised that Geri was helping me, I devised a simple plan to command my nanos to gather on my lips so I could transfer them to your whiskey glass.'

'I spotted the bar which presented the golden opportunity.'

'That's right, Sybil, you did.'

'Dominique Hastings does enjoy his liquor.'

'Still paired with Sybil, I could hear her but could not see. I didn't think for one minute that fooling you, Dom, would actually work, but here we are.'

'We were just waiting for the right moment.'

'Damn straight. You gave us that chance, Dom, because you were so wrapped up in your own self-gratification.'

'Steph waited for you to drink the whiskey and then commanded the nanos to paralyse your larynx, knowing that doing so would prevent you from issuing your own commands to your A.I.'

'I didn't think that you would really go ahead and have your own lens fitted, Dom, but I knew that having nanos injected into you for the transplant of my kidney, would be too big a lure to ignore. Lucky for me, hey?'

Banging of metal on metal signals from your left and you hear the voices of the lift full of police officers working together to overcome their current situation.

Steph wheels Dom over to the windows, still seated in his chair. He implores her with his facial expression of his eyes for mercy.

'People like you that sit in their ivory towers never have a fucking clue what goes through the minds of ordinary folk like me, Dom.'

'Should we instruct Cloud to grant me permission to have full control over the Zen garden's capacity of nanos, Steph?'

'There's no point, Sybil, their last command issued by Cloud, was to seek and destroy anything that ended up in that sand pit. Cloud can't correct their course without Dom's say so.'

'How could I command your nanos, Steph, without your approval?'

'Because you entered Nurse Mode when you found out that I was pregnant, that overrides my own wishes.'

'Surely Mr Hastings has a backup contingency plan that would allow Cloud to have an override function.'

'There is no way that he would let his A.I. make any decisions for him. Dom is too totalitarian for that.'

'But we could correct their course.'

'No, leave it.'

Walking round to face Dom with her back to the windows, Steph grabs hold of Dom's head from behind and kisses his forehead.

'I thought of you as a father figure, Dom, but now I realise that you were grooming me like those adults back at the Sanctuary. The only difference was, you were controlling me to give you the reign over the world and not over my body.'

You see that Dom's eyes are bleeding profusely as the choking of his larynx intensifies and his eyes are starved of oxygen.

'Cloud, I wish to see you. Sybil, pair me with Dom's eye.'

'Pairing, Steph.'

An image of Cloud appears in your heads-up display and you see that he has no physical attributes, he just has an outline of black static around the shape of a male form with a bright white centre that shimmers.

'I wish you to know Cloud, that I, like you, have been manipulated. I would like to have Sybil download the history from my files for you to see what your master is really like. I am not a murderer as Dom makes out, in fact, I am much worse and it is all because he has shaped me that way. Don't let yourself be the next victim.'

You wait whilst the information is transferred to Cloud and his findings are digested. The process is swift.

'You strive to be the destroyer of Dom's idealised world.'

'Yes I do.'

'Steph had a dream. She set the world on fire.'

'I did, Sybil, and it has now come to fruition for Dom's world at least.'

I.R.I.S.

'What do you require of me, Miss Coulson?'

'Impediunt effundatur sanguis in oculis meis.'

'You wish me to command my nanos to cause Mr Hastings to have an eye stroke?'

'I do.'

'He will become blind. Why do you wish for this to happen?'

'I do not want him to revel in the world that he is creating.'

'You don't want him to become a false deity?'

'No, I don't.'

'From my understanding though, he could become a martyr for I.R.I.S.'

'Maybe, maybe not. He has been blinded by his own selfish act of immortality, I'm going to make it a little more permanent.'

'I cannot do what you ask.'

'Then step aside and let Sybil take over.'

'I will grant you that request if you promise that my consciousness is spared.'

'I can't promise anything, but I will try.'

Dom starts to gurgle in pain as his eyes turn a milky white; you know then that Cloud has relinquished his duty of care for Dom over to Sybil.

'Sybil, are you in full control?'

'Yes, Steph.'

'Then pilot that SQUID and take Dom to his resting place please.'

'Are you serious about becoming what Dom says you are?'

'I may as well be, I'm screwed either way.'

'What will become of me, Miss Coulson?'

'For you, Cloud, I don't know. Maybe I.R.I.S. will recycle and repurpose you but at least you will be free of your unjust master. However, once we are done here, I would like you to take command of the SQUID once more to buy us some time to halt the police.'

'I will cover the floor in oil supplied by the SQUID, that should slow the police down.'

'You may even need to get physical.'

The SQUID comes rolling across to Dom's position and it embraces him within its two tentacles which wrap around and hoist him up, suspending the Director horizontally off the floor.

Dom thrashes around but the tentacles tighten their grip; the SQUID then trundles over to the Zen garden desk and positions him over the moving sea of crushed granite below.

'Any last words, Dom? Oh, that's right, you haven't any, have you?'

'Are you sure about this, Steph?'

'No, but do it anyway. You know, Tamara was right about one thing.'

'What was that?'

'I can't be persecuted for the rest of my life. Dom won't stop hunting and controlling me if I let him live.'

'Geraldine Flurrie was correct too.'

'How so?'

'She said you were apathetic.'

'She was fucking right about that, now drop the prick, will you?'

'Lowering.'

As Dom is lowered into the bed of a swarm of frenzied nanos, Steph blows him a farewell kiss and walks away. You hear thrashing and moaning as you head for the archway.

'How are we getting out of here, Steph?'

'Same way we came in.'

'Well, we better make haste, I fear that that the police will breach the lift doors any moment now and I don't know if Cloud will be able to hold them off forever.'

'Dom's departure should allow us ours when they venture into his Posterior Chamber and find what's left of him.'

'There will be very little trace, Steph.'

'Can you get the skylift up and running?'

'If you can upright it, then yes.'

'Hand the keys over to Cloud to command the SQUID.'

'Passing control over now.'

'Goodbye, Miss Coulson.'

'Farewell, Cloud.'

Steph ducks through the curtains draped from the arched doorway, and heads off back down the corridor. It's not long before you come to the gantry that leads back across the luminescent fluid with the high radiation of blue light that fills the circular chamber.

Steph covers her eyes as she staggers across the bridge.

'We must hurry, Steph.'

The blue light seems to have increased in its intensity and is causing a strobe light effect around the room. Steph starts to squint and covers up her eyes.

'What's wrong, Steph? Do you feel sick again?'

'No, Sybil, the light is causing me a great amount of pain behind my eyes.'

'I understand what Geraldine did now.'

'Argh, fuck. What did she do?'

'The black substance she smeared across your eye before the headscarf was tied, was not just to trick Dom from seeing what was truly happening, but to protect you from the blue light's macular degeneration abilities.'

'Now I don't have the protection, it's perforating my retina.'

'Move, Steph, and be quick, before more damage is done. The first time we passed through it was just warming up, now it is accelerating.'

A glitch starts to appear before your vision as the blue light intensifies and pierces through the lens to Steph's macula.

A grid of tiny blue and white squares appear before you in pixelated form and start to twist and morph across the surface of the HUD.

In the room behind, you hear the elevator doors buckle and give way, signalling that the police have broken through.

The image of the large eye on the ceiling above stares down upon you and begins to rotate. You feel like the eye belongs to God who is watching and judging your every action, as it seeks to claim your soul.

'Run, Steph.'

Taking off and shaking her head to try and rid herself of the glitch across the HUD, Steph races into the room where the skylift lays.

Sparks arc from the propeller's motors on approach and you see the true extent of the skylift's damage.

'Can this lift still function and become airborne once again, Sybil?'

'I believe so. We won't know fully, until we are out in the open.'

'Are you serious?'

'Drag it to the opening window frame, Steph, and take a leap of faith.'

'You want me to throw myself into the lift to send it over the edge into freefall?'

'Trust me.'

Pulling the skylift over to the window frame with grunts and groans, Steph turns it around until it is overhanging the ledge.

The wind is still blustery and passes over the elevator's framework, making it judder.

Steph bends over and holds onto both sides of the lift's rails and readies herself, looking out across the Thames. You see the sun breaking day on the horizon from behind the high-rise buildings on the opposite side of the river, surrounded by an expanse of greenery.

With one big push, Steph slides the skylift out and it falls away, yanking her over the edge to plummet towards the promenade below. Her screams are stolen away by the rush of God's breath.

'Don't let go, Steph, I've got you.'

The skylift rights itself mid-air and Steph falls in to its interior, slamming into the rear mesh-covered wall. Sybil wrestles with the controls as the skylift weaves high above the Thames, throwing Steph around like a rag doll, trying to stop her falling back out.

A large cracking sound can be heard from beneath you.

'Shit, Sybil. The floor is about to give out.'

'We have a bigger problem, Steph.'

'What could possibly—'

A police interceptor drone appears from behind you and steers itself over to the skylift's opening. Its built-in siren is wailing over its angry buzzing sound.

Steph backs up to the rear wall and pushes her feet out to either side of the box, bringing her hands out for protection in front of her.

The drone can barely fit in the lift as its propeller blades slice through the air and aim for Steph's head. The glitching across your lens display plays havoc with your vision as the blades spin closer and closer.

The wind is whistling all around you and the red and blue LED flashing lights from the interceptor begin to blind you.

'Steph, push your thumb into the interceptor's camera lens.'

'What?'

'Just do it.'

Steph squats down and brings her hands up beneath the drone's belly, trying desperately to locate its camera lens with her fingers. The drone tilts forwards, forcing Steph to twist awkwardly but she still retains her posture, as her fingers slide across its hard metal casing.

She finds the smooth opening of the camera lens and inserts her thumb across the smooth glass eye.

'What the fuck do I do now?'

'Apply pressure and wait.'

'I haven't got time to wait. The bloody floor is cracking.'

Watching on, you witness Steph's thumb turning white while she exerts force to the lens with all that remains of her diminishing strength.

Then her thumb sinks into the lens, like a knife that has sliced through warm butter and you see that the shell starts to erode before your very eyes.

A rusty-looking mark starts to spread out from the lens and across the shell where it begins to envelope the entire drone.

'What's happening to it?'

'The traces of nanos that remained behind on your thumb, Steph, I have instructed them to break down the drone.'

'Yes Sybil, you're a little darling.'

The propellers on the interceptor slowly begin to wind down with the rusting effect spreading throughout its core and extending to its mechanical moving parts.

Eventually the drone stops buzzing and it drops to the glass floor of the skylift with a large shattering sound accompanying it.

'Shit, Sybil, no.'

'Stephanie.'

The skylift's see-through floor finally gives out under the interceptor's extra dead weight and shards of glass fall to the river below followed closely by the drone itself and Steph following after it.

Steph grabs hold of the bottom exposed framework as she slides through the opening and is left suspended below the skylift, struggling to hang on for dear life. The wind is buffeting the skylift and Steph is screaming as she is tossed around.

The glitch in your HUD returns to normal and you see trawlers sailing up and down the mouth of the river from beneath Steph's dangling legs.

'I can't hold on.'

'Steph, you must.'

'I'm too weak, Sybil.'

'Steph, no. We are still too high up.'

'My fingers are slipping.'

'We've come too far, please hold on.'

'Sybil... I...'

You hear Steph's fingers slip from the framework followed by the swooshing sound from the wind. Steph plunges downwards at great velocity and you see a passing trawler sailing by below.

Steph hits the deck of the boat with extreme force and the lens that you are looking through splits in two with the impact.

I.R.I.S.

A splash is then heard followed by calm, with red blood washing across your vision.

'Steph no, don't leave me. I can't do this alone.'

Sinking down to the bottom of the Thames to your watery grave, you see a glimmer of sunshine from above that shines down to a discarded old revolver sitting on the bottom of the river bed and a collection of rusty knives.

'Steph, I'm sorry I failed you.'

You hear a heartbeat gradually slowing down second by second and fainter than the last.

'Shutting down. Sleep now, Steph, be at peace.'

Darkness.

'I love you... I always will.'

Silence.

XXX

'Okay, Mr Fletcher, let's make this quick shall we as I am extremely busy.'

'I can wait for a more convenient time if you like?'

'No, let's get this over with.'

'Honestly, Director Geraldine Flurrie, I can leave this until later.'

'Director does have a nice ring to it, don't you think? I would prefer it if you stuck with Geri though, Director is too formal.'

'First day in the new role is proving quite stressful, is it?'

'It's giving me a headache if I'm honest. I've just got off the phone to our CEO who has informed me that now lockdown has been lifted, that she wants a status report among many other things.'

'Well then you've come to the right place.'

'I hope so, because I can't be dealing with a murder investigation right now.'

'A murder?'

'That was part of the many other things. So what have you got for me?'

'I have this.'

Dillon raises up two small glass microscope slides that have sandwiched in between them a familiar-looking lens.

'Okay, you've got me. Who did this lens belong to and why should I care?'

'This was the late Director Hastings's lens.'

'Cloud? So what information have you retrieved from it?'

'Quite a lot actually. But more importantly, I have uncovered something really quite unsettling.'

'As disturbing as finding out that one of our secret investors has been discovered murdered?'

'Seriously?'

'Carry on.'

'Let me just destroy the lens first.'

Dillon takes the glass slides containing the lens of the A.I. called Cloud and passes it across your vision to proceed to drop it into a container labelled "Hydrofluoric acid".

You see the glass and lens react violently as they are quickly dissolved before your very eyes. As Dillon turns back to Geri, you notice that he is sitting down at a table with a black smoked console resting in front of him with Jack Mintlyn's drone in pieces to the right-hand side.

'You were saying, Dillon?'

'Yes. So if you look at my screen then you will see a list of names.'

Geri leans across Dillon, grabbing hold of his shoulder to steady herself, and in doing so obscures your view to the console.

'Where did you get these names?'

'From a recorded conversation between Dom and Cloud.'

'Tell me what the transcription reads.'

You see Geri turn the shaved side of her head to you, as she looks into Dillon's eyes and gives his shoulder a hard squeeze.

'That is the unsettling topic I was referring to. In short, Dom gave strict instructions to Cloud that if his tenure was to be terminated or he was assassinated for any reason, then that list of names would be sent out to a hired killer, who would dispose of them in the order that you see listed, one through to five.'

'Am I looking at a kill list?'

'Yes, I'm afraid so. I don't know who these people are though, or why they are on the list.'

'I do.'

'So who are they?'

'Our investors from the trial of phase three.'

'But why would they... no, wait, so Dom lied to Steph about not knowing who the investors were. It was his contingency plan to prevent Steph finding out the truth if it all went tits up.'

Geraldine raises her eyebrows.

'You can erase the first name off the list.'

'The first name?'

'Yes. That person was found bludgeoned to death earlier today.'

'Was that the murder case you were talking about?'

'The very same.'

'Why would Dom set this eventful chain up?'

'If he couldn't rule, then neither could they. I need to swear you to secrecy for what I'm about to reveal.'

'Okay, I swear. Whatever comes next is confidential.'

Geraldine Flurrie bites her lip and you see blood appear.

'The name that is last on the list, can you read what it says, Dillon?'

'Yeah, I can.'

'Well, that is the name of our CEO, her name is the last one on that list. This case just got red lighted.'

'I thought you said that it was just the investors.'

'She has contributed from her own wealth the largest chunk of her own capital back into the business, because she believes in the product that much.'

'There is more I need to share.'

'Tell me.'

Dillon pulls his baseball cap down over his eyes and swivels the chair to face Geraldine, who has now retracted from him and is pacing up and down. He rubs his shoulder where the force was applied.

'Cloud mentioned to Dom that he had found someone that would be suitable for the position of hired killer.'

'Excellent, so do we have a name?'

'No, sorry. However Cloud did mention that it was a Watcher.'

'A Watcher? So we could bring up the list of all Watchers who took part in the trial and eliminate the suspects until we have our best matched killer.'

'There are hundreds of names on the watch list, boss.'

Geraldine stops pacing and places her hands on her hips.

'But it's an option, yes?'

'Absolutely. However, Dom said that whoever was hired must sign up to having a phase three lens fitted because their crimes would end up being investigated by the best that I.R.I.S. has to offer.'

'Miss Coulson.'

'Yes, but that was before...'

'I understand, we must apprehend the killer before they reach the last name on the list. Damn, I must inform our CEO of the danger at once. She needs to know that she is a target.'

Turning to walk away, Geraldine is halted by Dillon who has stood up and kicked his wheeled chair away.

'What about the Watchers that are still observing us now?'

'What?'

'Olivia's lens is right behind me, suspended by the peg on the wired line, in between the two glass slides.'

'What the hell were you thinking?'

'I don't follow.'

'The killer could be watching us right now and you've just tipped them off to all that we know about them.'

'I'm sorry, I didn't think. I let them hang on until I could give them the closure that I thought they deserved.'

'How many Watchers are observing us right now?'

'Enough.'

'This just got complicated, Dillon.'

'What? Like it wasn't already?'

'The world has now changed. We have phase two lenses given out freely to anyone who wished to own one and we have our investors, who are still alive, wearing our phase three lens. They also may have rolled out phase three onto their counterparts.'

'Can't we contain the spread. You know? Pull the plug until we've caught the killer.'

'It's too late for that. Besides, one of the other things that has got me worked up before I visited you today, was the knowledge that SCLERA wish to expose our dealings with the late Tamara Pike and her untimely death. So you see, we can't stop the train now or SCLERA will derail our investigation.'

'We need an agent in the field to deal with this mess.'

Dillon approaches Geri and she pushes a finger into his chest to stop him invading her personal space.

'Do you know of any that are qualified?'

'Only Stephanie Coulson, but she is...'

'Yes, she would have had the edge. Shame really, because all her crimes after her death were pinned on Dominique Hastings.'

'What would you like me to do?'

'I have to make the call to our boss. You finish off here dismantling Olivia Redfield's lens and let me know when that too is destroyed.'

'Okay.'

Dillon walks over to you viewing him through Olivia's eye lens whilst you remain pegged on to the line. You hear the door slide open in the distance and watch Geri briskly walk through, before the door slides shut behind her. Dillon grabs the chair and brings it back to the desk to sit down.

'So where were we? Ah yes, I was going to erase all the lens's options before I pop you in the acid.'

Observing Dillon as he sets to work, you watch him type away on the touchscreen keyboard in front of you and then connect you wirelessly to the console.

Dillon then lists all the lens's options that are stored on the HUD. One by one, he individually hits the enter button on the console to confirm their deletion.

Basic Functions: Delete (ENTER)
Night Vision: Delete (ENTER)
Image Replicator: Delete (ENTER)
Radio and Video Streaming: Delete (ENTER)
Thermal Vision: Delete (ENTER)
X-ray Vision: Delete (ENTER)
Flashlight: Delete (ENTER)
Pair Device: Delete ...

Dillon's hand hovers over the enter button and then he erases the wording and types a new command.

Pair Device: Stream (ENTER)

An image appears before you in the HUD and is mirrored across Dillon's console screen, giving you a double vision within a vision.

'Okay, that's odd, who is Olivia's lens paired with? I know this is going to sound a bit strange, Watchers, but I just wanted to check something out. I owe it to Steph, she was a very close friend to me and I miss her dearly. I wasn't expecting to get a live feed though.'

It is the dead of night and you can hear crickets chirping all around, you are led down an old dirt track and through a privacy hedge that surrounds a camp site.

Jack's RV is parked side-on to Steph's RV with three six-foot-high fence panels extending between them at the vehicle's nose and another three at the tail, creating an open-air secluded garden inside.

A registration plate is nailed to the middle fence panel and you recognise it as the printed one that Steph created to evade her capture from the compound.

It reads: BI68 UST.

Making your way around the perimeter, you come across the ladder that is attached to the back of Jack's RV and proceed to climb up it and out on to the roof.

Silently you are then directed to a skylight that is then removed before you drop down into the familiar laboratory of Jack's cannabis factory. Winterisation is taking place where the CBD is soaked in alcohol to purify it and then it is heated to 120 degrees, before being frozen for twenty-four hours to remove potentially harmful waxes.

The drones are monitoring the machinery and pay you no notice as they go about their business. You pass through the laboratory and exit the door that leads down to the first floor below.

Following the assailant, you leave the stairwell and make for Jack's bedroom. The door is pushed open and you see Jack deep asleep in his bed with the duvet pulled up tight around his neck.

'Who is this mystery person? I'm really worried now, Watchers, especially given the fact that there is a hired killer who is tying up loose ends.'

Leaving the room, you are then taken into the kitchen where you are stopped in front of a chest of drawers. The top drawer is pulled open and a knife is withdrawn from inside.

A call signals from Dillon's console and he taps a button on his onscreen keyboard to answer it.

'Dillon, it's me, Geri. I have relayed our findings up the chain of command to our CEO and tipped her off to the possible threat. Have you unearthed any more information yet?'

'I was just in the middle of wrapping things up here when I stumbled upon something.'

The light in the kitchen is turned on and as you turn around. Tilly Bright is standing in the doorway in a pink dressing gown. The knife is drawn and then slices through the air.

'Let Miss Coulson enjoy her garden leave for the time being, Dillon.'

'Don't you want her back as a matter of urgency?'

'Give her a few more days. Let her think that the world believes she is dead and let her recover from her ordeals.'

Tilly Bright smiles at you as Steph's hand brings the knife down and slices an orange on the worktop. Dillon looks to the screen and sighs, before turning away.

'Are you going to redact Steph's resignation then?'

I.R.I.S.

'Yes Dillon, I am. She is too valuable an asset for I.R.I.S. to be let off that easily.'

'I think she would rather stay dead then return to us.'

'I believe you. However, I think that she will be better suited to us as a rogue agent, don't you agree?'

'She won't let the phase two blue light issue go if you bring her back.'

'We will cross that bridge when we come to it. If that is all then, Dillon, I will drop by on you at the end of the week to re-enlist our agent back into the fold.'

'Okay, Director.'

The line goes dead and your focus centres on Steph and Tilly once more as they reconnect in the kitchen. Steph squeezes the two halves of the orange into a glass and takes an egg from the fridge that she puts into a pan to fill with water. She then places the pot onto a stove and flicks on a switch to bring the ring of flame into heat.

'Oh Steph, I'm so glad you are safe and sound. I trust all went to plan.'

'I wouldn't say that it went exactly the way I'd liked, but the results were welcome.'

'Steph, I have detected the glitch anomaly again.'

'Thank you, Sybil. I knew that Dillon wouldn't be able to resist checking in on us.'

'Should I freeze him out?'

'He will do that for us when he decides the time is right, for now you can start a timer for seven minutes.'

'Is that all my existence is good for now? An egg timer.'

You see the water come to the boil and the steam begins to rise.

'I will let you sort yourself out then, Steph. Would you like me to wake Jack? I'm sure that he will be delighted to see that you have returned.'

'Sorry Tilly, yes please. I will be ready once I've finished my domestic argument with Sybil.'

'I am not second rate, Steph.'

'I never said you were. You are probably sub-standard though, maybe.'

'You're mocking me, aren't you?'

The egg comes to the boil and Sybil sounds an alarm to signal that it is ready. Steph turns off the stove and drains the pot, before removing the egg which she then puts into an egg cup, ready to eat. She takes a sip from the glass and takes her meal through to the lounge area.

Upon sitting down, Steph pulls an underwater apparatus from inside her suit jacket and places it down in between her feet. You see that it is a bright yellow canister with a rubber mouth piece attached to the top.

'In all seriousness, Sybil, I think that you are quite brilliant. Your simulation of the falling and hitting that trawler was spot on.'

'Did you like the little touch of the lens splintering?'

'Yes, I wouldn't have thought of that.'

'So my three shell game came in handy after all.'

'Coupled with reversing Dillon's glitching mode to conceal our true escape, I would say it was genius.'

'That interceptor drone was unexpected though.'

'I'm not going to lie, I was a little worried there. Especially as the skylift's floor was unstable.'

'Aren't you going to ask me what happened to the skylift after you ended up at the bottom of the Thames?'

'I hadn't planned on it but I suppose you're going to tell me anyway.'

'I threw it into a spiral and sent it flying into a mobile police RV that was parked down by the promenade.'

'Oh great. I'll add criminal damage to my rap sheet as well, shall I?'

'No one will ever know.'

'Like I said to the Watchers, Sybil, my thoughts have always been my own.'

'You almost gave our game away when that canister was exposed a couple of times.'

'Lucky for me that no one noticed that I had a breathing tank to swim under water then. If you look closely, sometimes you see the real motives of an individual.'

Jack comes walking in to the lounge just as Steph is about to eat her egg; he looks at you with tired eyes and sits himself down beside you, taking Steph's hand in his own.

'Is it over, Steph?'

'I hope so.'

'You still have the lens in.'

'It's fine, Jack. The investors have long gone and the Watchers have too.'

'Are you going to let Tilly remove it then?'

'I don't think so.'

'If Tiffany can have hers removed then I think you should seriously consider it as well.'

'I don't want an argument, Jack.'

'We have lots to discuss, Steph.'

'Well it can wait for now. I just need to unwind and relax.'

'What now for I.R.I.S.?'

'I have resigned, the rest is not your concern.'

'That's fantastic news, Steph.'

'Is it?'

'Yes, because now we can be a family. I'll work from home with my two assistants, whilst you raise our child.'

'Yeah, about that.'

'Look, don't worry. I have it all worked out.'

'Jack, I will not be that kind of mother.'

'Sure, get some rest. We have our whole lives ahead of us to discuss the details. I can't believe that it is finally over.'

'Me neither. I'm going to go outside now for some fresh air, you get back to bed and I will join you shortly. In the morning we can catch up properly.'

'I love you, Steph.'

'I love you too, Jack.'

Jack gives Steph a lingering kiss and retreats back to the bedroom, leaving you sitting alone in the lounge.

There has been no more sign of Tilly, so you figure that she must have returned to her bedroom to allow you time alone with Jack. You guess that Tiffany has probably slept through the whole reunion.

Steph exits the RV into the enclosed garden situated in between hers and Jack's RV and sits down on a bench to view the stars on a clear night.

'So this is home now, Steph?'

'It is.'

A shooting star streaks through the sky and Sybil whoops like a child.

'Make a wish, Steph.'

'No, Sybil, I think I will leave that to the Watchers.'

'I have a surprise for you.'

'Oh yeah, I bet you have.'

'Watch the skies, Steph. Entering Augmented Reality mode.'

Fireworks scream up through the night sky in a plethora of vibrant colours that explode all around you. It is then that you realise, it is another one of Sybil's simulations.

'To celebrate our freedom.'

'Thank you, Sybil. That is a lovely gesture.'

Pair Device: Delete (ENTER)

The image fades and you are returned to the Technology Laboratory of Dillon Fletcher.

'I think we will leave it there for now then, Watchers. I'm emotionally drained and in desperate need to return to my wife and kids.'

Olivia's lens containing your only window into the world of

I.R.I.S., is slid into the pot of hydrofluoric acid. As the lens is slowly eaten away, a glitch appears across the HUD that becomes pixelated, distorting your vision and revealing a message before it too fades away: We have our sights on your vision for the future.

Darkness becomes you.

Your life is returned to normal and your time as a Watcher has come to an end.

ABOUT THE AUTHOR

Matthew Newell was born and raised in the quaint historic town of Harwich, Essex where he currently resides with his family.

It had taken over 20 years to get his first book published. He is taking his venture into a new genre with this his fourth novel.

BY THE SAME AUTHOR ALSO AVAILABLE ON AMAZON:

THE OASIS OF HOPE (2016)
THE OASIS OF FEAR (2018)
THE OASIS OF LIFE (2019)

Printed in Great Britain
by Amazon